Benjamin Ward Richardson, Thomas Sopwith

Thomas Sopwith : with Excerpts from his Diary of fifty-seven Years

Benjamin Ward Richardson, Thomas Sopwith

Thomas Sopwith : with Excerpts from his Diary of fifty-seven Years

ISBN/EAN: 9783337018412

Printed in Europe, USA, Canada, Australia, Japan

Cover: Foto ©Raphael Reischuk / pixelio.de

More available books at **www.hansebooks.com**

THOMAS SOPWITH,

M.A., C.E., F.R.S.

WITH EXCERPTS FROM HIS DIARY OF FIFTY-SEVEN YEARS.

BY

BENJAMIN WARD RICHARDSON,

M.D., LL.D., F.R.S.

" Here is a dear, a true industrious friend "

I, HENRY IV.

LONDON:

LONGMANS, GREEN, & CO.

1891.

Printed by Hazell, Watson, & Viney, Ld., London and Aylesbury.

To

MRS. DAVID CHADWICK,

NÉE

(URSULA) SOPWITH,

THE CUSTODIAN OF HER BELOVED FATHER'S DIARY,

THIS VOLUME IS INSCRIBED,

WITH THE SINCEREST REGARDS

OF HER OLD AND ATTACHED FRIEND,

BENJAMIN WARD RICHARDSON.

PREFACE.

— ——

IT has long been known through the wide circle of his friends and acquaintances that the late Mr. Thomas Sopwith left at his death a remarkable Diary. Two years ago the members of his family, who had the Diary in their charge, requested me, as an old friend of Mr. Sopwith, to make a study of the work, with the view of preparing from it a modest treatise of some four hundred pages at most, to include, with a brief life of its author, excerpts of some of the incidents which he has recorded. With all the diligence I could command I have herewith carried out the task entrusted to me, in the hope of keeping alive the memory of one of the most estimable, able, and honest Englishmen to whom the nineteenth century has given birth.

25, MANCHESTER SQUARE, W.
  June 1th, 1891.

CONTENTS.

THOMAS SOPWITH, F.R.S.

CHAPTER I.

A PERSONAL INTRODUCTION.

IN the month of September 1856 it was my good fortune to receive an invitation from the late Dr. John Lee, LL.D., President of the Royal Astronomical Society, to form one of a company of scientific visitors who were to meet at his residence at Hartwell Park, near to Aylesbury. It was the fancy of the good Doctor to bring together, from time to time, a considerable number of men whose lives were devoted to the advancement of science, and to entertain them, not for a day merely, but for several days, so that they might get to know each other in the most friendly manner, and might discuss together, without hurry or excitement, those matters of practical and theoretical science which were at the moment engaging the attention of the scientific world. I remember that my invitation extended to fourteen days, but it was so arranged that any visitor who might have to leave for the day could do so and could return again. Carriages met every train in order to bring the visitors to the mansion, and carriages were despatched to every train with those who were leaving the mansion. In short, everything was made as free and homely as was possible.

1

During the visit in September 1856, to which I refer, as many as from thirty to forty visitors were brought into communion with each other, establishing acquaintances and friendships of lifelong duration. We were representatives of so many branches of sciences that we used to speak of ourselves, in a jocular way, as a British Association, in miniature, for the amusements of science. However, we did in some degree resemble the real British Association, by meeting every morning, under the presidency of Dr. Lee, in the library of Hartwell House, and holding a formal sitting. Mr. Samuel Horton, Dr. Lee's private secretary, read the minutes of the previous meeting, which the President confirmed, and then some one of the company was called upon—often without a word of preparation—to treat on a subject with which he was presumed to be familiar, and so to express himself that what he said could be discussed afterwards. These conditions, difficult to sustain, led occasionally to a great deal of embarrassment, mixed always with a compensatory dose of fun and good humour, and sometimes followed by the communication of useful information, which was none the less pleasant because of the piquancy incident to a little merriment and unexpected light of knowledge.

At one of these morning meetings I found myself by the side of a visitor who, up to that time, was unknown to me, but whose bright, genial smile soon made me happy in the acquirement of a new acquaintance who promised to be of the best sort. We began conversation, mutually, by discussing what was to be the subject of the coming debate, when the Doctor rose, and, after informing us that nothing had been arranged, said he was sure some one would volunteer a paper, or a suggestion that would lead to one. For a time no one did offer or

suggest anything, and at last the length of the pause
seemed to say no subject, therefore a dissolution. In
sheer fun I whispered to my new companion, who was
very much my senior, " Why not propose the financial
state of the Peruvians ? " He took up the suggestion
with delight, and, in the slyest manner, rose to say,
" Mr. President, my young friend here suggests, as a
capital topic, The Financial State of the Peruvians." The
proposal led to a general laugh, in which Captain, afterwards Admiral, Fitzroy joined so heartily that some
thought it had reference to one or other of his adventures
in one of his famous voyages, then the talk of the day.
The laugh ended in another period of silence, and the
President began to get quite uneasy, when, as luck would
have it, there appeared fresh on the scene a new visitor.
The Doctor seized the fact and worked it gloriously.
The new visitor, Mr. Thomas Dobson, if my memory is
not at fault, was a merchant, and knew all about curren-
cies. Called upon, therefore, by the President to open a
debate on the subject named, he accepted the duty in the
most artless manner, and in twenty minutes told us more
about Peru and its financial position than we had ever
heard of in the whole course of our lives. The success
was complete. Mr. Dobson got a hearty and well-
deserved vote of thanks for his instructive narrative ;
and, shame to say, according to a common accident of
getting honours thrust upon one, my new friend carried
a vote of thanks to me " for the happy thought which
had led to so excellent and so practical a discourse."

On the break-up of the meeting, my new companion
joined me in the other events of the day, and I found in
him one of the most delightful of associates. He was, it
turned out, about thirty years my senior, but he was so
young of heart that it did not seem possible for him to

be more than a fellow-pupil or schoolfellow of a past day belonging to an older form than mine. There was a quaint humour in him, also, which at once conveyed amusement and information. He told excellent stories, grave and gay, and he varied the part of a story-teller with that of a wise and philosophical teacher so readily that he seemed to have the power of changing his whole nature with a facility I had, at that time, never before seen, and have not many times seen since. But the most striking feature of all was the width and depth of his information on every conceivable subject. He had travelled extensively, and he had taken such careful notes of all he had observed, and had fixed his observations so thoroughly in his mind, that what he told rose before the listener as if it were seen as well as heard. Some one said of him that he was a cyclopædia of information. "Yes," said Mr. James Glaisher, who formed one of our party, "but he is a cyclopædia alive and kicking;" and the remark was duly recognised as true.

As I did not know to what profession or calling my new companion belonged, I made a kind of speculative study in order to guess the fact from his conversation. In passing through the mansion he spoke freely and correctly of its architecture, and compared the style so clearly by the side of another similar building which I accidentally referred to, that I took him to be an architect; but later on it occurred to me that he might be a Professor of Mathematics, for he had all kinds of calculations of the most curious nature at his finger ends,—how many generations of men it would take to cover, with their feet, every point of the surface of the earth: how many generations to make a raised block or terrestrial accretion of men, to rub shoulders with the man in the moon;

how many centuries had passed since the whole population of England was represented round one family hearth. That he was a first-class archæologist was also quite clear; and that he was well up in flint and geological specimens was equally obvious. To this he added a knowledge of many details of history. Thus in regard to Hartwell House itself he told me it was famous as having been for a time the residence of Louis XVIII. and his household. Our good host, Dr. Lee, had told us at breakfast a few facts, of a preliminary kind, regarding this residence of the king; but in a walk through the grounds my new friend told me many more. He was old enough to remember the period when this last royal and crowned descendant of St. Louis was a resident here. He remembered the incidents told of the return of the king to France after the banishment of Napoleon I. to Elba; how the king leaving Hartwell was accompanied by the English Prince Regent, afterwards George IV., to Dover, and by the Duke of Clarence, afterwards King William IV., to Paris; and how the long-exiled king on landing upon the French coast pressed the Duchess of Angoulême to his heart, and exclaimed, "I hold again the crown of my ancestors: if it were of roses, I would place it on your head; as it is of thorns it is for me to wear it." After luncheon my new friend and I—for I may now venture to place him on my list of friends—took a walk to the Vicarage at Stone, a village near by, to see the Rev. J. B. Reade, F.R.S., a most able man of science, and a Vicar in the Church of England,—a modern Hales in science. We found the Vicar busy at work on a new equatorial telescope of large size, which he had himself constructed. We were admitted into his laboratory, and were shown the new work he had accomplished in the art of photography, in the development of which he had taken a leading part. Once more I was struck by the knowledge of my companion. He was technically acquainted with the construction and use of telescopes, and brought out, to our pleasure, a sketch he had made on the previous night of the passage of the moons of the planet Jupiter, as seen through the fine instrument in the observatory at Hartwell.

The possession of all these learned faculties in one individual was, naturally, a marvel to me, a young and inexperienced man ; and my wonder was intensified, as we journeyed back to Hartwell, by the knowledge which my companion showed of men as well as of events and things. I said that I understood Robert Stephenson was to join us at dinner, and asked my friend if he knew Mr. Stephenson. Know him ? Yes ; he knew not only Robert, but the famous father of Robert, the great George, the " Pater Locomotorum " who took, so to say, the steam-engine out of the hands of James Watt and turned it into the all but living locomotive. Then we got on to a splendid topic of conversation. Here was a man who with his own eyes had witnessed the development of the art of steam locomotion into practice ; one who had seen it start in the mines, who had been carried down the Thames in one of the first steamers, and who had been present when one of the first great lines of rail was opened for public use. The whole was told so well, and with such natural truth and force, that we had got back to our destination before I was conscious of having traversed the distance between Stone and Hartwell. We parted on the terrace to go and dress for dinner. On my return to the terrace I saw Captain Fitzroy, wandering slowly with his hands behind him, in one of his thoughtful moods. Catching sight of me, he

came up and invited me to take a short stroll until
the dinner-bell should ring. He was rather depressed,
and asked me one or two questions of a professional kind,
which being answered to his satisfaction our conversation
turned on Hartwell and the present meeting. I told
him of the remarkable man who had been with me to
Stone, and described him to the best of my ability ;—a
rather short and stout man, with large head, broad
forehead, full features, bluish-grey eyes, kindly smile,
and though obviously a northern man, yet of gentle
speech ; a man whose practical knowledge seemed to
be universal.

" He is a capital meteorologist," said Captain Fitzroy ;
" Mr. Glaisher and he are great allies ; and we three have
been discussing barometers, with the idea of finding out
the best methods for making a cheap barometer for popular
use."

" You know him, then, pretty well ? "

" No, not much more than you do yourself. I
happened to travel with him part of the journey here ;
and as we found ourselves coming to the same place
and with the same intents, we got into friendly conversation, and I, like yourself, was quite surprised with
the breadth of his knowledge. He is one of those men
who are not only widely informed, but accurately informed also,—a rare combination."

" Very rare, I should think. But what is his name ? "

" Mr. Glaisher casually introduced us, but Dr. Lee
introduced me to him formally as Mr. Thomas Sopwith,
Fellow of the Royal Society ; for the Doctor, as you know,
never forgets the full titles belonging to his guests."

" What is his occupation ? " I enquired. " I have
made many guesses about that."

" And what is your best guess ? I am curious to

know, because I went through the same process of speculation for a considerable time."

"I took him first for an architect, next for a mathematical teacher or professor, but now I think he has to do with the manufacture of steam-engines or some other mechanical art on a large scale."

"And I took him for a professor of some mechanical branch of study also. But we are both a little away from the precise fact : he is really a mining engineer, and is the superintendent or chief of the greatest lead mines in the world, the headquarters being at Allenheads, in Northumberland."

And so, at last, I knew my new companion by name and profession, as well as by sight. I little thought then how often I should have to write the name, and hear the pleasant voice, in succeeding long years. Least of all did I think that the time would come when it would be my task to write a memoir of him and his works. At the moment I had to think of something very different ; for we had wandered far away from the house, and there was the dinner-bell ringing sharply. Captain Fitzroy, a sailor governed by the strictest views of discipline, was startled.

"We must return," he said quickly ; and he hurried me on with such speed that we were unable to sustain our conversation, even about so pleasant a subject as our new associate, Thomas Sopwith, F.R.S., Mining Engineer ; practical scholar in men, events, things ; and Northumbrian to the backbone.

CHAPTER II.

ONE of the most interesting and original features in the career of Mr. Sopwith, whose life and works I am now beginning to relate, is that he kept a Diary which extended over the long period of nearly two generations, namely, from the year 1822 to 1879, fifty-seven years. The diary consists of no fewer than one hundred and sixty-eight small neatly and strongly bound volumes and of three large volumes. Each entry is remarkable for the accuracy with which it is written, for the clearness of its style, and for the beauty of its penmanship. The pages read like the old manuscripts of the best kind, which came from the scriptorium, before the printer's art was known; and so carefully is every entry made, that throughout a whole volume there will not be found a single mistake or erasure. As to a blot, that were a thing impossible; I believe there is not one in all the series.

The mode in which these diaries were commenced is recorded by Mr. Sopwith in the first of the small series of volumes, written in 1828. When about twelve years of age, he says, he had a peculiar aptitude for descriptive writing, and amused himself with recording various data relative to the history and antiquities of Newcastle. At thirteen he copied a map of the Roman wall for Mr. Dalton, " an itinerant but highly respectable and able lecturer." He also wrote out, at this early period of his life, a series of notes on astronomical subjects, derived from the best sources of information attainable by him, with descriptions of observations he had made from a plain astronomical telescope constructed by himself, aided by a few opportunities of seeing and using a tolerably good instrument belonging to his schoolmaster, Mr. Henry Atkinson. In this same period of adolescence, he began to take notes of and draw up catalogues of coins and mineral specimens, employing, in his observations on the mineral specimens, a small microscope which, like his telescope, was constructed with his own hands.

From this methodical line of work he fell, naturally enough, into the way of keeping notes of his time, and of the details of his occupation ; following, in this respect, although probably quite unconsciously, the plan adopted in his early days by the famous Dr. Benjamin Franklin, a man, of all others I have read of, the most like himself in tone and character. It was not, however, until the year 1821 that he began a journal in a regular and permanent form. Then he was so fortunate, as he deemed it, as to obtain two or three account books or ledgers of considerable size, and containing a much longer space for writing than he had the means of getting in any new book,—manuscript books being at that time luxuries which we, of this day, can scarcely realize. Regardless of the red line for sums, he used these books for the purposes of his journal, and Volume 1. of the series covered an interval extending from October 28th, 1821, to June 2nd, 1828.

The father of Mr. Sopwith was a builder in Newcastle, carrying on a good business, and he, working industriously, with his eye directed towards engineering as his vocation through life, commenced his labours at six in the morning and continued them until six at night, with half an hour for breakfast and an hour for dinner. He had, therefore, not much time to expend on a journal, and, as he tells us, the details he had to enter were "of necessity trivial." Yet he found not only pleasure but advantage in the task, since it tended to fix his attention on different objects, enabled him to assist his memory by reference to a correct record made at the time, prevented him from depending on vague recollections, and, by inducing regularity of habit, increased the facility he possessed, naturally, of expressing himself precisely in descriptive writing. Two other good results followed the practice, namely, that the very occupation of writing led him to reflect on what he had recorded, and brought up the events of the past day, week, or month, to undergo, as it were, a formal review, which, in its turn, as an exercise of mind, induced a desire so to act, at all times, that he might feel a satisfaction from it whenever he came to the duty of recording what he was doing, or of reading what he had done. Those who knew Mr. Sopwith as I did will recall how notably this habit of order, learned so thoroughly in the commencement of his career, availed him all through his long life. He was the very soul of order and of exactitude, and came, I think, the nearest to the truth in all he said and did of any man I have ever known. I would not pretend, and I am sure he would have been the last to wish me to pretend, that this was from any particular goodness on his part. There was, no doubt, goodness in it and of it, but it was really a habit of accuracy, grafted upon a sound natural veracity. Many men perfectly truthful by nature are led away from the truth by a habit of loose observation on matters of fact. They trust entirely to memory, and, not taking sufficient time for fixing passing events properly in their minds, retain false impressions, which they are apt to give forth, often with much sorrow to themselves afterwards, in a form which does not bear the test of strict examination. Mr. Sopwith, truthful to the fullest degree by nature, cultivated truth methodically, and so became automatically truthful,—a high attainment.

CHAPTER III.

R. SOPWITH was born on the third day of January in 1803, and grew up a healthy boy. He was a very short time at school, and became, by the time he was of age, quite an adept in practical mechanical art. "I think," he once said to me, "that Sir Joseph Whitworth was not a better working engineer than I was;" and I once heard Sir Joseph, who to the last was proud of his own skill, say on his part, "I was quite as good with my hands, when I was young, as Tom Sopwith."

His elementary studies over, Mr. Sopwith, as a step onwards, began to study land-surveying; and gaining a practical knowledge of that art, he soon found opportunities of applying the knowledge he had acquired. In 1822 he was employed by the Corporation of Newcastle to make surveys, and as several private persons employed him in the same capacity, he carried out a considerable number of labours in surveying, and took an active part in planning the construction of a new jail in Newcastle. In this year, 1822, he was admitted a free Burgess of the Corporation of Newcastle, before the Right Worshipful William Wright, Esq., Mayor, and stood charged with a musket for the defence of the town.

The fact that he was admitted as a Burgess so early in life indicates that he had already made himself popular with the leading men of his native place,—a fact which is further borne out by the circumstance that a sum of ten guineas was voted to him by the Committee of the Town Council, with a complimentary message from the Mayor, and from Mr. John Clayton, the Town Clerk, a distinguished local man, whose death in his ninety-ninth year took place in July 1890, and was subject of comment far beyond the city and district in which he had flourished so long and won such golden respect.

He now finally determined to devote his life to the profession of an engineer. To this course his father assented, and on attaining the age of twenty-one he undertook to carry out a series of surveys for Mr. Joseph Dickinson, of Alston. At this time Mr. Dickinson, himself a surveyor of landed estates and mines, was engaged in surveying the lead-mines belonging to the Greenwich Hospital Estates. Into this work Mr. Sopwith entered, and a new world of wide extent lay before him, of scenery, geology, mining, in all of which he took delight. Once, when speaking to me of these early days, he told me, with a little touch of poetry, that his mental life rested at first on three supports: the mountain led him towards the skies and made him familiar with the stars; the earth kept him from becoming too aspiring, and in return made him familiar with the treasures of old which lie on her surface; and the mine took him under the earth, a still humbler sphere, to seek out knowledge in darkness, and the goods that are held in secret. So in some degree he became an astronomer; in some degree a geologist; and, in a

professed degree, a mineralogist. " And this," he added,
" embraced a great deal."

How he entered upon his majority is best told by the
following quotation from his diary, dated January 3rd,
1824.

" This day completes the twenty-first year of my age, and
terminates that period of life which all look back upon with
regret.   The amusements of childhood and the frivolity of
youth are now to be superseded by the more serious reflections
and pursuits of mature years. On taking retrospective views of
this interesting period of life, what varied scenes present themselves to view ! What happy days are past and gone for ever,
—ah ! never to return, but fondly registered in that memorial
of past affections where every day the leaf is turned to read
them ! How many in that time have been taken from the
troubled storms of life to the silent mansions of peace, solemn
instances of the uncertainty of life and of the rapid approach
of that period when the enjoyments of human life must fade
in the shadow ! "

With the money he had saved, and a small gift
from his father, he remained a year at Alston without salary or any other emolument. In the second
year he became a partner with his employer, and
commenced an independent life of activity, which,
as he often declared, was pursued onwards " with
comfort and happiness to himself, and he hoped with
some return of good to those by whom he was
surrounded."

In another memorandum, made in the year 1856, I
find him writing the following commentary on the
subject of his life at the period under description. It
is a commentary made in some happy moment, evidently
after perusing his first diary.

"I have, in looking over these pages, the opportunity of reviving as it were very distinct images in my mind of former days. I find recorded here the genuine thoughts and reflections which passed through my mind. I find much which I can rest upon with thankfulness and joy; but it is only too true that an exact and honest review of life cannot be made without seeing in bold relief the weakness, vanity, and imperfections of even our best efforts. Life indeed is a shadow, a vapour which passeth away, and the very ink on some of these books has already faded away. Yet how varied are those shadows; how diversified those vapours, like changing clouds,—sometimes heavy, dull, and hopeless, then bright and massive; at other times gay and fleecy, flashed with resplendent hues. Even so is life. We live that we may learn. The chiefest of all learning is to learn to live, and the foundation of all such learning can only be safely based on a humble, constant, and earnest faith in the never-failing goodness of God our Creator, our Preserver, and our Redeemer."

I have copied these simple words in all their simplicity and in all their purity. Had their author formed the least conception that they would one day be sent out to the world to be read, criticised, approved, or disapproved, he might have delivered them with more care and more effort at refinement. But no skill with the pen could have imparted the sentiments expressed with greater sincerity, or with greater sweetness of character. They reveal the man just as he was in his native worth.

The journal of Mr. Sopwith, extending over the long period already named, is something more than a mere diary. It contains a diary, with notices and occasional details of occurrences that came under his observation; but there is other matter also, consisting of extracts from MSS., scarce books, and miscellaneous collections copied at leisure hours at Newcastle-on-Tyne and at Alston. These include collections of pedigrees; copies of, and extracts from, correspondence; a common-place book, and plans and MSS. relating to public buildings and antiquities in Newcastle.

As to pedigree, it is necessary only to say that the Sopwith family had been located in Tyneside for three hundred years, and, as bearing on the proclivities of our present representative of it, that in 1735 one of its members, in company with Mr. Ennington, another well-known Northumbrian name, opened up and worked a lead-mine in the neighbourhood of Hexham. His father Jacob was born at Newcastle on May 23rd, 1770, and married Isabella daughter of Matthew Lowes.

Many curious incidents are related in the early diaries, showing the social life of the old English towns New castle and Durham at the commencement of the century. An account of the assize held at Durham, and of the outside ceremonial in 1823, is quaintly told. It was once customary to present the Mayor of the town on these grand occasions with a dagger, actually for his defence. The custom had ceased by this time, but the remembrance remained in the fact of the continued payment of a sum of money as "dagger money." At an assize at Newcastle this same year, Mr. Sopwith is an observer of Mr. Brougham, previous to attending the trial of Mr. Carr, the Captain of the Watch. Brougham, then rising towards the zenith of his fame, is described as "a tall, thin, dark, coarse-featured man, with nothing in his appearance indicative of those abilities which he so eminently possesses." In this same month (July 30th, 1823), a curious ceremony is described as taking place at Newcastle, namely, the Festival of St. Crispin, or, as

2

some called him, King Crispin. The festival had not
been held for many years—not, indeed, in the current
generation of Newcastle at least—and the streets of the
town were as much crowded as they had been at the time
of the coronation of the King, George IV., or at the time
of the visit of the Duke of Sussex. From the accounts
that had been rumoured forth about the splendours of
the pageant, something tremendous was expected. But,
alas! the grandeur was not realized. A number of
persons, the representative subjects of King Crispin, met
as the court of that monarch in the Freeman's Hospital
at nine a.m., and from thence marched through the
streets for three hours. At the Mansion House, the
Mayor had the privilege of drinking wine with the traves-
tied sovereign; but "the respectability and dresses and
numbers" of the actors "fell far short of the general
anticipation," and the antics of the paltry eccentric show
" became the laughing-stock of the public."

In this same year Mr. Sopwith seems to have been
unusually busied in many labours and exercises, which
brought him largely before his fellow-townsmen. He
made copies of "John Wesley's medal," and of his epitaph,
to be inserted in a volume of autograph letters of that
enthusiastic divine. He made the personal acquaintance
of the famous McAdam, of road-construction celebrity;
he learned to play on the organ, and occasionally
officiated as organist at All Saints' Church; and he took
part in the carrying out of many local improvements
in the town.

During the year 1825, Mr. Sopwith continued to work
at engineering with Mr. Dickinson, and was engaged
in the then novel employment of conducting a railway
survey. Respecting this work he has left some interesting notes, having reference to the early experience of

engineers in railway surveys, as well as to the arguments *pro* and *con* regarding the introduction of railways as lines of transit.

It was the birth-time of the railway system. Steamers had been put on rivers, and the idea was becoming common, amongst advanced and intelligent minds, that the whole country would have to be interlaced with railways for land transit, with the iron horse for the motor. This, however, meant the doom of the old coach, and all the associations connected with it. Many and varied interests, and sentiments which virtually are also interests, told against the new innovation even amongst those who were inclined, on scientific grounds, to be its advocates. The time had now come when some one was wanted in Newcastle-on-Tyne to take the practical steps towards the realization of a local scheme, and " to effect a more desirable communication across the island by a canal or a railway." The merits of a canal were very ably set forth by Mr. William Armstrong, a merchant of Newcastle ; but the general opinion was for a railway. During this period of indecision, in order to bring about the best information on the subject the services of Mr. Telford, an eminent local engineer, were called into requisition ; but as his numerous professional engagements prevented him from entering into the task for a twelvemonth, and bias in favour of a railroad increased, a committee that had been established to advance a railway scheme, and that had obtained shareholders very readily, called a meeting on May 21st, 1825, and completed an organization for the railway. A portion of the necessary work for the design was given to Mr. Sample, of Anick, near Hexham, and to Mr. Dickinson ; they were to undertake the construction of the line between Corbridge and Haydon Bridge ; and

for them Mr. Sopwith took part in the preliminary
inspection of the route that was to be followed.

Before undertaking these, his new duties, he returned
for a few days to Newcastle, and during this time visited
the exhibition of paintings and other works of art held
at the gallery in the house of Mr. T. M. Richardson. It
seems to have been a fine collection, the honours of which
were carried off, he reports, by Mr. Good, of Berwick, for a
picture of a fisherman with a gun. This picture was
bought, the first day, by Mr. Berkely, for twenty guineas;
a sum which another would-be possessor offered to increase by four times, without success. I mention this
note as indicating how early in life my friend began to
take an interest in artistic works.

CHAPTER IV.

1826.

THE year 1826 was welcomed by Mr. Sopwith with actual enthusiasm. He commenced his diary with a review of previous years, and added a list of the different persons of note with whom he had become acquainted, some of whom he had also entered on his list of friends. He was, at this stage, according to his own simple estimate, a fortunate man. He had entered a profession which was most congenial to his tastes and aspirations; he had won the respect of many connected with his native town; he had sent in his first account of fees, amounting to £16 16s., for surveying and plans, for the Corporation of Newcastle, per John Clayton, Town Clerk; and since then his pecuniary prospects had continued to brighten. With Mr. Dickinson he remained on the best terms, with promise of new arrangements for continued work in land and mine surveying.

He was now staying at Alston, and enjoying the quiet of the little place to his heart's content. He resided at "Mrs. Morris's." His time was chiefly occupied in drawing plans of mines and lands, and occasionally surveying both. A circle of intelligent and agreeable friends afforded many opportunities of profitable con-

versation ; and the skill of some of these in music
afforded him other opportunities of learning, practising,
and preserving his attachment for that most delightful
of all recreations. In brief, the information, good sense,
and hospitality which he received in Alston were most
grateful to him, and were indelibly engraved on "that
page where every day the leaf is turned to read, and
where the grateful recollection long exists."   Again,
somewhat after the manner of Benjamin Franklin, Mr.
Sopwith at this time kept a small book, in which he
entered with scrupulous care the minor details of each
day, and by this reviewed and shaped, day by day, the
course of his life.

In the early part of this year (1826) Mr. Sopwith,
for the first time, appeared as an author, by the publication of a descriptive historical account of All Saints'
Church, in Newcastle-upon-Tyne, illustrated with plans,
views, and architectural details.   From having been
engaged in the summer of 1824 to renew the plans of
freehold property in All Saints' Church, he determined
on the publication of an engraving of the church,
accompanied with some notices of the former and of
the present structure. In the prosecution of his design
he was favoured with the sanction of the clergy and
churchwardens, who readily communicated to him information bearing upon his subject. In his description he
added such particulars as local circumstances afforded,
collected from various sources : from documents in the
vestry of All Saints, from historical notices of the old
church by Bourne and Brand, and from personal inquiry
of those who remembered the old and nearly-forgotten
structure, to which he added the particulars of the erection of the present church. To many other engravings
he added a representation of a very curious brass plate,

formerly on the monument of Roger Thornton ; two plans to illustrate the architecture of the steeple ; and five plates of the armorial bearings in the cemetery, with the drawings and description of which he was favoured by Mr. M. A. Richardson.

The history of the church extends to one hundred and thirty-one closely-printed pages, and is not only a laborious but really a most interesting and historical essay, full of quaint observations and touching local stories and incidents. In one of these incidents some details are recorded of the life of a local celebrity named Captain William Hedley, who met with his death in the old church. At that time, a considerable portion of the body of the church having been taken down, the eastern extremity of the chancel was suffered to remain, and was afterwards enclosed for purposes of utility during the erection of the new church. The demolition of the steeple was unfortunately the cause of the fatal event long remembered. Hedley, in company with several other gentlemen, was inspecting the ruins of the building on the evening of September 2nd, 1786. The firm manner in which several parts of the tower were cemented rendered it necessary to have recourse to the operation of blasting with gunpowder, and one of the explosions not producing any immediate effect, the company drew near the place ; Mr. Hedley incautiously stepped within the great west door, when some stones fell from the upper part of the wall upon his head, causing a severe concussion of the brain, which deprived him of sense and in a few hours of life.

This accident was rendered the more deplorable because of the estimable qualities of Hedley, and an exhibition of bravery by him under the following circumstances, which made him the object even of national gratitude. The infant son of a wealthy person in Bordeaux having fallen into the river there, no inducement could prevail on any of the numerous spectators to attempt a rescue until Mr. Hedley plunged into the water and reached the child. The cries of admiration at his bravery were succeeded by lamentations for his supposed loss on seeing both the infant and himself disappear. With considerable difficulty, however, he succeeded in getting to the shore, and in restoring the child to its agonised parents. To their grateful acknowledgments he replied, "It is I who am most happy in giving consolation to a worthy family, and you owe me nothing, since this event has procured me a pleasure I shall never forget. There are few men who would not do what I have done." He then burst from them amidst the acclamations of the multitude, and cautiously eluded all the inquiries which were made with a design to pay due tribute to so brave a man. The following is an extract from an eulogium published in France concerning him :—

"All that could be learned was that his name was HEDLEY. Let this name then be consecrated on the records of humanity. May these trifles dictated by sentiment fall into the hands of this respectable Englishman, and may he not regret this tribute of gratitude paid him through me. My countrymen will not contradict me. Behold, ye of all nations and countries, such an eulogium as the heart ought to seek to be made known to the world. Without doubt we ought rather to preserve the name of Hedley than that of a warrior followed with blood, or of a politician whose negotiations are but a string of his perfidies. Unhappy mortals, will ye never be dazzled but by a sort of brightness which you yourselves lend to infamy, in decreeing it the honour of that immortality which ought only to be the recompense of those who do well? Bury therefore in eternal oblivion the oppressor, and all who are dishonourable to their species. Virtue alone deserves our remembrance."

The sentiments of this eulogium, Mr. Sopwith tells us, were also elegantly expressed in a piece of poetry which, as he was not aware of its having been previously published, he sent, many years before, to the *Newcastle Monthly Visitor*, in which magazine it was inserted in November 1816.

Taking it altogether, the diary of my friend for the year 1826 shows a life of continued enjoyment in the midst of work often of an arduous kind. He concludes his notes of the year with the observation that during the whole of the time he has been chiefly engaged in land and mine surveying with Mr. Joseph Dickinson. In May he completed the publication of the "History of All Saints' Church." He enjoyed good health and agreeable society, was for the most part very happy and contented, and ended the year with sentiments and opinions similar to those with which he commenced it.

CHAPTER V.

1827.

THE year 1827 presents Mr. Sopwith once more enjoying the monotony of a quiet country life. His working time was occupied with business through the day, and occasionally through the evening. His leisure time was chiefly spent at home, in writing and drawing, in architectural or geological studies. He retained his love for the practice of music, and essayed to play on the pianoforte, but soon devoted himself exclusively to the organ, which with him was "the king of instruments." A little later in the year, namely, in the beginning of March, he was seized rather suddenly with what was then called an attack of acute inflammatory fever. The record of this illness is remarkable, as indicative of the practice of medicine then in vogue. He tells us that the pain in his knees and limbs was extremely severe, and that two days afterwards, on attempting to go down stairs, he became faint, and was overpowered by a peculiarly suffocating sensation in his breath. In the evening he was too feeble to be able to return upstairs, and went therefore to bed in the "low parlour." Here he passed a restless night, and at five on the following day he was

attended by a surgeon of the name of Shaw, who bled
him to eighteen ounces, gave him a calomel pill, a dose
of Epsom salts, afterwards a dose of opium, and, on
the following day, a mixture of digitalis, antimony, and
tartar emetic every four hours to reduce the circulation.
He says he perspired profusely, and was very restless
until four in the morning, when Dr. Shaw, being sent for
again, took from him eighteen ounces more blood, after
which he was removed upstairs to his own room, where
he went to sleep and awoke about two the following
morning greatly relieved. This was on a Sunday. He
remained " variable," getting little rest and taking no
solid food, until the following Wednesday. On Thursday he got up at three p.m., and sat until bedtime. On
Friday he arose at nine a.m., sat until night, commenced
to take a " mixture of columba," and rapidly returned to
his natural state of health. Curiously enough, a little
later in the same month his own father was seized in a
somewhat similar manner at Newcastle—" attacked with
severe pain in his breast "—and was greatly relieved by
being freely bled.

On September 28th, 1827, Mr. Sopwith describes the
visit of the Duke of Wellington to Newcastle. The Duke
was this day presented with the freedom of the town, on
a large platform erected on the front of the Exchange,
in the presence of many thousands of people. The Duke
reviewed the yeomanry troops on the Moor, dined at the
Mansion House, and, after visiting the Assembly Rooms,
went to Ravensworth Castle. In a letter added by a
sister of Mr. Sopwith, the Duke is described as by no
means realizing the anticipation of the hero of Waterloo.
" He had very white hair, was carefully dressed in an old
and plain surtout, ornamented with a Waterloo medal,
and wore a round hat. He did not court the popular

observation, and the sovereign people seemed to take it rather amiss that his Grace took so little notice of them who did so zealously disturb themselves to take notice of him."

In a summary to the memoranda of this year, Mr. Sopwith adds some curious social facts bearing upon this period of his life. He observes that in 1825 the Stamp Duty was nominally 4*d*., but a discount of 20 per cent. was granted by Parliament against heavy Excise duties, which reduced the duty to 3¼*d*. per sheet. The price of paper was 70*s*. per thousand for the large papers, or rather more than 4⅓*d*. per sheet. The stamp and paper, therefore, cost rather more than 4*d*.

The 7*d*. London newspapers were sold to agents at 13*s*. per quire (technical of 27 papers), or 5⅑*d*., so that about 1¾*d*. was all that remained for remuneration and expenses, the agents receiving 1⅖*d*. on each paper. The regular salaries paid by the editors and proprietors of morning papers amounted to £5,000, £6,000, and even £7,000 per annum. The expenses of procuring reports of parliamentary proceedings for the daily papers was upwards of £3,000 per annum. Ten or fourteen reporters were employed, and each was engaged in the House for three-quarters of an hour to an hour. Formerly 250 impressions could be struck off in one hour, but now by steam-power 2,000, and even 2,500, could be struck off in the same period of time.

He adds to these some other statistical accounts.

In Great Britain, the number of men from 50 to 60 years of age, capable of rising in arms *en masse*, was 2,744,847, or about 4 in every 7 males.

There were about 90,000 marriages every year,—that is to say, about 246 every day,—and in 63 marriages three only were without issue.

The number of deaths in Great Britain yearly was 332,700 persons; monthly, 25,592; weekly, 6,398; daily, 914; hourly, 40. The proportion of the deaths of women to that of men was as 50 to 54. Married women lived longer than unmarried women.

In country places, the average number of children born of each marriage was 4. In cities and large towns the proportion was 7 children to two marriages, or $3\frac{1}{2}$ to one.

Married men formed three-fifths of the male population, but married women formed one-third of the female population.

Four out of five widows re-married.

The number of old persons who died during cold weather, to those who died during the warm weather, was as 7 to 4.

Half of all who were born in Great Britain died before the age of 17 years.

The proportion of twins at a single birth was 1 to 63.

The small-pox in the natural way carried off 8 in 100, and by inoculation 1 in 300.

The proportion of males born to females was 26 males to 25 females.

In 1801 the male population of Great Britain was 5,450,292, while the female population was 5,492,354, or 100 females to 99 males. The total population of the metropolis at that time was 1,099,104 persons, in the proportion of 100 males to 128 females.

In 1812 1 male in 10 in England and Ireland was under arms.

It appears from tables extending from 1772 to 1778 that nearly 1 in 8 cases of insanity arose from religious fanaticism.

Under the head of "Extracts from Brand's and Bourne's

'Antiquities,'" Mr. Sopwith makes some curious comments on the " Soul Bell," adding the following particulars on the use of the bells of the churches in the populous town of Newcastle-upon-Tyne. There, he says, the church bells have not been confined to ecclesiastical uses. They have also with great propriety been adapted to civil purposes. The tolling of the great bell at St. Nicholas' Church there was an ancient signal for the Burgesses to convene a Guild-Day, and likewise on the day of electing magistrates. The little carnival on Pancake Tuesday commences by the same signal. A bell, usually called "the Thief and Reever" (reever = a robber : to reeve, to spoil, or rob) bell, proclaimed the two annual fairs. A peculiar kind of alarm was given by a bell for accidents or fire. A bell was rung at six in the morning, except Sundays and holidays, with a view, it would seem, of calling up the artisans to their daily labour. There was also retained the vestige of the old Norman Curfew at eight in the evening. The bells were muffled on January 30th, for which he could find no precedent. Their sound on this occasion was peculiarly pleasant. Had my friend enquired more carefully into this matter he might possibly have discovered that the muffled bells on January 30th were the continuous mourning for the death of Charles I.

Distinction of rank, he observes, was preserved in Newcastle in the tolling of the Soul Bell. A high fee excludes the common people and appropriates to the death of persons of consequence the tolling of the great bell of each church. A bell also was tolled, and sometimes chimes were rung, a little before the burial, and while the body was being carried to the church. They chime or ring too, sometimes, when the grave is being filled up.

In another note made by Mr. Sopwith in this same year I find some calculations which he has collected relative to the importation of tea into England. In 1669 the quantity of tea imported was 143 pounds; in 1678 it had risen to 4,713 pounds. In 1700 it had become 20,000 pounds. In 1721, 1,000,000, and in 1816 it had reached 36,234,380 pounds.

On the same page he writes down a very good receipt for a scent-pot given to him by Dr. Dyer of Newcastle, as follows :—

" Calamus root .	. $1\frac{1}{2}$ ounce
Orris root	. 1 ounce
Musk	. 15 grains

To this add lavender flowers, damask rose leaves, and bay salt, as much as you please."

CHAPTER VI.

1828.

THE year 1828 was eventful for my friend. At the commencement of the year he was still residing at Alston, where he began to learn the art of engraving. The results of his labours in this direction ended in the publication of his work "Geological Sections of Mines." This work was illustrated with plates, and exhibits the subterraneous workings of the mines in the Manor of Alston Moor by a horizontal or ground plan, and by an upright or vertical section. These plans were intended to assist mining proprietors and those interested in the study of geology, by supplying numerous records of established facts on the disposition of strata, the position of mineral veins and their productiveness under various changes. The plans he executed for this work, some of them beautifully coloured, were of the most practical nature, and connected with the undertaking he showed a warm enthusiasm. He expressed the opinion that similar plans should be made in every mining district, and quoted from the celebrated Werner in his theory of the formation of veins, that a collection of geological plans, with the plan and description of a district, would

form a most instructive volume. To which he added :—
"If our ancestors had left us such documents for two
centuries past, or even for half a century, what advantage
would it not have been to us ! From what doubts would
it not relieve us ! With what anxiety do we not turn
over the leaves of ancient chronicles in search of information, often very imperfect, obscure, and uncertain ! With
what pleasure do we not receive the least sketch or plan
of some ancient mine ? With what pains do we not rake
up heaps of rubbish brought out of old excavations, to
discover pieces which may afford us some idea of the
substances which were formerly worked out ? Yet between these documents and those which we might obtain
in the way pointed out in the preceding paragraphs, there
is as much difference as between night and day. Would
it not be an obligation, a duty, for us to collect and leave
to future generations as much instruction and knowledge
as possible on the labours carried on in our mines,
whether it be in those that are still worked, or in those
which have been given up ? "

In the beginning of April he left home for the first
time for a long journey, paying a visit to Scotland, and
taking various places on his way, travelling by coach.
On April 3rd he passed through a vale of beautiful
scenery from Longtown to Langholm, and thence through
the mountainous district of Ewesdale, where he had the
pleasure of meeting Sir Walter Scott and his daughter.
In the evening he arrived at Hawick, and next day went
on a coach called the "Sir Walter Scott," by Selkirk to
Edinburgh.

The visit to Edinburgh is related by Mr. Sopwith in
the diary with much detail. It lasted for three weeks,
during which time it opened up many very pleasant
and important friendships. The distinguished actor

Vandenhorf was at Edinburgh at the time, with his wife and daughter, and showed him many courtesies. Of this family he speaks in the highest terms, dwelling particularly on the scholastic and accomplished character of the great tragedian. He was also introduced to some of the famous professors of that day, and attended the lectures of two of them, namely, Professor Wilson, who then held the chair of Moral Philosophy, and Professor Hope, who held the chair of Chemistry. The contrast which he draws between these two lecturers is as amusing as it is interesting. Wilson was all verve, animation, and yet condensation; while Hope was calm, deliberate, slow, with a delivery so low and a method so technical, it was difficult to follow him. Hope, at this time, had the largest classroom in Edinburgh. It would receive over six hundred students, and on one occasion when Mr. Sopwith was present there were over three hundred present.

The lecture is thus briefly described :—

"Ten minutes of the hour elapsed before he (Dr. Hope) entered, and his method seemed anything but that which gets through a great deal of business in little time. Much of the lecture was on the nature of soap, and its composition and qualities were exhibited in some experiments; the nature of volatile oils was then discussed, and a very neat exhibition of instantaneous combustion from the mixture of cold liquids shown. The low tone of his voice prevented me following him in a discourse so much compounded of technical language. A few of the students, I observed, took brief notes, but in the more important parts of his course, a few weeks ago, a friend informed me that nearly all the students made notes. As many of them attend several classes, of which the lectures closely follow each other, and each occupy an hour, very strict punctuality is required, which in this class was developed in a somewhat singular manner. The bell rings at the close of the hour, the janitor throws open the door of the classroom, and if a train of artillery loaded for their annihilation was about to enter, it could not send them more speedily on their departure than did the mere opening of the door. Up they rose *en masse*, helter skelter over forms and benches, and left the worthy Professor apparently wondering at this uproarious and instantaneous departure in the midst of his discourse. The effect was to me very odd. 'Gentlemen,' said Dr. Hope, 'to discover the purity of this liquid, which is often adulterated, you pour a few drops on paper and hold it to the fire;' and suiting the action to the word, he was about to do so. 'Now, gentlemen, if it evaporates——' But oh the uncertainty of human life, which most truly does pass away as a vapour! At that moment the folding doors flew open, and the class, regardless of the purity of the spirits of turpentine, more speedily evaporated than even the volatile fluid which remained in the Doctor's hands. It was in vain that he attempted to stem the current by a few words, which the noise did not allow me to hear distinctly, but there were some rather expressive words about 'great hurry' and 'doing it again.' But even this, seconded by the more eloquent countenance of the Professor, was in vain."

The reports of Professor Wilson's lectures on moral obligations, internal piety, self-interest, obedience to the Divine will, involuntary affections as a part of virtue, influence of the affections, observance of moral rules not the only essentials to virtue, the affections as duties, prudence and courage, view of mankind, remaining excellences of human nature, high moral sentiments, general sense of moral obligations, and union of religion and morals, are admirably epitomised in several pages of the journal. Still more interesting is the account he gives of a visit he paid the Professor at his residence, No. 6, Gloucester Place, in Edinburgh, on Sunday,

April 20th, 1828.   Lovers of "Christopher North" will be
grateful for this little bit of new light on the character
and manners of this brilliant scholar.

"On Sunday evening, April 20th, 1828, I spent part of the
evening with Professor Wilson, at his house, No. 6, Gloucester
Place, Edinburgh.   He was in a spacious room, without any
fire, and had two tables covered with books and manuscripts
before him; a paper on which he had written a few lines,
and a small book of poetry, were apparently occupying his
attention when I entered.   He was carelessly dressed in a
large and coarse great coat and waistcoat, no neckcloth to a
shirt seemingly worn two or three days, and a beard neglected
for the same period; his hair also disordered.   He is a tall,
rather stout, and good-looking man—much more so in his
lecture-room than the study; speaks with rapidity, but very
distinctly.   He walked quickly backwards and forwards in the
compass of a few paces, and took snuff from a paper on the
table.   The conversation, though brief and hurried, included
the following subjects: Highland scenery, Heber, Hugh
Moises, Hodgson's 'Northumberland.' York Minster, Sir
Walter Scott, Brougham's treatises, Grecian and Gothic architecture, Bewick, Nesbitt, Harvey, and wood engraving.   He
also enquired after Doubleday, Losh, Turner, Adamson, and
others.

"He had travelled, he said, a good deal on foot, and was
very fond of seeing strange places. . . . Had been at Alston.
. . . April rather too early for the Highlands, but May and
June very favourable.   Some prefer autumn and yellow-tinted
trees, but 'for my part,' said he, 'I love to see Nature in her
native and gayest colours, her beautiful green; and as for
diversity, trees naturally vary in colour at all times.'

"'Heber was one of the most amiable of men, and a fine
poet.   I knew him when at college.   He was of a very cheerful, lively, playful disposition; so much so, indeed, that it was
feared it might tend to idleness; in other respects he was

clever, and a very amiable character. . . . Mrs. Heber is a
very clever woman; I had no conception how clever. . . . I
wrote an article in *Blackwood's Magazine* a few months ago
on "Heber's Hymns," and received a very affecting letter from
her, with a copy of his "Indian Journal."'

"We spoke of the Rev. Hugh Moises, of the late and
present Bishop of Durham, and of Hodgson's 'History of
Northumberland.' He seemed much interested in the account
I gave him of the plan, and of the various details wrought up
in it. . . . He promised to see it. . . .

"'I have been in most of the Cathedrals in England, but
York Minster excels them all. . . . I first saw it when going
to college at seventeen years of age, and till then had no idea
that so magnificent a structure existed. . . . It alone is well
worth going a long way to see.'

"When speaking of Sir Walter Scott, I enquired whether
he was intended for the Church, as seems intimated in one of
the stanzas of 'Harold the Dauntless,' beginning,

'Grey towers of Durham, there was once a time.'

He said he was not aware of it, but thought it very likely that
this might have been at one time his intention. 'He is not
much attached to law, but in Scotland it is almost the only
profession that a man can get well forward in. Sir Walter
is not a member of the Church of England, but has a great
liking for it. You were fortunate in the coincidence of
meeting him on your first entrance into Scotland, and amid
so romantic scenery. I well remember it, being once detained
by an accident several days at Mosspaul.'

"I mentioned the treatises of the Society for Promoting
Useful Knowledge. 'I have only seen eight or ten numbers.
I think them very clever, and written by very able men.'

"We had some conversation on the architecture of Edinburgh, on the splendid Roman models of Adams, and on the
defective Gothic in St. George's Chapel by the same. I mentioned an idea that occurred to me several times, viz., that the
same combination of Gothic designs (as is common in the

Grecian) would produce a pleasing contrast, and have the imposing character of an immense cathedral pile.

"He made many enquiries about Bewick. 'My children will have his books alone. They are often lying on my breakfast table and other places, and I always look at them with renewed pleasure.' This observation is made in *Blackwood* about six weeks after, in these words, 'Have we forgotten the genius that dwells on the banks of the Tyne? . . . No . . . his books lie on our parlour, bedroom, dining-room, drawing-room, study tables, and are never out of place or time. . . . Happy old man! the delight of childhood, manhood, decaying age; a moral in every titlepiece, a sermon in every vignette.' This coincidence seems to indicate the Professor to be the writer of the article in which it appears, and which is a very favourable review of his brother James Wilson's 'Zoology.'

"On leaving, Mr. Wilson assured me he would call if he should again visit Alston. . . . On the whole, I was much pleased by his courtesy, and greatly admired his amazing penetration and intelligence."

Another very interesting interview was held by my friend whilst he was in Edinburgh with a man destined to play a leading part in the working literature of this country; one also whom we had the pleasure for many years to call our mutual friend, and about whom we often conversed in later days—I mean the distinguished Robert Chambers. Mr. Chambers, at the time when Mr. Sopwith first made his acquaintance, was in business in Edinburgh, and a note respecting his call is here given. It is a short but bright picture of the author of the "Vestiges of Creation" at the commencement of his hopeful and striking career.

"I called at the house of Mr. Robert Chambers, author of the 'Picture Book of Scotland' and other works, and had some conversation with him. He is a young man, and has lately travelled upwards of two thousand miles in various parts of Scotland, chiefly on foot, notwithstanding a slight lameness."

To this interview Mr. Sopwith, some time afterwards, added, in reference to the famous journal which William and Robert Chambers commenced :—

"The ability and moral influence of the well-known journal conducted by him and his brother are beyond all praise. Not only is that publication one of the most attractive means of improvement and refinement of the age ; but the energy and judgment of its conductors, so strikingly displayed in every number, are likely to effect a reformation of many abuses which exist in periodical publications, and to give a new and decided tone, which may operate in a very powerful degree towards the general welfare and happiness of society, not only to this but to other nations."

In our friendly gossipings on men and events, Mr. Sopwith and I often spoke and thought of events and sayings relating to Robert Chambers. I remember, as if it were but yesterday, telling Mr. Sopwith of my last meeting with our friend ; how one fearfully cold and stormy day in winter time, after paying a flying visit to St. Andrews on business connected with the University Court, I met Dr. Chambers (who then resided there) on my way from the University to the railway station ; how he insisted that on so bleak an afternoon I should not pass his house, but should rest there for the night, and "see his books, and talk of old friends and past times ; " and how vexed he was that a fixed engagement to lecture that very night in Edinburgh on my way back to town rendered it impossible for me to accept the gracious hospitality. "That was Robert Chambers all over," said Mr. Sopwith; who thereupon entered warmly on "the work that man has done. And remember what I say," he continued prophetically :—

"He is certain to turn out to be the author of the ' Vestiges.' I have reckoned him up page by page, comparing that book with his other works, and if I were put in the witness-box as an expert in calculations, I could prove the thing to the satisfaction of any intelligent jury."

Taking it altogether, the journey of Mr. Sopwith to Scotland was rich in interest of every kind, and an extremely useful lesson to him in this part of his career. He returned home, visiting on his way all the principal places on the Scottish border, and records with much care numerous particulars of place and history ; sometimes correcting, sometimes expanding, what others have said. For example, in describing Yevering Bell, a hill in the neighbourhood of the Cheviots, he corrects Hutchinson, commonly considered an authority of good repute.

"Yevering Bell, in this neighbourhood, is a steep, conical hill, and is remarkable for the extensive vestiges of antiquity on its summit, and which are commonly supposed to be of Druidical origin. There are two eminences, on the higher of which is a large cairn, or collection of stones, surrounded by a ditch ; and the whole is surrounded by the ruins of a wall of vast dimensions, which now occupy a breadth of about six yards, and varying in height from one to three feet. Hutchinson describes this hill as being two thousand feet in perpendicular height above the level of Milford Plain ; but, from observations which I made, I do not think it exceeds eight hundred feet in height."

A visit to Flodden Field afforded a striking though

rather broken picture of that memorable place. He tells
how he and his companions rode up a steep hill (which
is now planted), and observed the remains of the entrench-
ments where the Scottish army lay encamped for some
time previous to the battle. The summit was covered
with earth and mounds, and commanded an extensive
and most beautiful prospect southward as far as Wooler,
and on the north and east also a beautiful country, seen
spreading out to a great distance. He expresses himself
as very much struck in contemplating the transactions of
that fatal conflict on the very spot where it occurred, and
especially the fatality which overwhelmed the extraordinary advantages of the Scottish army, and rendered
the very precautions for their safety the immediate cause
of their defeat and ruin. He crossed a small stream, on
each side of which was a gentle declivity, and here the
thickest part of the conflict took place, according to
tradition, which the position itself seems to indicate.
He considers that no correct estimate has ever been
given of the numbers slain ; but though the loss on the
English side was trifling, that of the Scotch included
their king (James IV.), the flower of their nobility—
amongst whom were the Archbishop of St. Andrews, two
bishops, four abbots, twelve earls, seventeen barons, four
hundred knights, and many esquires and gentlemen.
The entire loss on the Scottish side has been calculated
from five to seventeen thousand, while upon the English
side it was about fifteen hundred. He concludes his note
with a happy allusion to the happier time in which he
lived, when civil war and bloodshed were known only by
tradition, and cultivation smiled over a scene which for
a few hours was once a scene of death and desolation.

Getting nearer home, he visited Hulme Abbey, and
found it undergoing repairs of some interest to the

admirers of Sir Walter Scott. The repairs were suggested to the Duke of Northumberland by Sir Walter. The ivy which covered a large portion of the walls had been taken off, and the stonework pointed with Roman cement, by which process the walls presented the appearance of a badly-built barn rather than of venerable ruins. With all his admiration for Scott, Mr. Sopwith maintains his own love for ivy. "Ivy," he says, "though sometimes destructive, is a great ornament; and he was not surprised to hear a general expression of opinion that tearing it from the walls of Hulme Abbey had greatly impaired the appearance and beauty of the building."

CHAPTER VII.

1828-29.

RETURNING to Alston in May, 1828, Mr. Sopwith resumed his engineering labours in his usual methodical style. His diary presents no point of special interest until September 2nd; there then occurs this important entry :—

" Married by license at Alston Church, by the Rev. Anthony Hedley, A.M., Thomas Sopwith to Mary, eldest daughter of Mr. Thomas Dickenson, of Spency Croft, near Alston, and principal agent to the Greenwich Hospital Estate and mines in this district."

The engagement had lasted for five years, and was, in every sense of the word, one of sincere affection. The marriage was followed by a short honeymoon, and then a return to work.

1829.

In February Mr. Sopwith was occupied in writing a brief account of the burning of York Minster by Jonathan Martin, which account was published in the *Newcastle Courier* on February 13th as a bit of cotemporary history. The more important extracts from this long-forgotten article call for repetition here.

"The strong suspicions which were excited of Jonathan Martin being the author of the destruction of the Choir of York Minster, have been confirmed by the apprehension of that remarkable individual, who, by an act of daring intrepidity impelled by religious frenzy, has secured an inglorious notoriety, equalled only perhaps by that of Erostratus, who to perpetuate his name fired the temple of Diana at Ephesus, over two thousand years ago.

"The ruin of the finest portion of the most splendid edifice in the kingdom has excited universal regret and an intense feeling which renders every particular of its destruction interesting. The following particulars were given by Martin himself while at Newcastle, exactly a week after the event. At the conclusion of the evening service at the Minster, on Sunday, February 1st, 1829, he, Martin, secreted himself in one of the recesses of the clustered columns which support the central tower. About nine at night he went to the belfry, in one of the western towers, where he lighted a candle by means of his razor, matches, and tinder-box. He drew up a bell rope, which he cut, and having coiled it, brought it down to the nave, when he put out the light and knotted the rope, which he made use of to enter the Choir. He spent three hours in arranging the folio books, cushions, and other combustibles in two heaps on either side of the organ; and having prepared, by tearing the leaves from the books, the most effectual means for completing his scheme, he set fire to both heaps at once, and on seeing the conflagration fairly commenced, departed by means of a rope through a window, breaking it with a pair of pincers which he took for that purpose that he might not cut his fingers. He assigned as his reason for destroying so beautiful a building that they did not preach the true doctrine of Christ, and that it was for the honour and glory of God. In answer to the question, 'Do you not expect to be punished for this great offence against the Church?' he replied, 'That is between the Almighty and me; I am willing to suffer any punishment for the glory of God.' He said that when in the Cathedral he felt quite comfortable, and in no way oppressed with that solemnity and awe which the venerable pile usually impresses upon spectators, and which to a mind capable of reflection must have been singularly awful in the darkness and silence of the night.

"Poetic imagination can hardly conceive a more distressing or remarkable scene than this poor idiot wandering alone in the vast aisles of the glorious structure, the last and only spectator of that magnificent Choir, on which the beams of light had shed their parting rays, and the chords of the organ had sounded their rolling thunders and sweet melodies never to be again heard! The holy and beautiful house where our fathers worshipped about to be burnt with fire, and the noblest monument of the land about to be destroyed!"

Twenty-five years after this event Mr. Sopwith described it to me at the house of a mutual friend, where, during our visit, we met one of the nearest relatives of the unhappy man who had been the cause of so much alarm. Mr. Sopwith knew another brother of the same family, William, who lived at Newcastle, and whose mind went wrong under the impression that he had discovered perpetual motion, on which discovery he published a new system of natural philosophy on the principle of perpetual motion (Newcastle, Preston, 1821). Later on (namely 1829) this brother published another work, entitled "William Martin's Challenge to All the World as a Philosopher and Critic," in which work he includes "The Flight through the Universe into Boundless Space; or, The Philosopher's Travels of his Mind," with another chapter, "A Critique on All False Men who pretend to be Critics, and not being Men of Wisdom or Genius." The same man also, after making an attack on the distinguished astronomer Dr. Nichol of Glasgow, turned round upon a religious sect with "A Stumbling-block to the Unitarians, proving Three in One in Everything."

While pitying these two unhappy brothers, Mr. Sopwith had unbounded admiration of a third brother of the same family, the marvellous John Martin, the painter, whose works as an artist were, he thought, even surpassed by his suggestions as an engineer, by his plans for improved sanitation, and by his hopes of securing a healthy world. "Truly," my friend said, as he closed the history, "in this case it is literally the fact :—

"'Great genius is to madness close allied.'"

Coming back from this short digression, I am brought to the record of a first domestic calamity, one which threw, for a time, a cloud over Mr. Sopwith's life. On July 21st, 1829, he spent the day with the Rev. Anthony Hedley, of Whitfield, by whom he had been married, some ten months before, to Mary Dickenson. The two gentlemen devoted their time to the study of several manuscripts, which Mr. Sopwith had written at intervals, on mining records, and a descriptive account of Alston for Mr. Davidson's intended work on Border excursions. Three days later, namely, on July 24th, an event happened which he thus records :—

"At eight o'clock this morning my dear Mary was safely delivered of her first-born child, a fine boy, at Loaning House, near Alston. The afternoon was one continued and dreadful storm of thunder and rain. Gilderdale and Thornhope bridges were carried away by violent floods."

Seven days later is the next mournful minute :—

"July 31st.—The remains of my dear Mary have this

evening been interred in the Chapel yard of the Independent
Congregation of Alston."

The particulars of this bereavement are given at great
length in a special chapter of the diary and in one of
the most touching of narratives I ever remember to have
read.   There is an account of the correspondence between
himself and his wife, of the trust they put in each other,
of their mutual fondness for particular pursuits, of all
others the "delights" of music.   Then come the
details of the catastrophe.   The child is born on
Friday morning, and all goes well until Sunday, when
the happy mother is so amused with some story a kind
lady friend tells her, that she has to be checked in her
mirth.   Then she expresses a desire that her child
shall be named after Mr. Sopwith's father, Jacob,
but soon after is seized suddenly with excruciating
internal pain, which continues with little intermission,
and in the presence of her husband and parents she
sinks into death on Tuesday afternoon, July 28th.
With the practical common sense which marked him
in all his life, Mr. Sopwith met his terrible bereavement
by holding himself close to his work.   He summoned
resolution to walk a great deal, to endeavour to take his
meals as usual, to converse with all the cheerfulness he
could command, and to sleep as regularly as was possible.
Happily for him, just at this juncture a new and, as it
may also be called, a novel duty came to him, by his
being invited, through his friend the Rev. John Hodgson,
to undertake a commission for Sir John Swinburne
to survey from Otterburn to Newcastle.   Undertaking
this duty, he was led by it to visit Capheaton, the
seat of Sir John Swinburne, to receive his instructions for the survey.   Here he met with a most kind

reception from all the family, and forthwith started on
a survey, the novelty of which served as a most useful
diversion to his mind.

On October 16th Mr. Sopwith began to be closely
engaged in his new duties, in making parliamentary
surveys for two lines of railway. He left Newcastle with
much regret, owing to the circumstance of his father,
Mr. Jacob Sopwith, being extremely ill; and on the 20th
received a message at Newham Edge that his father had
experienced an apoplectic seizure, with which his life had
terminated. By this event he became the possessor of
all the property and stock connected with his father's
business which he at once determined to continue at
least for a time.

In the course of the following month, Mr. Sopwith
was admitted to the freedom of the Joiners' Company;
he paid for the honour £5 11s., namely—fees, £4 9s. ;
stamp, £1 ; and warden 2s.

In many senses, the year 1829 was eventful and painful
to my friend. He had sustained two severe domestic
losses in the deaths of his wife and father, each of which
had affected him severely. On the other hand, he had
secured many advantages, that were to him sources of
special pleasure. He had, as we have seen, met distinguished men in Edinburgh, and to these he had added
other friends, such as Campbell, the African traveller;
Ward, the writer of a work on Mexico; and Sir John
Swinburne. He had also been engaged in labours which
were most congenial to his tastes. He had engraved
plans of mines in Mexico for Mr. John Taylor, had drawn
geological plans of mines near his native place, and had
become one of the first of the engineers connected with
the gigantic development of railway industry. To him,

at that time, this last-named industry appeared as a kind
of dream certain to be true and yet seeming quite impossible of attainment to the full result suggested. I
heard him once express regret that he did not at this
period take exclusively to railway engineering, inasmuch
as the field was open to him. But towards the close of
this eventful year his mind was at times gloomy and filled
with forebodings, "as if a dark cloud hung over him,"
as he expresses it in a passage in his diary, and for a
season was even "embittered." In the midst of this he
was enchained by local sympathies; so, although the
opening of the Stockton and Darlington Railway a short
time before, and the forthcoming opening of the Liverpool and Manchester line, had stirred in him a warm
enthusiasm, which was intensified somewhat by his own
work of parliamentary surveying, he let the opportunity
go by of being a leader in railway enterprise, and limited
himself largely to mining, as a branch of his profession
that was to occupy him chiefly through the remaining
portion of his active life.

CHAPTER VIII.

THE early part of 1830 found Mr. Sopwith re-domesticated in Newcastle, with his hands very full of business indeed. He began by inventing a new cabinet for business papers, which afterwards, with various improvements, became one of the most ingenious and useful office cabinets that was ever produced. He arranged his cash books in three volumes ; one for his every-day business, another for surveying, and a third for miscellanies. He commenced also the systematic study of geology under the Rev. Robert Turner, and undertook much surveying in in-clement weather and under difficult circumstances. At this time he continued, in more methodical form, his diary so as to give it permanency of character.

On February 2nd he left Newcastle at six o'clock in the morning in the "Chevy Chase" coach for Edinburgh, and in the midst of snow reached the last-named place after a journey of fifteen hours and a half. On the following morning, with a four-horse coach, he drove to Kerswell House, Lanarkshire, to obtain Mr. Lisle's assent to the Otterburn line. He returned to Edinburgh the same night, dined with Professor Pillans, and the next day got back to Newcastle.

In March Mr. Sopwith paid his first visit to London, to give evidence in reference to a Bill at this time before Parliament ; and as a memento of travelling sixty years ago I give the story entire from his diary.

"I left Newcastle in the Wellington coach on Sunday morning, March 7th, at 5 o'clock. Darkness and a well-known country afforded little to occupy attention, and having no companions I had abundant scope for reflection.

"I was really surprised to find myself at Durham so soon, for the awe of a comparatively long journey seemed to have taken away all idea of length of time, or distance from lesser portions of it. A hazy morning obscured the distant view, but on crossing Framwellgate Bridge and observing the rugged battlements of the Castle, the smooth surface of the Wear, the Prebend's Bridge, the woody banks, and splendid towers of the Cathedral, I felt convinced that a more admirable combination of interesting and picturesque objects would rarely be equalled, and probably in no part of England excelled.

"The road in the county of Durham is at present in no commendable state of repair.

"On entering Yorkshire, the roads are much better and the country flat. Northallerton Church is a venerable Gothic edifice ; from thence to Thirsk, the view on the right is confined, but on the other side is extensive and beautiful. The village of Lawton is delightfully seated on a luxuriant hill-side, and an extensive and cultivated view is terminated by the range of moorlands, on which much snow was yet remaining.

"The milestones hereabouts are extremely neat, made of wood or cast iron, and having raised letters of metal upon them.

"As we approached Thirsk, the beauty of the country was enhanced by the increasing fineness of the day, and at one o'clock a most interesting prospect of rugged and snow-clad hills, limestone cliffs, and a luxuriant valley of well-cultivated land was brightened by the smiles of an unclouded sun and clear azure sky.   The neighbourhood of Thirsk in summer must be extremely beautiful, the land is of good quality, and the whole face of the country thickly studded with hedgerow trees ; the church is a very beautiful Gothic structure.

"On arriving at York I spent the half-hour allowed for dinner in viewing the exterior of the Minster.   The sun shone brightly on the west front, and thus presented in the most favourable light a scene of architectural magnificence far surpassing anything of the kind I had ever before seen.

"The very excellent delineations, however, not only of the main features, but also of the most minute details in halfpenny and other books had so familiarised me to them that I can hardly say that it either surpassed or fell short of my anticipations ; the latter would indeed be an almost impossible case, for what but very accurate representations could incite anything like a just conception of so truly noble a fabric ?   The watchman of the Minster (at whose door I chanced to ask whether admittance could be gained) went with a key to two doors, but they were bolted within by the vergers, who were not to be found. A young man came up to me, and very civilly explained several particulars of the building before parting, and on my naming that I came from Newcastle, he said he had a brother in that town, a Mr. Wilkinson of the Asylum.   He kindly offered to show me the localities of York if I should again visit it.

"The old bridge over the Ouse and the picturesque houses which adjoined it are now removed, and a very stately bridge of elegant and massive architecture, and modern erections, supply their place.

"The country near York is mostly very flat, well wooded, and in summer must indeed be beautiful.   Its attractions were not however (at this season) powerful enough to recompense the severe cold of an outside seat, so after passing Tadcaster I resumed my inside place for the night, wrote these few notes, and read the ' Pictures of London ' until dusk.

"That anticipation and remembrance of pleasing events or interesting scenes form a very large portion of human happiness is universally admitted, and have generally been considered to afford both a more intense and longer-continued pleasure than the immediate enjoyment of them. Indeed the latter is frequently unaccompanied with much gratification, and seems as if merely furnishing the means of the enjoyment itself.

"The sight of York Minster was a treat I had always anticipated with much pleasure. I *had* beheld it with great pleasure, and the limited period of twenty minutes for viewing it seemed to have elapsed in the compass of as many seconds. The light colour of the stone, the boldness and clearness of the details, and the brilliant lights and shadows of the setting sun on the west front, left a vivid impression on my mind, which, after night had closed external objects from attention, afforded the most agreeable remembrance; its beauties seemed heightened by imagination, and at intervals through the night the image of this holy and beautiful house seemed like a golden dream to occupy my thoughts, and required some' exercise of thought to remember that the object of these waking visions actually existed, was the work of men's hands, and that its light and airy form, instead of being a bright delusion, really and commonplace-like 'stood upon the ground.'

"The exterior exhibits few indications of the lamentable ruin which in 1828 befel its beautiful Choir. Several new pinnacles and cornices have replaced those which were destroyed; their lightness and beauty, the crispness of ornament, and the bright sunshine on them, gave them an effect as if springing up from fairy rather than human hands, and most incontestably prove that architecture requires the means but wants not the power to equal the most splendid works of former times. My young friend informed me that parties frequently visit the interior by moonlight, especially at midnight, when the lunar beams flow directly through the marigold window,—spectacle beside which even the 'Fair Melrose' must hide its diminished head.

"Near Tadcaster two hats, with a lady appended to each, succeeded in gaining admission to my hitherto solitary berth. A few commonplace remarks, the addition of a gentleman grievously ill of lumbago, and eventually a profound silence, afforded so little interest that I willingly resigned myself into the more attractive arms of Morpheus, and slept soundly all the way to Doncaster.

"After a most comfortable tea and supper, I resumed my journey under very favourable auspices.

"The hats and lumbago were gone, and in their room a most tremendous white great coat formed an excellent pillow, on which, with few exceptions, I slept almost as comfortably and soundly as if in bed, till morning. Now and then the rattling on a pavement, the coachman's horn, and the houses 'whizzing' past the coach windows, betokened a town, and but for excessive cold the sight of these and of the country by the unclouded light of the full moon would have rendered an outside seat very pleasant.

"Doncaster seems to contain many excellent houses. At Bawtry I looked out for the division of the counties, and entered Nottinghamshire at eleven o'clock. After this I was little wiser of my journey until six o'clock, when another hat and its inhabitant entered with the grateful intelligence that we were only ten miles from breakfast. Not finding her disposed to be communicative, I took another doze, and awoke on entering Stamford. This is a large well-built town, with a handsome Gothic church, and two or three others, of which I only saw the spires.

"After washing and making a hearty breakfast, I entered the coach again, quite as little fatigued as at the commencement of my journey twenty-seven hours before.

"At the south end of Stamford is a beautiful entrance gate to the park and pleasure grounds of Burghley Park, the seat of the Marquis of Exeter, which extend over a vast space of ground, and are filled with numerous herds of deer. The general character of all the country hereabouts is flat; the fields large; hedges good; the land mostly of superior quality, diversified with plantations and scattered trees; windmills very abundant, and churches every here and there.

"At Wansford Inn is a sign of the bridge, and under it 'What? Wansford in England!'

"On approaching Huntingdon the road is more hilly, the surface is formed of gravel, is in good repair, and of great width. A large tract of country appears to the west, which on a clear summer's day must be very beautiful. Stokesly is a pleasant little village with a most picturesque ivy-covered tower to a Gothic church.

"Huntingdonshire County Gaol stands a short distance north of the town of Huntingdon, in some fields east of the road; it is of modern erection, has a neat front to the south, and an apparently limited area; is inclosed on the other three sides by a lofty stone wall, strengthened with numerous narrow buttresses; which seems exceedingly injudicious, as I believe there are few sailors who would find much difficulty in climbing either up or down them.

"Huntingdon seems a very clean and neat town, at least that portion of it which we passed was remarkably so; many of the houses are stuccoed, the pavement good, and numerous trees and gardens gave a very beautiful effect to the whole, even at this season; in summer it must be very beautiful.

"The first symptoms of 'London' now appeared in the shape of a gentleman driver, son of one of the proprietors, who, in a black dress-coat and top-boots, took the reins from thence to London, a distance of about sixty miles. The country continues extremely beautiful until we approach the northern border of Hertfordshire, when, being incumbent on chalk beds, the soil is cold and poor, the surface bare and treeless, and a naked ridge of hills presents an uncomfortable aspect. The road here is nearly straight for many miles, and is on the site of the Roman military way; on passing Royston it climbs a steep hill, and from the summit the prospect south, though somewhat improved, is still very bare and uninteresting.

Nothing could now exceed the extreme clearness of the air and the enlivening effect of a bright sunshine, which presented the country in a most enchanting manner, but (for in this there is always a but or an if) the cold was very piercing, and confined me to the inside until the attractions of the immediate vicinity of London, and the desire to see as much as possible of that magnificent city, induced me to prefer the outside.

"From sixteen miles from London the road seems one continued country village, with only a few intervening spaces of road for two or three hundred yards. It was dark as we entered the stone-paved streets of London, where the brilliant effect of the gas and the bustle of the people very much corresponded with the idea I had formed of London. At seven o'clock we reached the Bull and Mouth Inn, after a journey of 273 miles, performed in 33 hours."

The following memoranda of the expenses of this and of one or two subsequent journeys are curious as contrasted with the charges of railway travelling in our time.

The inside fare of the Wellington Coach from Newcastle to London was £4 10s.; breakfast at Ruthyford was 2s.; dinner at different stages 7s.; tea at Doncaster and breakfast at Stamford 2s. 3d. and 2s. 6d.; the fees to guards and drivers were 17s. Total expense £6 0s. 9d. for travelling 273 miles in 33 hours.

On the 17th of the same month (March, 1830) the expenses from London to Newcastle were: inside fare, £5 15s.; breakfast and dinner, 6s. 6d.; and guards and drivers, 17s. 6d.; being in all £6 19s. The distance 273 miles; time 30 hours.

On the 22nd of the same month, on a journey in the mail from Newcastle to London, the sums were: inside fare, £6 6s.; breakfast, dinner, and tea, 9s.; guards and drivers, 17*s.*; in all £7 12*s.*   Distance 273 miles ; time 32½ hours.

The mean of these is £6 17*s.* 6*d.*, or at the rate of 6*d.* per mile; and the mean time, including stoppages, 8·15 miles an hour.

In conversation in later years Mr. Sopwith was very fond of comparing the facilities and economics of travel in these days with what existed in the earlier periods of his life.   He told me once that under these influences he had no doubt he had lived to see the amount of travelling by the community more than quadrupled, and the safety and convenience proportionately increased.   At the same time he had a kind of lingering love for the coach and four horses ; and he believed that, as time afforded greater pleasure of life, the old turnpikes might still have a new career, either with horses as of yore, or more likely with steam or electric engines as the motor powers.   Richard Trevithick's steam-carriage ride from Bath to London at twelve miles an hour in the beginning of the century was, he thought, good ground for his prophecy.

CHAPTER IX.

LONDON SIXTY YEARS AGO, FROM A NORTHUMBRIAN'S FIRST VIEW. NATIONAL REPOSITORY OF ARTS. GREENWICH HOSPITAL. LONDON CURIOSITIES.

1830.

AT the close of the last chapter we followed Mr. Sopwith into the metropolis, in the year 1830. He alighted, as we have seen, at the famous Bull and Mouth Inn, which, with characteristic voraciousness, swallowed him readily. It did not, however, retain him long, for after taking a cup of tea, feeling no fatigue from the journey, he set out on his peregrinations through London.

The particulars of this visit to the metropolis he has written down in his journal with great precision, and as the narrative of London, sixty years ago, is extremely interesting I submit it as it came from his pen.

" After consulting my map, I took a walk round St. Paul's Cathedral, which (and the same occurred to me at York Minster) seemed scarcely so large as I expected. It is, however, a truly magnificent fabric, and those who would ' view St. Paul's aright' should 'visit it by the bright sunlight.' I was, however, glad of an opportunity of seeing it by moonlight, and, great as were my expectations, they certainly were in no respect disappointed.

" As to its apparent dimensions, that I had often heard commented on, and the deceptive effect of huge masses, whether mountains or buildings, had often before excited my surprise. That the Campanile towers of St. Paul's are twenty feet higher than the steeples of St. Nicholas' and All Saints' in Newcastle, and the dome a hundred and fifty feet higher than the great tower of York Minster, is what well-authenticated statements may inform us, but what the most attentive examination and comparison of the objects themselves seems to be incapable of confirming.

" I continued my walk along Ludgate Hill, down New Bridge Street, and along Blackfriars Bridge to Southwark. From Blackfriars Road I went westward by Stamford Street, returned to London by Waterloo Bridge, went to Drury Lane Theatre, and, finally, returned to the inn, without ever once asking my way or missing my road.

" What a difference a penny makes ! Blackfriars Bridge was crowded, Waterloo Bridge seemed, and indeed was at this time, a most delightful and almost unfrequented walk. A peal of eight bells in Southwark sounded very like those of All Saints' in Newcastle.

" The broad surface of the Thames, the magnificent front of Somerset House, and the heavy gloom that seemed thrown like a mantle over this vast metropolis, excited a train of interesting thoughts, all concentrated in the one vast and comprehensive and inexpressible idea of ' London.'

" I had the happiness to enter Drury Lane in the very plenitude of a most uproarious tumult. Kean had that night appeared for the first time as King Henry V., and four acts of that play had been represented; eighteen minutes had, however, elapsed, and no symptoms of the remaining act. The clamour was deafening, and at length the curtain rose. In vain was the attempt to perform ; a whole scene acted with resolute perseverance passed in dumb show, and at length Kean was compelled to come forward. After much clamour he said, that for twenty years he had had the honour of appearing before them, and been honoured with their approbation, and now (I understood him to say), for the first time, stood before them in disgrace. On this the yells were repeated, and much noise and confusion interrupted his apology. When I again heard him, it seemed to me a rhodomontade about being an Englishman, and, striking his breast, appealed to them 'as Englishmen' ! ! This did the business; the incensed and justly irritated ' John Bull' first melted into pity, and, with genuine consistency, honoured the offender with loud and repeated plaudits.

"The fifth act, however, was completed very speedily, and a great deal omitted, owing, I strongly suspect, to some alteration of the chief performer. This contraction of the play was too obvious not to excite dissatisfaction, but, happily, the rising storm was quelled by the able execution of the magnificent overture to *Der Freischutz*, which the audience had the good taste very loudly to applaud. I was much pleased with the music of this piece, especially the laughing and hunting chorus. But the scenery, and very singular stage effects produced, were beyond anything that my imagination could have previously conceived.

"The scene of the Incantation was gradually wrought up to a most horrible, hideous, and truly appalling spectacle. A large owl flapping his wings, green dragons, and ill-omened birds hovering in the air, with fiery serpents, green lights, etc., moving in all directions; fiends with burning faces; skeletons, and a livid picture of Pandemonium, with a falling shower of fire and demoniacal screams, completed the horrid climax.

"Drury Lane presents a semicircle of four galleries; the lowest has panels richly painted and gilt, the upper three have gold ornaments in bold relief, on a salmon-coloured ground. The ceiling is a flat ellipse, divided by gilt ribs into seventeen compartments, with golden ornaments in relief. A very handsome glass chandelier is suspended from the centre. The galleries (part of which are the boxes) are supported by metal columns, extremely light and elegant, and richly gilt.

On each side of the stage are two very splendid Corinthian columns, so made as to have all the richness of real columns, while, at the same time, they do not greatly intercept the sight. The frontispiece is very deep, and has a splendid effect; it represents a crimson velvet curtain, with the Royal Arms and medallions of George and the Dragon in gold. The drop scene is a fine Ionic colonnade, and classic landscape.

"The theatre was very well filled. I made the following hasty computation of the number of people that may with ease and comfort be contained in it.

	Persons.
The Pit	600
Boxes and Galleries . . .	1,800
Stage Boxes and Gallery above . .	120
	2,520

"The orchestra consisted of thirty-six musicians.

"The staircase and lobby of this theatre are very beautiful; in the latter is a fine statue of Shakespeare.

"The saloon is a magnificent apartment; a considerable portion of the sides is covered with plate looking-glass, and thus 'many reflections' are cast among the 'gay and licentious crowds' who resort to this seat of luxury, forgetful how little conducive is the pursuit of mere pleasure to the real welfare of man.

"On Tuesday morning (March 9th), I rose at six, and wrote till nine, breakfasted with Mr. Percival Fenwick at 15, Featherstone Buildings, Holborn, and went with him to Mr. Bramwell's office. We afterwards looked into the Court, where the Master of the Rolls was presiding, and into Lincoln's Inn Hall, where we saw the Lord Chancellor. His lordship is a healthy, vigorous, good-looking man, far from being 'stricken in years,' and seemed, by frequently changing his position and looking very indifferent and unconcerned, as if he would willingly hear the end of a long and seemingly very uninteresting story which a learned gentleman was relating to him.

" Above the judges' seat is a large painting of Paul before Felix, either a copy or the original by Hogarth, most probably the latter.

" After engaging lodgings at 42, Wilmington Square, Spa Fields, and removing my luggage from the inn, I went, after calling at Mr. Ord's, to meet Fenner, agent for the Bill, in the lobby of the House of Commons. On leaving him I walked through the interior of Westminster Abbey, an edifice which, in many respects, falls very short of my expectations. I speak with humility in anything that has been directed by superior taste and judgment, but I cannot help thinking that the interior of the Abbey and King Henry VII.'s Chapel might, at no great expense, be rendered far more beautiful and imposing than it now is. The organ is a plain, commonplace looking instrument, no way suitable to so august a pile; and the waxworks seem to me in miserable taste. In extent, solemnity, and slenderness of the columns, the whole interior disappointed me. Not so the monuments; they are truly magnificent and deeply interesting. Deep, and powerful, and holy are the impressions they are calculated to make; the greatest, the wealthiest, the worthiest, the most learned and able men that adorn the annals of our country here repose in one sleep of oblivion.

" The splendid memorials erected to perpetuate their memory speak many a lesson to the contemplative mind, and who can stand on the slab that covers the mouldering temple of so much wit and genius, and read the simple inscription,

'GEORGE CANNING,'

without feeling, with acuteness, the destiny of all the human race?

" Many of the monuments excited great admiration, but none more so than that of Lady Nightingale. It is a truly inimitable design, and great as were my expectations of it, they were most abundantly fulfilled.

" There is no longer reason for complaint on the score of

exorbitant charges for seeing this structure and its interesting contents. For the moderate sum of fifteen pence the visitor has not only the privilege of seeing every part of the building, but is also attended by one of the vergers, who points out the most remarkable and interesting features, and relates some particulars of their history. It is obvious that a gratuitous admission would render the place a thoroughfare for the rabble, and as the attendants are strictly prohibited by a public notice from demanding further fees, those who for so high a gratification as should be derived, object to so moderate a fee, may have at least this consolation, that they lose an enjoyment which a narrow and parsimonious mind could derive a small share indeed of gratification from.

" After calling at Mr. Topham's, in Bermondsey, I returned by London Bridge, saw the magnificent structure intended to supersede the present bridge, and on passing had a 'keek at' the 'pearl o' the City.' I spent the whole evening at my lodgings, and in the ease and comfort of a cheerful fireside, with plenty of maps, books, and papers to occupy me, I find as much, nay more, real peace and true enjoyment than in the gayest and most splendid fascinations which have yet attracted my notice.

" *March* 10*th.*—Rose at seven, wrote and breakfasted till nine, hired a hackney for an hour, made several calls, and attended Divine service at St. Paul's Cathedral at ten.

" The vast and splendid interior of this magnificent Cathedral excited great admiration, and the impression was much heightened by the rattling echoes of the organ pealing from vault to vault, and filling the august pile with deep and solemn chords. The Choir, though certainly beautiful, is both less appropriate and picturesque than that at Durham, and to me afforded a convincing proof that Grecian and Roman architecture is incapable of the solemn and venerable character so peculiar to the Gothic style.

" The organ of St. Paul's is suitable in design to the character of the building, but to me seemed far less attractive than the

old and venerable-looking one at Durham. As to their comparative merits in a musical point of view I am in no way
adequate to judge. St. Paul's seemed very powerful, and is
allowed to be a very fine instrument, but it did not impress
me with those ideas of richness and sweetness of melody which
I have so often been delighted with at Durham.

"As to the chanting in St. Paul's I was miserably disappointed.
I did not expect that it would excel, and scarcely expected that
it would equal, that at Durham; but so wide a difference, so
very decided and indisputable an inferiority, I was in no way
prepared to expect. On many, certainly on nearly all things,
I would give an opinion with much diffidence in powers so
incompetent as mine are to form a judgment on such subjects,
but, in this particular instance, diffidence or hesitation in
advancing the opinion I express would only be hypocrisy.
The harsh, I had almost said unmusical, chanting which I
this day heard in St. Paul's can never be put in comparison
with the heavenly cadence and exquisite harmony of Durham.
To hear the one I have often gone many miles, to hear the
other I would not go as many yards.

" After leaving the Cathedral and making some calls, I went
to Southwark Bridge, and spent an hour with Miss Scott at
her father's in Thames Street. I afterwards heard the
Appollonicon, and was much pleased with the performance. I
then walked by Pall Mall east to Regent Street, and by it to
Regent's Park, where I saw the Diorama and Colosseum,
walked round Regent's Park, and returned home, where I
drank tea, and spent the evening writing, etc.

" When it is considered that the paintings in the Diorama are
drawn with critical accuracy, and the effect so striking as to
seem a perfect reality, it was to me very interesting to see such
a representation of the interior of St. Peter's at Rome on the
same day as that of visiting St. Paul's.

" The Appollonicon is a musical instrument invented by
Flight and Robson, organ-builders to his Majesty, and is
exhibited at their manufactory in St. Martin's Lane. It is, in

fact, a very large organ, with a great variety of pipes and other musical accompaniments which imitate different instruments. It is capable of great nicety of modulation, and its full powers are tremendously effective. It performed, by machinery, the overtures to *Figaro* and to *Der Frieschutz* with astonishing brilliancy, and to all who have any love for music the Appollonicon can scarcely fail to afford a most agreeable entertainment. In front of it are several sets of piano keys, by which five or six performers can play at the same time.

"Waterloo Place and Regent Street present an imposing exterior (the design of which cannot but excite much admiration), and if they were constructed of real stone would, as streets, be unparalleled for grandeur and magnificence. The want of stone which has rendered it necessary to have recourse to stucco, is a great disparagement to London, and in this respect the Scotch have just reason to boast of a mighty superiority in their northern capital.

"It seems to me, that the stamp of true greatness cannot be affixed to any work where 'Imitation' is a prevailing feature, and this idea has been very much confirmed by observing the stuccoed buildings of London. In colouring those houses also, a very marvellous bad taste and want of management occurs, in making the middle of ornamental columns the line of division, so that where a pillar of one dingy hue might seem to be of stone, a partial colouring of it tells to every passing stranger, 'I am not what I would be thought to be.' It must, however, be admitted that stucco is a vast improvement to a brick building when architectural embellishment is introduced; when this is not the case I would prefer the humble but 'honest' face of brick before the more specious and deceptive covering of stucco.

"The Diorama of the interior of St. Peter's gave a very excellent, and I doubt not a very accurate, idea of that noble structure. The imposing effect and reality of these works of art can only be appreciated by eye-witnesses, and show to what an amazing extent human industry and perseverance can go.

An organ playing some of the beautiful symphonies of the Italian service would have added much to the interest of the scene, and by partly attracting the imagination would in some measure heighten the pictorial illusion by diverting the eye from the sole employment of scrutinizing it.

"But beautiful and interesting as was this and the other view of the Diorama, they were far exceeded by the representation of London in the Colosseum.

"The accounts which I had frequently read of this exhibition, had raised very high expectations, but no description, however minute and accurate, and no anticipations, however sanguine, can afford a correct idea of this surprising work. The dimensions of the building are such as to create astonishment; it is polygonal, having sixteen faces, each 25 feet in length, and the external diameter is 126 feet. The interior of the wall of the Colosseum is covered with a panoramic representation of London as seen from the top of St. Paul's. It is painted on 40,000 square feet of canvas, nearly an acre in extent. In the centre is an ascending room which would contain from ten to twenty persons, and is raised by machinery to the first gallery.

"This gallery has balustrades resembling those round the upper gallery of St. Paul's cupola; beneath this gallery is a projecting frame of wood, so formed and painted as to resemble the great dome of St. Paul's, while a projecting canopy above conceals the roof of the building. The range of vision is thus confined to that portion of the wall which is entirely covered with the painting. No language can describe the extraordinary effect produced on this amazing surface of canvas, and nothing but a perfect conviction that it really is painted on a flat surface could counteract the impressions of distance it is calculated to give. If the effect is wonderful, still more wonderful is the surprising accuracy with which every minute object in this extensive view is delineated, and almost incredible is the industry and perseverance by which alone such a painting could be executed. The first sight of it is calculated to create, and does almost invariably create, much astonishment. An Irish gentleman who came in when I was there inquired several times if the dome below us was that which he had seen from the outside; when assured that it was not, and that it was in the interior of the building, nothing could exceed his amazement. Gazing with convinced but wondering eyes, he involuntarily exclaimed, ' Lord God Almighty ! is it possible ? '—a testimony of his wonder which, though very objectionable, seemed a most unfeigned expression of the very highest surprise and admiration.

"*Thursday, March* 11*th.*—Made several calls and saw a great portion of the western part of London.

" Went in the afternoon to the House of Commons ; got four franks * from Mr. Ord, and spent the evening at home writing letters, and with one or two friends who called.

" One of these friends was Mr. R. S. Richardson, with whom in former years I had spent many pleasant hours, and for whom I ever entertained much respect. His intention to leave England had led to cessation of correspondence, and to find him again, in good health and comfortably situated, afforded me more genuine pleasure than I had experienced since my arrival in London.

" *Friday, March* 12*th.*—Waited on Mr. Percival Fenwick, and after preparing some estimates and other papers required by Parliament, walked with Mr. Clennell to Mr. Bramwell's office in the Temple. Called upon Mr. Bell at his house in Wimpole Street and attended a Committee of the House in the smoking room. Sir M. W. Ridley, Mr. Ellison, Mr. Liddell, Mr. Bell, Mr. Ord, and Mr. R. F. Wilson were present. The Committee adjourned till Tuesday following, in consequence of a Petition from the Free Burgesses of Newcastle respecting the Town Moor.

" By Mr. Ord's recommendation I was admitted into the gallery of the House of Commons, and from the front seat of the Strangers' Gallery had an excellent opportunity of observing the proceedings. But for previous information, the interior of St. Stephen's would certainly strike a stranger as being

---

* The frank or free postage granted by members of Parliament before the days of the postage stamp.

both small and mean as compared with the importance of the matters transacted in it, and but for the same preventive of surprise, the method of transacting those matters, guiding, as they do, the political destinies of the world, would excite still greater surprise.

"The House of Commons is a plain, ordinary-looking place. The Speaker's chair stands on the floor, and has a high back and cover, surmounted with the Royal Arms; in front of it is a large table, at which three clerks of the House are seated. It is covered with red cloth, has a number of books and papers lying promiscuously upon it, and at certain times the mace is laid on it.

"On each side of the Speaker's chair are ranges of seats, rising from the floor to the wall, five on each side. Those on the right of the chair are usually occupied by Ministerial members, and those on the opposite side by the Opposition. There are also cross benches behind the chair, common to both parties, and galleries, which are rarely occupied.

"Opposite the chair is a gallery for the public, to which admission can be had at any time for 2s. 6d., or by an order or verbal 'pass' from a member to the door-keeper. The back seat of this gallery is appropriated for the reporters, a situation which would almost seem to prevent them either seeing or hearing anything of what is going on below. Behind it is a gallery communicating with two staircases, one of which is for the ingress, the other for the egress of the public; so that when the gallery is cleared for a division, those who, having a back seat, get first out, stand the best chance of being first in again when re-admission is permitted. The reporters, however, have a retiring room allowed them. The extreme *sang-froid* of Mr. Speaker in the execution of his duties is very amusing. A venerable old gentleman with an immense parchment roll pointed to the Speaker, was most impressively mumbling a relation of the 'why and wherefore,' while Mr. Speaker, the party formally addressed, was directing his attention to quite another subject.

" On the Gloster and Avon Railway Bill a very animated discussion arose, in which several members took a part. A verbal understanding had, it appeared, been entered into, two years ago, which 'solemn compact' it was contended was sought to be violated by one of the parties now applying for the Bill before the House. Mr. Bright of Bristol spoke very vehemently on the question, and most warmly contended for the sacredness of the engagement formerly made. He called on Mr. Speaker, and he called on the Honourable House, to show ' Honourable Gentlemen ' that such engagements could not thus be set aside ; and all the while Mr. Speaker, insensible to the flow of oratory thus poured upon him, was most coolly and pleasantly discoursing to a gentleman beside him, and with his face quite in a different direction to that in which the stream of eloquent exordium was flowing. All of a sudden, a bustling noise, and several members walking out, with 'Walk out, gentlemen—quick, walk out, walk out,' were the outward and visible tokens of a division of the House, and consequent clearing of the gallery. The routine of receiving petitions and reading Bills is, to a stranger, I think I might almost say farcical, if such an expression be allowable for what, on the stage, would certainly not fail to create much amusement.

" Every now and then Mr. Speaker rose and quickly repeated a brief form of words, to which not one of the members seemed to be paying the least attention. The form, as well as I could make it out, was this (a strong emphasis and protracted tone distinguishing the words written larger) : ' You that are of opinion that this Petition be received say AYE ; you that are of a contrary opinion say No ; THE AYES HAVE IT.' And this as fast as the sentence can be uttered, without any real ayeing or noing on the part of the members ; so that of a number of Petitions and Bills read, probably eighteen or twenty in number, the *Ayes* always *had it.*

" I had an opportunity of hearing and admiring some observations made by Lord Lowther ; they related merely to a private petition and afforded no scope for eloquence, but I was much pleased with the ease and gracefulness of his manner.   By gracefulness I mean that courteous and dignified address which so well becomes a British senator, and one who may in time be one of the chiefest nobles of the land.

" If I had returned into the gallery I would have heard a number of very interesting debates and many excellent speeches by the principal members.   Mr. Liddell introduced the Northumberland petition, and many highly interesting subjects were to come under discussion.   Of this I was aware, and yet I preferred returning home and spending the evening there.

" Home (even a temporary one) has attractions powerful at all times, but when vivid impressions of sorrow remain, when the mind, even in the midst of the most splendid and powerful attractions, will revert to scenes that fly on memory's wings like shadows of departed joys,—at such times,—and who has ever been entirely free from such impressions?—home, sweet home, that calm, and tranquil, and holy temple of the wounded mind, is the only place congenial to such feelings, the only place where, at such times, real peace and happiness can be found.

" On the following day I called and spent part of the forenoon at Mr. John Scott's.   Being in the immediate vicinity of the Monument, I took this opportunity of ascending it, and the prospect amply repays the labour of ascending so great a height. Accompanied by Miss Scott I then spent some time in seeing the monuments and other treasures of the great lion of London lions, St. Paul's.   Every visit to this stupendous and magnificent structure increases my admiration of it.   There is only *one word* that can convey a true idea of its grandeur, and that *word*, if attentively read and diligently attended to, cannot fail to afford a vivid, a correct, and an indelible impression of the glories of this august temple.   That word is inscribed on the monument of Sir Christopher Wren at the entrance of the choir, and must there be read.   It is—

" ' CIRCUMSPICE ! '

"The notes of the ' deep-labouring organ ' rolled from vault to vault, and its magnificent tones were heard to great advantage from the Whispering Gallery. My companion had previously visited the upper galleries of the great dome, and declined again undertaking the laborious ascent to them. Having provided her a comfortable seat by a warm fire in the library, she remained until I had made the ' grand tour ' of this mountain of architecture. I went up alone, and carefully examined the curious construction of the inner cupola, cone, and timber framing. The climbing into the ball reminded me very much of the rises in the lead mines; and the civilities (eighteen pennyworth) of my conductor as forcibly called to my remembrance the friendly admonition of the miners, ' Take care, maister, and dinna fall down the rise.'

" After returning to the library we visited the models, clock, bell, and finally the crypts or vaults, the pocket sweating pretty freely all the while; though, after all, when the great convenience of constant attendance on visitors is considered, I do not think the charges exorbitant.

"The vaults I consider well worthy of the stranger's attention; a deep and heavy gloom fills their long aisles, and well does this solemn effect accord with the sepulchral reminiscences that crowd upon the mind. Mere ' sight-seeing ' is an occupation of which both eyes and mind soon grow weary, and one bright and magnificent and attractive object succeeding another, and then, again and again, superseded by similar scenes, soon creates a sort of vacancy in the mind, or want of aptitude for that species of enjoyment. The dark chambers beneath the cathedral afford that transition which the mind seems to long for, and fill it with mournfully pleasing and interesting associations. The magnificent marble sarcophagus of Nelson, the tomb of Collingwood, the little spot wherein is laid the rearer of this mighty fabric, these and many other objects offer much to occupy the contemplative mind, and to impress the deepest convictions of the destiny of man, and of the shadowy nature of all earthly pomp and glory; for in the splendid tomb of Nelson we see what was erected by and

intended for the remains of him who might well exclaim, as
has by Shakespeare been attributed to him, ' Vain pomp and
glory of the world, I hate ye ! '

" Surely the pomp and glory of so august a Temple above,
and Wolsey's 'self-intended monument' below ; the triumphant
flags of victory hung proudly round the stupendous dome, and
the mouldering ashes that silently rest in the vaults beneath
them ; the gay and stirring crowds that throng around and
in this great temple, and the darkness, and silence, and loneli-
ness of these chambers of the dead, eloquently and fervently
proclaim the truths which, above all others, the living should
lay to heart.

" On the following morning I attended St. Paul's during the
musical part of the service, which, from the grandeur of the
organ, re-echoed from the stupendous vaults above, was very
imposing, but much less attractive than the Durham service.
I was much surprised that no anthem was sung after the
third Collect, according to the usual custom of cathedral
service, and still more surprised that the whole should seem so
devoid of that grace and beauty of expression which elsewhere
prevails, and which ought certainly to be found in the metropolitan church of the kingdom.

" I then went to Bishopsgate Church in expectation of
hearing the Hon. and Rev. Edward Grey preach, but was
informed by a gentleman that Mr. Grey was to preach at St.
Sepulchre, in Snow Hill. Thither I hied with all speed, and
arrived just as the service commenced. I got an excellent seat,
and seldom have I experienced more gratification than was
afforded me by the excellent discourse of Mr. Grey and the
admirable music of a very excellent organ.

" The sermon was for the benefit of a Girls' Charity School,
the scholars of which sat in the organ gallery, and in their
simple attire, and with sweet and modest looks, seemed like
cherubs sent to awaken compassion in the hearts of men.

" A printed copy of a hymn, composed for the occasion, was
handed to me, and never will I forget the inimitable, the soul-

stirring sweetness with which these lovely babes sung their humble praise. It was a simple but very devotional piece, and every note impressed the most lively sensation of delight and sympathy with the helpless choir. I even shed tears which I could not control, and my heart earnestly responded that benediction of our Saviour, 'Of such is the Kingdom of Heaven.'

"Mr. Grey is, beyond all comparison, the most admirable and impressive preacher I ever heard. His discourse was truly excellent, and was delivered with that solemnity and power which surely well becomes a Messenger of God,—a Legate of the skies. Chaste, and simple, and dignified, and expressive, the sermons of Mr. Grey seem to me as almost perfect models of pulpit oratory; at least I can truly say that his sermons, more than any others I ever heard, have had a lasting influence on my mind, and some of his eloquent passages seem indelibly impressed on my memory. The doxologies were all chanted, that too in a very superior manner. I think it greatly relieves the monotony of our long liturgy, and as they happened to sing two very favourite chants, the pleasure of hearing them, added to the other and much higher gratifications of the sermon and hymn, made me truly thankful for the incivility of a St. Paul's verger, but for whom I should have been immured in the gallery of that Cathedral the *whole* of the service, and only have seen the delivery of an inaudible sermon.

"I dined with Mr. Topham at his house in Southwark. My father had stood sponsor for his eldest child, and I was requested now to undertake that office for his youngest one; with which, as it was particularly urged, I complied. Mr. Topham had a numerous and intelligent party of friends on the occasion. Immediately after tea I begged to be allowed to leave, and returned home to my lodgings, where I spent the evening very pleasantly among my books and papers.

"On Monday, March 15th, I went to the British Museum, with a letter to Mr. Barber, one of the principal librarians, who procured me a ticket for the Reading Rooms. It was fully my intention to devote a portion of my time to copying some extracts for the Rev. Mr. Hodgson, but unforeseen and unexpected occurrences prevented me then, and numerous engagements will, I fear, render it almost impossible for me to devote any considerable portion of time to the seclusion of this most author-like tabernacle, where books may be said to be cut and dovetailed together with persevering and unfailing diligence.

"The room in which the King's Library is placed is truly magnificent. After viewing it I went through the Museum, and found, as every one must find, a great deal to excite astonishment and admiration. The Gallery of Sculptures was a most delightful treat, and I longed for a week, and an intelligent friend, to view its matchless contents.

"After leaving the Museum I dined at the Café Colosseum, and proceeded to the House of Commons, where I attended a Committee of the Lowgate Road Bill. I heard on this and some other afternoons when at the House, the afternoon service in the Abbey. The chanting is sweeter than at St. Paul's, and they sing an anthem. The interior of this venerable structure gains upon me every visit; my first visit greatly disappointed me, and I candidly set down my ideas; but ideas change. It somehow or other falls short of my expectation, and though it would be folly to dispute its claims to venerable grandeur and solemnity, yet I think its general effect might be improved by a uniform colouring like York Minster. Artists may decry colouring as they like, and those who greatly admire naked stone have much to confirm their views, but I think that in an ornamented interior the architectural enrichments and composition are seen to greater advantage when of a uniform colour. Westminster Abbey, and Henry VII.'s Chapel, with coloured and clean walls, and clean and dark-coloured, brightly-varnished oak, would, I imagine, be much more imposing in its effect than it now is; but yet the picturesque and gloomy grandeur of its long aisles and fretted vaults cannot fail to excite much deep and solemn feeling, and this feeling in me has certainly been increased by every successive visit.

" At Mr. Martin's establishment, 104, Holborn, I saw by far the finest specimens of lithography I ever met with or heard of. They equal copper-plate etching in the fineness of the lines, and can scarcely be distinguished from it. He gave me some specimens, and showed me how very many impressions had been taken from some of them without injury to the tenderness and clearness of the ' hatching.' Professional men who have seen the specimens are equally surprised and pleased.

" On this afternoon (and also on some others when attending at the House), I returned to my lodgings by a very circuitous route, by Vauxhall Bridge, Belgrave Square, and Hyde Park, the principal places I fixed on before leaving home in the morning, and took a small list of streets to guide me from one to the other. In the town itself, after a few days, I felt little or no difficulty in steering my course to any part of it, and very seldom enquired my way. These long rambles soon made me familiar with all the leading thoroughfares of the western portion of London, and as I marked each day's route out upon a map I could easily observe by it in what direction and by what lines of streets I would be able to see the most interesting squares or other principal streets. They had the effect also of rendering home and tea very comfortable, and as I had several estimates and other papers to examine, as well as books and pamphlets to read, I never thought of leaving them, but enjoyed with them the occasional company of my friends Richardson, Newton, Davison, and others,—as much real enjoyment as at this time could have been afforded me by the most gay and attractive amusements.

" On Tuesday morning I went to Greenwich in a small boat. The morning was very fine, though cold, and the face of Old Father Thames in parts was ruffled with the wind.

" I had an excellent view of the bridges, especially of New and Old London Bridges. The former is truly a magnificent erection, and worthy of the first city in the world. The rapids at the old bridge have a somewhat alarming appearance, and are considered dangerous; the boat shot through like an arrow, and I understood from my guide that it was then less dangerous than at some other periods of the tide. Flatness is the general feature of the shore of the Thames, which, fringed with miles of active commerce, and its auxiliary ships, wharves, docks, warehouses, and manufactories, fill the mind with almost overpowering ideas of the greatness of the British Empire.

"I took with me the mathematical writings in MS. of my respected master, the late Henry Atkinson, to his brother-in-law Mr. Riddell, master of the Naval Asylum, with whom I dined, and returned to a Committee of the Lower House at 3 o'clock. After another long ramble I returned to my lodgings, and had the pleasure of Mr. Davison's company in the evening.

"I was on this day informed by the Parliamentary Agent that my continuance in town was no longer essential, for though it might be as well to comply strictly with the Standing Orders of the House, yet if anything required my presence in Newcastle I could on signing certain documents be dispensed with without any material inconvenience."

During his residence in the metropolis, Mr. Sopwith lodged at 42, Wilmington Square, a part of London which, although, as he said, not even then very fashionable, was exceedingly convenient, quiet, and comfortable. The work on which he was engaged was congenial to his tastes; and from the circumstance that it brought him into communion with persons of great intelligence and influence, he looked upon the visit almost in the light of a holiday. Moreover, it was the first taste of the great city; and as a centre of enchantment the great city bewitched him. He was fond of Newcastle from its local associations and the many friendships which were connected with it; but had the opportunity offered itself, had it seemed to his prudent mind a good arrangement to settle down in London, the temptation would have been very great, and would perhaps have been followed by a more brilliant if not more useful career.

The news of the death of his uncle, Mr. James Sopwith, caused him to return to Newcastle. The details of the return journey by mail coach contain little of interest. He had not been long at home before he received a message from London requiring his attendance on a Committee at the House of Lords. He therefore left Newcastle again by mail coach on Monday evening, March 22nd, 1830, and read and slept all the way until he was safely set down at the new Post Office on Wednesday morning at 6 o'clock. He was so little fatigued and felt so little inconvenience that he went direct to his lodgings and from them to Spa Fields Bath, took a bath, breakfasted, and proceeded to the House of Lords, passing some time very pleasantly on his way at the National Repository of Arts. Here he found for the first time introduced some patent globes which would go into the pocket when collapsed, but inflated with air would form fine globes, four feet in diameter. He also found Rolff's patent self-acting pianos, which played with brilliancy and force. Here, also, was Chevalier Aldini's defensive dress against fire, a strong woollen dress, saturated with saline material and covered with armour and shield of wire gauze. This dress Mr. Sopwith spoke of with commendation quite late in his life. It was, he said, so cheap, light, and portable, he wondered all firemen were not clothed in it. It enabled a man to go literally through fire without being burned. Aldini, I take it, was the famous nephew of the still more famous Galvani, from whom we obtained the word galvanism. In this same repository there was being exhibited at this time the piece of sculpture from Thorwaldsen, entitled the Triumph of Alexander.

In the afternoon he attended the Committee of the Lords in the Robing Room, after having been previously sworn at the bar of the House. Lord Shaftesbury was in the chair, and that meeting terminated the professional engagements of Mr. Fenwick, another engineer, and himself. Everything ended in the most satisfactory and pleasant manner, after which he and his colleague went to the Café Colosseum, where, according to custom, they finished up the day by an excellent dinner. The Café Colosseum, which was situated at Regent's Park, was, he tells us, a place worthy of remembrance. It was easily reached by the "Paddington Stage" running between Paddington and the City. Its cuisine was admirable, and was memorable in that it seems to have first turned out the famous soup called mock turtle.

A neat little picture is given, in this stage of the journey, of the magnificent entrance to the House of Lords called the King's Entrance. During his survey of this entrance the Duke of Wellington passed them, plainly dressed in a blue surtout and making his way towards the Lords. Another picture, very interesting, is a description of a visit to Greenwich Hospital.

"On Saturday (March 27th, 1830) I went on the 'Stage' to the City, and went solus into a number of offices, large and small, in the Bank of England. I then went on a coach to Greenwich, where I spent the remainder of the day.

"Everybody knows that Greenwich Hospital is one of the finest, most magnificent, most uniform and extensive structures of the kind in Europe. It is, in fact, a little city of palaces, and has a little nation resident in its walls. The painted hall is exceedingly and delightfully beautiful, and the chapel is one of the most elaborate, magnificent, and costly structures I ever beheld. A fine organ is supported by six columns fifteen feet high, formed of one solid block of white marble; they cost £600 each,—the guides lay on another £400 each by way of making the thing sound better,—and Mr. Locker, who gave me this item, also assured me that the interior of the chapel cost upwards of £60,000, which is more than twice the cost of All Saints' Church by £6,000 or £7,000. I was truly surprised that my friend Mr. Collison, who at Alston exclaimed, 'What, live within forty miles of Keswick and never seen the Lakes!' had never yet seen the interior either of Greenwich Chapel or Westminster Abbey. I visited the Chapel twice, and was allowed to remain in it as long as I chose. I spent upwards of an hour alone viewing the matchless yet chaste and beautiful enrichments of this splendid chapel.

" I went into the dining-rooms which are below the painted hall and chapel, and saw several hundred pensioners at dinner. Such a feeding as this of His Majesty's 'Old game cocks,' as they style themselves, I never yet beheld. I went into the kitchens and saw the cooking apparatus; in the eastern one, which is the largest, there are three immense cauldrons and a large open fire grate.

" An old tar gave me the following particulars of this august mess. In one great copper 5 cwt. of potatoes are boiled three-quarters of an hour by steam every day. In another 7 cwt. of meat is boiled every week day and 8 cwt. on Sundays—four days mutton, three days beef; boils about an hour and a quarter. At the grate only some 20 or 30 lbs. of meat are roasted for such petty officers as choose roast, and in a cauldron 45 lbs. of cocoa and 42 lbs. of sugar in the morning, and in the evening 8 lbs. of tea and 36 lbs. of sugar, are the materials for about 180 gallons of these respective beverages.

" I wandered through a great many of the hospital wards, and entered into conversation with some of the old veterans; to one I said, ' Well, these are all very good things, and you should be very comfortable;' with true British modesty he replied, 'Aye, true, sir, they're all well enough, but then we *deserve* it, ye see, or else we wouldn't have been here.'

"In the dining-room I copied a printed board, which I supposed at first was some of Mr. Locker's doings, if not in composing, at least in placing it there. But to Mr. Locker, who in the evening copied it from my notes, it was as new as to me; he had neither seen nor heard of it, and joined with me in admiring its point and brevity : it was headed,—

COUNSEL AND ADVICE.

Hear			To be silent.
Be silent	and		To understand.
Understand	learn		To remember.
Remember			To practise.

All that you	see, judge / hear, believe / know, tell / can do, do	it not !

Before you speak—think,
and regard well
what you speak, where you speak, of whom you speak, and to
whom you speak.

Religion / Generosity / Injustice / Wickedness	you	lose / impoverish / enrich / profit	not.

If you lose	Property, some / Health, much / Reason, more / your Soul, all	is lost.

"I then spent nearly two hours in ranging through the Park, amidst the venerable and richly-fretted trunks of many large and aged trees. The day was serene, and fair, and sunny, and nature shone in a bright and beautiful garb. After greatly enjoying a long and circuitous walk through the various lawns and avenues, I traversed several of the streets of Greenwich, and then took a sail on the Thames for half an hour, and saw the royal fabric in all its different bearings ;

being high water, it seemed very singular to behold so amazing a pile so very near the surface of the river. Having sailed about half a mile lower down, I returned, and at five o'clock dined with Mr. Locker, with whom I spent the evening until ten o'clock.

Some other points of sight-seeing in London in 1830 lead to a conclusion.

"On Wednesday (March 31st) Mr. Davison breakfasted with me. I afterwards called at Mr. Pratt's, thence on to Mr. Barber at the British Museum, thence at Boosey's music shop in Holles Street, then on to Thomas Phillips, Esq., Professor of Painting, about Sir John Swinbourne's portrait, and then at the Papier Maché Manufactory in Edgware Road.

"I next called on Mr. Ord of Whitfield, then went through the museum of the Zoological Gardens in Bruton Street, and a very admirable museum it is. I next spent an hour at the Western Bazaar, and saw Haydon's pictures of Eucles and Punch, with which I was much pleased, and also with the sculptured figures of Tam o' Shanter and Souter Johnnie, which Mrs. Locker had particularly recommended to my notice. I then visited the beautiful and extensive exhibition of paintings, models, and sculpture at the galleries of the Society of British Artists; and after much too hasty an inspection of these, which well deserve a whole day's examination, I went to the Royal Menagerie at Charing Cross (removed from Exeter Change),—I saw the lions and other principal animals fed. The collection is very interesting, and the ravenous disposition excited by hunger, in most of the animals, is truly terrible. I returned by Fleet Street, where I purchased a very good pantographer, and then returned straightway to my lodgings.

"In the evening I went with Mr. Davison to Covent Garden Theatre, and heard the sacred oratorio of 'Messiah.' This, and Drury Lane on the first night I spent in London,

were the only theatres I visited. I was much gratified with
the music, but the choruses have not full and overpowering
magnificence.

"I visited the Excise Office in Broad Street, and spent some
time at the East India House, the museum of which was
certainly among the most curious and interesting sights I saw
in London. The Eastern manuscripts in particular are highly
deserving the attention of the stranger.

"I went to see the animals in the Tower, and as a
menagerie the thing was much more confined and insignificant
than I expected. I deferred seeing the armouries and jewels
to another visit; and having completed all my parliamentary
business, and had many opportunities of seeing the varieties of
London, I left in one of the stage-coaches at four on Saturday
afternoon, and went outside as far as Huntingdon, where we
arrived about eleven. There I got inside for the remainder of
the journey, having suffered very much from the intense cold.
The ground was covered with snow, and the following day was
very cold and cheerless. Travelling along the London and
Edinburgh road for the fourth time is a rather tiresome
operation. *Once* is more than sufficient to see all that is
worth seeing, with the exception of two or three places."

CHAPTER X.

1831-33.

THE year 1831 becomes again eventful in a personal point of view. On January 31st Mr. Sopwith started for Ross in order to be married to Miss Jane Scott of Ross, whom he had had the good fortune to woo and win. He travelled in a storm of excessive violence, accompanied with a heavy fall of snow. The marriage ceremony was performed in Belford Church, after which the married couple started in a chaise and four for Berwick, but the weather was so tempestuous that both were made ill by it, and "a more deplorable wedding jaunt has seldom perhaps occurred." They reached Berwick at last, but could get no further for some days. They carried with them a letter of introduction to Sir Walter Scott at Abbotsford, but the storm prevented them getting so far. They returned to Ross on the 12th, and thence to Newcastle on the 17th.

On April 12th Mr. Sopwith took an active part in the opening of the Scotswood chain bridge. On April 20th he attended a large meeting of professional and amateur

artists to form the Artists' Conversazione at Newcastle-
upon-Tyne, of which institution he was made President.
In August of this year he was seized with illness, and
suffered from congestion and inflammation of the lungs,
which proved extremely serious. During this year he
remarks on the public uneasiness existing in Newcastle
in regard to the Reform Bill, and records that after the
Bill had been thrown out by the House of Lords he met a
countryman who was reading an account of the rejection
from a paper edged with deep black. He also refers
to an outbreak of Asiatic cholera which took place in
Newcastle, the deaths from which were very appalling.
One death occurred next door to him, but neither
Mrs. Sopwith nor himself felt any apprehension; which
circumstance, he thinks, contributed greatly to their
escape, a view respecting contagious disease he maintained consistently all through his life.

On November 8th of this year he spent an evening
with Captain James Glencairn Burns, son of Robert
Burns, at the house of Mr. Dunbar. He seems to have
been much struck with Captain Burns, and greatly
pleased with his acquaintance.

At the close of his journal for this year 1831 he adds
that the year will ever hold place in his memory. He
observes :—

"The year 1831 will ever hold an honoured place in my
memory, as having added greatly to my happiness by my
union with a most esteemed and amiable girl, who has proved
a most affectionate companion, a prudent manager of household affairs, and a most tender and diligent guardian of my
dear boy. . . . The event of next moment was my illness
which for three months kept me from business and brought
me to the verge of the grave. And here let me record with
much affectionate regard the inestimable value of the constant

and judicious attention of my dear wife, that if any of my
posterity should hereafter read these pages they may, if she be
living, honour and esteem her, and, if departed, may seek for
grace to follow the good example she has shown."

1832.

In January 1832 Mr. Gray, the Governor of Newcastle
gaol, and Mr. Forsyth, the Town Marshal, called on
Mr. Sopwith, to view the model of the gaol for which
he had received a premium from the Commissioners in
1822. The visit evidently gave him great happiness,
and he continued actively employed, restored completely
to his ordinary healthy state of mind and body. On
March 17th a daughter, Ursula, was added to his family.

In the spring of this year he commenced a systematic
study of isometrical perspective, and on May 21st read a
paper on this subject to the Natural History Society. This
afterwards gave origin to a well-known and valuable
treatise by him on isometrical drawing.

He was next busied in surveying a new line of road
up the Derwent, on which subject he published a short
and very practical essay, entitled "Observations to
Accompany a Map of the Vale of Derwent in the County
of Durham." The map itself is admirably drawn, and
the description is carried out with all the precision and
attention to details for which its author was so much
respected. He also wrote a review in the *Newcastle
Journal* of Hodgson's "History of Northumberland,"
and was engaged by the publishers of a series of views of
Fountain's Abbey to write an architectural and historical
description of that venerable ruin. For the local journals
and for " Dunbar's Catalogue" he wrote a brief biography
of one called Blind Willie, a well-known local minstrel,
who died in All Saints' poorhouse on July 20th, 1832, aged

eighty-four or eighty-five years. Mr. Dunbar, the sculptor, made a statue of this celebrity, and Mr. Robert Gilchrist commemorated him in the songs of the bards of the time. Amongst local events witnessed during the year Mr. Sopwith dwells on the first lighting of Newcastle by gas and a further outbreak of cholera.

In the autumn, at the request of Mr. John Clayton, the Town Clerk of Newcastle, Mr. Sopwith undertook the survey of a railway from Durham to Shields, being associated in the labour with Mr. John Buddle, the eminent engineer. They commenced the survey on October 9th, and rapidly completed their work.

Mr. Clayton was a man after my friend's own heart. He won the highest social reputation in business and in local affairs generally, taking a very active part in the development of railway enterprise; but his life was most devoted to Newcastle, and the growth of it from a comparatively small to an enormous centre of industry was, Mr. Sopwith thought, due to his, more than to any other person's, individual efforts. He had also antiquarian tastes, and was proud of his possession of the remains of five Roman camps along the great Northumbrian wall raised by the Roman forces. The friendship remained to the end, but Clayton, as we have seen in a previous chapter, long outlived his companion.

Mr. Sopwith's *résumé* of 1832 is quite joyous in its tone. He rejoices in excellent health, considers his domestic happiness perfect, and lays special stress on the advantage he has obtained in making the friendship of his colleague, Mr. John Buddle.

1833.

In the new year of 1833 he made the acquaintance of an accomplished and excellent man, Mr. Surtees, and on

January 3rd, that being his thirtieth birthday, Mr. Buddle
called upon him with an official letter from Mr. Milne,
of the Woods and Forests, relating to a proposed survey
of the mines in Dean Forest, a duty which he accepted.
He left Newcastle on the evening of February 10th,
arrived at Boroughbridge at six the next morning, took
postchaise to York, proceeded next day to Leeds, thence
to Sheffield, Birmingham, Worcester, and Gloucester,
and so to the Forest of Dean, which was reached on the
13th. On the 18th, in his pit dress, he went with his
assistants to the Hopewell Colliery in Dart Hill to make
his inspection ; but some opposition being offered to the
survey by a local magnate, his assistants had to return
home, and he, writing to Mr. Buddle for further instructions, took the opportunity of staying a day or two
at Bristol and Bath on his way to town, where he arrived
on the 22nd, and on the 26th had an interview with Lord
Duncannon at the Office of Woods respecting the Forest
affairs. On the 27th he looked in at Chancery Lane to
see Lord Brougham. On March 4th he viewed the
Thames Tunnel, then the great engineering feat of the
day, and on the 7th commenced his journey home by
way of Manchester, Liverpool, and back by way of Leeds
to Newcastle. This journey was purposely a deviation
from the direct route in order to visit the Manchester
and Liverpool Railway. On Friday the 8th, he visited
the magnificent scenery of Matlock in Derbyshire,
and arrived at Manchester in the evening. Next day
at seven he went on the Railway to Liverpool. He
minuted the quarter-mile posts and found them as follows: 56″, 50″, 38″, 41″, 54″, 65″, *the whole journey
of thirty miles scarcely occupying two hours*. He
returned to Manchester in the evening and went to
the theatre. The following morning he left for Leeds,

dined there, and proceeding by night coach homewards reached Newcastle on the 12th.

He was occupied in Newcastle until May 4th, on the evening of which day his workshops were burned down, with a loss of about seven hundred pounds. Fortunately for himself he was insured, and fortunately for his employés a subscription was raised for them through the benevolent and active exertions of the Rev. Robert Green. A day or two later he was called to London, as a witness before the Committee of the House of Commons on the Derwent Road Bill.

The diary of May 7th contains the following entry :—

" On this evening I was elected a member of the Institution of Civil Engineers, an honour which I chiefly owe to the voluntary offer and subsequent proposition of the celebrated Mr. Telford, the President of the Institution."

On May 11th he visited the Royal Academy, and on the 12th went to hear the Bishop of Hereford, Dr. Grey, preach in Bow Church. On the 14th he attended the Institution of Civil Engineers for the first time; on the 15th went to Richmond by steamboat; and on the 19th spent the day at Windsor and visited the Castle—the ballroom of which he considered the noblest apartment he had ever seen. The tapestry he thought " inimitably beautiful." At eleven he went to the Chapel Royal with his friend Mr. Collinson, where they were seated nearly opposite to their Majesties, whom he thus quaintly describes:—

" We saw them as they walked out of chapel arm in arm. The King (then William IV.) is stout and fresh-looking, but walks rather lamely; he was dressed as a plain country gentleman, and his coat was somewhat shabby in appearance, its newness having long departed. The Queen (Adelaide) was plainly dressed in a green hat and white feather, blue sleeves and white gown, without any jewels. The choir performed 'Lift up your heads,' from Handel's 'Messiah.'"

On the 20th he was sworn at the Bar of the House of Lords as a witness, and on the 22nd he left Blackwall at ten in the *City of Edinburgh* steam packet, in which, after a pleasant voyage in calm weather, he arrived safely at Newcastle.

In July he visited Edinburgh, renewing the acquaintance of Dr. Boswell Reid and Professor Pillans. Of his journey there and back he made many notes, antiquarian, professional, and social, one of which, relating to the Roman Station at Housesteads and the Roman Wall, must be introduced.

"I left the coach at Bardon Mill at twelve, and had a pleasant walk to the beautiful and sequestered cottage of my respected friend the Rev. Anthony Hedley, where I dined, and at two o'clock rode to the Roman Station at Housesteads; here I found the Rev. John Hodgson, the Rev. A. Hedley, Mr. Turner, Jun., of Blagdon, and Mr. John Hodgson superintending an antiquarian research in the foundations of the eastern gate of the Station, from which six or seven labourers were employed in removing the soil and loose stones.

"Two worn paths were laid bare, but no remarkable remains of the former occupants had been discovered.

"The Rev. Mr. Hodgson then accompanied me on a view of the Wall from Housesteads westward to Craglough, and as this was the first time I had ever made an exploratory visit to this most singular relic of Roman warfare, it was truly gratifying to have so able and intelligent a guide as the author of the 'History of Northumberland,' whose intimate acquaintance with the localities and extensive knowledge of antiquarian subjects added the greatest interest to the feelings of surprise and admiration excited by a view of the Wall and adjacent cliffs.

" We first viewed the station, which Mr. H. minutely described, and then ascended to the summit of Housestead Crags. The Roman Wall here stretches along almost on the very edge of precipitous cliffs formed of fine basaltic columns, and winds a tortuous and often very steep course up and down the steep sides of a succession of prominences called the ' Devil's Teeth.' It is impossible not to be impressed with the strongest admiration at the fine grey columns which form so stupendous a foundation for the Roman barrier, which, however magnificent as a work of art, sinks into insignificance beside the proud basaltic wall which forms the north side of the ridge. I made a sketch of a fine square column of basalt, which, like a stately tower of a vast castle, rises on the face of the cliff a little west of Housesteads, showing a distant view of the winding course of the Wall over Sewingshields Crags. The prospect from the summit of Housesteads and neighbouring crags is very extensive; to the east and south the lands contiguous to the Vale of Tyne have a rich and diversified aspect.

" The southern horizon presents the commencement of the high lands bordering on the Pennine Chain. The stately Castle of Langley, the romantic banks at Staward, and numerous other interesting places may be distinctly seen, the view extending over Whitfield and Allendale to Alston Moor, and bounded on the south-west by Cross Fell mountain. The west view chiefly comprises a succession of lofty basaltic ridges, on which the course of the Wall may be distinctly traced; and on the north the eye rests on one vast and broad unbroken extent of desolate moors, the waving lines of which grow more and more dreary as they recede, until lost in the horizon formed by the Cheviot Ridge; a few loughs, or lakes, and a solitary cottage or two being almost the only objects which appear scattered over this wide and solitary domain. This district, I was informed by Mr. Hodgson, was the Forest of Lough, or Lowes, whence the latter family name had its origin.

" We next slid down the steep escarpment of the cliff to the plain below, where I made a drawing of the face of the basaltic scars, on finishing which we pursued our ramble along the Wall on the top of the Cliffs.

" This interesting relic of antiquity is here in surprising preservation, being in height from four to five feet above the surface, and showing the entire breadth, which is about seven feet. It is built of a white and close-grained freestone (brought from quarries about half a mile down the hill on the south side), in regular courses on the outside, but filled with whin and grouting within; the cement contains many small pieces of limestone, and is extremely hard. The military way of the Romans is very observable lower down on the south side, and still further down, adjoining the turnpike, are the Agger and ditch of Hadrian ; I made a sketch showing a long unbroken line of the Wall, with singular offsets in it of about nine inches. On proceeding further west I was suddenly struck with admiration on beholding the romantic appearance of Crag Lough, and the bold perpendicular face of basalt whence the name is derived, and which rises from its southern shore.

" At Holbank farmhouse (the property of John Clayton, Esq.) I had a drink of Gilsland Spa water, and on arriving at the summit of the Crags I selected one of the most prominent points of view, and sketched one of the magnificent series of columnar blocks of basalt which form the northern side of the Crag.

" No description can convey an adequate idea of the grand and imposing effect of the view from the edge of these cliffs. The rippled surface of Lough Craglough was studded with broad leaves of the yellow water lily, and a gabled mansion, lately built for a shooting box by Sir Edward Blackett, is here added to the few objects which appear on the broad moors of the Forest of Lough.

" Nearly opposite Holbank farmhouse are the very observable remains of one of the Castra, or forts, which were built

at intervals between the stations, and another of these forts
occurs in a hollow immediately west of Craglough. They vary
in size, but the two which are here alluded to are about eighty
feet in extent and nearly of a square form.

"The upper surface of the Wall is covered with a fine soft
bed of grass, in which lady's-bedstraw, sheep's-scabious, and
wild thyme plentifully abound. I made a sketch of Craglough
and adjacent scenery while sitting on this comfortable place of
rest, on the Wall immediately behind Bradley. After walking
down the lough, we examined a portion of the Wall which is
built in horizontal courses, and not, like many steep parts of
the Wall, inclining with the surface of the ground. In a section
of the wall where the courses are level, the manner of building
exhibits more care, the inner work being arranged in layers
corresponding with the outer course.

"From Craglough a fine range of basaltic cliffs extends
westward."

The description of the Roman Station is followed by
that of a modern cottage belonging to his friend Mr.
Hedley, and affords not only a contrast of an historical
kind, but a good illustration of Mr. Sopwith's powers as
a natural and picturesque writer.

"Chesterholme is the name given by Mr. Hedley to a
spot of ground about an acre in extent, a flat or 'holme'
immediately beneath the Roman station of Little Chester
(Vindolana), around which the ground rises steeply on every
side, excepting the narrow outlet of a small and most romantic
rivulet which runs down a steep channel of limestone rock. The
hill side on the south of the holme is steeper than the rest;
the lower part was planted twelve or fourteen years ago, and
the higher portion of it is a broad and lofty fell of considerable
height, from the summit of which is an extremely beautiful
and interesting prospect.

"The cottage which adorns this romantic and sequestered

little valley was erected about three years ago by Mr. Hedley, from a design given by Mr. Green, sen., architect. It is built with steep gables, with large boards and ornamented chimneys. Some parts of the walls are built with stones brought from the station which crowns the rising ground opposite. The grounds are laid out with exquisite taste, and the whole scene is more like the beautiful creation of a poetical mind in visions of Fairyland than a rustic dwelling in a northern clime, and in a wild and moorland country. A profusion of roses, shedding their fragrant odours around the walls they so richly adorn, add the last and highest finish of romantic loveliness and beauty, which, to be fully appreciated, must be seen. Still more attractive is the character of its amiable inmate, whose widely-known and acknowledged worth have procured him the admiration of all who know him; and it reflects but little honour on the zeal and integrity of the political party he has so long and ably supported, that in the day of prosperity PROMISES, *unasked* and *unlooked-for*, have been his ONLY reward.

"The interior of the cottage is fitted up with butternut, a Canadian wood, which resembles oak, but is much cheaper. The library is both extensive and select, and the views from it are romantic and beautiful. In front is a rustic porch, under which are several Roman altars and other antiquities found in the adjoining station."

Towards the close of July Mr. Sopwith commenced a survey of the Durham Junction Railway at Pensher and of a bridge over the river Wear; and, in August, he went to work in earnest with his treatise on isometrical drawing. In September he records with much regret the death of his friend Mr. Surtees. In the latter part of the same month he began the survey of the Blaydon and Hebburn Railway.

Towards the end of October of this year he received

a letter from the Office of Woods referring to Dean
Forest and inquiring when he could resume his survey.
The latter part of the year was fixed upon, and he
left Newcastle on December 12th, taking with him, as
assistants, George Johnson, William Smith, and N. Sey-
mour. They arrived at their destination on December 15th,
and the following day proceeded with the mineral survey
of the Forest of Dean, commencing with Hopewell Colliery
in Dart Hill, in which they surveyed all night on the
Wednesday and Thursday preceding Christmas Day.
Christmas Day was spent with Mr. Davis at Lydney.
Then work went on again until,—

"after continuing the subterraneous survey, and making
various plans and sections on Monday and Tuesday, another
year at the close of the latter day was completed, and gave
rise to many reflections connected with the progress of time,
with the events of past years, and anticipations of years
to come."

CHAPTER XI.

1834.

A GREAT accumulation of business came to Mr. Sopwith in the beginning of the year 1834. Of one hundred and fifty-one hours occupied in January in passing from Newcastle to Coleford in the Forest of Dean,—where his three assistants were still engaged,—and to other places, sixty-four were passed in travelling, eighty-two in resting or detention, and five only on the special business of his expeditions. In six consecutive days he was in Newcastle; for three hours he was at Harrogate; nineteen at Leeds; seventeen at Burnley; two at Manchester; five at Liverpool; seven at Coleford; twelve at Gloucester; one at Bristol; three at Bath; eight at Salisbury; two at Poole; and three at Swanage. Considering that this was a man who never loitered in business, the record tells us strikingly what time was lost in travelling before the railway system came fully into operation.

In February he made a special visit to the Forest of Dean, for the purpose of continuing his labours there, proceeding on February 12th from Newcastle to Harrogate, in order to meet the Bishop of Durham, to gain his ssent to some concessions concerning the Blaydon and

Hebburn line. The interview was fixed for nine in the
morning, but such an interview "as he shall never forget."
The Bishop assented to the railway passing through his
lands between Blaydon and Hebburn, but throughout
was irritable up to actual rudeness and unkindness.
Never in any similar application had Mr. Sopwith experienced anything at all approaching to the harshness
and "uncourteousness" which on this occasion caused
him surprise, but not uneasiness. The manner in which
my friend bore this infliction is best told in his own
words, recorded in his journal almost immediately after
the interview. His words breathe a spirit of independence combined with a gentleness it would be difficult
to find surpassed.

" He had not heard of the death of Mr. Surtees, and there
was a melancholy interest in being the first to communicate
the loss of the historian of Durham to the Bishop of the
diocese.   His lordship had no ground of objection to the
railway, nor any fault to find, otherwise than a most unreasonable and unbusinesslike displeasure at my bothering him with
railways and such like, of which ' he knew no more than a
child.' He pushed the plan away from him, but I informed
him that the law of the land required me to state upon oath
the fact of his having seen it, and he then cast a hasty glance
or two over it. It fortunately happened that my duty was
plain and simple, and I steadily adhered to a respectful and
courteous behaviour, undisturbed by a treatment which I was
conscious of not having merited ; and I left with feelings of
perfect astonishment and regret that a shepherd could set so
poor an example to one of the humblest of his flock.

" The Bishop of Durham has the general reputation of being
a man of great literary and scholastic attainments, and many
describe him as a good and charitable man. The deportment
alluded to above, doubtless, must have in a great measure, if

not altogether, arisen from nervous irritability caused by illness, but its marked and peculiar character was such as will ever associate very strange ideas with the name of bishop in my ears."

From Harrogate he passed to Leeds, where he found electioneering in full swing, and where he was compelled to stay all night.

"The town was perfectly mad electioneering, and I saw an immense procession of the Blue party (Sir John Beckett's). This is the second time the boon of Reform has given the inhabitants of Leeds the fancied advantages and practical evils of a popular election. No one can be more anxious than myself that electioneering and every other privilege of Englishmen should be placed upon such a foundation as may best promote the welfare of the state; and the measure of Reform conceded by the present administration to the wishes of the people of England was doubtless intended to effect a better mode of election and a better transaction of public business in Parliament. The great simplicity of the Reform poll is justly admired and approved by all parties, but the general purity of election and the proceedings of the House do not yet present the decided improvement which was hoped for by the friends of Reform.

"The gross waste of time, the breach of regular industry, the cessation of business, the notorious existence of the most depraved and dependent party spirit, the noise, confusion, and drunkenness which prevailed in Leeds on this occasion, is a most deplorable contrast to what an election would be if ever the people of England shall by the blessing of God become wise and enlightened.

"In occupying a leisure hour before bed-time 'in mine inn' with the writing of these brief memoranda, let it not be supposed by any one whose eye may glance over them that I either profess to study or care about politics. I have known

7

many excellent men of all parties, and in confiding any interest or property of my own to the care of any one, I would look out for an honest and respectable man, on whose general good feeling and integrity I could confide, and select him as a proper person to be the guardian either of my private or public interests.

" To the ranks of either Whig or Tory I have no desire to attach myself, and in my humble station my only desire is to be at all times a sincere and hearty lover of my country. If I were to venture at imitating the example of the great mass of His Majesty's lieges by commencing business as a statesman, I would so far meet the popular cry as to adopt for my motto Annual Parliaments, Universal Suffrage, and Election by Ballot, but then it would be by a very different mode of operation to what is now practised. My plan would simply be to have good, strong, capacious chests placed in the Town Hall of every county town or borough, or other place of election, and on a given day in each year every individual in the kingdom man, woman, and child, should have full liberty to vote as often as they chose, by putting money in the box appropriated to their respective candidates.

" This genuine test of their favour, however unreasonable it may at first appear, would be as rational a mode of expressing public opinion as any other. The extensive contribution of the great mass of the middle and lower classes would insure a proper influence from the populace, and the large sums of noblemen and capitalists would give to property its just influence in what so greatly concerns the welfare of the country. The money thus collected I would apply to the payment of public rates, taxes, etc., in the respective districts, and thus the disagreeable task of tax-paying would become a means of expressing political sentiments, and an annual contribution of this sort would doubtless raise no trifling sum throughout the kingdom. Bribery and tax-gathering would thus be almost or entirely abolished. A candidate might vote for himself with a thousand pounds, and give his friends as many ten or fifty pound notes as he thought proper; all would go to a good cause, would relieve the public burdens, and in this as in all other matters it would doubtless be found that the best member would fetch the highest price.

" It is clearly inconsistent that the vote of a man who employs fifty thousand pounds in business should weigh no more than the vote of one who has little or no interest in the permanent welfare of the country. The mere *number* of votes is manifestly no criterion of fitness. Moral worth and integrity ought to stamp a weight on votes far exceeding the vote of a thoughtless or profligate person, but this in society is impracticable; neither is the Member of Parliament so much the representative of mind as of property, of private worth as of public interests.

" By the plan I propose the successful candidate would either represent a very extensive and strong feeling of the many, or the vast and important interests of moneyed men and great landowners, but most probably the heaviest box would often be formed by the united contributions of these two classes of society. By way of a finish to my scheme it would be no bad plan to bestow on the successful candidate a moderate percentage of the contents of his own box; this would induce candidates to be more free in the honest bribery of their friends, would relieve them of much expense, and would encourage men of plain good sense and moderate fortune to aspire to that station which they are most eminently qualified to fill. Every voter would enjoy all the secrecy of balloting, for his contributions should be known to himself only, and the poor but honest tradesman might safely promise every candidate a vote."

A day or two later on I find my friend offering some new reflections on railway travelling in 1834.

" I left Burnley next morning in the mail, and slept nearly all the way to Manchester, which town we found enveloped in the brown and greeny darkness of a London fog. I breakfasted

at the Palace Inn, and went to Liverpool on the railway.   In
this journey nothing particular occurred different to what I
had seen before, but three things forced themselves much on
my attention :—

"(1) A worse engine than last year.

"(2) More jolting on rails than ditto.

"(3) The vast local improvements along the line.

"Each of these ' unfold a *tale*,' but I have not time to
detail further than by remarking that the enormous expense of
good engines and keeping the railway in perfect repair seems
indicated by their being both suffered to deteriorate, and if
such be the case with this railway very few places in the
kingdom can afford speed on railways.   Horse or engine
travelling of ten or twelve miles an hour is probably the most
economical speed, and is sufficiently quick for most purposes;
but the march of intellect will never rest satisfied with this,
and they are now scheming a velocity of forty miles an hour.
The immense traffic between Liverpool and Manchester furnishes funds for all manner of experiment and improvement,
but other poorer concerns must beware ere they attempt to
follow the example."

From Liverpool Mr. Sopwith proceeded across the
Mersey in the mail steam packet, and then went by mail
through Chester (where he was much amused with the
singular style of building) to Shrewsbury, Hereford, and
Monmouth.   From the latter town, which he reached at
nine on Sunday morning, February 16th, 1834, he went,
after breakfast, in a phaeton to Coleford, and greatly
admired the romantic scenery of the banks of the Wye.

At Coleford he found his three assistants ready for
church, and after dressing he accompanied them.   In the
afternoon he looked over the plans done during his absence
in the north, and found them, as well as the progress
of the survey, highly satisfactory.

At five on Sunday evening he drove in a phaeton to Gloucester, and next morning rose at six and had a delightful walk to see the Cathedral. The beauties of the exterior of this fine structure were almost new to him. The morning sun gilded the fine crisp edges of the minute architectural enrichments of the tower, and presented them in a very favourable aspect.

At nine he went in a coach to Bristol, and from there to Bath, where he saw Sir Thomas Clavering, and had a walk in the Pump Room and in Great Pulteney Street, and then dined at York House. At seven he left in the mail, and after a very comfortable journey arrived at Salisbury or New Sarum at midnight.

On Tuesday morning, February 18th, having had a look at the Cathedral, he went in a coach to Poole, and after dinner sailed in a packet for Swanage. Poole he describes as an active, bustling little port, having one of the finest quays in England. The harbour is very spacious, and if its entrance were as safe as its interior is capacious it would be one of the finest in England. A sail of two hours in a packet brought him to Swanage.

The hotel at Swanage is a very spacious and handsome structure, the property of Mr. Pitt. He stayed here until the following morning, and left at eleven in a gig for Wareham to meet the coach for Dorchester.

From Wareham he had a pleasant ride on a coach to Dorchester, whereas, finding that no coach proceeded to Bristol until Friday morning, and that from Weymouth, he resolved to spend Thursday in seeing Weymouth and the neighbouring Isle of Portland.

At Dorchester he found very comfortable quarters at the King's Arms Inn, and at ten next morning went on a coach to Weymouth, passing the extensive Roman station called Maidon Castle. The bay and adjoining walk or "esplanade" at Weymouth were extremely beautiful, and the long range of well-built houses had a noble appearance, but he was disappointed by their being built of brick instead of stone, as he expected they would be, from the vicinity of Portland Island.

The day being delightfully pleasant, he walked to Sandsfoot Castle, and thence to a ferry which took him across to Chesil Bank, a beach of eighteen miles in length, composed entirely of small rounded pebbles; it was formerly from eleven to thirteen feet higher, and narrower, but was spread wider by a tremendous gale in November 1825, when several houses were destroyed in Chesil and many lives lost.

He walked to Chesil, and made an exploratory journey round the island, visiting the quarries and Rufus Castle. Near the south point or "Bill" of Portland he found a modern castellated mansion, once the residence of William Penn, son of the celebrated William Penn; and in front of it, on the steep and rugged declivities facing the British Channel, the remains of a church with several monumental stones.

From this date onwards up to the end of May Mr. Sopwith remained engaged on the Dean Forest survey, but making meanwhile several visits to London, and thoroughly enjoying all that passed before him. In London he listens to Paganini at the Adelphi Theatre, is delighted with the elder Mathews and his monologue, makes the acquaintance of Dr. Birkbeck, and in the early part of June returns home to Newcastle, after an absence of four months, to find another daughter added to his family. He now continued to work on the treatise on isometrical drawing, and on September 10th brought it before the world. The object of the work was to offer a general view of the nature and advantages of mineral plans and surveys, the construction of geological maps, and regular series of working plans and sections of mines. It also gave familiar explanations concerning plans of mines, roads, and estates, and at the same time supplied the libraries of gentlemen with a book of reference and information on several details of plans and sections of which no popular description had yet been supplied. The mode of drawing suggested enabled the reader to apply the method to representations of gardens and pleasure grounds, so that not only a correct plan of the various flower beds and walks could be shown, but also the height and pictorial appearance of trees, shrubs, greenhouses, and the like. The use of isometrical rulers would, he thought, be found an agreeable occupation to amateurs as well as artists, and especially to ladies, who would combine the beauties of landscape, architecture, and flower-painting with correct and useful delineations of pleasure grounds, houses, and gardens.

The book met with marked success, and it is somewhat a matter of surprise that it has not to this day retained its place as an educational work.

The remaining portion of the year 1834 was spent by Mr. Sopwith chiefly in railway surveys, in some of which he was associated with other engineers. On November 14th he made the acquaintance of Professor John Phillips, an acquaintanceship which ripened into a friendship lasting through a long series of years, and in which it was my own good fortune, in some measure, to take part. Professor Phillips and Mr. Sopwith were admirably fitted for friendship. Their tastes were congenial and their pursuits similar. Sopwith's love for geology lighted up in him immense admiration for Phillips' special and classical knowledge on that subject ; and Phillips' appreciation of Sopwith's breadth of knowledge on all subjects was often warmly expressed. They were both fond also of quiet humour, and were not afraid to indulge in a little fun on their own peculiarities.

Throughout all his career Mr. Sopwith's love for geological science was unabated. The study seemed to come to him naturally, although, according to his own view, it resulted from his practical work in the mines. "But all miners are not geologists," I remember hearing said to him by one of our clerical friends, the Rev. J. B. Reade ; "and you, I believe, are the only one I ever met." "That may be," responded Sopwith; "but miners are by occupation in the bowels of the earth, and the bowels of the earth are the galleries of the geologist. Perhaps they are too much occupied with their own pursuits to observe the natural history around them." "Yes," continued our jocular cleric, "and see what such men lose. Just think, Doctor, what Jonah might have told us about digestion if he had only looked out when he was in the belly of the whale." "You are too hard on Jonah," said the medicus addressed, "for he had no light, not even a safety-lamp." "That's one for Jonah," added Sopwith, with his merry laugh; "and the doctor has beaten the parson on his own ground."

CHAPTER XII.

1835-36.

IN 1835 we may consider Mr. Sopwith a thoroughly established man in Newcastle-upon-Tyne. He was engaged in many lines of occupation. He carried on still the business of his father; he was actively employed in surveying; he took a lively interest in local affairs, and continued to educate himself more and more in subjects scientific and practical.

On March 25th he was called to London, and travelled by the Wellington coach. In his notes on this journey he records the curious fact that he was in the company of fifteen convicts, and that, notwithstanding the singular companionship, he had a perfectly comfortable journey. It was a new chapter to him in the history of human life, and opened up many curious reflections.

His business to London in this visit was to give further railway evidence before the House of Commons, but he found time to go to the museum of Sir John Soane in Lincoln's Inn Fields, and to make the acquaintance of the eccentric founder of that institution, through the introduction of Mr. Britton, the architect and well-known writer on architecture. Returning to Newcastle at the close of

March, he became very unwell from rheumatism, and continued ill all through April and May. On May 30th he was compelled to go to London, although he had to be lifted into the coach, but managed the journey pretty well, being accompanied by his " dear Jane." On June 4th he was examined before the House of Lords Committee, but had to be seated while giving evidence. On June 14th he got back to Newcastle, and soon afterwards went to Berwick, where under the influence of baths and pure country air he recovered, and in July and August visited the Trossachs and many places of historical interest in Scotland.

On September 13th he came again to London, this time in the Highflyer coach. He started at half-past nine a.m., and reached London at eight p.m. on the following day. From London he went to Dean Forest, and from there to Gloucester. On September 21st he commenced levelling the Forest of Dean, that is to say, taking levels for sections, for which purpose he planned a new levelling instrument, which saved much time and ensured great accuracy as compared with instruments then in use. The survey lasted till the early part of October.

Towards the close of this year Mr. Sopwith was proposed and nominated as a Councillor for the west ward of Newcastle. He was not elected ; many of his friends declining to vote, from a conviction that either the duties of the Council would interfere with his professional work, or that the continued attention to his professional duties would interfere with those of an official kind. In returning thanks to the gentlemen who supported him he acknowledged the justice of the defeat. He had abstained, he said, from asking even a single vote, and would always follow the same plan, though he would be ready to serve if elected.

In the early part of 1836 Mr. Sopwith was engaged largely in travel, or, as he calls it, " in excursions to obtain assents," that is to say, to submit railway plans to owners and occupiers of lands and houses near to which intended lines of railway had to pass. At this particular period in our national history the railway interest was the all-absorbing topic, and opinions respecting every new line proposed to be laid down were divided in the sharpest manner. The old fashions, and what may be called the Conservative instincts of the people, were against the innovation, and a host of objections having relation to ownerships of properties, privileges, and businesses stood in the way of any such radical change as that of a railway. In some instances the majority of a large town would rise, and without foreseeing the future, blind in fact to its own future interest, would protest against the innovation in the most determined manner, and sometimes with success. Mr. Sopwith's excursions, therefore, to obtain " assents " proved, he tells us, " an interesting occupation, leading to introduction to a great number of persons of every rank, from the peer with his wide domains to the humblest cottager or occupier." In this way his time was spent in the north of England until February 7th, when a longer excursion was requisite on the same business. He left Newcastle on the evening of the 7th in the mail coach, and visited York, Tadcaster, Leeds, and Manchester. From Manchester he went to Northampton, from there to Cambridge, and from Cambridge to London, where he remained until February 21st, when he left in the Highflyer coach, and reached Newcastle in thirty-five hours. The coach fare was £4 4s. ; the guard's and driver's dinners, £1 8s. 6d.; the entire

cost of the journey £5 12s. 6d. In March we find him
at Harrogate examining the geological conditions relating
to the sulphur wells, and in the same month he con-
tributes a paper to the *Mining Review* on "Civil and
Mining Engineering."

Work connected with the Great Northern line of railway
now occupied a great portion of his time, and he was
soon summoned to London again to appear before the
Parliamentary Committee. On May the 2nd he gave
very strong evidence on the manifest intention of the
" erroneous section " to deceive the Committee. For this
he received much but ineffectual abuse from opposing
counsel, whose case, however, broke down, to the great
chagrin of the opponents of the line. From London he
travelled to Bristol, thence to Chepstow, Catford, and
Dean Forest, then to Gloucester and Cheltenham, returning (on May 10th) to London, where he dined with Mr.
Fisher, the well-known publisher, and afterwards went
to the Institution of Civil Engineers to hear Mr. John
Martin, the great painter, explain his plans for improving
the river Thames. With the suggestions made by Martin
he was very greatly impressed, and I have heard him say
that the whole plan indicated an advance of the most
remarkable order,—an anticipation, indeed, of the improvement that has been made in what is now called the
Thames Embankment, and including other projects not
less important, and still unfulfilled. After returning for
a short time to Newcastle, he was called back to London
in the early part of June, and was detained until the 20th,
when he proceeded on business for the Great North of
England Railway, leaving by the Halifax mail and going
to Leicester, Manchester, and Wigan.

On July 13th, at seven in the evening, having hired a
commodious travelling carriage, Mr. Sopwith, accompanied

by Mr. Buddle, Mr. George Johnson, and Mr. Nicholas Wood, proceeded to Sedburgh, Lancaster, and Wigan. They posted all night, travelled all day on the 14th, dined at Preston, and reached Wigan at nine at night. The occasion of this journey was to view the *locus in quo* of an important reference case, *Clayton* v. *Greyson*, in which about £32,000 depended on the construction to be put on the single word "level," in a lease of the coal under the property. On the 16th they went to Liverpool, where on the 19th the matter was arranged by the payment of £8,500.

On August 10th he attended a meeting of the Great North of England directors at Darlington, and in September he was surveying the boundaries of Sir Edward Blackett's manorial properties near Haydon Bridge.

In addition to other work carried on this year he prepared a plan of a proposed arrangement by Mr. Grainger for concentrating the terminal lines of the Newcastle and Carlisle, the Great North of England, and the projected Edinburgh railways. Newcastle was to be the centre for this combination. He concluded this year at his offices in the Arcade, Newcastle, where he had been chiefly occupied during the year, except when taking one of the journeys to which reference has been made. The year, he tells us, " was one of great activity, and, at times, of extreme exertion, both bodily and mentally ; " but his health was good, his spirits lively, and he rejoiced greatly in the comforts of home and the plenitude of many blessings from the Giver of all good.

CHAPTER XIII.

1837.

IN January 1837 Mr. Sopwith, accompanied by Mr. Buddle, proceeded to Edinburgh on railway business, and in February he was called southward on engineering work connected with the proposed line from London to Brighton, where he arrived on the 22nd, returning on the 23rd, by Epsom, to London, and so again by the Highflyer back to Newcastle. In March he attended a trial at York on the "Harrogate Well Case." The case was heard on March 14th. Amongst the witnesses were the famous Dr. John Dalton, the "father of chemistry," as he has been called, and the discoverer of the atomic theory; Dr. William Smith, the well-known and admitted "father of English geology;" Professor Daniell, the inventor of the Daniell battery; Professor John Phillips; Mr. John Buddle; Professor Johnstone, the chemist; Mr. John Johnstone of Edinburgh, connected under Government patronage with Elkington's system of drainage; Dr. Clanny of Sunderland; and Mr. West, a chemist at Leeds, with others. West is noticed as being a Quaker who prided himself on having no name or title of any scientific distinction. When asked for his designation to be written down on an affidavit, he replied, "William West, Chemist, Leeds; lives in an alley and is nobody." But some years afterwards, when he became a Fellow of the Royal Society, he changed his tone and was always F.R.S. On March 13th, in a consultation with Mr. Creswell,—afterwards the well-known judge,—Mr. Sopwith described the geological details by means of a model, and induced Mr. Creswell to recommend an arrangement on the following morning, when the trial came on at York before Judge Alderson.

On the following day, March 14th, the scientific witnesses dined together,—a memorable dinner, which Mr. Sopwith reports as follows :—

"The addresses made after dinner by Dalton and Smith were in the highest degree interesting. It was indeed an event of no ordinary occurrence that two men so highly distinguished as original observers should be induced to favour the company as they did with very curious details relating to their respective connection with the advancement of chemistry and geology. Their healths were proposed separately. The company was sufficiently numerous and of a scientific character enough to justify a little formality in this ceremony, and in the addresses of thanks which followed the respective speakers both seemed to consider the parties present as friends to whom they could speak with freedom as well as with a degree of formality. Hence, the recital which they each gave of their discoveries was listened to with great attention and respect. I was particularly pleased with the hearty, open, and very friendly communications of Dr. Smith, and gladly took such opportunities as occurred from time to time to enjoy his society, and to derive benefit from his useful and instructive observations, which, with a liberality often found in the greatest minds, he was always most ready to communicate to others."

A curious and interesting conversation is reported by

Mr. Sopwith at this period of his life between himself and the Russian Count St. Aldegonde. The narrative is best told in his own words.

"I received instructions from the solicitors of the South Eastern Brighton Railway to be in attendance on the Committee on April 6th, and made arrangements accordingly. Previous to my departure I received fresh instructions which admitted of my remaining at home until the 8th; of this I would gladly have availed myself, but my brief visit to home was again shortened by a message from the Great North of England Railway Company, which required me to be in London on April 8th. I therefore secured an inside seat in the Wellington coach for Friday morning, April 7th.

"While I was engaged in my office on Thursday, the day previous to my departure, Mr. Morton, of Lambton, the agent of the Earl of Durham, called and wished me to accompany him to the George Inn, to be introduced to the Count St. Aldegonde, a Russian nobleman, who had brought letters from Lords Londonderry and Durham. I could ill spare time in this the eleventh hour of a hurried visit at home, but Mr. Morton was so anxious for me to go, that I was induced to do so, and was forthwith introduced to the 'Count de St. Aldegonde.'

"On our way to the inn Mr. Morton informed me that his visitor was a General in the Russian service, intimately acquainted and on terms of personal friendship with the Emperor, and much interested in scientific researches. I devoted three hours to visiting several places with him, and found much pleasure in doing so, inasmuch as his manners were in the highest degree pleasing, and his numerous and intellectual observations were instructive and entertaining.

"He expressed a wish to see some iron and glass works, the manufacture of locomotive steam engines, and the refining of lead, and especially Mr. Pattinson's recent discovery. I sent a note to Mr. Pattinson, who called at my office while

we were out; he left a specification of his patent, which I
gave to the Count, and made an arrangement to wait upon him
the following Saturday.   After showing this Russian General
various plans and sections at my office, and among others the
isometrical plan in Mr. Buddle's office, with which he was
particularly pleased, we walked to Mr. Grainger's new market.
This he greatly admired, and pronounced it far superior to
anything of the kind he had ever seen, either on the Continent
or in England.   I took him to the office, where Mr. Wardle
showed him several plans, elevations, and models of the new
streets, and gave him copies of some of them, which the Count
said he would show to the Russian Emperor, who would, he
was sure, be delighted with them.*

"I next took the Count to the Literary and Philosophical
Institution, and showed him the Law and Medical Libraries,
the Lecture and Apparatus Rooms, the General Library,
Reading and Committee Rooms, the Natural History Museum,
Geological and Antiquarian Rooms, and the Gallery of Roman
Altars, with which he was much pleased.   I introduced him to
Mr. Hutton and Mr. Fryer, and in the course of conversation
an arrangement for the interchange of minerals, etc., was
suggested, as a probable means of obtaining for the museum
a valuable accession of Russian and Siberian geological
specimens.

" From some incidental remarks it appears that the Count
has a private collection of minerals of considerable value.
He was particularly interested in viewing the sections of
coal strata presented to the Institution by Mr. Buddle, and

---

* It may here be observed that the Emperor of Russia inspected
Newcastle in December 1816, and several of the principal manufactories.   He also visited Wallsend, where Mr. Buddle explained to
him the nature and extent of the colliery operations.   The intention of
the party was to descend a pit, and an aide-de-camp was sent down the
day before to make the necessary arrangements as to dresses, etc.   Some
matters of etiquette, however, and a sight of the pit, proved obstacles
to this subterranean expedition.

also with the model of coal workings, by means of which I explained to him the mode of ventilation introduced by Mr. Buddle. He expressed a great wish to meet this eminent miner, of whom he had heard so much, both in England and abroad.

"I then walked with him to Hawthorn's Steam Engine Manufactory, and left him with Mr. Wm. Hawthorn to view these extensive works. On returning to the office, I sent George Shadforth, who accompanied the General to Cookson's Glass Works, and conducted him back to the George Inn, where I called upon him and bade him adieu.

"We had a long conversation on mineral surveys, and I gave him copies of some mining sections. It is contemplated to make some extensive surveys of this description in the south of Russia, with the view of establishing coal works."

This suggestion about a mineral survey in Russia was but a hopeful one for that great country. We once had a casual conversation on this subject *à propos* to a short essay of mine on the food resources of Russia, published in the *Journal of Public Health* for December 1855. This essay dealt with the food resources of the Empire, exclusive of Poland and Finland, in 1849—that is to say, shortly before the great war between France and England against Russia. At that time the surface of the Empire embraced 1,675,492,948 acres of land, rather more than one-fifth part of which was under cultivation. About 24,000,000 acres were private domains; 218,387,516 were devoted exclusively to arable purposes; 107,971,138 were pasture land; 393,277,413 were covered with forest wood; and 932,052,138 were waste. Deducting the waste and forest lands from the whole, there were left 350,163,397 acres of cultivated soil; which on a uniform rate of distribution to population would have given a proportion of more than six

acres and a half to each one of the 53,000,000 of the
then existing inhabitants. From these resources it was
inferred that the produce of the Empire was sufficient
to supply all the people with those elements of food
which are really essential to life ; but there the produce
finished, for beyond the production of food very little
indeed was done with the soil. Mr. Sopwith's view was
that in such vast tracts of country the most precious
mineral wealth must needs abound, especially in the
southern districts, and he thought that the whole question
of advancement of the peasants lay in making them
miners on their own soil rather than in Siberia. He
would have rejoiced to have been the first British
mining engineer in Southern Russia.

A reference to his library and to a list of books to be
sent to the binder leads to some notes in the diary of
April 1837 bearing upon the books which most attracted
the attention and the taste of my friend. He is warm in
his admiration of the works of Bishop Berkeley, whom
he names among his " chiefest favourites." " The clear
and chaste composition, the admirable metaphysical tact,
the philanthropic sentiment, the genuine piety and the
abundance of deep and interesting philosophical and
literary research, which prevailed in the writings of this
highly gifted prelate, entitle his volumes to an honourable place in every library. His singular ideas and
acute reasoning upon materialism are as entertaining as
they are instructive, and if the force of his arguments
fails to convince, it at least affords a clear insight into
many of the most beautiful phenomena of nature, and
eloquently teaches how narrow a range is permitted to
the human understanding when it attempts to fathom
the deepest mysteries of the universe."

Another favourite writer was Sterne. Putting aside

the quaint absurdities of this writer, which are nevertheless often attractive, Mr. Sopwith found much in him that was also useful. He speaks sensibly of the sermons of Sterne, sermons eloquent and forcible, which he expects in this day are well-nigh forgotten altogether. Gilpin's " Forest Scenery " is spoken of as an admirable exposition, with graphic descriptions and well-executed engravings of forest trees. He does not estimate Gilpin one jot too highly, for his work in its way has never been surpassed, and is as readable as it was in the day it was published. Gregory's " Mathematics " seems to have afforded him much instruction, and Zimmermann's " sweetly written " book on Solitude runs side by side with the " Vicar of Wakefield."

A work called the " Curious Book " comes in for warm praise. It is " well named ; " it contains a rare and well-collected assemblage of anecdotes in various departments of history, biography, and science. Washington Irving's tales afford him great delight, they are so accurate in regard to minuteness of detail, and his pictures of English manners present graphically every circumstance of sound and sight to the very ears and eyes of the reader. Phillips' " Geology of Yorkshire " he regards as the best work on social geology that had appeared at the time named, and McDiarmid's "Sketcher" is a book he valued, not only for its intrinsic worth, but also from the fact that he had spent an evening with its author in Dumfries, had heard that author speak of his intimate friend Robert Burns, and had drunk out of a goblet which had been for many years the property of the Scottish bard.

I may state in this place that the taste which Mr. Sopwith displayed in these early days for literature continued until the end of his life. He was always an industrious reader, slow in reading, but grasping thoroughly every detail of matter and point of style. He continued always to gain delight from the works of Washington Irving, and when Dickens, Thackeray, Lytton, Kingsley, Macaulay, Dixon, Froude, and other writers whose works engrossed the mind of the nation came on the field, he followed them with equal avidity, committing their best parts almost to memory. He had a keen sense of the humorous, and sometimes succeeded, if I may so say, in making new humour out of old, that is to say, of giving humour to the imaginary persons of the author beyond what the author himself conceived.

In the diary for April 7th of this year (1837), there is an account of another journey to London, by the old passenger coach, which account, as it gives the modern reader a perfect picture of what travelling was in the immediate pre-Victorian era, had better be given in its entirety.

"On Friday morning April 7th, 1837, I left Newcastle in the Wellington coach to visit London for the fourth time this year. The morning was cold, and snow showers fell on this and the following day. I had the good fortune to have for a fellow-passenger Thomas Fenwick, Esq., of Dipton, an able and experienced coal-miner, agent for the Bishop of Durham and the Dean and Chapter's Collieries, and author of a very ingenious treatise on Subterranean Surveying. His great vivacity and extensive range of information and anecdote tended much to beguile what might otherwise have seemed a long and tedious day. As regards travelling, however, custom has made it in me a property of easiness, and I now think nothing of the journey between Newcastle and London, which once appeared a very serious undertaking. I have learnt to read, to write, and to sleep well in a coach, and in addition to these have usually the good fortune to find some intelligent and conversable fellow-passenger. In this respect I have been more than usually fortunate this year, having in stage-coach journeys become acquainted with Cipriani Potter, the President of the Royal Academy of Music, and with the Rev. William Vernon Harcourt, a son of the Archbishop of York, as well as other agreeable and interesting persons, ladies as well as gentlemen; and the acquaintance, though brief, was in every instance highly agreeable, and seasonable as a relief from the fatigues of a long journey. My companions on this journey were Mr. Fenwick, Mr. Richardson, solicitor of York, and my clerk. The Wellington coach is well conducted, and travels nine miles an hour, including all stoppages except for meals; it leaves Newcastle at half-past nine. The passengers have half an hour for dinner at Northallerton about two o'clock, and the same time for tea at York at seven, breakfast at Grantham a little after six, and dinner at Harrington about two; it reaches the Bull and Mouth at half-past seven, being in all thirty-four hours. The Mail (the rival coach) is thirty-three hours going up, and twenty-nine hours coming down. The fare *in* the Mail is £5 up and five guineas down. *In* the Wellington the fare is £4 10s. The other expenses by the Wellington are as follows, but subject of course to very considerable variation according to the liberality, economy, or it may be parsimony, of passengers :—

	£	s.	d.
Dinner at Northallerton .	0	3	0
Driver at ,,	0	1	6
Guard at York .	0	2	6
Tea at ,,	0	2	3
Brandy at Tadcaster	0	1	3
Driver at Ferry Bridge .	0	1	6
Driver at Newark .	0	1	6
Breakfast at Grantham .	0	2	3
Driver at Huntingdon .	0	1	6
Dinner and brandy at Harrington .	0	3	9
Guard at London .	0	5	0
Driver at ,,	0	2	6
Porter .	0	1	0
Hackney coach	0	1	6
	£1	11	0

This journey to London was again on railway business, and examination before the parliamentary Committee, with evidence in favour of the London and Brighton Railway. The evidence is remarkable as showing what difficulties were thrown in the way of a line from London to London-super-Mare. Mr. Wood, who afterwards became Sir William Page Wood and finally Lord Hatherley, was the cross-examining counsel, and treated the witness with unusual severity; but the witness was a tough one, who never made a statement he was not prepared to substantiate, and who came off in triumph as the result. He stated his opinion of the line from an engineering point of view, and as affording peculiar facilities of intercourse, not only between London and Brighton, but also between London, Newhaven, and Lewes; also between these several towns and Brighton, Dover, and the central districts of the county of Kent. During this visit to London there is an account of an evening spent at Mr. Newton's in company with the "father of geology," Dr. William Smith. Blue cloth cloaks were now all the fashion, and as the weather was cold, Mr. Sopwith wrapped up the "father" in his own blue cloak, "taking good care, however, to get it again before we parted." At Mr. Newton's the geological father became very entertaining. He wrote his name in an album with some curious specimens of inverted writing. He was proud of this caligraphy, and observed that a person has no more right to alter the form of letters in writing than he has to alter the current coin of the realm.

To carry out all the instructions he had received, Mr. Sopwith again went to Brighton, and took up his residence there for a short time, making surveys of the different points where the line would have to pass, and where

stations would have to be erected, as at Lewes, East-
bourne, Newhaven, and Hastings. In the survey conducted by himself and his friends and his coadjutors,
they found several fossil branches in the green sand
under the chalk. At Lewes they came upon extensive
chalk quarries, and learnt some very curious particulars
from a workman there who had sustained a terrible
bereavement. In the previous winter there had been a
great fall of snow, which, accumulating above the chalk
cliff, had come down like an avalanche, killing the wife
of this man, the mother of eleven children, and doing an
immense deal of mischief. The scene of this avalanche
is still pointed out to visitors.

A note dated April 18th, 1837, gives a graphic account
of an express post journey from Brighton to London. It
runs as follows :—

" We pursued our inquiries and observations, and at twenty
minutes before 4 p.m. we passed St. Peter's Church on our
way to London, and reached Westminster Bridge at 10 past
8, being just 4½ hours for 52 miles, including stoppages. Mr.
Anderson reached town in time for a consultation, and I sat
up till two writing my reports, and making drawings, etc., to
illustrate the case.

" As our journey was altogether one of minute observation,
and as the time of travelling forms an element, we were desirous,
both on this account and also in order to prepare notes for
counsel, to expedite our return as much as possible. The
details were as follows :—

" We passed St. Peter's Church at Brighton at 3.40 p.m.
and reached Hickstead at 4.34, being 12 miles in 54 minutes
(change occupied 5 minutes). From Hickstead at 4.39 to
Crawley 5.28, being 10 miles in 49 minutes (change 4 minutes).
From Crawley at 5.32 to Red Hill at 6.14, being 9 miles in
42 minutes (change 5 minutes). Left Red Hill at 6.19 to

Croydon at 7.17, being 11 miles in 58 minutes (change 5 minutes). From Croydon at 7.22 to Westminster Bridge at 8.10, being 10 miles in 48 minutes. The following is a *Summary*.

$$
\begin{array}{llll}
12 \text{ miles} & 54 \text{ minutes} & = 13\frac{1}{4} \text{ an hour} \\
10 \quad,, & 49 \quad,, & = 12\frac{1}{4} \quad,, \\
9 \quad,, & 42 \quad,, & = 12\frac{7}{8} \quad,, \\
11 \quad,, & 58 \quad,, & = 11\frac{3}{8} \quad,, \\
10 \quad,, & 48 \quad,, & = 12\frac{1}{2} \quad,,
\end{array}
$$

" The expense was £5 17*s.* 6*d.*

" The above may be considered as the maximum speed which can be obtained on post roads without previous and special arrangements."

The return to Newcastle was on April 24th, soon after which Mr. Sopwith was busily occupied in planning a Town Hall for the town of Thirsk. In May he was in London once more on parliamentary business, enjoying, as a bit of his recreative break from Committee work, a concert by Ole Bull.

" *Friday, May 19th*, 1837.—Joseph Scott breakfasted with me at Wood's Hotel. I called at Manchester Buildings, and was sworn at the Bar of the House of Lords on the Great North of England Standing Orders Committee. In the evening I went to Ole Bull's concert at the great concert-room, King's Theatre. This proved a very great musical treat, and I was delighted to have an opportunity of hearing a violinist of whose extraordinary powers I had heard so often. The vocal performers were Madame Pasta and Mdlles. Blasis and Ostergarde, Misses Cooper and Bruce, and Signors Rubini, Tamburini, Giubelei, and Lablache. Among the instrumental performers were M. Franchomne, first violoncellist to the King of the French; Master Taylor, a young harpist aged nine years; Signor Liverani; and M. Rosenhaim, who performed on the pianoforte with Ole Bull; and a numerous orchestra led by Sir George Smart.

"The concert began with the magnificent overture to *Der Freischütz*, which had a very fine effect. A variety of pieces followed, all of which afforded me great pleasure, and especially the playing of Ole Bull, which, to my imperfect judgment of music, seemed more wonderful than Paganini's performances, and I was glad on a subsequent occasion to find this opinion confirmed by the experienced judgment of Mr. Buddle. The song of songs of the evening was by Miss Cooper, 'She never told her Love.' It was exquisitely sweet and appropriate; sung in a subdued and solemn tone, it partook of that 'refreshing melancholy' which Anthony A. Wood speaks of. It was true to nature, and both composer and singer seemed in my humble estimation to do justice to the immortal bard who penned the brief but most expressive and inimitable words of the song. As the song proceeded it seemed to conjure up to the view the striking and highly poetical incidents of a secret love,—a pining in thought, a fading of the damask cheek, and of a fair saint of heavenly patience 'smiling at grief,' a fair flower withering in the shadow of death.

"This song was followed by another favourite piece of music played by Master Taylor on the harp; this was 'Kathleen O'More,' and it was played with great sweetness and simplicity. I was truly delighted with its wild and plaintive melody; although unaccompanied by the voice, its notes seemed to tell a plain and sad tale so true to nature as in my estimation to rank among the most expressive pieces of national melody.

"Mr. Bull was prevented by illness (that was the plea), or by a thin attendance, from playing his *Polacca Guerriera;* but I soon after heard him play it at Cipriani Potter's concert."

In another entry we have accounts of two other performances in which celebrated characters of the past played their parts.

"*Friday, June 2nd*, 1837.—Went to Manchester Buildings, and took a walk with my cousin, Thomas Sopwith, to see the House of Commons, Westminster Hall, etc. I called and saw

Mr. Provis, and, after taking an early and very plain dinner at Gregory's Hotel, I went to Cipriani Potter's concert at Hanover Square rooms at two o'clock.

" This concert was very numerously attended by a fashionable audience. Madame Pasta sang twice. Mr. Kröff sang ' Der Wanderer ' with great feeling and expression. Miss Clara Novello sang ' From Mighty Kings,' a piece which requires great skill in modulation, and I admired her performance of it very much. Mr. Ole Bull played his *Polacco Guerriera,* a most extraordinary performance, which Mr. Buddle, who is a good judge of violin-playing, thought superior in execution and in ' honest fiddle-playing ' to the much-talked-of performance of the celebrated Paganini. Dragonetti Lindley and various other eminent instrumental performers were present, and Mr. Potter played some concertas with great clearness and skilful execution. An original overture composed by him was also performed and very favourably received.

" In the evening Mr. Donkin gave Mr. Buddle, myself, and Charles a treat to Covent Garden, where we heard Pasta and De Begnis, and saw Macready perform Wolsey in *Henry VIII.* With this I was altogether disappointed, inasmuch as I think he entirely failed in exhibiting either the pictorial or moral portrait of that celebrated priest and statesman. Liston played in the farce. He has taken leave of the stage at his usual place of acting (the Olympic), and it is said that he will only once more appear on the London boards. To the provincial stage he long ago bade adieu."

Nothing of special moment occurs in the diary until June 8th, when two events of importance come before us: one a visit to the famous Dr. Buckland—father of the late Frank Buckland—at Oxford; and a second, the projection of a School of Mines, arising, as it seems, out of that visit. Mr. Sopwith and Mr. Buddle were at Oxford, on railway business, when both received invitations to breakfast from Dr. Buckland. As they were short of time they were unable to accept the invitation, but they called before the breakfast as related below.

" Dr. Buckland's house is one of those venerable fabrics which form the principal quadrangle of Christ's College. As soon as the old-fashioned door is opened abundant evidence is presented that the residence is that of a zealous disciple of geology. A wide and spacious staircase has its floors, and even part of steps, covered with ammonites, fossil trees, and bones, and various other geological fragments, and in the several apartments piles upon piles of books and papers are spread upon tables, chairs, sofas, bookstands, and no small portion on the floor itself. In the drawing-room I found a young lady of ruddy, cheerful aspect, and of unassuming and agreeable manners. Dr. Locke, Professor of Chemistry in Cincinnati, was present, and explained a very ingenious apparatus named in the doctor's note, on which the action of heat is so moderate that the *approach* of the hand or the touch of a finger induces a magnetic movement of a 12-inch needle. Dr. Locke also described a mode of measuring vertical angles by ascertaining the degrees covered by his hand, or by one or more fingers when held at arm's length.

" I saw the large painting from which the engraving of Dr. Buckland has been taken. In the breakfast-room Dr. Buckland introduced me to Mrs. Buckland and to Dr. Davies Gilbert, and shortly after to Mr. Edward Bigge, who joined the party. Dr. Buckland said that he had been applied to to recommend some one as a proper person to undertake the office of Mining Commissioner on the part of the Free Miners. ' I told them,' said the Doctor, ' that they must have nothing short of Newcastle, and I named Mr. Buddle and yourself.' I sat next to Dr. Gilbert, and had with him and Dr. Buckland a conversation on the subject of a School of Mines. Dr. Gilbert said that great advantages had been derived from the Institution of a Polytechnic School in Cornwall, of which he has been an active promoter. I assured Dr. Buckland that Mr. Buddle and myself felt highly gratified and obliged by his present of the 'Bridgewater Treatise on Geology;' to which he replied that he felt more indebted for information he had received from us. Before leaving, he made me write a minute to the effect that Mr. Buddle and I should dine with him at the Geological Club in London on the following Wednesday.

"At ten I left Oxford on the Blenheim coach, which was filled with young Oxonians. The road by Wycombe and Uxbridge and its beautiful scenery was new to me, and I enjoyed it very much."

Friday, June 9th, 1837, records rather an amusing incident.

"This morning our usual breakfast party of Mr. Donkin, Mr. Buddle, and myself was enriched with the addition of Mr. Reinagle, an eminent artist and Royal Academician, who had come the preceding evening to Mr. Buddle, bearing a letter from Lord Ravensworth. Mr. Reinagle astonished us not a little by declaring that he had found a simple and infallible mode of at once doubling the profits of the northern coal owners, but our faith in this consummation was somewhat lessened as the worthy artist, with great clearness and simplicity, disclosed the data on which his scheme was based. The first and principal assumption was, that the coal owners sell two tons for *one* (an idea formed, I suppose, from the different values of 25 and 53 cwt. in the London and Newcastle chaldron). When Mr. Reinagle was made to understand that a ton at Newcastle was 20 cwt. as well as at London, it seemed in some degree to shake his scheme, but, like a genuine romancer, he found in other wild and visionary imaginations a refuge from this trifling misconception. The conversation at length merged into an extravagant satire on various projected improvements, and Mr. Buddle with his usual facility and caustic humour devised some Munchhausen-like plans which bore very hardly on the extravagant conceptions of our well-meaning but visionary artist, who took all in perfect good humour, and subsequently forwarded to Mr. Buddle his plans for the Company."

A visit to the Royal Academy at the National Gallery on June 13th, 1837, forms a pleasant episode in the diary. In this exhibition Chantrey's statue of Dr. Dalton and Ramsay's portrait of Earl Grey are much commended, but the rooms are stamped as very unsatisfactory. They were too much like common dwelling-rooms, whereas, by means of large doors and archways, a continued gallery might have been formed. The sculpture room was most objectionable, the busts and statues being jumbled together as if intended to be packed for wholesale exportation, instead of tastefully arranged in separate groups on appropriate pedestals.

On June 14th the geological dinner with Dr. Buckland came off at the Geological Club; Whewell, the President, being in the chair. After dinner Mr. Sopwith and Buckland walked together arm-in-arm to the Society's rooms in Somerset House, Buckland, as was his wont, carrying his umbrella and a blue bag. Thereupon comes a story about this bag. Sopwith wishes to relieve the Professor of it, which, after a time, is permitted, and then the story.

"The greatest honour," said the Doctor, "which my bag ever had was when Lord Grenville insisted on carrying it ; and the greatest disgrace it ever had was when I called on Sir Humphry Davy three or four times one day and always found him out. At last Sir H. D. asked his servant, ' Has Dr. Buckland not called to-day ? ' ' No, sir; there has been nobody here to-day but a man *with a bag*, who has been here three or four times, and I always told him you were out.' "

In the retrospect of the year 1837 Mr. Sopwith recalls many other pleasing passages beyond those referred to in the last two chapters. He was in London during some parts of eight months in the year, and found his frequent journeyings opening up many new scenes and personal introductions. He sat for his portrait to Mr. James Ramsay, went to the bottom of the river Thames in a diving bell, and was much gratified in making the personal acquaintance of Cipriani Potter. He devised various plans for the improvement of Newcastle-upon-Tyne, and spent a few hours a day, now and then, in the contrivance of a writing table with a flat top which would contain fifteen drawers, two closets, and three spaces for books and papers, all of which could be opened by one key. This effort ultimately led to the construction of one of the most ingenious literary cabinets ever invented. He many times showed me this remarkable piece of furniture, which seemed almost automatically to put before you everything you wanted at a moment's notice ; and the more he experienced the great saving of time effected by this contrivance the more he became convinced of its value for professional and official purposes.

A very interesting geological survey about Newcastle carried out by himself and Dr. William Smith in connection with the new lines of railway then springing up occupies a good space in the journal, and introduces us to Sir William Jackson Hooker, the eminent Professor of Botany in the University of Glasgow.

But the most interesting event of a personal kind was his accidental introduction to the famous Mrs. Somerville. He had come to London after a long excursion in Dean Forest, and on his way back to the north met this distinguished lady.

"I left town in the Edinburgh mail at 8 o'clock. An elderly, stout gentleman, a lady, and a young gentleman, were my companions.

"*Thursday, Sept.* 14*th*, 1837.—After leaving Grantham I discovered that the elder gentleman was well acquainted with the leading scientific men of the day. From having seen the name 'Dr. Somerville' on the luggage the preceding night, from the occasional use of the word 'Mary,' and finally from a striking resemblance to the bust I had so often admired at Chantrey's, I conjectured that the lady was no other than the far-famed Mary Somerville, the authoress of 'The Mechanism of the Heavens,' 'Connection of the Physical Sciences,' etc. I took an opportunity of making the inquiry, and my conjecture proved to be correct; he said the bust was considered one of Chantrey's best efforts, an opinion in which I quite agreed with him. Dr. S. said that when Mrs. Somerville was very young she overheard her brother's tutor teaching him Euclid's Elements; she was so pleased with it that she pursued it unknown to the family, and soon mastered the 'Elements' and imbibed a taste for mathematical knowledge. While she thus outstripped both her brother and his tutor, she paid a due regard to domestic duties, and through life she has never been led to deviate from that plain and unpretending line of conduct which best beseems the feminine character.

"Mrs. Somerville received a handsome present from the Emperor of Russia, and while the bearer of it was waiting for a receipt, another gentleman called to ask permission to name after her a large vessel then being built at Liverpool intended for the China trade, offering to be at any expense for a portrait or bust to ornament the head of the vessel with a correct likeness. Permission was readily granted by Mrs. Somerville, who prized far more highly being thus identified with the commerce of the country than the gift of the Russian autocrat. Some time after, a chest of tea arrived as a present to Mrs. S. from the owner of the ship, and directed to her per the *Mary Somerville*.

"Nothing can be more plain and unassuming than the manner and conversation of this highly-gifted lady; the bust by Chantrey is a striking resemblance of the general expression of her features, but the smoothness of a marble surface, and its having probably been done a few years ago, causes it to have the appearance of a younger and more beautiful countenance than that of Mrs. Somerville, the interest of which chiefly consists in an agreeable, complacent, and highly-intellectual expression.

"*Friday, Sept. 15th*, 1837.—Dr. and Mrs. Somerville arrived at Newcastle at six this evening, and accepted my invitation to partake of such hospitality as I could offer. I was truly glad to entertain as a guest so distinguished an ornament of English literature as Mary Somerville, a name which is destined to occupy a high and honoured place in the annals of science. Mrs. Somerville expressed herself very highly pleased with my writing cabinet; she also expressed great admiration at the application of isometrical drawing to geology and mining, and was much pleased with the isograph and projecting ruler."

Another entry is also very interesting. It is dated from London on Thursday, November 9th, 1837.

"This was a very momentous day in the metropolis of the world, the young Sovereign having accepted the invitation of the citizens to dine in Guildhall on Lord Mayor's Day. Public expectation was roused to a pitch of enthusiasm which can scarcely be conceived without having witnessed its extraordinary results. The greater part of the business of London might be considered as being suspended. About a quarter of a million is said to have been expended on the banquet and illuminations in the City, and there is little doubt that at least another fifty or sixty thousand pounds was expended in illuminations in Westminster.

"A great part of the money was spent in extra wages on the urgency of the demand for workmen, and this may be considered as being therefore very improvidently spent, leading, it is to be feared, to intemperance and excess.

"A still larger part of these large sums went to enrich the oil merchants and gas companies, and nearly the whole may be considered as expended in such a manner as to leave no sub-

9

stantial tokens behind; no memorial of the vast labour and
exertion which had been bestowed on the brief pageant of a
procession, and a splendid dinner enjoyed by comparatively few
persons. The gratification of seeing and welcoming a Sovereign
might be enjoyed without this enormous machinery and waste
of time and money; the pleasure of seeing a fine procession and
beholding the blazing refulgence of illuminations is surely not
worth so large a price.

"I am far from denying that the procession was interesting. I
admit that both the appearance and the sentiment conveyed by
the illuminations were highly pleasing, but this pleasure, I consider, was more than counterbalanced by the concomitant circumstances. Among these may be briefly mentioned that danger and
even death were known to be almost inevitable; that the peace
and security of the metropolis was more or less hazarded by such
extraordinary occasions of public excitement; that the person of
the Sovereign was exposed to the possibility of danger, and that
the presence of an armed force was deemed necessary as a means
of protection. Now what pleasures or what advantages are
derived from a royal visit that can be put in comparison with
these great public dangers, this temporary destruction of social
order, this enormous, unmeaning waste of money? If the
Sovereign of the kingdom condescends to be entertained by the
citizens of London, would it not be infinitely better in taste, in
propriety, and in moral influence that the entertainment should
rather be based on the substantial comforts of citizenship, than
on a rival display of the splendours of a Court? Suppose that
every person who desired to honour his Sovereign subscribed in
money one-half or one-third of what was spent in lamps, in loss
of business, in idleness, in exposure for hours to the raw and
miserable air of a foggy November day, to the risk of health
and life: a very large amount would have been available for the
erection of some great public work, the endowment of a school
or hospital, and the construction of an architectural building
for the purpose which in letters of gold should record the event
of Her Majesty's welcome to the City of London. The list of

these subscribers I would have printed in legible characters, describing their several professions and trades, and this list I would have preserved in the palace of the Sovereign, in the public courts and assembly rooms, etc., throughout the kingdom, and widely and gratuitously distributed. These would be trophies worthy of an enlightened Sovereign, and productive of benefits to the various parties who might thus exhibit their loyalty. Another demonstration of joy, and a delightful subject for public observation, would be to give dinners to the poor in large numbers.

" These views are not Utopian speculations on what might be done ; they are merely applications of what has already been done in my native town. In 1809 the inhabitants of Newcastle, instead of wasting their money and creating idleness, danger, and confusion in the streets by an illumination, gave public dinners to the poor ; and never will I forget the delightful scene. They subscribed also sufficient funds to erect a handsome school on the Doric Portico. Their sentiments, and the fruit of that good work, yet flourish by imparting sound and valuable blessings to the poor children of the district.

" I walked to Temple Bar, and along the Strand to the Office of Woods ; this was closed, and Cockney-land was all ' agog.' However, I found Mr. Gardiner in his office ; but for every kind of business I found it a ' *dies non.*'

" I procured a seat in a first-floor window in Cockspur Street, where I saw the procession pass ; I had a good view of the several personages in their respective carriages, and especially of the Duchess of Kent, the Duke of Sussex, and the Queen. I afterwards walked from Temple Bar eastwards to the Bank through the illuminations. In the evening I went with Mr. Davison in a van to see the West End illuminations. The crowd was truly astonishing, and as to carriages, cabs, omnibuses, carts, drays, and vans, the streets were actually one solid and often immovable mass."

Two more entries in this year deserve notice.

"*Sunday, November 19th,* 1837.—Attended service at the Chapel Royal, St. James's, and afterwards called and sat an hour with Dr. Somerville and his daughters. I had an opportunity of seeing Mrs. Somerville's paintings by daylight, and I admired them very much. I spent the evening with Mr. Milne, at his house in Whitehall Place.

"*Monday, Nov. 20th,* 1837.—In the morning I prepared a preamble for the Dean Forest Bill. At eleven a Mr. Coram called; he has taken out a patent for converting small coal into aggregated masses. At twelve I went to Mr. Ker's, where I met Mr. Gardiner, and after an hour's consultation I went to Whitehall and saw Mr. Milne. In Parliament Street I saw Queen Victoria go in state to open her first Parliament; I saw the procession to great advantage both in going and returning. I had an excellent view of Her Majesty, who appeared to be in splendid spirits. On returning I saw crowds of people running towards and loudly cheering a gentleman on horseback. This I immediately supposed must be the Duke of Wellington; my conjecture proved right, and he soon after rode close past. I joined in a most hearty cheer for the hero of Waterloo."

CHAPTER XIV.

1838.

SOME time in 1837 Mr. Sopwith made the acquaintance of that remarkable man Robert Owen, whose attempts to establish a theoretical and practical system of social reform are particularly important in this day, when socialistic tendencies are becoming so popular. Owen had had a kind of chapel in Burton Street, and Mr. Sopwith passing it had been rather astonished to find that the chapel had changed both its name and its character. On inquiry he found that Mr. Owen had moved the establishment to Great Queen Street, and on asking what was the present occupation of the place, was told politely that it was now a chapel of the Swedenborgians or New Jerusalemites, so that Mr. Owen's enthusiastic plans seemed to be marching backwards, and his millennium of truth, reason, and equality as far distant as ever.

The first entry of moment in the diary of 1838 has reference to Mr. Owen, who was at Newcastle.

"*April 25th*, 1838.—Spent the evening at Mr. H. L. Pattinson's. Mr. Owen, Mr. George Burnett, Mr. Lee, and Mr. Carrick were present, and we had a long and interesting conversation on Mr. Owen's benevolent and sanguine but theoretical prospects of the improvement of society.

"*April* 26*th.*—Mr. Owen and I walked to Mr. Donkin's, where we breakfasted. Mr. D. expressed himself highly delighted with the schools and discipline of New Lanark when he visited them some years ago, and Mr. Owen detailed several very interesting particulars of his interviews with Prince Metternich and other European diplomatists.

" Mr. Owen is very communicative, and is willing to answer any questions, which he always does with a distinct reference to his particular views. His notions of classifications of society, although based in some measure on the results of his own practical experience at New Lanark, and comprising many very enlightened and benevolent arrangements, are yet so very Utopian that it is difficult to attribute his sanguine anticipations to any other cause than monomania or a delusion on that particular subject. Even those parts of his plans which may be considered practicable as improvements in the general habits and constitution of society, will, in my humble opinion, require the lapse of ages to be accomplished,—I would say two thousand years at least ; and this opinion I have always urged on Mr. Owen. In contemplating a change so great as he imagines will take place, I cannot but think that it affords as strong an evidence of delusion as can possibly exist in a cultivated and intelligent mind, which, in an eminent degree, Mr. Owen possesses. His opinions on religion are such as the generality of persons would consider it a duty not only to disapprove, but to condemn in the strongest and most unqualified terms. My intercourse with a varied circle of society has, however, taught me to be very cautious in forming extreme opinions on speculative subjects. Claiming, as a Protestant, the right of free opinion, I consider it a duty to tolerate the same in others ; religion is a matter between God and man, and all history and observation point out the unhappy results which have flowed from the interference of men with the religious opinions of their fellow-creatures. Mr. Owen is very open and unreserved in expressing his opinions on religious topics, but I cannot say that they present a pleasing prospect."

A considerable number of minor events carry us on until June 18th, when one of considerable, and we may almost say national, importance was presented, namely, the opening of the Newcastle and Carlisle Railway from Blaydon to Carlisle, a distance of sixty miles. The whole of the engines belonging to the company were put into requisition, and a vast number of trucks fitted up with temporary seats were provided for the public accommodation. The procession of trains was intended to start from Redheugh at 11 in the morning, but after various delays, and a considerable stoppage at Blaydon, a final start was made at 1.50 in the afternoon. Carlisle was reached at 5.30, sixty miles being accomplished in three hours and twenty minutes.

The description of the arrival in Carlisle and of the departure back again is recorded in the next entry, dated June 18th, 1838.

"Immediately on being liberated from the carriage I hastened with all convenient speed through the gay and crowded streets of ' Merry Carlisle,' past the venerable Cathedral to the coffee-house where ' luncheon' was provided by the Directors. The entrance was by a narrow passage, and notwithstanding the exertions of the police, the crowd and consequent pressure were very annoying.

"In the large Assembly Room three tables extended length-ways down the room from a cross table, in the middle of which the Mayor of Carlisle presided over this hungry and disorderly assemblage. The Queen's health was drunk with great en-thusiasm, and followed by three cheers of that hearty and cordial gratulation which prevails at feasts in general, but especially at gratuitous entertainments. ' Success to the Rail-way' was received with a similar demonstration of goodwill.

" In the meantime I hastily helped myself to some cold beef and bread, and after drinking the preceding toasts I went to the railway station at the London Road; this was at half-past six o'clock, and it was generally understood that the trains were to start at seven.   I took the first opportunity of getting into one of the same description of carriages that I came up in, and had Miss Frances Burnup, Mr. Thomas Dunn, Mr. Anthony Nichol, and Mr. Cuthbert Burnup for companions. It was not, however, until ten o'clock that we got fairly started, and during this long period by far the greater portion of the vast multitude were exposed on the outside conveyances to a very heavy and long-continuous rain.   After various stoppages we reached Redheugh at three o'clock, but some of the trains did not arrive until six or seven o'clock.   Much alarm was therefore created in many families by this detention, and for several days the discomforts and apparent want of method of the whole expedition were the general theme of conversation, and of very strong reprehension by many who had suffered the inclement exposure and fatigue of a midnight and stormy ride in the light dress of an expected summer-day excursion."

Coronation Day, June 28th, is referred to briefly.   The day was observed as a general holiday at Newcastle, as elsewhere.   In Newcastle there was a Radical meeting on the town moor.   The Council accompanied the Mayor to church, where the Vicar preached a political sermon against the progress of Reform.   The military were reviewed on the town moor, and the yeomanry fired a *feu de joie* on the sandhill.   About 170 persons dined with the Mayor, and a few places were illuminated.

On July 2nd the Diary records the birth, at Newcastle, of a son,* Thomas Sopwith.

In the summer of this year Mr. Sopwith published a short treatise on the proposed line of road from Shotley

---

* The present Mr. Thomas Sopwith, of 6, Great George Street, Westminster.

Bridge to Middleton in Teesdale, to form, with existing roads, a direct and easy line of turnpike roads from New-castle-upon-Tyne to Lancaster, Preston, and Liverpool. A good map illustrated the route.

Several other publications came through his hand about this time, including a series of topographical questions on quarry work, a descriptive essay of the Monocleid or writing cabinet, "The Stranger's Pocket Guide to Newcastle-upon-Tyne and its Environs," and a second edition of his "Treatise on Isometrical Drawing."

The essay on the Monocleid writers' cabinet describes a series of improvements on the writing table referred to in a previous chapter. The Monocleid was a very hand-some piece of furniture, and I know nothing with which my friend was more pleased than with this invention. Very shortly before his death he devoted an hour in explaining to me the "ins and onts" of the ingenious piece of mechanism, by which the whole of the drawers, closets, and partitions could be opened by means of a single lock, yet were so arranged as to be easily accessible to any one seated in front. The cabinet was in no way liable to get out of order, and was less costly than one in which the locks used are on each drawer.

The pocket guide-book to Newcastle-upon-Tyne con-sisted of one hundred and two pages. In it nothing of moment in regard to the town is omitted. It formed an excellent reference book for the members of the British Association for the Advancement of Science, which held its eighth meeting at Newcastle, commencing on August 20th of this year, 1838.

Some useful details are given in the diary respecting this meeting of the British Association, and special reference is made to Mr. Garnett's paper, read in the Mechanical Section, on the Telegraph. The advanced men of science

at this time were just dreaming of the practical application
of electricity to telegraphic purposes; but when some
thought, Mr. Sopwith told me, of sending a word a
hundred miles in a minute, "then we had to pick our
company;" by which he meant that such a seeming
miracle could only be told to a select few. At the meeting he made the acquaintance of many distinguished
persons, and at his breakfasts entertained Dr. and Mrs.
Buckland, Mr. Charles Babbage, Mr. (afterwards Sir
Charles) Barry, Dr. Reid, and other eminent persons.
He took also a great part in the geological work, having
by this time been elected Fellow of the Geological Society.
The following entry bears date August 25th :—

"I drove with Mr. Barry, the architect, to Falfield, and had
a very interesting conversation with this highly-gifted architect. We went to the Durham Junction or Victoria Bridge,
which was opened this day. As we approached this splendid
bridge, Mr. Barry greatly admired its general aspect and noble
proportions, but he condemned the small arches at each
end, which impair the general solidity so essential to the
character of the design. While we were viewing the bridge,
we heard one of the railway trains approaching with a great
number of persons present at the ceremony of opening the
railway. This train stopped at the south end of the bridge, and
a few minutes after another train approached at so quick a
rate as to threaten a violent collision. This in a few seconds
took place, but the result was much less seriously felt by the
passengers than might have been anticipated. Some accidents
occurred, but no lives were lost ; and in about half an hour the
party were enabled to proceed to Shields, followed by a train
of no less than a hundred and twenty coal-waggons.

"After walking along the bridge, we found Mr. George
Stephenson, the eminent engineer, Mr. William Brandling,
Mr. James Walker, the President of the Institution of Civil
Engineers, Mr. Nicholas Wood, and others, to whom I

introduced Mr. Barry. After some conversation, in which Mr. Walker deplored the innovation made on his design by the substitution of three small arches instead of one large arch at each end of the bridge, we proceeded to Pensher Quarry, and after viewing it we returned to Mr. Buddle's house. Here we found Dr. Buckland, Sir Charles Lemon, and Mr. Edward Bigge. We returned through Lambton Park and arrived at Newcastle, and Mr. Barry dined with me.

"Dr. Buckland and Sir Charles Lemon came in the evening, and we spent some time in considering the best mode of bringing the subject of an application to Government, on Mining Records, before the Association."

In the autumn of this same year Mr. Sopwith was appointed a Commissioner for the Crown under the Forest of Dean Mining Act. On the part of the free miners Mr. Probyn was appointed Commissioner, and Mr. Buddle was nominated as umpire. Mr. Sopwith often expressed the great satisfaction he felt at this appointment. It was a post of great honour and responsibility, and it came to him altogether unsolicited, which rendered it the more satisfactory. On September 5th the first meeting of the Commissioners was held at the King's Head Inn, Coleford, at twelve o'clock ; but the room not being large enough, there was an adjournment to the Angel Inn, where he took the chair, and explained the object of the meeting. On September 10th the Commission sat at what is called the Speech House, distant three miles from Coleford, and situated in the midst of the royal Forest of Dean. Here a very numerous assembly of gentlemen, solicitors, and free miners was collected. Mr. Sopwith opened the business. The sittings continued for some time, with various disputes and arguments in regard to possession of what is called "a gale." The whole history is very curious, but is matter long gone by. Suffice it to say, that he acquitted himself in the delicate negotiations which took place with what Mr. Buddle described as perfect diplomatic skill, and that he left the Forest divided in opinion as to whether its scenery or its people were most to be admired.

A curious little entry of September 22nd, 1838, has reference to the Zoological Gardens in London. He walked with Mr. Probyn to the Gardens, and found the selection so meagre that it could scarcely be considered as having commenced. But the walk to it was pleasant.

September 29th yields us a pretty bit of philosophy, the first paragraph being a copy of a letter addressed to Mrs. Sopwith, his "dear Jane" :—

"I always endeavour to be happy and comfortable, and as much as possible *at home;* and in this I am very often successful in whatever part of the kingdom or amongst whatever class of persons I happen to be placed for the time being. This appears to me to be a part of the philosophy of human life. Every day, nay, every hour, is a beneficent gift bestowed upon us, and requires and richly merits all the improvement we can bestow upon it. These and similar reflections are often suggested to my mind when I think of my family and home,— of a cup filled to overflowing with every comfort I desire, and above all a disposition to enjoy the present time whether at home or abroad. These enjoyments are often closely combined with my professional pursuits, and I often consider them in reference to that clear, and elegant, and most useful rule of life contained in the Church Catechism : 'To learn and labour truly to get mine own living, and to do my duty in that state of life to which it shall please God to call me.'

"This train of reflection is one which I often find both a pleasing and a profitable occupation of my mind. The miseries of human life are a fruitful source of dissatisfaction and of complaint with a large portion of mankind; but it has ever appeared to me that the misfortunes of men are in a great measure chargeable upon themselves, and that if right objects are pursued with a proper disposition of the heart towards God and man, the general tenor of human life is that of cheerfulness and contentment. The condition of our nature, it is true, is necessarily mixed with a portion of suffering and privation; but even these, nay, even the most severe afflictions, are found to promote some lasting cause of happiness. As regards the experience of human life, however, our own mind is the only source which we can exercise any reasoning upon, for the thoughts, and consequently the happiness or misery, of others are hidden by an impenetrable veil; but in our own minds we can trace the operations of moral causes, and discover many of the secret springs of good and evil. Rest in the conviction that a God-given soul, as Wilson expresses it, has been bestowed upon us to admire and adore the bountiful Creator of all things, and above all to rely on the designs of an inscrutable Providence which ' shapes our ends, rough hew them as we will.'

" The two points on which happiness mainly depends are the regulation of the mind and the proper employment of time; the former of these is the *source* and the latter the *result* of that inward satisfaction which is the only solid basis of a happy life. Once secured, this happy frame of mind serves as a rock, over which the stream of existence flows with an equal current, which even the storms of adversity cannot disturb.

" There is not in the whole range of nature any type of human life so striking as that of a river traced from its fountain head, pursuing a devious and obscure path until it widens into a noble stream, passing by mountains, plains, and cities, and finally losing an individual existence in the vast abyss of ocean,—the emblem of eternity. The placid surface of such a stream reflecting the light of heaven, and the verdant aspect of nature, are beautiful emblems of a mind delighting in the love of nature; and in like manner an ill-regulated mind is not unfitly represented by such a stream when

' Fouled with stains,
And swoln with torrents and descending rains.'

"The regulation of the mind is greatly promoted by such reflections as are here alluded to, inasmuch as by tracing the past we are enabled in some measure to anticipate the future. It is in this respect that I have often thought my journals of some use, by recalling to my memory the scenes and adventures of former years, and recording the impressions which were then made upon my mind. The most important use of this has been to show what circumstances were productive of present comfort and future happiness, and hence the futility of many pursuits which occupy mankind has been made apparent. My convictions on some of these matters have occasionally gone beyond what many persons consider as prudence; but which term, as often understood, has but a slight relation either to piety or wisdom. To depend on others instead of ourselves is often a source of great unhappiness, and I count it a peculiar blessing that the lesson of self-dependence was enforced by my father from his own knowledge of its inestimable value. In marrying I carried this feeling so much into effect, that I was then, and am still, impressed with the idea that a fortune would have been a positive disadvantage. There is no reason why it should be so; but when the motives are known to be purely disinterested, there is a solid ground for much happiness, and that my own experience has largely proved.

"The pursuit of riches is another wide mistake and fruitful source of evil; for when once the love of gain has taken possession of the soul, a long and sad farewell may be given to all those charms which

> '. . . work the soul's eternal health,
> And love and peace and gentleness impart.'

There seems, indeed, in the general disposition of events, a continual disappointment which accompanies the pursuit of improper objects, and that disappointment is often greatest when that pursuit is apparently crowned with success.

"To the pursuit of riches, and of every object of hope which is selfish, this lamentable complaint very strongly applies. If disappointment, in the ordinary sense of the word, ensues, there is little solace for the loss; and success too often brings with it the total destruction of every fancied charm. This holds good throughout the whole framework of social order, and it exhibits in the moral dispensations of Providence that same aptitude of design and harmony of purpose which is so admirably displayed in the arrangement of physical nature. These considerations lead to deeper sentiments, which are better fitted for the recesses of our own minds than for being recorded in a journal of this kind.

"Next to the due regulation of the mind, the employment of time is the grand element of human life. The hours spent in my professional pursuits have always been agreeable to me, inasmuch as they blend many interesting pursuits in one harmonious whole. For the pen and pencil abundant occupation is afforded. A frequent change of scene gives variety of company as well as of picturesque beauty, which has ever been a great source of delight to me; and hence the useful and the sweet go hand in hand. In this manner business has proved not only a source of profit but of pleasure, and occasional relaxation from it is enjoyed with a zest unknown to those who are accustomed to vigorous and active business exertions."

In another note, dated September 27th, there is a record of an evening party at Mr. Probyn's, at which the music seems to have been extremely good. To his great delight, Mrs. Probyn played on the violin, which led Mr. Buddle, who was present, to state that he had always held that the violin was both an elegant and appropriate instrument for a lady. In this opinion Mr. Sopwith joins, and comes to the immediate conclusion that it shall be no want of exertion on his part to make his eldest daughter, Ursula, a good fiddler.

It strikes me, in reading through these pleasant memoirs, that my good friend, in doing so much for the railway system, did a great deal to destroy the pleasure connected with ordinary travelling ; for anything more delightful than his description of his many thousand miles a year of coaching and posting it were indeed difficult to conceive.

Two more entries must bring this chapter to a close.

"Called on my friend Hervey, the eminent designer and engraver on wood. Half an hour passed away very delightfully in his *den*, as he called it—a small sitting-room in which he pursues his avocations. The group consisted of Mr. and Mrs. Hervey, Mr. Smith, a very able engraver on wood, Mr. Robert Allison, myself, and, though last certainly not least curious, a Bedouin lady, arrayed in true Oriental costume. She was tall, handsomely formed, and with a tolerably pretty face. She stood in one corner of the room in a very commanding but somewhat theatrical posture. Strange to say, that though she frequently changed her attitude, she never spoke, nor even when I took hold of her beautiful hand and finely-pointed and flexible fingers did she offer any resistance. She has been for some time an inmate of Mr. Hervey's house, and assists him greatly in his professional pursuits. Nor has she ever made any mischief in the family. Mr. Hervey bought her in Paris for £40. She has very pretty feet and fine ankles, which Mr. H. especially directed my attention to ; and as to her head, its contents may truly be said to be very solid, and not like that of some ladies—full of emptiness. Her history is a very curious one, but too long and marvellous to be inserted in these pages.

" I called upon Mr. (afterwards Sir Charles) Barry at his office in the Speaker's house. He showed me some of his beautiful plans, and his still more beautiful model of the new Parliament House. This was indeed a treat, and I obtained Mr. Barry's permission to bring any friends to see it on my future visits to London. I spoke to him about Costello, and detailed at great length all that I know of his capabilities and high character. Mr. Barry said his establishment was tolerably complete, and that he had innumerable applications; nevertheless, this should really have his best attention, and I felt persuaded from his candid and kind expressions that his promise will not be forgotten. Mr. Barry regretted that I could not visit him at his house this time, and made me undertake to do so on my next visit to town—an invitation I shall certainly not forget, as I very highly enjoy the agreeable and unaffected manners and intelligence of this most highly gifted architect."

Few great architectural works in this country have been subjected to more severe criticism than the present Houses of Parliament, and few probably will live longer to attest the genius of the architect who designed them and superintended them to their completion, if not to their perfected beauty. In this view Sir Charles Barry had always a powerful advocate in Mr. Sopwith.

CHAPTER XV.

ABOUT the middle of October 1838 Mr. Sopwith received a letter from Liverpool asking him to undertake a mineral survey of the west of Ireland. He acceded to this on the condition that he should have a full week for preparation; and on October 30th he set sail in the *Queen Victoria* steam-packet for Dublin, accompanied by Mr. Mackay. On board there were about four hundred Irish labourers returning from the harvest in England, who paid three shillings each for their passage on deck to Dublin. They were nearly all men, but a few women, children, and infants were amongst them. They each returned home with an amount of savings averaging about £2. They seemed for the most part to be exceedingly quiet, and to exhibit a quiescent cheerfulness, which now and then became more mirthful in spite of the comfortless condition they were placed in. One or two manifestations of a contrary feeling seemed likely to create an uproar; but this was exceptional. They landed at North Quay, Dublin, at eight o'clock a.m., the voyage lasting eleven hours. The fare in the best cabin was 12s. 6d., with an additional steward's fee; and provisions not included in the fare were very moderate.

One of the first persons called upon by Mr. Sopwith in Dublin was Sir Richard John Griffiths, F.R.S., the distinguished geologist, whose name has been rendered so familiar to us, even to the present time, through his land-valuation scheme. He turned out to be a very agreeable man, and described with great care the general structure of the district near Ennis about to be inspected, the nature of the mineral deposit, and the progress made in the mines there by Mr. Taylor, of London. He said he had been staying a month with Mr. Spring Rice, the Chancellor of the Exchequer, at Mr. Trenchard's; that the model of Dean Forest had been a subject of conversation, and had given great satisfaction.

A great many sheets of the diary are here extended in details connected with the special business of the visit. These details I must omit, in order to give in full a summary of conclusions of a very clear and unbiassed observer of Irish life and character half a century ago. They cannot fail to be instructive at a crisis like the present.

"GENERAL NOTES ON MY FIRST VISIT TO IRELAND.

" 1. *Travelling.*—My journey from Newcastle was merely a repetition of former ones in the stage-coach called the 'Lord Exmouth.' From Liverpool to Dublin I enjoyed the comforts afforded by the very excellent steamship *Queen Victoria*, belonging to the City of Dublin Steam Navigation Company. In point of dimensions and every substantial comfort, it would be difficult to imagine a more convenient or elegant means of accomplishing this voyage of a single night; but yet the mail-packet *Urgent*, on which I returned, was certainly superior. In both, however, I enjoyed an excellent night's rest. The sea was smooth on both occasions, particularly on our return, when not the slightest heaving of the ship was perceptible.

"On landing at Dublin, the Irish car had the claim of novelty, and I found it a most convenient mode of calling at different places, inasmuch as you step at once from the seat to the ground. The Irish mail-coaches I found to be very much like those in England, both in size, in comfort, and in speed. During my stay in the county of Clare, I had very excellent travelling accommodation afforded by Mr. Scott's britzska and phaeton, Mrs. Scott's phaeton, Mr. Macbeth's car and gig, etc., all of which were good in their way, and particularly the britzska, which was built at Bristol, and was a remarkably elegant, comfortable, and noiseless carriage. The public car from Ennis to Williamstown was quite a treat in the way of public travelling; a leather strap, and afterwards a branch of a tree, sufficed for a whip, until an innocent country lad was coaxed into an exchange *pro tempore*—that is to say, he very good-naturedly lent our driver his whip on a simple promise to return it, and took the branch instead. Although half an hour too late at starting, our loquacious conductor assured us that we would arrive in due time at Williamstown to meet the packet, 'barring accidents,'—which was well put in, for the wheels were once or twice so hot and the horses so lazy that a stoppage at one time seemed inevitable.

"A voyage in a large steamboat of one hundred horse power was quite a novelty to be enjoyed in an inland piece of water, and I greatly enjoyed both this and the voyage up the Shannon, in a less steamboat of twenty-four horse power. I had never in my life travelled in a canal passage-boat, and the voyage therein from Shannon Harbour to Dublin was described by a Limerick attorney as a nuisance, horrible beyond endurance. I have never, however, been disposed to rely so much on the opinion of others as on my own experience, and therefore I resolved to try the voyage. Never was I more agreeably surprised than to find, after sailing in it eighteen hours, I arrived at Dublin *too soon,* so far as the pleasantness of the journey was concerned. I heard the best Irish songs and recitations, and had a most interesting account of Irish scenery and superstitions from Mr. Dennis Leonard, of Kilrush; besides this, I had a very comfortable night's rest, and was altogether much interested and pleased with my first journey on a canal.

"On my return to England I travelled on the Dublin and Kingston Railway, the Liverpool and Manchester, and the Newton, Wigan, and Preston Railways, and from the latter town by coach to Newcastle; so that in the course of my tour I travelled by land, by sea, and on rivers, lakes, and canal, by no less than fourteen different modes of conveyance, viz., two stage-coaches, company's steamship, Dublin car, two Irish mail-coaches, private car and gig, britzska, two phaetons, public car, large and small steamboats on the Shannon, canal passage-boats, three railway carriages, and several hackney coaches. So far therefore as a brief visit afforded an opportunity of comparing different modes of travelling both in England and Ireland, I had ample materials so far as vehicles were concerned.

"Travelling in the mail in Ireland differs from the same mode of travelling in England only in respect of the fees, which are more moderate in Ireland than in England. There is fully as much importunity from porters, etc., at the coach; but they are satisfied with a smaller sum, are good-natured, and not so thoroughly dogged and impudent as English porters when repulsed. Of course I can only speak from a very limited experience, but my object was to observe, however brief the opportunity; and this impression was produced during the only coach journey I had in Ireland, viz., from Dublin to Limerick, and from thence to Ennis. Steamboat and railway travelling are on the same footing as in England and Scotland. Posting on the great lines is said to be very good; and as I travelled from a hundred to a hundred and twenty miles by post, I can add my encomium of the goodness of the horses furnished at Ennis. The post-boy presented an odd contrast to the generality of English postilions, by the exceeding shabbiness of an old and ragged brown coat, which hung so loosely upon him that he seemed more like a pauper than a post-boy. An Irish post-chaise is said to comport in some degree with the coat I have mentioned, but I had not an opportunity of travelling in one.

"The travelling equipments in Ireland, so far as public vehicles are concerned, are, with the exceptions I have named, very far inferior to most of the public conveyances in England, and many of the car-drivers in Dublin are arrayed in a series of ragged vestments which even the shabbiest of London cabmen cannot compete with.

"It only remains for me to observe on this head, that travelling is cheaper than in England, the usual car fare being eightpence a mile, and a fee of twopence per mile to the driver, and for this four persons may travel very comfortably in dry weather from one end of Ireland to the other. This applies to the Irish mile, eleven of which are equal to fourteen English miles, which for a party of four is about twopence per English mile each; so at this rate a journey of one hundred miles, exclusive of gates, would only cost about sixteen shillings and eightpence. The roads in Ireland, so far as I saw, are generally good; those in the county of Clare particularly so.

"2. *Scenery.*—To attempt to describe the varied scenery I viewed in the course of my tour would be to write a volume on the sublime and beautiful; to descant on the rich and varied attractions which abound in the 'Green Isle' requires an abler pen than mine, which is unblest with either powers or leisure to do justice to so interesting a theme. In this brief retrospect my only object is to record a memorandum of the leading points without entering upon minute details, and hence any allusion to the various beautiful and interesting scenes I beheld will appear rather as a catalogue than a description of them.

"The dreary wilds of Stainmore and the lofty mountains near Sedbergh have become familiar to me. Not so the broad bosom of the Mersey, and the still wider surface of the silvery sea which reflected the light of the full moon. The ocean is always grand, always beautiful, and I enjoyed its beauties by moonlight at night and a splendid sunrise in the morning.

" My first view of Ireland was an interesting sight. The Bay of Dublin and the approach to the city were also exceedingly interesting.

" The Phœnix Park is a magnificent piece of ground, and the scenery of the Zoological Gardens is a paradise on earth.

" I greatly enjoyed my moonlight ride through the interior; and in passing through Tipperary, which is at present in a disturbed state, as if to give character to the lonely landscape, a man lay in the middle of the road, and a delay of some minutes occurred before we could ascertain whether he was living or dead. He was quite insensible; but his stupor was at length ascertained to be the result of intoxication, a vice too prevalent in this and indeed in every other country. The country on approaching Limerick appears to be extremely interesting; but a very dull and rainy morning prevented me from forming a correct estimate of it or of the town of Limerick, through which we passed, and I saw no more of it than in walking a short distance from one coach-office to another. The scenery near Ennis is varied, some parts being well wooded, and others quite bare. Cahircalla is a lovely spot. Quin Abbey, a most inimitable subject for the antiquary and the artist. The bare limestone rocks were quite a novel feature to me, especially when developed on the ample slopes of the mountains in the Burrin district. These are truly sublime, and are of the highest interest in a geological point of view, inasmuch as they in all probability are the depositories of mineral wealth which, if diligently pursued and successfully worked, would greatly contribute to the prosperity of the district in which they are situated. The views at Burrin, the shores of Galway Bay, the mountains of Connemara, the bold, bleak, and rocky promontory of Blackhead (' O'ill luck to it,' says Paddy, our post-boy; ' may it be a long day before I see its ugly face again'), and the coast of the Atlantic were all fraught with deep interest.

" Different in character, more pleasing, but not less interesting, were the views of the Shannon from the heights near

Cahircon, the beautiful woodlands and lawns near that mansion, the splendid view of the Fergus and its islands from Mr. Arthur's fine seat at Paradise, and again the beautiful lake and hills at Scarriff. The inland ocean of Lough Dearg and the lofty mountains in its vicinity present a rich treat to all who delight in the attractions of natural scenery. I might enumerate many other highly interesting points regarding the landscape beauties of the interior of Ireland, but will only observe that my whole tour was a succession of interesting, sublime, or beautiful scenes, which in summer must be still more delightful.

" 3. *Buildings.*—I had heard and read and in pictures seen much of the architectural grandeur of the public buildings in Dublin. They are on a magnificent scale, and there is much lightness and grace in the style of many of them, particularly the Bank of Ireland and the Post Office. The interior of the chapel at the Castle is truly splendid, and the stranger finds easy access both to it and the interior of the Castle when the Viceroy's family are not occupying it. Nelson's Pillar affords a noble view of Sackville Street and of the city generally. I viewed with much interest the venerable aisles of St. Patrick, and the stately Doric interior of the Marlborough Street Roman Catholic Church.

" The abbeys at Quin and Corcumroe, and the hall and lodge at Cahircon, were the principal buildings that attracted my attention in the county of Clare. A vast number of ruins of castles are scattered over the country in every direction; but the most melancholy sights connected with the subject of Irish buildings are the *huts* of the peasantry. It is truly deplorable to find human beings lodged in such wretched abodes, and it seems next to a miracle that life can be preserved throughout a severe winter in so defenceless and exposed a situation as these poor cottagers are placed. I was prepared to witness much misery; but imagination, however fertile, will never picture the sad and horrible and gloomy aspect of these dwellings of the Irish poor. The Roman Catholic chapels which abound in Ireland form striking features in many land-scapes. Those which I visited were large, plain, and unadorned, the interior barnlike, and the whole presenting a cold and poor and cheerless aspect.

" 4. *Institutions.*—My journey being one of business, and not of general observation, I had little time to attend to public institutions. The principal ones that I visited were the Dublin Asylum for the Blind, where much good is done, but which at one time was nearly suspended by discord on religious topics. I was much gratified by attending the first meeting of this winter's session of the Royal Irish Academy, especially as my friend Sir William Betham was the principal party in the evening's discussion. Tea and coffee are provided in an ante-room as at the London Geological, and Civil Engineers' Societies.

" The Zoological Gardens are quite perfect as regards situation and arrangement. Few vicinities of towns afford so beautiful a site as has, in this instance, been selected; and the highest credit is due to the contriver and designer of the several cages, cottages, stables, etc. It is quite a model institution in this respect, and far superior to the Liverpool Gardens and the beginnings at Cheltenham; and many of the arrangements are more picturesque, appropriate, and convenient than even the splendid establishment in Regent's Park, London.

" Of schools I had no opportunity to observe, except two in the county of Clare. Both of these were in very remote districts which are seldom visited. In both instances the school-masters were remarkably courteous, and acquiesced most readily in my request to hear the scholars read, etc. I must say that, considering the scanty recompense, the solitary and unrewarded nature of their toils, and the apparent success of their labours, I felt much interested in them, and left them with very sincere feelings of respect. It is true that the system of education, under such wretched circumstances as that at Glanamana and Finare, is by no means perfect; but I was prepared to make a large allowance, and I found it better than I expected. My brief inspection of Irish schools and schoolmasters left on me a most favourable impression; and if I ever visit Ireland again, a visit to the country schools will certainly be one chief object of my attention.

"As nearly allied to the nature of a public institution, I may mention the Imperial Hotel at Dublin, which I understand belongs to a large company. The management is excellent; and any stranger visiting Dublin will find every reasonable gratification afforded by the ample premises, the elegant and convenient coffee and dining-rooms, comfortable bedrooms, prompt attention, Irish civility, and, though last not least, moderate charges.

"5. *Religious Services and Ceremonies.*—My first Sunday in Ireland was chiefly spent in the Temple of Nature during a journey of thirty miles, in which the lofty mountains, the beautiful little lakes or tarns, the Bay of Galway, and a lovely moonlight night could scarcely be viewed without many sentiments of reverential awe and admiration which the worship of Nature never fails to inspire. Sunday travelling is objected to by many on the score of religion. So far as my own feelings are concerned I have not this objection; for some of my Sunday journeys have been productive of many feelings and sentiments more closely allied to devotion than the eloquence of the preacher can produce. I was glad to find the cottagers neatly attired, and this alone reconciled me to my journey on this occasion. I was very anxious to go to a Roman Catholic chapel at Ennis, but was dissuaded on account of the crowd, and the possibility of coming in contact with the fever which at present is prevalent in the district.

"I have noticed in my journal the prayers offered up before the pictures or stations in the chapel of Glanamana. Sincerity in any garb is to be viewed with respect, and it is very possible that these services may not be wholly unproductive of some wholesome influence on the heart.

"I was much amused by the *naïveté* of the answer given by a Roman Catholic gentleman when I inquired if these prayers were to expiate part of his sins. 'It is,' said he, ' upon that speculation.' Viewed in a philosophical point of view, the apparently earnest and sincere prayers of these people are in their own view a meritorious work. Such is the opinion formed in their minds in the situation in which Providence has placed them; and if the heart in any degree accompanies the aspirations of the lips and the humility of the bended knee, doubtless they depart not unimproved.

" An Irish funeral, and the remarkable custom of *howling* or making a loud and frenzied lamentation for the dead, came under my own observation, and the ceremony was too singular ever to be forgotten. Those who delight in wild and horrible romance need not on earth expect to find anything more truly romantic and harrowing than the advancing wailing of an Irish howl in a dark and lonely place. Mrs. Mahon, of Cahircalla, who appears to have an admirable taste in the sublime and beautiful of Irish scenery and manners, states that she once heard an Irish howl set up on the borders of a lake along which the funeral advanced, and the scene was one of the most painfully interesting she ever heard. If ever witchcraft and infernal agency returned to earth, an Irish funeral howl would be a truly appropriate herald of its approach.

" At Dublin I attended the Roman Catholic chapel in Marlborough Street, where mass only was performed. The music was very good, but no anthem was sung. The ceremony to me was altogether unmeaning, for I heard not one word of it. The congregation seemed very devout while the ceremonial lasted, and very talkative and lively the moment it was ended.

" A moderate fee of a few pence secures the stranger admission, and I got a most excellent seat near the altar.

" The service at St. Patrick's, as a performance of fine music, merits a visit, but, the ordinary service is not superior to some of the daily cathedral services at Durham, York, Gloucester, or Westminster. Even as a musical service some very considerable improvements might be made.

" 6. *Hospitality.*—A pen capable of doing justice to Irish hospitality must indeed be an able one. Mine, however, would

certainly be negligent indeed if it were not to attempt, however
feebly, to record a brief memento of the kind civilities and
attentions I met with.   First on the list I must place my friend
Sir William Betham, who on my first calling upon him gave
me an admirable specimen of true hospitality.   He left his
engagements and walked with me to the Museum of the Royal
Dublin Society, which on that day was not open to the public.
He introduced me to Dr. Scauler, the eminent geologist and
mineralogist, to Sir William Hamilton, and various scientific
persons.   He begged me to arrange so as to be in Dublin at the
first meeting of the Royal Irish Academy Club, and I became
his guest on that occasion ; and there, if time had permitted, I
might have laid the foundation of many other hospitalities,—
the only one which I could accept was the invitation of Charles
Wm. Hamilton, Esq., to breakfast.

" At Ennis I was truly at home in the hospitable mansion of
Mr. Macbeth, and was delighted with his children, especially
the eldest, James, who is a remarkably thoughtful and engaging
boy.

" At Cartron and at Cahiracon we had a plenteous abundance of every comfort and luxury, accompanied by a welcome
too cordial and unaffected to be misunderstood.   I must not
omit to add that the companionship of Mr. Mackay and his
hospitality at Liverpool, with that of Mr. Hasleton, and the
songs of Mr. Samuel Lover sung by their author and composer,
made a valuable addition to the hospitalities of Ireland, and
that a most grateful recollection and sympathy will always in
my own breast be a memorial of the kind attentions and
civilities which met me at every step.

" I had several introductions which I could not avail myself
of for want of time.   Among these were Mr. Owen, of the Board
of Works ; Mr. Owen, of Limerick ; Mr. Spaight, of Limerick ;
Sir Lucius O'Brien and two of his brothers ; and the Chancellor
of the Exchequer.   So that for so short a visit I was well
provided with opportunities of observing and enjoying society
of various ranks in Ireland.

" 7. *National Character.*—Time and experience can alone enable a stranger to understand the peculiarities of character in a new country,—I mean in a country new to his observation. The hospitality which I experienced could not fail to make an agreeable impression as regards the upper classes; and I must say, so far as my limited means of observation extend, I entertain a very favourable opinion of the Irish character generally. The peasantry are placed in such a desperate state of wretchedness and indigence, that one might well expect to see a dark and frowning gloom hang on their countenance, and giving ferocity to their general expression. It is not so, however. You enter Paddy's miserable hovel; your heart sinks at the appalling want of even the commonest comforts of life. A wife and a numerous progeny seem to render the burden still more hopeless, for a life in such circumstances is surely a burden, and one so heavy as few Englishmen and probably no West Indian negro slaves have ever yet conceived. But Paddy brightens up; his face seems free from every care, and he welcomes ' your honour ' with right good-will. If you inquire your way, ' Och, I'll go with your honour ; ' and after trudging a mile you have no solicitation for money, nor apparently does he even think of such a thing. I saw many instances of this, and the contrast with Englishmen is by no means in favour of the latter. There is a general cheerfulness prevalent among the lower orders of the Irish which seems ever ready to break forth even under the most untoward circumstances.

" Doubtless, however, there are some large deductions to be made from the brighter page of Irish character. Revenge is said to be cherished with fatal perseverance, and the cruelties which have been inflicted in the disturbed districts are dreadful to think of. A vast allowance, however, must be made when we consider the imperfect education and the wretched condition of the peasantry. Under favourable auspices I can have no doubt that the leading points of the character of the peasantry are highly calculated to promote general comfort and happiness.

" Improvidence and love of gaiety in the rich, and improvidence and love of whisky in the poor, are but too prevalent.

" 8. *Religion and Present Condition and Prospects of Ireland.* —The title of a volume, but a volume which could only be written by one who has studied Ireland for years and visited its different provinces. Viewing the subject with a mind disposed to be impartial, I am not of opinion that the Roman Catholic religion is adapted to promote the spread of those liberal and enlightened views which are the brightest feature of genuine Christianity. On the contrary, I think that the freedom of inquiry and independence of mind which is the very basis of Protestantism are admirably calculated to promote political freedom, and to break down the barriers which unhappily exist between different persuasions. I have avoided all topics connected with the theological part of the question, and have looked at the religion of Ireland in that spirit of Christianity which commands us to do to others as we would they should do unto us. Looking at the subject in this broad and unexceptionable point of view, and speaking only of the districts which I have myself seen, candour compels me to say that I view with regret a system which compels a population of nearly three thousand persons to pay three or four hundred pounds a year to the clergyman of ten or twenty persons. Even these ten or twenty have no clergyman, have no church save the ruins of one, and no service on Sundays, and no resident minister. Will any one who has any claim to fair and impartial judgment say that this system partakes in any degree of the spirit of common honesty, much less of religion? It is, in fact, a *treble* premium given to Roman Catholicism; it is a premium given by the indirect influence of a bad example which even the poorest peasant can understand and condemn; it is a desertion of the cause which the Protestant clergyman is paid for advocating; it leaves the Roman Catholic chapel as the only place where any Christian can attend public worship; and it is the greatest of all premiums, viz., persecution and injustice, under the influence of which Satan himself and his ministers of darkness would flourish and maintain a place from whence liberality and justice would sweep them with one fell swoop. The property of the Established Church applied in this manner can never fail to be a fruitful source of discord; and in a case to which I allude—the parish of Abbey, in the Barony of Burrin—there is an injustice so manifest, that it appears to me to be quite apart from all considerations either of religion or policy, and to be indispensable on the broad and plain foundations of common fairness and honesty. Let any Englishman ask himself the question if, in a parish of two or three thousand Protestants, he would see the tithes to the amount of three or four hundred pounds a year sent to a Roman Catholic clergyman living at a distance, and having only some ten or twenty disciples, and they without any ministrations of religion? Can there be any doubt as to his feeling indignation at so preposterous an abuse? At present there appears to be a decided barrier between the Protestant and Roman Catholic religions in Ireland. The one is supported by the aristocracy, and possesses the property which the others formerly owned. Whatever may be the opinion of Protestants as to the errors and superstition which they attribute to the Catholics, can they wonder at their continuance, when the field is wholly abandoned to them, and an example shown of a clergyman deserting his post and receiving his hire without performing the labour required of him?

"The long continuance of this state of things has engendered so much ill-feeling that amendment can only be a gradual process, to be effected by the influence from which alone any permanent benefits can flow, viz., that of pure and active and earnest benevolence. In such a case as I have mentioned, nothing but a name and an abuse of an establishment exists. The Roman Catholics are in possession, and likely to keep possession, of the entire population of the parish above named. They are, in fact, deterred from becoming Protestants by the exhibition of what is manifestly unjust and disreputable, and hence an attachment to their own religion grows with their growth and strengthens with their strength. It is not by abuse and neglect and contempt that any good is to be effected; and these, it is to be feared, are but too largely exercised towards the Roman Catholics of Ireland.

" Depending almost entirely on the lower classes, the Catholic priesthood are described as becoming a less educated and consequently less liberal class than they formerly were; and their remuneration, scanty as it is, is a heavy tax on the Irish peasantry, who in a portion of their exorbitant rent pay the minister of the Protestants, and again in their earnings contribute to the support of their own Church. It is indeed a fruitful theme for contemplation to consider this and other features of the present condition of Ireland. Its resources are undoubtedly great, but capital is wanting to bring them into successful operation. Its inhabitants possess many agreeable and excellent traits, but it is to be feared that improvidence has greatly impaired its prosperity, and cast a dark cloud over its future prospects.

" A general system of education, with especial reference to sound morals, and commercial habits of calculation and economy, with a liberal and benevolent and candid endeavour to conciliate all parties by equal justice as regards the revenues of the Church, together with the introduction of English capital, and the cultivation of a liberal and friendly feeling between these two countries, are the chief points which occurred to me as likely to promote the welfare of Ireland. So far as the introduction of capital is concerned, I have some reason to believe that my visit to the county of Clare has not been unproductive of some beneficial result, and my report on the minerals of that county will probably lead to the expenditure of at least fifteen hundred or two thousand pounds in mining adventures. Of the prudence of such an undertaking my opinion is best expressed by the circumstance of my having joined the parties along with Mr. Scott, of Cahiracon, making in all twelve in number, and which I have proposed to denomi-

nate 'The County of Clare Mining Company.' Of this, however, there can be no doubt, that the expenditure of such a sum,
if it fails to be productive of profit as a mining adventure, cannot
fail to be highly beneficial to the district in which it is spent.
And so far as my share is concerned, I look at the speculation
as shrouded in that uncertainty which hangs over all mining
adventures; but I shall not regret its loss if I have afterwards
to remember it only as a willing contribution—a humble but a
hearty one—towards the prosperity of a district which I shall
always recollect with feelings of deep interest."

It will be seen from this chapter how thoroughly
Mr. Sopwith anticipated the disestablishment of the
Irish Church, as well as the best of the arguments on
which that great political change was finally brought
about. Could his sensible ideas, formed in 1838, have
then been carried out, the troubles of to-day and of many
days still in the future had long since, possibly, been
forgotten troubles of the past.

CHAPTER XVI.

A DAY IN OXFORD. DR. BUCKLAND AND MR. JOHN RUSKIN.

1839.

IN the early part of February 1839, Mr. Sopwith, after paying a very pleasurable visit to Dean Forest, arrived on the 5th of the month at Oxford, and became the guest of Dr. Buckland. A description of this distinguished Doctor's lecture-room is admirably pourtrayed,—a room in which dear Frank Buckland, whom we knew so well, then a lad of twelve or thirteen years of age, assisted his father by bringing him "the respective specimens as they were wanted," a sort of holiday amusement to Frank, who was to return to school on the following Thursday.

Amongst other specimens Dr. Buckland at this time was specially pleased to exhibit to his visitor was a large slab showing casts from the impressions of the feet of the Chierotherium. When wetted the indications of rain having fallen upon it were quite perceptible on the stone. Another specimen indicated the direction of the wind at the time the surface was formed.

In the evening, after a walk in Christ Church meadows with his host, they returned to dinner, where they met Dr. Wilson, Professor of Sanscrit, the Rev. Edward Bigge, and Mr. John Ruskin. The history of this meeting

with Mr. Ruskin in the earliest part of his career must
be told by Mr. Sopwith himself.

" Mr. Ruskin was invited because Dr. Buckland thought
I would be pleased to make his acquaintance, as a very
intelligent person and admirable artist. Some descriptions
convey too high an idea, and Dr. Buckland spoke so highly
of Mr. Ruskin's drawings that nothing but a sight of them
could have given me a better idea of them.

" After a very pleasant conversation, during which Dr. Wilson
related several very interesting particulars concerning India
and its natives, we had a new stranger introduced on the
dinner-table. This was a live salamander which Dr. Buckland
found at Liège, and which crawled about very peaceably on
the tablecloth. I described the East India Company's maps
to Dr. Buckland, and while we were talking the loud tones
of the Great Tom of Oxford fell on my ears. This bell, the
largest in England, hangs in the tower of the gateway of
Christ Church, near to that part of the quadrangle in which
Dr. Buckland resides. I went to the door, and stood for some
time listening to its tremendous tones as they rolled through
and reverberated from the gloomy walls of the spacious quadrangle of venerable buildings of which Dr. Buckland's residence
forms a part. In the drawing-room I had some conversation
with Mr. Ruskin. He asked my opinion about the principles of
perspective drawing recommended in Mr. Parsey's book, and
I told him very freely my opinion of it. I said I had bought
his book for twelve shillings, that I thought myself very foolish
for throwing away so much money on so useless a production,
and had never supposed that it would occupy any share of the
attention of any intelligent person. The subject, I said, had
been discussed at London's table, where I laughed heartily at
the manner in which Candidus rode rough shod over Parsey
and his whimsical perspective. I explained my views at full
length, both as to the theory and practice of this method of
perspective, and was glad to find that Mr. Ruskin was the

author of the able papers which have appeared in *Loudon's Magazine* under the title, or rather signature, of Katá Phusin (according to Nature). It was truly delightful for me to become acquainted with the ingenious author of these very able papers, and still more so to find that we exactly coincided in opinion. His essays on the 'Poetry of Architecture' range exactly towards the same feelings and objects as those which influenced me in the composition of the papers on the 'Principles of Design' in the same magazine.

" Dr. Buckland's house is truly characteristic as the residence of a geologist and a scholar. The exterior is a plain, low, rustic, time-worn Gothic wall, being part of the large quadrangle of Christ Church College. A low and very plain-looking door opens, and you behold a very wide and short staircase, almost covered with fragments of rock, specimens of fossil remains, an immense tortoise, and a stuffed wolf.

" In the breakfast-room are a series of piles of books, boxes, papers ; in short, such a combination of book-stands, chairs, sideboards, boxes, all blended together in one mass of confusion, which, I was informed, had not been invaded by the dust-cloth for the last five years. The drawing-room at Dr. Buckland's has its share of variety, of great interest, and of a tolerable deal of confusion, through which a person might range a whole day, and find some new index every moment pointing to weeks and months and years of occupation. One of the round tables is formed entirely of coprolites ; another presents on its highly polished surface all the varieties of lava, etc., found at Mount Etna.

" But the most interesting part of this interesting mansion is the domestic comfort which so eminently prevails. The children are five in number. Francis, the eldest, is about thirteen, a fine, good-looking, active lad, full of movement and vivacity. Edward, Marian, Elizabeth; and the youngest a fine thriving lad, who rejoices in the truly geological name of Adam Sedgwick Conybeare Buckland. I must not omit to mention my humble eulogium on the kind hospitality, the amiable character, and the literary and scientific talents of Mrs. Buckland, who, it has been often observed, has been expressly intended for the Doctor.

"Having finished my sketch of the house and family, I have only further to say that I closed the day at midnight, and enjoyed a most comfortable night's sleep. I shall always remember it as a red-letter day, and noted in the calendar of my memory as A Day in Oxford.

"*February 6th.*—Dr. Buckland invited Mr. Ruskin to breakfast, and requested him to send his drawings for me to look at. He also formed a most admirable programme for the day, which he detailed to me, and I was delighted to find that I was to have the honour as well as the great gratification of his devoting the whole day to my amusement.

"As soon as we had breakfasted we commenced an inspection of Mr. Ruskin's drawings. These are contained in four large folio volumes. They consist entirely of original sketches in England, Scotland, and various parts of the Continent. Most of them are in pencil, on tinted paper, and touched with a few slight effects of light or colour.

"Architectural subjects prevail, and comprise very clear, minute, and exceedingly beautiful details of some of the most celebrated cathedrals, churches, ruins, etc. There is great spirit, richness, and freedom of touch in his style of drawing, which are peculiarly adapted for elaborate architectural drawing; and some of his views, as Roslin Chapel, for instance, are one mass of sumptuous decoration arranged in just perspective and in good keeping. They appeared too extravagantly rich by daylight, but in the evening they showed to more advantage by candlelight. The colouring was after the fairy-like and aerial tints of Turner and Martin, and some of the mountain views had great depth and sublimity; one of them in particular seemed like a vast and glorious prospect of immense mountains bursting on the sight through a hazy atmosphere, an effect in which the judgment is at a loss to determine whether the vision is of the eye or of the imagination. Those who delight

in seeing correct and vivid portraits of distant scenery, in
beholding splendid architectural combinations, and in admiring
the highest efforts of art, will readily appreciate my enjoyment
in looking over these beautiful volumes.   The Apprentices'
Pillar at Roslin; an old oak hall, with a forest seen through
the window; interior views of chapels, etc., with red sunsets
and rich purple tints; the magnificent tower and spire of
St. Mary's, or University Church, and of Merton Tower in
Oxford,—these and many other similar drawings are inimitable
examples of that accordance with nature which Mr. Ruskin
has so ably and so eloquently advocated in *Loudon's Architectural Magazine* under the signature of Katá Phusin.   Many
of the landscape views were commented upon by Dr. Buckland
with reference to the geological features.

" I had a long and agreeable conversation with this excellent
amateur artist, who is now residing at Oxford as a gentleman
commoner; and it was no ordinary gratification to lay the
foundation of a further acquaintance with him under such
favourable auspices as an introduction in the house of
Dr. Buckland."

Amongst his many admirers the distinguished author
of " Fors Clavigera " had not one more earnestly sincere
than Mr. Sopwith. One night, at the Society of Arts, Lord
Shaftesbury in the chair, we had a discussion in which
Mr. Ruskin ran a-tilt at steam engines, arguing that
they did the work which should alone be done by the
human engine. I reported this to my friend with some
glee, knowing his admiration of the steam engine as
well as of Ruskin. He thought a little while, and then
observed, with his characteristic sly humour, " Well, the
human is the best engine, and if Ruskin could get the
same amount of work out of it he would be right."

CHAPTER XVII.

1839.

N February 7th Mr. Sopwith left Oxford in a
stage coach for Tring, a distance of thirty-
four miles, and then by railway train to
Wolverton, a distance of twenty-one miles
accomplished in fifty minutes. Here the train stopped
ten minutes for refreshment, from whence it proceeded
to Coventry, passing through a tunnel of considerable
length. He did not experience any disagreeable effects
as regards the air of the tunnel, but the darkness and
sudden glimpses of light while passing the shafts produced a peculiar dazzling effect. Proceeding onwards he
reached Birmingham at five in the afternoon, where,
finding he could not get on to Preston, he stayed
all night, putting up at the Railway Hotel.

In his way to Preston the following day by mail train
he met Mr. Taylor and the Rev. George Kennard, the
last-named warm in his description of a patent railway
invented by Mr. Kolman, an organist and an excellent
musician. Mr. Kennard related a good story of Dr.
Buckland, to the effect that Buckland and a friend
riding towards London on a very dark night lost their
way. Buckland thereupon dismounted and, taking up

a handful of earth, smelt it. "Uxbridge," he called out to his friend, "his geological nose telling him the precise locality." Mr. Sopwith reached Carlisle at nine o'clock, slept there all night, and on the following morning returned home, pleasantly, by rail.

Sopwith was a born traveller; everything about travelling brought to him happiness and health. At the close of his journal for 1839 he writes on this topic :—

"I enjoy travelling on many accounts; it agrees well with my health; every year seems to improve both my strength and spirits. Headaches, toothaches, and a tedious train of minor grievances seem totally banished by the refreshing influences of change of air and scene. This must ever be subject of gratitude, while at the same time it is incumbent ever to remember that in the midst of life we may be on the verge of death. Happy is it for us that the day of our departure from this world is unknown to us, and that a full reliance on the wisdom and goodness of the Supreme Disposer of events reconciles the mind to a contingency which experience shows to be very remote. In practice, however, I prefer acting rigidly on the possibility of sudden death by arranging matters from time to time, and at this time of the year by seeing my life insurance paid on the very day it becomes due. It is impossible to travel so much as I do without recollections of this kind often presenting themselves to my mind.

"Travelling is, to my mind, one of the most interesting occupations that can be pursued during the middle period of life. It affords many opportunities of intellectual as well as physical enjoyment, and combined as it is in my case with duty as regards my professional employment, it is at once a source of pleasure and profit. The past year has, as compared with the preceding year, been a good deal spent at home, but in the two years I have travelled upwards of three thousand miles, entirely in Great Britain."

In March my friend visits Ebbw Vale to make a valuation of mines, of which he leaves in his diary some curious and important details. A little later in the month he is in London dining at the Geological Club (March 13th), where he meets, in addition to Dr. Buckland the President, Mr. Justice Haliburton, author of "Sam Slick's Sayings and Doings," the Marquis of Northampton, President of the Royal Society, with many others. After the dinner there is an attendance at the Geological Society, when Sedgwick, De la Beche, Roderick Murchison, and Phillips are present. After the meeting they adjourn to Lord Cole's to supper, where they stay till two o'clock in the morning, and where some of them, including Mr. Sopwith, meet again at breakfast, in order to be introduced to Mr. George Rennie. On the following day he is at the College of Surgeons, inspecting the Hunterian Museum and making the acquaintance of the illustrious man at the head of it, Professor Owen.

March 15th contains an entry in which the views of the famous Mr. Babbage on literary property are described.

"I dined at Mr. Greenough's in the Regent's Park. It would require a long description to convey even a slight idea of the extent and sumptuous elegance of this mansion, which may indeed be described as a palace rather than a private villa. It was built by Decimus Burton, the younger, and is figured in several architectural works, both in England and on the Continent. We had a small, but very agreeable dinner party, consisting of Professor Babbage, Robert Hutton, Esq., M.P. for Dublin, and Mr. Jukes, who is going out to Newfoundland on a geological survey. We had a conversation on various subjects, but chiefly on copyright and photogenic drawing. Mr. Babbage considers that a literary work is the production of labour equally with the acquirement of land by trading, and that so long as land is transmitted from generation to generation, so ought the copyright of every original literary production. As to identity, a word altered in each and every sentence would satisfy him as the criterion of a work being different, and with this as a limit the work might be altered, enlarged, improved, condensed, or whatever else was thought necessary by any other writer. Inventions, he thought, were different, for it was probable that an invention would at some time occur to another person, but the same literary ideas would never be expressed in the same language."

An entry immediately follows, rich in social interest; a very faithful description of one of the famous evenings of fifty years ago, given by Mr. Babbage at his residence at the foot of Manchester Street, Manchester Square.

"*March* 16*th.*—At nine I went to Mr. Babbage's soirée. There was a great assemblage of nobility and of scientific persons, amongst whom I had the pleasure to converse with the following: the Marquis of Northampton, President of the Royal Society,—his manners are extremely pleasing, and expressive of kind and amiable feelings; Mr. Talbot, the inventor of a kind of photogenic drawing in which the object appears white and the rest of the surface of the paper is very dark,—some very admirable examples of which were lying on a chiffonier and attracted great attention: the finest films of vegetable form, and the minutest threads of the finest lacework, are shown with surprising delicacy and clearness; Sir Francis and Lady Chantrey, G. W. Wood, M.P., Robert Hutton, M.P., Professor Phillips, Professor Wheatstone, Bellender Ker, George Rennie.

"Of those whom I only knew by being pointed out were: Admiral Codrington, M. Van de Weyer the Belgian Ambassador, Professor Faraday, Mr. and Mrs. Collidge, Mrs. Marcet, Lady Charleville, Wentworth Buller, Lady Chatterton, who wrote "My Aunt Dorothy," Charles Darwin, Charles Lyell,

Sir William Gossett, Mrs. Rothschild (widow of the famous stockbroker), Mr. Hawes, M.P., Dr. Holland, Lady Monroe, Mr. Macready the tragedian, Lady Nugent, Admiral Sir Charles and Lady Ogle, Sir John and Lady Shelley, Sydney Smith, Lady Mary Shepherd, Lady Vincent, Wilkie the celebrated painter, and many others of whom it may be truly said, in newspaper fashion, their names are 'too numerous to mention.'"

A further entry is a curiosity in reference to the Babbage calculating machine.

"*March 17th.*—I went at eleven to Mr. Babbage's and remained till after four. A large portion of this time was occupied in an inspection of the drawings and plans of the calculating engine, which are very elaborate and present an extraordinary combination of machinery. Mr. B. detailed at great length the history and prospects of this invention. After thirteen or fifteen years' labour, and an expenditure of twenty thousand pounds, the engine was suspended for lack of further funds five years ago, and it is yet uncertain whether it will be completed. I saw a portion of it which was placed in the drawing-room, and performed the operation of cubing eighteen in *thirteen seconds* by merely *grinding*, or rather by moving a handle backwards and forwards twice. The result was of course correct; the following are the figures, viz., 5832. Mr. Babbage is now employed in constructing plans and very voluminous details of another and very superior engine, which will, he says, perform the most complicated problems in the highest departments of arithmetic and algebra. A multiplication of thirty figures by thirty figures is done in three minutes. He showed me his writing table, reading chair, work room, mode of keeping his letters, warming his rooms, the classification of his library, and many other very interesting matters, with which I was much gratified. Many of these arrangements are similar to those which I have pursued at home.

"I dined and spent a very pleasant evening at Mr. Murchison's, the talented geologist of the Silurian region."

The record in the diary for the rest of the year 1839, rich in local matter, and rendering an account of various journeys to London, Cheltenham, Ebbw Vale, Forest of Dean, Gloucester, Denbigh, St. Asaphs, Birmingham, Holy Island, Durham, Stratford-on-Avon, Warwick, Berkeley Castle, and the Severn, affords but few points that would be of interest to readers of this day. A brief notice is given of the Chartist Riots in Birmingham in July, and mention is made of similar riots in Newcastle. An excellent account is written of Stratford-on-Avon, and a very graphic description of Warwick Castle, but there is no attempt at anything that is specially new. There is, however, a note about Robert Owen which deserves notice. On November 19th Mr. Owen called upon him to unfold the plans of his proposed community buildings. Mr. John Hancock joined them, and remarked on the bump of benevolence in Mr. Owen's head, while Mr. Sopwith expressed his opinion that the plans were entirely visionary, but that he wishes all theorists would advocate their views with Mr. Owen's good nature and perfect candour. The conversation then turned on Mr., now Lord, Armstrong's application of water power.

At times in the year he was busy with invention, and was greatly taken with Mr. Jordan's experiments on photogenic registration, the first starting-point of what is now likely to become one of the most beautiful and wonderful of the works of science. He suggested the application of a lens to lessen the size of the record and to increase its clearness by additional intensity of light. This method of Jordan, with his own suggestions upon it, he expounded to Dr. Nichols, of the Glasgow

University, and author of "The Architecture of the Heavens," who was much struck by both these advances. In this year he took part also as a lecturer and essayist as well as reporter on the mineral districts of the County of Clare, Ireland, and he wrote a paper for the Polytechnic Society on his method of recording states of weather by descriptive symbols. On November 6th I find him at Durham University delivering a lecture to the students on certain points connected with plans, sections, geological drawings, and models. It must have been a strikingly practical and useful lecture.

He first remarked on the frequent use, the great importance, and the extreme accuracy required in levelling as applied to the selection of lines of road, the formation of railways, the drainage of fens and other districts, to geology, and to mining. In all these pursuits facility is highly important, first, in taking the observations, and, second, in recording them in the field and on drawings. He then described the different forms for such records, and gave a specimen confined simply to the two differences and the lengths in levelling. He next explained the method of constructing geological sections, and the mode of observing and delineating the rocks, etc., by plans, sections, and isometrical drawings. He exhibited models in detail to illustrate the construction of geological models, so as to afford a clear idea of complicated geological structure; and he commented on the method and advantages of preserving mining records.

On November 23rd we discover him delivering a lecture for the Popular Lecture and Musical Society of Newcastle, before an audience consisting of from seven to eight hundred persons; the subject, "Some Outlines of Astronomy." A good portion of the lecture was of the usual historical character, with some refined

and yet serious touches bearing on the grandeur of the
science as a study. He afterwards entered into details
known to astronomers respecting the sun, the moon,
and the planets; and then, in his own homely and
original manner, described the distances of the planets
from the sun by a comparative scale, in which one inch
should represent the diameter of the earth. The sun
would then be 110 inches or 9 feet 2 inches in diameter;
Mercury, $\frac{3}{4}$ inch; Venus, nearly 1 inch; the Earth, 1 inch;
Moon, $\frac{1}{4}$ inch; Mars, $\frac{1}{2}$ inch; Jupiter, $11\frac{1}{2}$ inches; Saturn,
10 inches; Herschell, $4\frac{1}{2}$ inches.

The proportion of distances would be by a scale of
feet:—

Mercury .	.	36 millions of miles	.	360 feet.
Venus .	.	68 ,, ,,	.	680 ,,
Earth .	.	95 ,, ,,	.	950 ,,
Mars .	.	144 ,, ,,	.	1,440 ,,
Jupiter .	.	494 ,, ,,	.	4,940 ,,
Saturn .	.	906 ,, ,,	.	9,060 ,,
Herschell	. 1,812 ,, ,,	.	18,120 ,,

125 inches = 1 million, but in the above 120 inches was
assumed, or 10 feet as an approximation.

As a further illustration of the immense distance of
the planets, he explained the time it would take to count
a million, thus: 60 per minute, 3,600 per hour, for nine
hours a day, would require upwards of a month, but say
one month; then to count at this rate the distance
of the planets from the sun would require as follows:—

For Mercury .	.	3 years and	3 weeks.
,, Venus .	.	5 ,, ,,	8 months.
,, Earth .	.	7 ,, ,,	11 ,,
,, Mars .	.	12 ,, ,,	3 weeks.
,, Jupiter .	.	41 ,, ,,	2 months.
,, Saturn .	.	75 ,, ,,	6 ,,
,, Herschell .	.	151 ,, ,,	1 month.

From the earth to the moon 7 days $3\frac{1}{4}$ hours.

Another illustration was afforded by taking a velocity with which the public were familiar ; and as every one was not conversant with locomotive speed, he supposed a body moving from the sun to the planets with the velocity of the mail coach,—ten miles an hour. The time such body would arrive at the several planets after it left the sun would be as follows :—

At Mercury	.	.		.	360 years.
„ Venus	.	.		.	680 ,,
„ Earth .	.	.	.	.	950 ,,
„ Mars .	.	.	.	.	1,440 ,,
„ Jupiter	.	.	.	.	4,940 ,,
„ Saturn	.	.	.	.	9,060 ,,
„ Herschell .	.	.	.	.	18,120 ,,

He defined, by a diagram, the relative velocity of the planets, in minutes, in their course round the sun, as follows :—

Mercury	.	1,824 miles in a minute.					
Venus	.	1,335	,,		,,	or 80,110	miles per hour.
The Earth .		1,135	,,		,,	or 68,130	,, ,,
Mars .	.	920	,,		,,		
Jupiter	.	498	,,		,,	or 28,895	,, ,,
Saturn	.	368	,,		,,		
Herschell	.	258	,,		,,		

He closes the year 1839 in his library, reading-room, and writing-room. His dearest Jane is reading beside him. His family of three girls and two boys are well, but Ursula has not long recovered from a severe illness. He has been busy with his accounts, which show a good return, and his hope is that succeeding years may be as happy, as comfortable, and as prosperous as the one just passed.

CHAPTER XVIII.

*CLEGG'S ATMOSPHERIC RAILWAY. MRS. ROBERTSON.
SIR FRANCIS CHANTREY. THE "GREAT WESTERN"
STEAMBOAT. REMINISCENCES.*

1840-41.

THE year 1840 was a busy one, and almost all devoted to professional work. In the course of the year Mr. Sopwith travelled six thousand miles. His duties as a Commissioner on the part of the Crown for the Dean Forest mines required him to make several visits to Dean Forest, in nearly all of which he had the agreeable and instructive society of his esteemed friend and brother-Commissioner, Mr. Buddle, of whom he always speaks in the warmest terms of respect and affection. His engagements led him to Pontypool, Swansea, and the valley of the Neath, where he viewed some valuable property belonging to the Duke of Beaufort, and made a model of the mountain Alt-y-grey. He also went to Midsomer Norton to survey the mine belonging to the Dean and Chapter of Christ Church. Similar professional business took him to Denbigh, Flintshire, and Shropshire, to Holy Island for a survey for the Government, and to Alston Moor in company with Dr. Buckland.

Of men of note whom he met at this time he mentions first Mr. Robert Stephenson, a man very agreeable in his manners and a master on a variety of topics. Stephenson had just been on a tour through Italy and Switzerland. Another gentleman to whom he makes special reference is Mr. John Taylor, whom he deservedly ranks as one of the most enterprising and enlightened miners that this country has ever produced ; a man of great abilities, and at the same time of the most amiable and pleasing manners ; who has for many years been extensively concerned in mining in Cornwall, Wales, Ireland, and Mexico. Dr. Kay (afterwards Sir J. Kay-Shuttleworth), Secretary to the Committee of the Council on Education, was another friend of whom he speaks in very warm terms; and on the Earl of Enniskillen, a nobleman as unassuming as he is learned and scientific, he grows quite enthusiastic. Sir Charles Lemon comes, in like manner, into the list of those whom he holds in the highest estimation, especially in reference to his (Sir Charles's) proposition to endow a school of mines in Wales.

An entry of September 5th gives us the first glimpse of the idea of an atmospheric railway. The inventor and patentee of this original design was Mr. Clegg, who took Mr. Sopwith to Wormwood Scrubs to see half a mile of the railway in operation there. The plan met with Mr. Sopwith's approval. The practicability of the plan seemed to him to be satisfactorily established. It possessed peculiar advantages tending to the speed, safety, and pleasantness of railway travelling, and probably also to economy. It is somewhat remarkable that after such recommendation from so cautious and able an observer as Mr. Sopwith, Clegg's plan should have been allowed to have passed into oblivion.

Under date of September 24th there is a record of the expenses of a journey of two hundred and seventy miles—one hundred and twenty by coach, and one hundred and fifty by rail; the summary of this showed that inside coach travelling cost fivepence and railway travelling threepence per mile.

A note on October 8th gives us an account of an American-built engine which had found its place on the Gloucester and Cheltenham line. This engine was shown to him and to Mr. Buddle by Captain Moorsom, the engineer of the line, who took them on the engine while it ran seven miles one furlong in fourteen minutes, and explained to them its construction. The particulars run as follow :—

"*October 8th.*—This engine (the Victoria, No. 84) is eight and one-third tons weight; and the ratio of the cost, including duty, as compared with English engines, is as seventeen to fifteen. The cylinders are outside, and are eleven inches diameter with a twenty-inch stroke. The wheels are four in number, and four feet diameter; they are not coupled. The whole rise from Cheltenham to Cofton is about five hundred feet. The inclined plane is above two miles in length, rising one in thirty-seven. Two engines draw ordinary trains up at twelve miles an hour; a single engine six miles an hour. Sand is used on the rails in wet or frosty weather. There are ten or eleven American engines and four or five English engines on the line. The iron plate of the fire-box Captain Moorsom thinks is not so good as in the English engine, and the tubes should be brass instead of copper."

On October 21st there is a note indicating that he went with Mr. W. G. Armstrong and Mr. W. G. Anderson to try a number of experiments on the newly discovered electricity of steam. "The experiments," he says, "were very curious and satisfactory," and greatly interested him. He quotes also a few lines from a letter by Dr. Buckland to intimate that the Doctor has shown some articles of painting and sculpture, sent him by Mr. Sopwith, to Sir Robert Peel, Lady Peel, Sir Francis Chantrey, and the elder Stephenson, "to their no small edification and amusement," and to which "the new post-office arrangements have afforded such facilities."

1841.

The amount of business which Mr. Sopwith had to conduct in London at this time necessitated the occupation of offices in Berners Street, in which he took temporary residence in the early part of 1841. On January 5th, 1841, he read, before the Geological Society, his well-known paper on geological models. On this occasion he made the acquaintance of Mr. (afterwards Sir Charles) Lyell. On the 8th of the same month he notices Dr. Reid's first attempt to ventilate the House of Commons. On the 17th of the month he drew a little picture of an artist whose name, now well-nigh forgotten, was then one of the well known.

" Dined at Mr. Robertson's, where I was delighted with the splendid specimens of art by Mrs. Robertson; this inimitable portrait-painter is better known on the Continent than in her native country. Her paintings are remarkable for the soul of poetry which seems to pervade them, and the rich harmony of colour corresponds with the music of Haydn or Mozart. During the last eighteen years she has painted no less than seven hundred portraits, some of them being oil-paintings of various sizes, the rest large miniatures. The largest size of her oil-paintings is the size which artists call ' Bishop's full-length '—viz., 9 feet high, and 5½ feet wide; for these her price is from three to four hundred guineas; and amongst her sitters for oil-paintings of various sizes have been Lord and Lady Milton, Lady Rolle (300 guineas), Lady Majoribanks and children (400 guineas), Lord Rivers (200 guineas), Mr.

and Mrs. Heneage (200 guineas each), Mrs. Leigh (200 guineas). As miniatures she has painted the Duke and Duchess of Northumberland, Duke and Duchess of Buccleugh, Marchioness of Lothian, etc.; these cost 100 guineas each. She is at present in Russia, where she has painted a Bishop's full-length of the Emperor (300 guineas), and two paintings of the same size of the Empress."

On January 21st Dr. Buckland suggested "Monocleid" as an appropriate name for the writing cabinet, and Mr. Sopwith accordingly adopted it in the printed description of it which he drew up, with wood-cuts by Miss Loudon, sister of the celebrated J. Claudius, London.

"On January 25th Mr. Lyell called and spent nearly three hours examining the hand models, and in conversation on general matters. He expressed a wish to introduce engravings of the models in his forthcoming edition of ' The Elements,' and I assured him that I felt a sincere pleasure in offering any contribution to one who had communicated so much information, in so pleasing a form, as he had done. Professor Sedgwick also called and examined the large section of the strata from Howne's Gill to the summit of Crossfell, which he honoured with the appellation of this ' gorgeous section.' I dined and spent the evening at Mr. Loudon's, where Miss Loudon instructed me in the first rudiments of wood-cutting, and under her able tuition I made a small and very imperfect wood-cut."

The Minutes of the Institution of Civil Engineers, bearing date of February 2nd, 1841, records that Mr. Sopwith called the attention of the meeting to the valuable geological sections presented by the railway cuttings and other engineering works now in progress.

On March 13th he is once more at Oxford, where Dr. Buckland assists him in the arrangement for the further description of his models. He suggested that

six might form one series, and be useful in conveying
a general notion of strata and denudation, while the
remaining six would be more appropriate as illustrating
more complex conditions. He read to Mr. Sopwith the
MS. notice of these models contained in his address to
the Geological Society in February last, and in which he
comments on the usefulness of such dissected models,
and the value of their adaptation to geological and
mining purposes.

In Dr. Buckland's society, Mr. Sopwith felt he was
with a man perfectly sincere, prompt, and generous in all
he said and did; he was in every sense practical, plain,
straightforward, and persevering; he had an intimate
knowledge of the world, and his acute observation was
in constant operation. To a fund of deep and original
thought he added an extraordinary degree of mental
activity and acquirement ; and all these were blended
with a cheerfulness of disposition and heartiness of
manner which rendered his company and conversation as
delightful as they were instructive and improving.

March 18th gives us an interview with Sir Francis
Chantrey.

" I showed him Ronketti's thermo-barometer, which he had
not seen nor heard of. ' I always,' said he, ' carry a thermometer when I go fishing, and the first thing I do is to
plunge it into the water. If the water is colder than the
air the fish will rise, and a good day's sport may be expected ;
but if the air is colder than the water, they know better than
to put their noses out.'

"Sir Francis expressed his approval of the monocleid cabinet,
the isograph, etc., and I felt much gratification in spending
two or three hours with this intelligent and truly eminent
man. He said he was anxious to avail himself of the aid of
the daguerreotype, in order to obtain exact representations of

his sculptured works, which, as he justly observed, 'would be good sitters.'"

Then follows, on same day, an account of a dinner.

"I dined this evening at Mr. Ord's, in Berkeley Square; Mr. Ord introduced me to one of the guests, but I did not catch his name. Mr. Ord said I had just come from Oxford, and this led to a conversation on the subject of Puseyism, of Mr. Newman and his style of preaching, and various other matters. I was not aware until dinner was half over that this guest was no other than the President of the Council, the Marquis of Lansdowne; I sat opposite to him at the table, and had some further conversation respecting Dean Forest, etc. Nothing could be more plain, unassuming, and agreeable than the whole bearing and conversation of this much-respected and highly-talented nobleman. Among the other gentlemen present were Colonel Clive, of the Guards, and Mr. Westmacott, the sculptor."

The grand event of this year, the building of the *Great Western* steamboat, is the subject of a note in the early part of May.

"*May 3rd.*—I attended a meeting at Messrs. Harford, Davies, & Co.'s office, in Small Street, and dined with Mr. Davies, of Cotebank, in the evening.

"I went this afternoon with one of the directors of the Western Steamship Company to see the large iron steamer now in progress at their establishment. The buildings and machinery belonging to this concern have been erected at a cost of £40,000, one moiety of which is to be charged to the leviathan of a vessel now in progress. The works are situated on the south side of the River Avon, midway between the Quay and the Clifton New Bridge. The building is of vast extent, and the machinery, by Fairburn of Manchester, is of first-rate excellence. The vessel, which the public, *pro tempore*, denominate the *Mammoth*, is now built up to the

height of her deck, with the exception of part of her stern;
so that by standing at the stern, or a little outside, a complete
view of the hull of the vessel is obtained.   Her length is 319
feet 6 inches; the breadth of course is various, but about 50 feet
is an approximation to the width of deck midway in the vessel.
The thickness in the plates of iron varies from $\frac{3}{4}$ inch to 1 inch,
the latter being the keel plates.   The ribs are about 2 feet
apart.   The keel is flat-bottomed, and her bows remarkably
thin and sharp.

"The outlay on the vessel alone up to this time is £30,000;
the cost is estimated at £80,000, which, with £20,000 share of
the building, makes £100,000; but this, like many other
estimates, will probably be exceeded.   The engines are not yet
made.   It is stated that her weight will be only four-fifths of
the weight of a wooden vessel of like calibre."

On June 22nd, after dining with Mr. William Cubitt
at 6, Great George Street, Westminster, Mr. Sopwith went
to the meeting of the Society of Civil Engineers, and read
a paper on the construction and use of geological models
in connection with civil engineering.   The paper was
divided into six parts: (*a*) application of modelling to
geological and mining purposes; (*b*) material to be
employed; (*c*) mode of construction; (*d*) scales to be
employed; (*e*) objects to be represented; (*f*) use of
models and connection with civil engineering.   At the
close the author observed that the avocations of the
civil engineer peculiarly qualify him for an observant
geologist; and that, being called upon to visit so many
different districts, the observations he could make ought
to be replete with instruction.   In speaking on this paper
Dr. Buckland, in instancing the utility of a knowledge
of geology to the engineer, mentioned that after the
Thames Tunnel had been commenced by Sir Isambard
Brunel, upon an assurance of those who made the

borings that they had reached the London clay, it was
found that they were actually traversing the sand of the
plastic clay ; hence arose nearly all the difficulties which
the engineer had to encounter, and in overcoming which
he displayed so much skill and perseverance.

On July 24th, the Dean Forest work being near its
conclusion, Mr. Buddle gave a dinner to the Forest
friends, to which thirty-eight sat down; and on the 26th
the Mining Commission was brought to a conclusion.

On August 29th Mr. Sopwith describes as a novel incident that he had his likeness taken by the daguerreotype
process at the Polytechnic Gallery.

"The operation only occupies one minute, and the charge is
a guinea for the miniature and a few shillings for the frame,
according to the taste of the person, who chooses it from a
large assortment kept on hand."

In the evening he went to a concert at Drury Lane,
where a novelty was introduced of exhibiting *tableaux
vivants*, or living figures clothed in white dresses closely
fitting the body.

On September 2nd he is at the Royal Gardens at Kew,
where he finds Sir W. Hooker, as usual, in great force,
full of activity and vivacity, and apparently thinking and
speaking and walking about four times faster than any-
body else.

In September he attended the meeting of the British
Association at York, and read a paper on the importance
of preserving railway sections. He also produced some
new and beautiful specimens of electrotype by his friend
Mr. Jordan. After the meeting he spent a few days
with Mr. Thomas Wilson at Banks, during which visit
he writes :—

"I walked with Mr. Skelton to some of the manufactories

of steel conducted by himself and partners. Iron is converted
into steel by the absorption of carbon, from eight to ten or
twelve tons being converted at a charge; and the process
occupies several days, varying according to the degree of
hardness required; and for some purposes the process is repeated two or three times. The introduction of carbon blisters
the steel, which is submitted to the heavy and exceedingly
rapid blows of the tilting-hammer. The activity and precision
of the workman who presents the heated bar of steel to be
formed and fashioned by this incessant and noisy monster is
such as can only be acquired by long practice, and hence such
men receive a high rate of wages, amounting, I was told, to four
or five pounds a week in some cases. The blows of the tilting-
hammer are sometimes as many as four hundred in a minute,
and are, as well as the rolling mills, worked by water-power
from reservoirs in the River Don."

A tour in North Wales with Dr. Buckland in October
of this year opens up some very pleasing passages,
including accounts of visits to Snowdon, the Menai Straits
with a view of the bridge, some glacial researches down
the Neath Valley, Bangor, Carnarvon, and Holyhead.
The journey afforded much information for both travellers.
In the same month, namely, on the 25th, he, in company
with Mr. Buddle and Mr. Robert Stephenson, went to
Bristol to inspect " the stupendous iron steamship " then
being built there, containing, without the engines, eight
hundred tons of iron. They started from Paddington
Station, and travelled at the rapid rate of fifty-three
miles an hour. In his reminiscences at the close of
1841 Mr. Sopwith dwells with much sympathy on the
death of his friend Sir Francis Chantrey, sculptor, who
left an impression on him never to be recalled without a
feeling of sincere attachment for the extreme sincerity
and amusing remembrances of his bright anecdotes on

fishing, on the sliding scale, and other subjects. He
speaks warmly also of Alexander Milne, Esq., one of Her
Majesty's Commissioners of Woods and Forests. Robert
Stephenson and John Buddle are again associated in his
recollections, together with Mr. Isaac Cooke of Clifton,
Mr. Benjamin Haywood Bright of Bristol, the Rev.
Henry Douglas of Durham, William Ord, and the artist
Sir William Harvey. Amongst men of science with
whom he came much in contact during the year he enrols
Sir Roderick Murchison, Mr. de la Beche, Professors
Owen, Phillips, Whewell, Bowerbank, and Basil Hall ;
with, as engineers, Mr. James Walker, President of the
Institute, and Messrs. William Cubitt, J. Rendel, Robert
Davison, J. Murray, and J. Macneil. He also places in
the list of his present friends Lords Lansdowne, Dun-
cannon, Fitzwilliam, and Sudeley.

In his professional work in 1841 he travelled over
seven thousand miles, all pleasant travelling, with many
agreeable and profitable hours spent in connection with
geological and mining pursuits.

CHAPTER XIX.

1842.

THE year 1842 presents few subjects of moment until we arrive at September, when there appears in the diary a peculiarly interesting account of a meeting at Wakefield of the West Riding of Yorkshire Geological and Polytechnic Society, at which some of the most distinguished living men were present. The description of this meeting is rendered in the following entry :—

" *September 7th.*—In the course of the forenoon I had the pleasure of meeting Mr. William West, an eminent chemist of Leeds, and several other friends who are connected with the Polytechnic Society, the Quarterly Meeting of which I attended at noon, and had the gratification to meet the noble President Earl Fitzwilliam, Dr. Buckland, and Professors Liebig, Playfair, and Daubeny, all of whom took an active part in the proceedings. I was called upon to explain the model of Ebbw Vale and Sirhowey, and also my set of twelve geological models, which were set on the table in front of the President. I did this verbally, and wished to be very brief, knowing that the time of the meeting was limited, and that an interesting paper on architecture remained to be read. At each effort to abridge, however, Lord Fitzwilliam urged me to go on, and appeared much interested. Afterwards Dr. Buckland rose, and describing some peculiarities of structure, pronounced an eloquent eulogium on the great importance of preserving mining records in a modelled form.

"At 3 o'clock I dined with the Society, Earl Fitzwilliam in the chair, and at 6 o'clock I went with Mr. West and another friend in a chaise to Leeds to a meeting which I had been invited to attend. It was in the music-hall, a large and elegant room, which was filled by a respectable company of ladies and gentlemen of what is commonly termed the middle classes. Earl Fitzwilliam presided, and Drs. Buckland, Liebig, Playfair, and Daubeny were present, as was also Mr. George Stephenson, the celebrated railway engineer.

"Several very interesting addresses were made, and especially one by Dr. Buckland, which was afterwards reported fully in the Leeds paper, and transferred to the columns of the *Mining Journal* under the heading of an 'Important Geological Address;' and such it certainly was, for it included a graphic description of the local phenomena of the structure of the carboniferous rocks, their adaptation to supply a great manufacturing district with coal and iron below, and with abundant fruits of the earth on its rich surface, and ascribed in very eloquent language these and similar arrangements to benevolent design.

"His observations were received with rapturous applause, and still more so was a long and very characteristic address by Mr. George Stephenson, who alluded to his defective education, and his still speaking what he calls the 'bad language of Northumberland,' meaning its dialect. He also referred to the difficulties of cross-examination before Parliamentary Committees, and said he would almost as soon face the gallows. He urged the importance of education, and alluded to many interesting topics, all of which afforded great delight, and gave rise to long-continued acclamation.

"I said a few words, as few as possible, in acknowledgment of the good wishes expressed by the meeting towards the Natural History Society of Northumberland, Durham, and Newcastle."

Another entry on the following day is curious.

"*September 8th.*—I left Leeds in a first-class carriage of the railway train which starts at six in the morning, and after a safe and pleasant journey to Sheffield, I hired a 'fly' and went directly to Middlewood Hall, distant about three miles from Sheffield.

"I then went by hilly roads over a very hilly country to Ecclesfield, and to Milton and Elsecar Iron Works. It rained in torrents, but this had not deterred the scientific party from their investigation of these places. I found Dr. Daubeny, who had taken shelter in one of the workshops, and afterwards we joined Buckland, Liebig, and Playfair. I was invited by Lord Fitzwilliam to dine and sleep at Wentworth House, but had previously promised to join my kind friends at Middlewood, and to this arrangement I adhered, although it would have been a great treat to have dined in company with three Presidents of the British Association, Harcourt, Fitzwilliam, and Buckland, and other eminent scientific guests assembled at the hospitable mansion of the noble Earl."

After the close of the Wakefield meeting Mr. Sopwith and Dr. Buckland made a tour in Yorkshire. Amongst the incidents of this tour I notice specially a description, very unique, of Clapham Cave, near Settle.

"*September 12th.*—Dr. Buckland sent a note to Mr. Jackson, inviting him to accompany us on our expedition to Clapham Cave, to which he returned an assent on a neatly embossed card. After an early breakfast we started at seven o'clock, accompanied by Mr. Howson and Mr. Jackson, and examined several rocks by the way. Limestone scars impend over the east side of the vale, and the Millstone grit thrown down by the great Craven fault passes along the line of the road or very near it.

"We had a pleasant drive to Clapham, a village at the base of Ingleborough, and walked up a beautiful valley called Clapdale. The great lion of the place is the cave, which Dr. Buckland pronounces to be probably the finest of its kind in the world that has hitherto been explored. About fifty yards from the entrance has long been accessible, but it was only about four years ago that attention was called to further exploration by a great quantity of sand and gravel being washed out after a heavy flood.

"The proprietor, James Wilson Farrer, Esq., of Ingleborough House, was absent, but his son and nephew, and a guide named J. Harrison, accompanied us on a survey of the subterraneous wonders of this magnificent and extensive cavern.

"It would require a large volume, and a vast number of drawings, to convey any tolerable idea of the beauty of this place. Every step presents some marvellous combinations, which excited the highest admiration and astonishment; here a stately column, there a noble dome, a clear lake reflecting beautiful groups of pendent stalactites, the water flowing in curious pulsations over round masses of rock, some places reminding one of the modelled ruins of an ancient city, and others presenting a fac-simile of Alpine glaciers. One strange projection of rock resembled the open jaw of an infuriated dragon; some of the pendent stalactites emit musical tones, which at a short distance have the melody of a fine peal of bells. Dr. Buckland suggested the name of Lady Chapel for a beautiful chamber in which festoons of stalactites descend like gracefully flowing robes.

"It is a marvellous, a transcendently beautiful, a deeply interesting and instructive lesson of Nature's silent but effective labours even in the bosom of the mighty hills, where unseen, unknown, unthought of, this cavern has from age to age been forming, and is now for the first time presented to the wondering eye of man.

"On our return we examined some scratched and polished rocks by the side of the lake, one of which Dr. Buckland suggested should be preserved by having a cover over it. We had luncheon at the hospitable mansion of J. W. Farrer, Esq., with his brother, his son, and nephew."

On September 27th there is a note on the Newcastle Musical Festival, and on October 22nd another note on an examination of students in engineering at Durham, with a brief reference to Professor Chevallier, who was present; and on October 29th there is an account of a visit to see the working of the " Centrifugal Railway." The experiment did not seem to be very satisfactory. One of the attendants went round safely enough, but a Mr. Rively, who tried the experiment, was thrown off. He was not hurt, but his escape was marvellous. I pass from these particulars to the description of the Armstrong hydro-electrical machine.

"*November* 15*th*.—Mr. William Armstrong has constructed an apparatus the electrical powers of which are most astonishing. A boiler 3 feet 6 inches long and 18 inches diameter, with fire-box below, is insulated by being supported on four glass feet on a carriage. The strength is very great, being capable of a pressure of 300 lbs. per inch, but in the experiments alluded to about 70 lbs. pressure is found to be as effective as a higher power. The result is attested by a discharging electrometer,—the capacity of the jar being $\frac{1}{2}$ a gallon—the balls $\frac{1}{5}$ inch apart. The number of discharges from a 3-feet plate machine being 26 per minute, that of Mr. Armstrong's steam, under exactly similar conditions, is 280 per minute, or more than 10 times as powerful.

" There are 14 jets, viz., 7 on each side, each jet discharging as much steam as would at 70 lbs. pressure pass through a circular aperture of $\frac{1}{16}$ inch; 7 jets gave 70 discharges in half a minute, hence 14 jets give 280 in a minute. The length of spark from the boiler is from 12 to 14 inches, without any proper apparatus for elongating the sparks.

"The hair or fingers held in the jet of steam are brightly illumed with electrical light, and the effects are not less beautiful than curious, new, and important."

On November 24th Mr. Sopwith delivered a lecture before the Geological Society of Manchester; and on the 26th he was taken by Mr. Kennedy, one of the leading men in Manchester, to call on the illustrious Dr. Dalton, the founder of the Atomic Theory. They discovered the philosopher reading a newspaper by the fireside. He was now infirm, and spoke with difficulty, but was most kind and cheerful in manner. On November 28th my friend went to Leeds, where he delivered a lecture, before the Mechanics' Institution and Literary Society, on Geology as evidencing benevolent design.

In the reminiscences of this year the loss of his child Mary Jane holds a prominent place, although her long and painful illness, and the sad prospect that she would never enjoy vigorous health in mature life, somewhat alleviated the suffering. The remarkable talents of Mr. William G. Armstrong,* a solicitor in partnership with Mr. Donkin in Newcastle, are referred to, with the observation that Mr. Armstrong ought to have been an engineer, and with the expression of the high opinion he entertained both of the head and heart of his ingenious and valued friend.

Again there is a reference to Mr. John Ruskin, whom he has met in London, and "on whom his feeble encomiums cannot convey the faintest idea of the consummate skill of an artist of truly amiable and pleasing character." "My visits" to his library, says Mr. Sopwith, "had the good effect of teaching me a lesson in humility which I shall never forget, for whatever I have done in

* Now Lord Armstrong.

sketching shrinks into insignificance when compared with his elaborate and magnificent works." The thousands of enthusiastic admirers of the John Ruskin of to-day will, without doubt, join with unanimous voice in crediting Thomas Sopwith with the prescience with which he estimated the talents of their master.

This early recognition of supreme talent is, however, not really remarkable, since it came from one who was himself by nature a gifted though not cultivated artist. Some of Mr. Sopwith's sketches are worthy of warm commendation. They are extremely faithful to nature; the perspective, when that comes into play, is good, and the colouring is always grateful. Here and there throughout the diary sketches and drawings of local scenery abound, each one conveying the usual touches of industry and fidelity.

Two final reminiscences afford him this year great pleasure—one, that in the first month of the year he received from the Institution of Civil Engineers a Telford medal, awarded for his communication on Geological Models ; and two, that in the last month of the year he found himself in the enjoyment of the best health and spirits, with from eight to nine hours' sleep, and great benefit from taking his breakfast directly after he has risen from bed.

CHAPTER XX.

1843.

THE year 1843 produced from Mr. Sopwith a report of an engineering expedition to Belgium for the purpose of a survey for the first Belgian railways. Previous to this, however, there are some records of interest on matters at home. In March he was led to comment on a movement then commencing in Newcastle, and having relation to the development of High Church principles and practice. A Broad Churchman himself, and fond of everything that is artistic, and especially of music, Mr. Sopwith held, it would seem, an independent and strong place in the controversy. He was most favourable to the introduction of music of a high class into the Church services, believing that the services would thereby be made much more attractive and beneficial. At the same time, he was opposed to all ceremonials that would bring the Catholic ritual into the Church of England. He was not opposed from any sense of bigotry to the services of the Church of Rome; on the contrary, he thought that the ceremony of the Romish Church was of itself magnificent. His objections related to the introduction of portions of it or imitations of it into the simpler English form of worship. I do not think he ever changed from this view, a view which has been and is largely held by many thousands of his countrymen.

In this month he speaks with great pleasure of a visit which he received from an excellent as well as an eminent man, Dr. Duncan of Ruthwell, Dumfriesshire. Duncan was the originator of Savings Banks, and author of " The Philosophy of the Seasons ; " in every sense an amiable, original, and accomplished man.

On March 31st I find him reading a paper at the Literary Institution at Newcastle on County Clare, in Ireland, and a thoroughly good practical paper it is, dealing not only with descriptive topics, but briefly with the condition of Ireland and the urgent necessity for better government for that unhappy country.

On April 8th he dined with Mr. John Claudius Loudon, a very remarkable man of letters, who died at Bayswater on December 14th this same year. Of him Mr. Sopwith reports, in speaking of his death :—

"It has very often been my good fortune to enjoy the society and friendship of this accomplished and truly amiable man. He was in a great measure self-educated, having gradually made himself a position, and surmounted all the obstacles which lay in his way from being a humble assistant to an enterprising cabinet-maker and publisher, to his being rightly viewed as one of the most industrious and able writers on Botany and other subjects. He was the editor of various works, such as the *Gardener's Magazine*, the *Architectural Magazine*, etc. But the most elaborate of his compilations was the ' Arboretum Britannica,' a work of enormous labour. By some wrong treatment when being shampooed, he suffered an injury which required the amputation of an arm, and the fingers of his remaining hand were contorted in such a way that he held a pen or pencil with difficulty. It may be safely said that, as regards the quantity of letterpress composition, and of pictorial illustration, which appeared with the express sanction of his name as author, editor, or publisher, few, if any, have exceeded London in productiveness. Take, for example, his ' Cottage, Farm, and Villa,'—what a vast mass of reading, what a great deal of minute reference to very accurate plans, sections, and other illustrations. I had for many years the privilege of dining with him at his plain family dinner any time I chose to go, and I not unfrequently had this very great pleasure. No ceremony as to dress. Conversation in a free and unmeasured and most friendly manner was the true charm of the feast."

Mr. London was a keen observer of nature, and possessed a considerable skill and taste in design. Ornamental gardening was part of his profession. On the day when Mr. Sopwith visited him on his sixtieth birthday, April 8th, 1843, he was overworking himself in order to recoup the losses he had sustained in publishing his " Arboretum Britannica."

In April and May Mr. Sopwith is in London again on parliamentary work. On April 13th he dines with the New Madrigal Society at Freemasons' Tavern, and after dinner, when the cloth is cleared, the Madrigals begin, and continue to the end of the meeting. A choir of boys from St. Paul's had great effect. On April 23rd he breakfasts with Mr. Ruskin, at Denmark Hill, in order to see water-colour drawings, which are much admired. We have become accustomed of late years to look on Mr. Ruskin purely as the art critic, but those who knew him in these early days were strangely impressed with his skill as an artist. Amongst these admirers Mr. Sopwith must be ranked, and I may add that he retained his opinion on this matter to the end of his life. The last time we ever spoke together about Mr. Ruskin he remarked, " A great art critic without a shadow of a doubt, but would have shone with equal light if he had kept to his natural gift—art itself."

On April 28th there is a note that Mr. Edwin Chadwick called at Berners Street to discuss with him some points on the health of towns. Chadwick, then in his prime, is attracted by the idea of getting a series of maps and models for sanitary purposes similar to the geological,—an excellent idea, which afterwards bore good fruit.

On May 15th he is at dinner with Mr. Robert Stephenson, at Hampstead; and on May 22nd a proposal comes to him from Mr. Fearon, with explanations from Mr. Cubitt, that he should undertake a series of surveys in Belgium for railway engineering purposes.

Returning to Newcastle in June, he received a visit from Mr. Moses Richardson, to look over sketches for the commencement of a work to be called the "Table Book;" and on June 25th (Sunday) he is at St. Thomas's Church listening to a sermon by the Rev. Richard Clayton, directed against the evils of the racecourse. The sermon, he says, was excellent, and free of all narrow prejudices and intolerance, but denouncing the misconduct which abounds, to a lamentable extent, not only at races, but at many other of the popular entertainments of the English people. Commenting on this matter in the note below, he gives us a good example of the advanced views he held on the important topic of recreation at the time specified, views which are only just now coming into practical application.

"It is, however, my belief that the mere denunciation of excesses will do little to repress the natural desire which is felt for recreation, and until more harmless amusements are provided we must not expect any material change in long-established customs, especially when supported, as racing is, by royalty, by the nobility and gentry, and by municipal authority.

"The school of evangelic reform, to which this excellent and zealous clergyman belongs, repudiates all attempts to substitute a harmless field of amusement in the way of museums, botanical gardens, etc., and deems them unsuitable occupations for Sundays; hence all rational hope of amendment is nipped in the bud, and the bulk of the public cling to whatever law and custom have left them of their favourite pastimes.

"A Race Sunday assuredly presents many demoralising scenes, but the opportunity for getting air and exercise tempts many to the tents on the town moor who would more willingly have gone to the quiet and fascinating enjoyments of a botanical garden, if such a means of innocent recreation had been afforded them."

On July 10th John Bright visits Newcastle to deliver one of his famous addresses on the Corn Laws. My friend is of the audience, and makes a critical note on the speech he has listened to. Mr. Bright is described as an excellent speaker, adapting his subject very ably to the comprehension of his hearers.

On August 19th Mr. Sopwith started for Boulogne, steaming across the Channel in the *Water Witch*. It was a steamer with two thirty-five-horse power engines, with a tolerably spacious deck, and a gloomy cabin. This was the first time he had ever left the British Islands, and it afforded him a kind of new view of life. He was uncommonly pleased, surprised, and instructed by his first visit to a French hotel, the Hotel du Nord, of which he gives a vivacious description, as he does also of the then existing theatre at Boulogne. To these he adds notes on the fair and the Haute Ville.

"*The Fair.*—This present Sunday, August 20th, is the last day of a fair which begins on the 5th and lasts fifteen days.

The fair is held on the esplanade; the wooden stalls are covered with lead, and are made so as to close at night; they were filled very much in the manner of an English fair, with toys, jewellery, etc.   There were a few shows of the diorama kind, with drummers, etc., but no crowd, no mountebanks, not much noise; and several *rouge et noir* tables.

"*Haute Ville.*—I examined the principal streets of the high town, saw the Palais Imperial, once the residence of Napoleon, but now shorn of all its grandeur.   I walked entirely round the ramparts, which are partially planted, and command very extensive views of the low town and harbour, the adjacent country, the sea, and the English coast.   The walls are of great height, and form a rectangle of about three hundred metres by two hundred metres, at the base of which are gardens and very pleasant promenades, planted with rows of trees."

The return from Boulogne was on the 23rd, and the next labour undertaken was an essay of very considerable historical value on the Free Miners of Dean Forest.

The essay sets out with the statement that if we look at a map of Gloucestershire, we see an angular portion northward of the spot where the river Wye joins the Severn, and abutting upon the Counties of Monmouth and Hereford.   In this angular portion is situated the Forest of Dean, which has been the property of the Crown from time immemorial.   At intervals the laws and customs by which this Forest is regulated have come under the notice of Parliament, chiefly in relation to the respective rights of the Crown on the one hand and the inhabitants on the other.   In the year 1838 an Act was passed by which three Commissioners, Mr. Sopwith, Mr. Buddle, and Mr. Probyn, were appointed to settle various disputes, and to place the government of the

Forest on a better footing. The Commissioners published an elaborate description of their labours in November 1841. They found that the Forest comprised an irregular area of about thirty miles in circuit, covered for the most part with timber, and containing extensive seams of coal and iron. From earliest times all male persons born in the hundred of St. Briavel's, in which the Forest is situated, have enjoyed the right of working these mines, subject to the leave or licence of the *gaveller* or the deputy-gaveller, and to the payment of an annual gallage rent or duty to the Crown. The share of the Crown has been reckoned as one-fifth of the produce. The Commissioners could not trace the origin of the custom, owing to its antiquity. There seems to be evidence that the Britons, and after them the Romans, worked the iron-mines of the Forest; but there is no evidence to show whether or not they worked the coal. At the time of the Norman Conquest the soil was in the possession of the Crown, and all the rights of a Royal Forest were in force. The persons by whom the mines were then worked were probably in a state of servitude, and therefore the " Free Miners," a term which had been in use for centuries, must have derived their right from some subsequent privilege. It has been supposed that the privilege originated in some such way as this :—That after a man had worked for a year and a day, or some other defined period, in the mines he was awarded the privilege of digging on his own account, provided he gave a portion of the produce to the Sovereign. The royal power was sometimes delegated. The manner in which a Free Miner exercised his right was exceedingly remarkable. He claimed the right to demand of the king's gaveller a "gale," that is, a spot of ground chosen by himself for sinking a mine; and this, provided it did not interfere with the works of any

other mine, the gaveller considered himself obliged to
give on receiving a fee of five shillings and on inserting
the name of the Free Miner in the gale book. The right
to the gale was considered by the Free Miners to carry with
it that of the timber for their works, but this extended
no further than to the use of the offal and soft wood, on
application to the keeper of a walk in which a mine is
situated.

When the Commissioners came to their inquiry they
found "foreigners" as well as Free Miners in possession,
the evidence about these being very conflicting. Some
witnesses alleged that none but Free Miners could hold
a mine either by transfer, consent, or partnership ; whilst
others maintained that a mine being originally galed to a
Free Miner might be sold, leased, devised, or passed by descent to an outsider. The outsiders, nevertheless, entered
into these mining speculations in a very extensive degree,
having up to 1835 invested £700,000, of which £200,000
were invested by one individual alone. To reconcile these
conflicting interests was the object of the appointment
of the Commission of 1838, and the general system
adopted has been a gradual transition from the antiquated
practice of past centuries to the more efficient modes of
working adopted everywhere else, with such protection
to existing rights both to the Free Miners and the
"foreigners" as could best be awarded.

In addition to the above labours Mr. Sopwith published
a careful little treatise on the Museum of Economic
Geology established in 1837. This treatise was considered of great practical service in advancing the formation of geological museums, and may be said to have
given a good start to those who have since been engaged
in the work of geological classification and arrangement.
It was often suggested that Mr. Sopwith's treatise should

be enlarged and republished in a more extended and
authoritative form, with new and original chapters on a
subject of which he was so good a teacher—mining
in relation to geology. His many other engagements
prevented the realization of this useful and practical
suggestion.

In the middle of August Mr. Sopwith went to London,
and received from Mr. Fearon his instructions for the
visit to Belgium, whence he proceeded to examine the
districts lying between the Sambre and the Meuse, with
reference to their mineral capabilities, and especially on
the bearing of such capabilities on the prosperity of a
new railway, or rather series of railways, in that part of
Belgium. He left London the last day of August for
Antwerp, and was occupied about two months in Belgium,
returning home on the 21st of October. The results of
his work, in which he was associated with Mr. Cubitt,
were embodied in a voluminous "Rapport sur le projet
du Chemin de Fer à établir dans l'entre Sambre-et-
Meuse, ainsi que sur la statistique minérale et commerciale
des contrées qu'il doit traverser." In this report every
detail required seems to have been given. He was most
cordially received on all sides, and had several private
audiences of King Leopold, whose skill and forethought
as a politician in regal command have always been acknowledged on all sides, but whose interest in scientific research
as applied to every-day life has not been generally
recognised. Speaking of one of his interviews with the
king, Mr. Sopwith says :—

"The pensive and serious expression of countenance which
is well pourtrayed in many published likenesses of King
Leopold strongly resembles the grave aspect for which Sir

Walter Scott was remarkable when silent; but, like that justly celebrated writer, no sooner does he enter into conversation than his face is brightened by great animation and an expression strongly indicative of cheerfulness and benevolence."

Writing on September 10th he says :—

"I have now had a survey of the entire length and breadth of the district of the Sambre and the Meuse intersected by the proposed railway. Captain Pernez's (one of the officials) time being limited, we have worked very hard, and on Friday I was much fatigued, but I feel no ill effects from the journey and was never in better health or spirits.

"I could have wished for more time on the line, but as I shall probably have to go over part of it again with Mr. Cubitt, or visit portions of it, it is well that I am enabled at once to sit down to my Report over the documents, plans, and sections. This I shall do at Charleroi.

"There seems every prospect of my accomplishing my survey to the satisfaction of all parties, and so far as scenery, society, fine weather, and good eating and drinking are concerned, I never spent a pleasanter week in my life. Indeed each day has unfolded new beauties, and every object has the charm of novelty.

"The idea that comfort is known *only* in England is a delusion, and hence I have been more prolific in illustration of the reverse as regards what I have myself observed.

"The roast beef of 'Old England' is another fallacy, for they cook beef and all other meats in so savoury and palatable a manner, that if roast beef had been waiting I do not think I would have preferred it to the dishes provided. So far everything has been most satisfactory to me. I like the general character of the people very much."

As a matter of course Waterloo was visited, and was described in a letter dated September 17th, 1843.

Visit to Waterloo.

"I write this at the base of the Belgic Mound, on the plains of Waterloo. A most lovely day. I have just descended from the very summit of the mound, which is 200 feet high, and 509 paces round. It commands a most perfect view of the field of battle. I had an excellent large map showing the disposition of the forces,—but I must continue my letter when more at leisure.

"Resumed on September 18th, 1843.

"*September* 17th.—I rose at half-past four, and left Charleroi at half-past five, in a cabriolet. At this early hour the shops were open. I was accompanied by Master Gustav le Bon, who speaks a little English. We travelled along on the paved road at a rate of about five miles an hour, and at Lodinilsart passed a coal waggon with eleven horses, *i.e.*, eight pairs and three leaders.

"The morning tints were exquisitely beautiful, and they lighted a district remarkable for its agricultural beauty, as well as for the vast number of mines and manufacturing establishments. The suburbs of Charleroi and adjacent villages extend for some three or four miles like a continuous street; the houses are well built, and the people generally well and always comfortably dressed. Reached Pont-à-Mellet, six miles, in an hour and twenty minutes, but part of the way was up hill; Frame, nine miles, in two hours, *i.e.*, four and a half miles an hour.

"My friend is nephew of Baron le Bon. One of his uncles was killed at Waterloo; and his father also served both there and at Salamanca. We had breakfast at Gemappe, the town where Bonaparte's carriage was taken. The charge for coffee, eggs, etc., was sevenpence halfpenny each. We went to see the interior of a handsome but unfinished church. Gustav asked me if I was a 'fervent Protestant.' I said not so strict as many in England, and especially in Scotland; and great was his surprise to learn in how strict a manner the Sunday is observed,— shops closed, no music, no travelling, etc.

'Oh la, la, la, la,' he exclaimed, 'so, so, so, so,—it is un-supportable.'

"At eight o'clock we reached Quatre Bras, and I made a drawing of the farmhouse. After resting a short time, we proceeded very pleasantly on our journey.

"I can scarcely describe my emotions of delight and of deep feeling when I viewed for the first time the FIELD OF WATERLOO. I sat down and made a coloured sketch to keep as a memento. I had excellent maps, and traced every spot, every line; the place where Bonaparte slept, and stood, and pitched his observatory. Here was General Cooke's division, there General Clinton's; here fell Sir William Ponsonby, and there the brave Sir Thomas Picton met his death.

"We pass La Belle Alliance and reach La Haye Sainte, thus immortalised :—

> "'La Haye I bear witness,—sacred is its height,
>   And sacred truly is it from that day,
> For never braver blood was spent in fight
>   Than Britain here has mingled with the clay.
> Set where thou wilt thy foot, thou scarce can tread
>   Here on a spot unhallowed by the dead.
> Here was it that the Highlanders withstood
>   The tide of hostile power, received its weight
> With resolute strength, and turned and stemmed the flood.

"We passed the very spot where Wellington stood at the commencement of the action, and on reaching the base of the mound I found four friends, Mr. and Mrs. Piddington, with Elizabeth and Rose, who had just arrived, although no particular arrangement had been made. We ascended the mount. This artificial hill, surmounted by a lion on a pedestal, is said to have cost £160,000; it stands on nearly level ground, and is, including the lion, two hundred feet high. From it I viewed the field, having before me a good map, and a description of the battle.

"It was a view of views, and a day of days gloriously bright and clear. We had a *déjeuner* at Mount St. Jean, and then drove to the village and church of Waterloo, nearly two miles from the field."

The remainder of this visit to Belgium was devoted to inspections for the report on Belgian railways then in preparation, and affords no incidents calling for particular notice. After completing his preliminary surveys, Mr. Sopwith returned to Newcastle for the rest of the year.

One sad event is recorded in the journal of this year, namely, that on August 10th at Lancaster, where he was giving evidence at a trial in company with Mr. John Buddle, he saw that gentleman for the last time. Mr. Buddle died somewhat unexpectedly, and the news of his death was a cause of deep regret. Amongst all his list of friends I think there is not one towards whom Mr. Sopwith has expressed a more sincere admiration and regard than towards this distinguished and original engineer, companion, and tried friend.

CHAPTER XXI.

1844-45.

N January 11th, 1844, a meeting of the Health of Towns Commission was held in Newcastle, over which Commission Mr. Sopwith was appointed Chairman of the first or A Committee. In this capacity he drew up the Report appertaining to the construction of dwellings, and assisted in some of the other departments. At this point of his diary I find mention made of several names which have, to some little extent, passed out of memory, but which deserve the brief note he has made respecting them. I refer to Messrs. Donkin, Cubitt, Walker, Fearon, Cheney, Milne, Baxendale, and Sir Henry de la Beche. Of them he writes under date of February 20th :—

"MR. DONKIN was a man of unusual activity and energy in his profession as a solicitor, and occupied a very influential position in Newcastle, where for several years I had the happiness to have his friendship and frequent society. This warm and generous friendship ended only with his death.

"MR. CUBITT (afterwards Sir William Cubitt) was, at the time now referred to (1844), taking a high rank in his profession as an engineer. He removed from the small house in Parliament Street to a much more commodious and elegant mansion in

Great George Street, London ; and the drawing-room in which I spent many happy hours was an engineering office. My friendly intercourse with him was connected with important railway and other business, and was continued as long as he was able to exercise his professional talent. As age advanced his memory failed him, yet in a quiet and elegant retirement at Clapham he passed the evening of his life, and to the last retained his great friendliness and hospitality.

" Of SIR HENRY DE LA BECHE I took occasion to make honourable mention in an address given to the Naturalists' Field Club at Newcastle, when I was President of that society. He stood in the front rank of geologists, and effected practical objects which will be the means of perpetuating his name. He was the sole originator of the Museum of Geology in its economic departments.

" JAMES WALKER, many years President of the Institution of Civil Engineers, was by virtue of that position considered as the nominal head of the profession, and his influence both with Government and with the profession was considerable. I always felt honoured by his friendship and hospitality, both of which it was my good fortune to enjoy,—the former during a friendship of several years, and the latter on many occasions when I visited his house.

" Of JOHN PETER FEARON I may truly say that he was at once one of the most able, amiable, and accomplished men I have ever known. He was actively engaged on several of the early railways, and I was much thrown into connection with him on the business of English and foreign railways. At a later period he became solicitor to the Attorney-General, and I fear that it was intense and incessant work that at length overcame him, and caused indisposition which closed his latter days. In society he was most elegant in manners, most refined in conversation, most effective in argument, and of unwearying perseverance in whatever he undertook. His words were few, but they were words of wisdom, and the excellence of his character was reflected and continued in his amiable family.

There was a charm of sweetness about his home, and about his memory is a halo of pure and holy light.

"With Mr. ROBERT CHENEY I had the pleasure and honour of a very friendly acquaintance, and much correspondence on matters which resulted in a considerable augmentation of the income of estates belonging to his family, and placed in a great measure under his care. My last interview with him was at Alnwick Castle, under the hospitable auspices of Algernon, the Sailor Duke, as he was sometimes called, of Northumberland. Cheney was a man of high accomplishments, and a skilful painter, both in oil and water-colours,—a most agreeable and steady friend.

"ALEXANDER MILNE was a Commissioner of Woods and Forests, a Board with which I had much connection for nearly twenty years. During all this time I was on terms of great intimacy with Mr. Milne and other officers of the Department of Woods and Forests; and to the kind confidence of his colleagues and himself I owed the honour of being appointed Commissioner for the Crown, under the Dean Forest Mining Act. Very frequent were the occasions of my having official intercourse and correspondence with him on Government business, and very frequent also were the occasions when his hospitable table and social hospitalities were available to me.

"It was at this time (February 20th, 1844) that I met Mr. BAXENDALE for the first time. He was then Chairman of the South-Eastern Railway (of which Mr. Cubitt was the Chief Engineer), and thus a special train was readily obtainable for our journey from London to Folkestone. We met at the railway station, and after Mr. Cubitt had introduced me, we all three got into the carriage appropriated for our sole use. I may add that Mr. Baxendale was at this time also the head of the vast mercantile carrying concern 'Pickford & Company,' and was not unfrequently called 'Pickford' by his friends when in familiar conversation. He had a great deal of humour, and rejoiced in jokes and anecdotes.

"'Now then,' he said, 'I suppose I may say here are three

14

of the cleverest fellows in England!' 'You come from New-castle?' he said, addressing me. 'Now I am under great obligation to a Newcastle man whose name is unknown to me (or, 'not in my recollection'), 'but whose advice enabled me to receive £500 a-year from a small estate in Lancashire, instead of £80 a-year which I had previously received.' 'Was it the Crowshaw Estate?' I asked. 'Yes.' 'Then I am the man,' I replied. I had given my opinion of the value of the property, and my valuation of £10,000 had been received by Baxendale."

On April 25th there is a curious entry, connecting for the last time in his mind the old and the new mode of travel : —

"I left the railway station at Gateshead precisely at noon. Reached Durham in one hour and five minutes by the railway, and went from thence at the rate of about ten miles an hour to Southchurch near Bishop Auckland, and after this and an omnibus ride of eleven miles, went by the Stockton and Darlington Railway to Darlington, where a detention of about an hour takes place, viz. from three to four. I took a place to London, reached York in two hours, and stopped about forty minutes. At Derby another stoppage of about an hour occurred ; and ten minutes were allowed for refreshment at Wolverton. As this is nearly the last stage in the transition which has been for some years in progress, from coach to railway travelling, it may be interesting, and perhaps useful also, to note down a few of the particulars as regards the important elements of time and expense.

"First, as to time. From Newcastle to London by the above route now occupies exactly 17 hours, including all stoppages. These are as follows: at Darlington 1 hour; at York 40 minutes; at Derby 40 minutes usually, though on this occasion it was an hour; at Wolverton 10 minutes; in all $2\frac{1}{2}$ hours ; so that $14\frac{1}{2}$ hours only are occupied in actual travelling, being very little more than 20 miles an hour.

" Cost. The present cost of travelling from Newcastle to London is as follows :—

First-class Railway and Omnibuses to Darlington	0	8	0
First-class Railway Darlington to London . .	3	15	0
Total, Newcastle to London . . .	£4	3	0

Another entry on May 1st of this year refers again to the atmospheric railway, and may be useful to some future historian.

"Breakfasted with Mr. Clegg, the inventor of the atmospheric railway, and had a long conversation with him on the subject. The atmospheric system is decidedly making progress, and I have little doubt will eventually fulfil the expectations I formed when I visited the first experiments at Shepherd's Bush. It may at some future period be interesting to know that Mr. Clegg recognises, and recommends as the best recent description of the atmospheric railway, an article in the sixteenth volume of the *British and Foreign Review; or, European Quarterly Journal*, page 304 (published April 1844)."

On May 3rd we are introduced to Rowland Hill of postal fame.

"I went this evening to dine with my valued friend Mr. Rowland Hill, the celebrated originator of the Penny Postage System. There was a small but very agreeable party, and among them were Mr. Shuttleworth, of the Stamp Office, Manchester, and Mr. Chadwick, Secretary to the Poor Law Commission. Mr. Hill is very quiet and unobtrusive in his manners generally, but, as may be imagined from what he has done, is extremely shrewd and intelligent."

One or two other personal entries deserve insertion.

"*May 6th.*—I had luncheon and a long conversation with Mr. Robert Stephenson this morning. He is as agreeable and communicative as he is clever, and his society is always a great treat to me. He gave me the outline of his views on the atmospheric railway, his report on which is now in the press, and he promised to send me a copy of it as soon as it is completed.

"At Mr. Fearon's I was introduced to Mr. Anderson, who, it had been proposed, should proceed to Belgium to conduct the final negotiations with the Government respecting the Sambre and Meuse Railway."

"*May 7th.*—Called at Mr. R. Stephenson's office, and had some conversation with Mr. George Stephenson, who wishes Dr. Buckland to join me in a visit to him at his house near Chesterfield. He is looking remarkably well, is very animated, and displays great kindness of manner in those directions where he has formed a favourable opinion. On the other hand he is said to be equally unbending under opposite circumstances. Be this as it may, he is unquestionably a man of extraordinary powers of mind, and to his vigorous exertions it is that we owe in a great measure the introduction of railway travelling on a large scale. However idly the world may dream of conquerors and heroes, few men at any period of known history have conferred greater benefits on their fellow-creatures than the originators of locomotive travelling and cheap postage,—the one almost annihilating time and space in bringing together persons from distant parts on business, or for friendly intercourse, and the other enabling every class of society to rejoice in that next of social blessings, frequent correspondence."

On May 26th Mr. Sopwith is again in Belgium, when he had an audience with King Leopold, which he thus records :—

"Mr. Anderson and I were shown into a large room, with some good paintings. Presently two aides-de-camp in full dress, with stars, etc., came, and very politely explained that the King had not yet returned from church, but was expected very soon. In a few minutes His Majesty and suite arrived; he bowed as he passed, and we were shown into an adjoining apartment; the aides-de-camp retiring, we were left alone with the King, who wore a dark-blue military dress, gold epaulettes, a profusion of orders, and a handsome sword.

"After the usual complimentary bowing, the King observed that he understood we intended to be interested in some occupation in this country. I replied that the information which Mr. Cubitt and I had obtained in our former surveys had inspired with confidence parties who were disposed to execute extensive works, and that Mr. Anderson and I, representing these parties, were pursuing the requisite negotiations. Mr. Anderson said that great assistance and facility had been given by the Minister of Public Works, whose consideration and talents were of great value. In this commendation the King very heartily joined, and said: 'Although the Sambre and Meuse Railway is not so great as many of your vast English works, yet in my opinion it is a very solid and useful one, and the calculation of its trade has been derived from the actual experience of many years.'

"I replied, 'That, your Majesty, is precisely the opinion that has been formed—viz., that if it hold out less brilliant prospects than many new undertakings, yet it is more surely based, and is certain to be of great public utility.'

"Mr. Anderson said it would be highly satisfactory to the parties in London to know that His Majesty entertained this opinion. The King entered at considerable length into details connected with the subject, as the extension to Sedan, the difficult navigation of the Meuse, etc., observing that though its scenery was very magnificent, yet, what with floods in winter, and shallow water in summer, it was very bad to navigate.

"I observed that the district of the Sambre and Meuse was the very heart of Belgium, containing in vast abundance those minerals which constitute the foundations of national wealth; that in a small compass there were coal, iron, marble, slate, and yet a great part of this district was unopened, nay, almost inaccessible.

"Referring to the exports of coal to the Ardennes, His Majesty observed that this railway was the only mode by which they could obtain an increased supply. He also referred to the marbles of Dinant, and was pleased to hear that I had visited the manufactory there, and at Rame. I said that I had placed specimens of these marbles in the Museum of Economic Geology in London, and I presented to His Majesty my account of that Institution (having previously requested permission to do so in writing). He accepted it with great complaisance, saying, 'I am greatly obliged, I am grateful; it is a very interesting subject, and one that I am very fond of.' Looking at the section on the back, he added, 'There are very interesting sections like this as you travel on the railway towards Charleroi.' I informed His Majesty that I had seen them, and that the section on the book represented coal mines belonging to the Prince of Wales, and which I had surveyed on behalf of the Duchy of Cornwall. He turned over the leaves, and when he came to the lithographed plate of models, I said that they represented models which I had made of wood to represent the principal geological features that relate to mining, and that I had given a series of them to the Museum in Brussels. 'It is very kind of you,' said the King. I added that I would feel greatly honoured if His Majesty would allow me also to present a series to him. To this a very kind assent was at once given. I said that the undertaking of foreign enterprise, and consequent investment of capital, the interchange of scientific research, and the development of the natural sources of wealth, afforded a solid prospect with reference to the peace of nations, and the increase of their prosperity. His Majesty assented very fully to these remarks, and expressed similar sentiments.

"These are some of the subjects, which I have made mention of as likely to recall distinct impressions of a very agreeable interview. Mr. Anderson joined from time to time in the conversation. Nothing could be more affable and winning than the courtesy and kindness of His Majesty, and we took our leave with the most agreeable sentiments of respect and regard."

On June 19th a new railway triumph is entered.

"On this day, for the first time, the whole railway journey from London to Newcastle was opened to the public.

"I left Euston Square Station with Elizabeth Piddington by the 9 o'clock train, and reached Gateshead, Newcastle, at 9.30 p.m., this being the first journey performed by a train for the conveyance of the public from London to Newcastle in 12½ hours.

"As it may be interesting at some future time to refer to the details of this step in the rapid march of locomotive travelling, I annex them from memoranda made during the journey.

"The day was remarkably favourable for the journey."

	Hours.	Min.	TRAVELLING.		STOPPAGES.	
			Hours.	Min.	Hours.	Min.
Left London	9	3	—	—	—	—
Arrived Tring	10	10	1	7	—	—
Departed Do.	—	11	-	—	—	1
Arrived Wolverton	—	50	-	39	—	—
Departed Do.	—	56	—	—	—	6
Arrived Rugby	11	58	1	2	—	—
Departed Do.	12	8½	—	—	—	10½
Arrived Leicester	—	42½	—	34	—	—
Departed Do.	—	48	—	—	—	5½
Stoppage, 34 miles	—	—	—	—	—	1¾
Arrived Derby	1	41	—	51¼	—	—
Departed Do.	2	20½	—	—	—	39½
Arrived Chesterfield	3	—	—	39½	—	—
Departed Do.	—	4	—	—	—	4
Arrived Masbro'	3	29½	—	25½	—	—
Departed Do.	—	35	—	—	—	5½
Arrived Barnsley	4	—	—	25	—	—
Do. Normanton	—	16½	—	16½	—	—
Departed Do.	—	22	—	—	—	5½
Arrived Castleford	—	30	—	8	—	—
Departed Do.	—	30½	—	—	—	½

	Hours.	Min.	TRAVELLING.		STOPPAGES.	
			Hours.	Min.	Hours.	Min.
Arrived Bolton and Tadcaster .	—	53½	—	23	—	—
Departed Do.	—	54	—	—	—	½
Arrived York	5	7½	—	13½	—	—
Departed Do.	—	57	—	—	—	49½
Arrived Alne	6	15	—	18	—	—
Departed Do.	—	19	—	—	—	4
Arrived Sessay	—	32¾	—	13¾	—	—
Departed Do.	—	33¼	—	—	—	½
Arrived Thirsk	—	41	—	7¾	—	—
Departed Do.	—	43	—	—	—	2
Arrived Northallerton . . .	—	57	—	14	—	—
Departed Do. .	7	2	—	—	—	5
Arrived Cowton	—	15½	—	13½	—	—
Departed Do.	—	17	—	—	—	1½
Arrived Darlington . . .	—	32	—	15	—	—
Departed Do. . . .	—	41	—	—	—	9
Arrived Rudd's Hill . . .	8	10	—	29	—	—
Departed Do. . . .	—	12	—	—	—	2
Arrived Belmont	—	30	—	18	—	—
Departed Do. . . .	—	38	—	—	—	8
Arrived Brockley . . .	9	5	—	27	—	—
Departed Do. . . .	—	11	—	—	—	6
Arrived Gateshead . . .	—	30	—	19	—	—
Total . .	—	—	9	39½	2	47¾

DISTANCES.

		Hrs.	Min.
London to Rugby . . .	83 miles in	2	48
Midland Counties . . .	49 ,, ,,	1	25
North Midland	64 ,, ,,	1	46½
York, and N. Midland . .	24 ,, ,,	0	44½
To Darlington	45 ,, ,,	1	22
To Newcastle (G. Station) .	38½ ,, ,,	1	33

In August he had a visit from Mr. and Mrs. William
Chambers of Edinburgh; and in September he was
engaged in surveys with Brunel, in Northumberland.
On September 7th he and Brunel went into the coffee-
room of the Queen's Head Inn, Newcastle, and en-
countered Mr. George Stephenson, who good-naturedly
shook Mr. Brunel by the collar, asking him what business
he had "north of the Tyne." Mr. Stephenson had been

for some time engaged in projecting a railway through Northumberland, to which the railway of Mr. Brunel was in direct opposition. Brunel, like Mr. Sopwith, was sanguine as to the final success of the atmospheric railway at some future day.

1845.

The year 1845 brought with it a great amount of work to my friend, who was in Newcastle, London, and Edinburgh, as if they were all his natural home. There is, however, but little matter of moment until March 8th, on the evening of which day he went to a meeting at Lord Northampton's, by whom he was introduced to Prince Albert, "a fine-looking man, with handsome face and good figure." The Prince, who was very pleased to make his acquaintance, spoke to him warmly of the geological models, the surveys of the Duchy of Cornwall which Mr. Sopwith had made for the Crown, and the interest which the King of the Belgians was taking in the mineral wealth of his kingdom.

On March 19th, in company with Mr. George Stephenson, Mr. Fearon, Mr. Piddington, and Mr. Benjamin Scott, Mr. Sopwith again left for Brussels on another railway survey. The journey all through was rendered very pleasant, especially by George Stephenson, about whom, on March 30th and April 4th and 5th, there are special entries.

" *March* 30*th.*—I may here observe that during our journey, and especially when resting in the evening at the hotels, I derived a large share of instruction and enjoyment from the society of my fellow-travellers. *One* of these, known in all countries, and to be known in all time as foremost in that march of improvement which has so eminently marked the present century, has long been known to me by occasional but brief opportunities of intercourse. The present journey has afforded an opportunity of becoming more intimately known to him, and of participating in that store of practical information, quick observation, and mental energy, by which Mr. Stephenson has climbed from a humble origin to the elevated position he now occupies.

" It is most interesting to hear him relate the anecdotes of his youth. They are chapters pregnant with instruction and encouragement. Commencing at so early an age as three years, his memory reverts back to a bird-nesting scene. He was carried to see a nest, and the impression caused by the little helpless inmates fluttering about induced an affection for birds which ripened with age, and has ever since remained. At one time he ploughed for twopence a day and breakfast; at another was toiling for twelve hours in an engine-house; then occupying his evenings with repairing clocks and watches, and so gaining money which he applied to the education of his son, the present distinguished engineer.

" Thirty-three years ago he constructed the first efficient loco-motive engine that had been made, and afterwards followed step by step in the construction of the first great railways in the kingdom. His graphic descriptions of many of these and similar incidents are so full of character, so plain, honest, and unassuming, and at the same time so marked by all the energy of true genius, that I rejoice here to record some faint memorial of them that may recall to mind the pleasant hours passed with this truly great man in the present expedition.

" It is most amusing to hear of his labouring to convince his fellow-workmen in early years that the world turned round, they arguing that at the bottom they would fall off! ' Ah!' said their more inquiring companion, 'you don't understand it.'

" Guided by a practical knowledge of geological structure, Mr. Stephenson purchased an estate containing valuable beds of coal, and in short his whole life has been so great an example of the value of practical application of science, that it is to be hoped he may some time employ his leisure in drawing up an autobiography, which would be of most surpassing interest, and would form the best memorial of his progress.

"Mr. Starbuck, who accompanies Mr. Stephenson, is largely concerned in the management of business relating to locomotive engines, etc. He has travelled much in various parts of the world, speaks French with great facility, and his society added much to the pleasure of a journey where our enjoyment, though heightened by external conditions of weather, scenery, etc., was chiefly derived from interchange of thought and cheerful conversation."

DINNER TO GEORGE STEPHENSON.

"*April 4th.*—We returned to Brussels, and at four in the afternoon accompanied Mr. Stephenson to a magnificent dinner which was given to him by the engineers of Belgium, at one of the principal restaurants in Brussels.

"The room was magnificently decorated; at one end of it were a number of flags surmounted by the Union Jack (six Belgian flags and five English). These surrounded a handsome marble pedestal with the bust of Mr. Stephenson crowned with laurels.

"The table was covered with luxuriant viands, and in the centre was an archway with a locomotive engine (*The Rocket*). Mr. Masni, the chief director of the Belgian railways, presided. Mr. Stephenson sat on his right hand, and I was placed on his left. About forty gentlemen were present, all of whom were connected with railway management. Nothing could exceed the enthusiasm with which they all joined in giving a welcome to the distinguished father of English engineering."

"*April 5th.*—Mr. Stephenson and I went to the Palace of Lacken, where we had the honour of a private audience with His Majesty the King of the Belgians. As on two former occasions when I have been in the presence of His Majesty, he stood during the whole of the interview, and conversed very freely on several topics. He thanked me for the models I had

sent him, and said I must have devoted much time to these
subjects.   When we took our leave his Majesty shook hands
with both, and said to me, 'I wish you success in all your
undertakings.'

"Throughout the interview he displayed a complete knowledge of the general structure of the Belgian coal-fields, and
spoke of the great importance of economy in a fuel which
had become indispensable, and which formed the basis of all
our manufactures, locomotion, and domestic comfort.

"In the evening we went to Ghent, accompanied by Mr.
Masni, and had a carriage appropriated to us.

"We examined the works at the new station at Brussels."

"*April 6th.*—We left Ghent in the private railway carriage
of Mons. Masni, the head director of State railways in Belgium.
Breakfasted at Ostend, and left at ten in the *Widgeon* steam
packet, and reached Dover at six, just in time to catch a train
to London, where we arrived at eleven, thus completing the
journey from Ghent to London in seventeen hours, nearly half
of which were spent on the sea."

A fortnight later he is once more in Belgium.

"*April 18th.*—Interview with the Minister of Public Works,
Mons. Deschamps, on the subject of negotiations for the
West Flanders railways.   I was occupied the whole day in an
attentive study of this project; and not approving of the lines
suggested in the several plans I have examined, I drew up
a new arrangement which appears to me to possess several
very important advantages, namely, by occupying nearly the
whole of the province of West Flanders with lines accommodating
the important towns of Bruges, Roulers, Courtrai, Menin,
Ypres, and Poperinghe in one line, and Furnes, Dixmude, and
Thielt in another.

"These lines I have studied with reference to future
extension, as well as local convenience, and in the evening I
had the satisfaction to find that the Minister referred to this
map only during an interview which lasted three hours, and

during part of which time he explained and advocated it to
the deputation from Bruges, headed by the Governor of West
Flanders; and upon this map the convention is founded, all
the terms of which were fully discussed on the following
day."

"*April 21st.*—Accompanied Mr. Chantrell to the office of
the Minister of Public Works, where the convention for the
West Flanders Railway was formally completed, and signed by
the Minister, myself, and Mr. Chantrell, my signature being
on behalf of William Parry Richards and John Peter Fearon,
from whom I held a power of attorney to conduct and close
this important step towards the establishment of railway
communication throughout the province of West Flanders.

"Immediately after receiving from the hands of the Minister
the official duplicate of the convention, I left Brussels, and
reached Ghent at two in the afternoon, accompanied by young
Chantrell.

"Left in the railway diligence and went to Bruges. A
carriage-and-pair was in waiting at the station, and I at once
started in it for Thourout and Roulers."

"*April 22nd.*—Left Roulers at five in the morning, and
reached Courtrai at half-past seven. After breakfast started
with a fresh pair of horses to visit Menin and Ypres.

"We returned to Courtrai to dinner, and afterwards proceeded to Ingelmunster and Bruges, where we arrived at
half-past nine."

"*April 23rd.*—Left Bruges at eight o'clock, and went by
railway to Ostend, and had a delightful sail across to Dover."

In the early part of May Mr. Sopwith revisited London
on business connected with the Newcastle, Berwick, and
Northumberland Railway Bills, together with other business relating to the Woods and Forests Committee. These
occupations left him but little leisure, concerning which,
however, he makes no complaint, but rather rejoices that
his time should be so well occupied. During this visit,

moreover, he was gratified by attaining a distinction which he had all his active life most wished for. On June 5th he was elected, and on the 18th was received, as a Fellow of the Royal Society. The reception of this distinction is recorded in a brief paragraph of the diary.

"*June 19th.*—Went to the Royal Society at Somerset House, Professor Owen in the chair (in the absence of the President, the Marquis of Northampton); and went through the formality of being admitted a Fellow of the Royal Society. If this, under any circumstances, be deemed an honour, I think it is still more so when brought about—as my admission has been—by direct invitation and persuasion of the President, and by the unasked-for suffrages of so many eminent Fellows. That kind influence was used by friends I have no doubt, but I entirely abstained from asking any one to vote for me."

Whilst Mr. Sopwith's numerous friends were congratulating him on having so honourably won what has been called the "blue ribbon" in science, an event leading to a new phase in the history of his active life was near at hand, as will be told in the succeeding chapter.

CHAPTER XXII.

A CHANGE OF CAREER.

1845-46.

IN July 1845 we enter into a new phase in the life of Mr. Sopwith. Up to this time he had been acting entirely on his own account in business, chiefly as an engineer and railway surveyor; but some little time before the date named a communication had been made to him by Mr. Hodgson, for whom he had the greatest respect, that he should become chief agent of Mr. T. W. Beaumont's lead-mines in Northumberland and Durham. The change meant his removal from Newcastle to Allenheads, disconnection from his large circle of miscellaneous clients in engineering and mining, and occupation for three-fourths of his time.

It was a serious question amongst his friends whether this new arrangement was or was not a prudent one, and much difference of opinion was expressed on the matter. In a retrospect which he made thirty-one years later in his life, he himself reviews the matter, adding a few reminiscences which are worth repeating as a good indication of the simple and genuine nature of the writer.

" First, and very far indeed beyond all other considerations, were those which related to the comfort of my family and my enjoyment at home. This indeed so far exceeded all other views as to leave me no option, and on this I shall add a few words of comment,—the result of actual experience and of frequent and long-continued reflection.

"It was quite true that at the time the proposition was made to me to take the agency of the Beaumont mines I had gained what I may fairly call a good position in my profession. I had conducted very extensive surveys, both on the surface and under ground, at Alston in Cumberland; and over a large portion of land in the centre of Northumberland. I had in 1829 successfully competed with McAdam, then in the zenith of his fame as a road engineer; and my line, after being approved by a majority of forty to one by the local trustees, received the assent of Parliament in 1830. Fifteen years of active employment followed, and my engagements assumed more and more of a public character, and of what may be called professional eminence.

"In 1832 I made the greatly valued acquisition of the friendship of Surtees, in addition to that of Hodgson and Hedley—names ever to be treasured amongst my richest memories. The generous friendship of William Ord, Esq., of Whitfield, and the equally warm and kind friendship of Sir John Swinburne, added much to my happiness.

"In 1832 I was elected a member of the Institution of Civil Engineers, on the special volunteer offer of proposal of Telford; and in that year I was much employed and consulted by the Commissioners of Woods and Forests. At this time my 'Account of Mining Districts' and 'Isometrical Treatise' were favourably received; and the latter work, though very technical, passed into a second edition.

"In 1833 I laid out and surveyed a line of colliery railway from Jesmond, near Newcastle, to St. Laurence on the river Tyne; and in 1835 I had made surveys of part of the Newcastle and Carlisle Railway from near Corbridge to near Hexham and Haydon Bridge. I had in 1845 been much employed in surveying and setting out lines of railway in England and on the Continent, and had a fair prospect of success in that very lucrative department of civil engineering. I had entirely accomplished a most important mineral survey of the Forest of Dean; and my large models of that, and other districts, had not only been much admired at the British Association meeting at Newcastle, but had won the honour of a Telford Medal at the Institution of Civil Engineers.

"Most unexpectedly, and entirely unsought for by me, I was asked by the Commissioners of Woods and Forests to take the high position of Commissioner on behalf of the Crown in the Dean Forest Mining Act, and in three years the duties of that Commission were brought to a satisfactory close.

"In 1844 the Coal Trade Committee of the North of England appointed a special committee of the most eminent members of their body to settle all disputes relating to the coal trade; and they further appointed a 'tribunal of appeal,' with the absolute power of final decision, viz. Messrs. John Grey, John Clayton, and myself.

"These appointments and employments were in the highest range of services connected with coal-mine engineering.

"In railway engineering I was among the very first who were largely employed in extensive and profitable surveys; and in lead mining, the position of Chief Agent of all the three districts of mines in Coalcleugh, Allendale, and Weardale was undoubtedly the first position open to a professional man. The offer of it to me was at all events a great honour, and my acceptance of it was based on considerations such as the following:—

"My professional avocations took me very frequently from home, sometimes for weeks, and even months. This separated me from my family, and it seemed likely that continued success in general practice would ere long render it necessary for me to remove my offices to London.

"To constant residence in the Metropolis my dear Jane had a great objection, on the score of health and domestic enjoyment. Upon this I made my determination. I was assured

15

that a new house should be built for me, with gardens, and open space of pleasure grounds for my children to play in.

"The prospect of comfort in the exercise of my duties at home, the reasonable prospect of quietude in the evening of life, was pressed on my attention. All this I now look upon as past. Twenty-six years have since been spent in active service, and for other five years I have had the quietude of retirement."

The duties of the chief agent of the Allenhead mines commenced on July 1st, 1845, but before settling down to them certain other matters of business had to be cleared up. One of these was the giving of evidence at Cardiff on the trial of Lord Dunraven *versus* Mr. Malins, for breach of covenant in working his mines. Cockburn, afterwards Chief Justice of England, was the opposing counsel, and with Mr. Frank Forster, a colleague of Mr. Sopwith's, was "exceedingly sharp." Mr. Sopwith's own examination followed, and he got off lightly.

"'You are paid for coming here, are you not?' said Counsel Cockburn. I said I had not yet been paid, but hoped to be so. —'Ah!' said C., 'what I mean is, you would not have come here without being paid!' I answered that I had done more romantic things than that in my lifetime. My examination now set in with the same aspect as in Forster's case, and to an early question I was pertly told to answer 'Yes' or 'No.' I answered 'Yes;' but I added, 'Unless I explain exactly what I mean by that answer, it may lead the jury to form an erroneous conclusion.' My keen interrogator would have gladly dispensed with any explanation, but the judge ruled that I might explain my answer, a decision gladly acquiesced in by the jury. I explained the matter in my own way, and when I finished, I was told I might go down!"

After some further delays in surveying Plymouth Iron

Works, and in visiting Edinburgh on matters connected
with the Lead Hills arbitration, during which he was the
visitor of Mr. Robert Chambers, he entered formally on
his duties at the W. B. Lead-mines, so called from the
initials of a former owner, William Blackett, the produce
of whose mines was specially well known in the markets
of England, the Continent, and elsewhere as W. B., or
sometimes as Blackett Lead. The commencement of
this new career is recorded in the subjoined entries.

"To Allenheads.

"*August 25th.*—I left Newcastle at five o'clock in the afternoon, and, accompanied by Mr. Delemaine, went to Bywell
Hall, and dined with Mr. J. G. Atkinson."

"*August 26th.*—Went with Mr. Atkinson to Allenheads,
calling at Allen Smelt Mills by the way. I had a meeting
with Mr. W. Crawhall in the house he has so long occupied in
his capacity as resident agent of Allenhead Mines; and a walk
over the premises was a kind of formality approaching to the
giving up of possession, but not quite so, as I most readily
assented to his remaining a few days longer, on his expressing
a wish to do so.

"The books of account and plans were handed over to me
in the office, when I was made acquainted with the assistants
and clerks, and may thus be considered as having been formally
installed into so much of my appointment as relates to East
and West Allendale, formerly, and up to even recently, in two
separate agencies, but now combined in one."

"*September 26th.*—Accompanied the inspectors of the mines on
their quarterly examination of the several workings preparatory
to arranging the prices for new contracts. This underground
survey is of great interest, as exhibiting the state of the veins
of lead, or the condition of rocks where levels are being driven
in non-productive ground, and I made notes and drawings of
the more prominent indications."

"*September* 27th.—Among the new occupations to which my agency at Allenheads introduces me is that of being considered as 'the master of the hounds,' the inhabitants of Upper Allendale having been from time immemorial, as it is said, fond of hare-hunting as an amusement, and, owing to the nature of the country, this amusement is more followed by persons on foot than by horsemen; the latter, indeed, being few in number, and the pedestrians being quite a multitude.

"This was the first 'meet' since I came to Allenheads, and, mounted on an excellent pony, I followed the hounds, and, for this day at all events, took an active share in the hunt, and in some of the subsequent festivities, as 'master of the hounds.' This position was willingly accorded to me, but the efficiency and general regulation of the 'hunt' practically devolved on Mr. Steel, with whom it remained until it gradually succumbed to a prevailing indifference among the community. Mr. Steel was a pedestrian hunter, and a surprisingly active one. It was amusing to observe his activity in 'louping' a dyke, and the glee with which he received the annual subscriptions."

"*October* 4th.—At Allenheads, where I 'let the bargains,' as it is termed, for the East Allendale Mines. This was followed by a dinner at the inn, at which all the inspectors, chief clerks, etc., were usually present, and at which I was expected to preside."

"*November* 6th.—In London. 'Meeting at Mr. Beaumont's, when the new house was determined upon and the scale arranged. I dined with Mr. Beaumont.' This is the brief memorandum as written at the time in my pocket diary. I had made the building of a new house, with spacious garden and ornamental ground, the sole condition on which I would accept the agency of the W. B. Mines. All other matters, such as amount of salary, arrangements as to time of residence, and, in short, all other details, I was willing to leave either in the sole disposition of Mr. Beaumont, or, at all events, as matters to be considered and discussed, but the new house was of the very essence of the agreement."

In December Mr. Sopwith visited Paris for the first time; but seems to have been less interested in that remarkable city than one would have expected. He returned to Allenheads to close the year, a year which he always re-surveyed with great satisfaction.

1846.

In January 1846, during a visit to London, he makes a note on certain reflections which occurred to him after a conversation with his friend Mr. Hodgson, at The Elms, Hampstead. He is satisfied, from the experience of his past life, that a plain and honest and straightforward path is the only one that can lead to permanent comfort and prosperity. To overcome all influence of prejudice and passion, to rise superior to the mere consideration of selfish interests, to look with charity and forbearance on whatever calls for indulgence, and to promote kindly feelings and generous sentiments,—these are objects worthy of daily perseverance, and productive of peace and happiness in the midst of all the career of business and the various and often deceptive fascinations of society. It has been truly gratifying, he adds, to find in Mr. Beaumont, and in those who immediately represent him in his absence, an entire accordance with those sentiments, and a desire to base every proceeding on a firm and honourable foundation.

An entry follows anent a visit to St. Paul's, Knightsbridge.

"*February* 1st.—Sunday. I went to St. Paul's, Wilton Place, where Puseyism reigns in all its glory, and a finger-post 'To Rome' might be appropriately placed in its chancel. This is the church of the noble and the great, of Lady Marys and Lord Johns, with here and there the crimson waistcoat of a favoured footman.　I never yet in any church found a silver key to fail; and as there appeared in Sunday notices on the door something like an unusual attention to details of the service, I was resolved to try an experiment here.

"Several pews close to where I stood had abundant room for myself and for one other person standing in the aisle, but neither the courtesy of the inmates nor the exertions of the vergers were so far extended as to offer the accommodation of a seat.

"Tired with standing, I left this goodly congregation of fine raiment and gold rings, enjoyed a most delightful walk in the park, had luncheon with the Dean of Westminster (Dr. Buckland), and met Mr. Calverly Trevelyan."

In February of this year (1846) Mr. Sopwith published a pamphlet of seventeen pages, entitled "Observations addressed to the Miners and Other Workmen employed in Mr. Beaumont's Lead-mines in East and West Allendale and Weardale." The pamphlet opens with the announcement of an increase of wages to the miners, followed by a suggestion for the formation of a fund for the relief of arrears, and by an urgent appeal in favour of paying ready money for everything. "Let me," he says, "most strongly and affectionately urge this on your attention; consider it well individually, canvass it with your friends, weigh it in the balance. If it be found wanting in reason, in prudence, in common sense, neglect it; if it appears to you to be reasonable and prudent, act upon it; advise your partners and your friends to act upon it; consider well the differences between the price of credit and of ready-money payments. You will assuredly find, in many cases, eightpence or ninepence ready cash buying as much as a shilling on credit; that for a shilling, paid after a year or half a year's credit, you only have got eight or nine pennyworth of goods; whereas if you spend a shilling in ready money, you get as much as you would have to pay one-and-fourpence for on credit. Do not consider anyone's interest in this but your own." Then, towards the close, touching on the subject of temperance, he adds, " To everyone who has a family, I would venture to say, Avoid the alehouse, and study the happiness of yourself and family at your own fireside."

" *February* 21*st.*—In the evening I attended the first soirée of the Marquis of Northampton, at his house (adjoining Mr. Beaumont's) in Piccadilly Terrace. This assemblage was considered to be as numerous and brilliant as any that has been held during the Presidency of the noble Marquis. I met a great number of highly valued friends, and by going soon after nine I had an opportunity of examining the various drawings and works of art and science which were exhibited. His Royal Highness Prince Albert came soon after ten, and spent some time in examining the various attractive objects which the tables presented. He especially devoted some fifteen or twenty minutes to the inspection of Parsey's air-machine, during which time I was at the side of the table opposite to the Prince, and had thus the opportunity of seeing and hearing all that passed. His inquiries were all of a sensible and intelligent character, expressed with great suavity and a becoming cheerfulness. The Premier, Sir Robert Peel, arrived about eleven, dressed in a Windsor uniform, and appeared in good health and spirits. The Dean of Westminster (Dr. Buckland) introduced the Dean of Llandaff (Conybeare) to Sir Robert Peel; but Mr. Conybeare thought he said Sir Robert Dean, and so the interview passed off as a mere matter-of-course introduction to some Oxford baronet, as the Dean of Llandaff assumed 'Sir Robert Dean' to be. These two geological deans and the scarlet riband and glittering star of Sir Roderick Murchison bid fair for the prospects of geology."

A note on March 6th and 7th introduces us to Faraday.

" All the world and his wife went to hear Faraday lecture on his new discoveries in electro-magnetism. I went an hour too soon, and so called upon him, and spent the interval very agreeably with the learned lecturer. The crush to hear Faraday outdoes the opera crowd, and the noble President of the Royal Society sits to hear the errand-boy of a few years ago bring forth the hitherto hidden secrets of Nature.

" On my return home, I found my friend W. G. Armstrong, of Newcastle. On the following morning, Faraday headed a recommendation of Mr. Armstrong to the Royal Society, and I accompanied him to Mr. John Taylor, Professor Owen, Sir Henry de la Beche, Mr. Phillips, and the Dean of Westminster, who all added their names to his recommendation paper. It was well said by Faraday, ' What is the Royal Society for if not for such men as Armstrong ? ' "

On July 14th Mr. Joseph Paxton comes on the scene.

" Dr. Buckland (now Dean of Westminster) came to my house at St. Mary's Terrace, Newcastle, on a visit, and very greatly did I enjoy his agreeable society.

" Much activity prevailed in Newcastle, owing to a flower-show and a cattle-show being held this week. Returning with some friends from the Cattle Show on Thursday evening, they accepted my invitation to take tea at my house. The party was a somewhat notable one, comprising the Dean of Westminster, Sir James Duke, Mr. George Stephenson, and Mr. Paxton (of Chatsworth). A most lively conversation occurred ; and I was not a little proud to entertain so many men of mark. Mr. Stephenson's humour was to call Mr. Paxton ' the Duke,' and Sir James was now and then spoken to by his surname of Duke. The servant hearing this, told Mrs. S. on her arrival at home that she did not know who all the gentlemen were, but that ' two of them were dukes,' an array of aristocracy which was alarming in so quiet an establishment. But no four dukes in the kingdom could have equalled the noble aristocracy of talent then assembled in my drawing-room. These four persons represent in an eminent degree Geology, Engineering, Commerce, and Agriculture.

" Dr. Buckland left on Friday morning from the station at Gateshead, where he introduced me to the Duke of Cambridge, with whom I had a short conversation."

The change of career into which Mr. Sopwith had now fully entered led to the necessity for him to have a fixed place of business in the metropolis, and in November he was in possession of chambers at No. 1, Chapel Place. In this month he brought to a close, I think with some regret, all his business transactions with the Office of Woods and Forests, and therewith we may consider that his professional life as an engineer in general practice came to an end.

On his own part he seemed soon to become reconciled to his new career ; and as he had stipulated that a house should be built for him at Allenheads with gardens around it, the whole designed by himself, his constructive genius relieved his mind from all regretful reminiscences.

CHAPTER XXIII.

1847-56.

SETTLED down in his new home at Allenheads, but retaining for a time the house at St. Mary's Terrace, Newcastle, and moving his chambers in London to Chapel Place, the life of Mr. Sopwith became, in his new sphere of work, very regular, and free of much of the previous rapid movement and excitement to which he had been accustomed. We find him, however, often coming up to London; and in 1847 there are records of a very interesting visit in town, with Mr. Robert Chambers and other friends as agreeable companions. So the year 1847 smoothly glided away.

1848.

In 1848 one or two little episodes are related: one of an adventure on February 16th with Mr. W. G. Armstrong and himself in a mine at Allenheads, where the two narrowly escaped being pounded into nothing by passing through a water-wheel, I had almost said, from one passage to another. Imagine a dark subterranean cave just large enough to hold the machinery of the engine. One of the attachments is a ponderous beam, which, worked by the regular action of a water-wheel, keeps slowly moving up and down, both movements completed in about ten seconds. The only mode of passing is to creep as flatly as possible from one side to the other in the short interval of about four seconds when it admits of passage. The two gentlemen did it at the impulse of the moment, one after another, and thought little of it at the time, but a great deal of it afterwards. A more pleasant episode is at Melrose Abbey, on May 13th, in company of Mr. and Mrs. Robert Chambers and Professor Pillans. The "old custodian" gives the party a full account of the abbey, got, he tells them, from " *Chammer's Jarnal.*" This is in the afternoon. Near midnight and in the bright moonlight they returned with Mr. Mainzer, a musician, and some of his musical friends. Mr. Sopwith was standing close to Robert Chambers in the very centre of the abbey, when the deep tones of a Gregorian chant broke upon the silence. The effect was one of startling novelty and grandeur. Mainzer, a proficient in this style of music, had gone to the place of the high altar, under the eastern window, and from thence his deep and expressive tones floated through the stillness. Chambers listened in astonishment to the end, and then exclaimed, " I feel just bathed in poetry. Few such moments occur in the journey of life."

On November 30th Mr. Sopwith and Mr. Donkin dined with the writers of *Punch.* There was much humour and anecdote ; but, none, he thought, excelled his friend Donkin, " in wit's worth " at Mr. Punch's table.

On December 20th of this year Thomas Wentworth Beaumont, Esq., the owner of the W. B. Lead-mines, died at Bournemouth. " He was," says Mr. Sopwith, " a kind employer and generous friend."

From January to May 1849 there was a strike of miners. According to quarterly contract, each miner undertook to work during the week for forty hours, in five eight-hour shifts. It was detected that the men did not work their full time, and when remonstrated with they struck work. Mr. Sopwith had interviews with them many times, but would not make any concession, although he remained on friendly terms with them all. They at last voluntarily came back to their occupation. One incident he records with much pleasure. In settling some wages whilst the men were on strike, £5 were paid them in excess of what was due, by an accident. The honest fellows brought it all back,—a touch of nobility which he never failed to honour when on any occasion the subject of strikes was under discussion.

A note on October 17th records the commencement of the Elswick Works of the famous Armstrong Company. The company consisted of five persons—namely, William George Armstrong, his father, Alderman William Armstrong, Alderman Donkin, Richard Lambert, and William Cruddace. With a moderate investment from each it was determined to commence the works which have since grown to such magnificent dimensions. Mr. Sopwith could, if he had pleased, have become a partner in this wonderful work; but he had made up his mind already that the superintendence of the Allenhead Mines should be his future care, and he was not the man to change his mind even for this most tempting offer.

The property had now passed into the possession of Mr. Beaumont's son, at the time a minor; so much the more the reason why his own experience should be devoted to the important work he had in hand.

He has a note, dated March 22nd, 1850, relative to the great forthcoming Exhibition of the Industries of the World; but, curiously enough, the course of the journal is broken or lost for several months at this point. A reference to the Theatrical Fund dinner, with Mr. Benjamin Webster in the chair, is the principal incident named in 1850.

1852.

A brief note on April 10th, 1852, conveys an excellent notion of Mr. Sopwith's views on the course of life.

" If it were possible to foresee what will happen, what will be important, and what will be insignificant, then of course I would concentrate my whole time and attention on that which is to happen, and leave all the rest to the oblivion and insignificance which fate, or Providence, or the order of events, by whatever name it is called, has destined ; but so long as we know not the course of future events, it is well that every matter in its turn be duly considered, be regularly recorded, and placed on such a footing as can be understood and acted upon by others if need be. This may be plodding and 'slow;' but if there is stability placed within our reach, it is only by order and method, not by lucky hits, that we can obtain stability."

In a subsequent entry another line of reflection is offered, bearing on the work of principles from details.

" It will, I believe, always be found that the harmonious and effective working of any great concern depends on a close and constant study of details ; but then such details taken separately are of no significance ; it is only when collected into groups of general facts and conclusions, and those groups, again, compared one with another, so as to present a clear view of the whole in its true proportions, that a collected and useful comprehension of the whole scheme can be formed. It is, in fact, only that habit of mind which can patiently consider the minute operations, and grasp them in large and general views, that can rightly understand the whole. No one who has not diligently worked in all the three kingdoms of nature with the microscope, and grasped the myriads of suns which the telescope unfolds, can form a just conception of the wonders of the universe; and so in like manner constant daily and hourly observation has the same relation to any succession of events that the microscope has to the development of minute structure in physical substances.

"The comprehensive retrospect of many years so occupied affords to the mind a certain capacity for forming conclusions; it brings into a focus, as it were, long series of events, of which the minuter details are lost, just as we lose all trace of minute objects in the view of an extensive landscape from a mountain-top. Hence it is that education and intellectual labour are indispensable to arrive at any tolerable degree of perfection in any department of art and science. It is this and this only which can give aptitude for any particular pursuit; and hence the serious errors which arise from what is called amateur legislation. Authority to do, without the power fully to comprehend the results, may well be said to make angels weep; and yet it is upon this system, in a great measure, that the legislative power is conferred on a class peculiarly ill-fitted for the acquirement of minute detail and for habits of patient investigation. I have had abundant opportunities through life of observing how much this holds good both in the transactions of public business and the management of large properties, and this train of thought is often present to me when following the routine of my daily duties."

At the close of 1852 Mr. Sopwith was a member of the Athenæum Club and of the Society of Arts.

1853-55.

In 1853, a pleasing event of Mr. Sopwith's life was a visit, in October, at Inveraray, to the Duke of Argyle, for whom he went to inspect a nickel-mine. The story of the visit is delightfully told.

The year 1854 is of interest from the circumstance that it deals with a journey which Mr. Sopwith made to Denmark and Norway, in company with Mr. Robert Stephenson, Mr. Illingworth, and Mr. Bidder. The account of his visit to Copenhagen, and to various other places in this tour, is racily told; but the strain of the narrative is most lively in relating all the honours heaped on Robert Stephenson, on whom was conferred, with great distinction, the Norwegian order of knighthood. Unhappily the pleasure of the visit was marred by a message received by Mr. Sopwith at Kiel, on September 7th, telling him of the illness of his beloved wife, to whom he immediately returned, to find her much prostrated, but recovering slowly from a serious illness from which she had suffered.

Mrs. Sopwith recovered considerably from this illness, and during the early part of 1855 the usual business of my friend progressed with very little change. In September, in company with Mr. Robert Stephenson, he paid a visit to Paris, in order to see the Great Exhibition there, where they both received a very hearty welcome. Returning home in the middle of September, he resumed the consideration of some proposed works of considerable magnitude connected with the mines; and on Thursday, October 4th, at Holmes Linn, he broke ground for a new shaft; Mrs. Sopwith also broke ground for a second, and his daughter Ursula for a third shaft, at Sipton Shield,—quite an eventful day in mining at Allenheads.

A few days later, while on a visit at Scarborough, he was recalled, owing to a relapse of Mrs. Sopwith. He arrived home on October 12th to find her in a very prostrate condition.　Her illness continued to grow more serious, and on November the 1st she passed away.　The narrative of this bereavement, as told in the diary, is most affecting.　It shows a combination of the tenderest sympathy with the most perfect resignation.　The loss was irreparable ; but with his usual strength of will he continued at his labour, and trusted to time as the only means of cure.

In May 1856 he is in London on a visit to Mr. Robert Stephenson, and is greatly pleased with a day they spent together, on May 29th, at Mr. Henry Stephens', of Finchley.　Mr. Stephens was himself a very remarkable man.　He was a fellow-student and friend of John Keats, the poet. and, as I have elsewhere related, was present when Keats wrote the famous line, " A thing of beauty is a joy for ever."　On another day he rode on horseback with R. S. to Albemarle Villa, Wimbledon, the residence of Mr. George Stephenson, and breakfasted with him.　On June 7th they went with a distinguished company to Greenwich Observatory.

During this visit to London he had the great pleasure of supping with Faraday and his very agreeable circle of friends and relations.

On July (14th) he records as a memorable event a visit which he received from Michael Faraday at Allenheads, which, as throwing a pencil of light over one of the most distinguished Englishmen of any time, must be given in full.

" Mr. Faraday came about one o'clock, and I was indeed glad to receive so distinguished and so truly welcome a visitor.　He remained until the forenoon of the following day, little more than twenty hours in all, and scarcely exceeding twelve hours of his company and conversation at Allenheads, with other two hours on our way to Haydon Bridge ; but these hours, few in number, were rich in interest, and I derived from them an amount of enjoyment which it would be difficult to describe without some appearance of undue partiality or enthusiasm.

"Those, however, who have been enabled to appreciate the world-wide fame of Faraday as a philosopher, or who have witnessed the charming simplicity and attractiveness of his domestic habits, will readily understand how much I was gratified to have the solitudes of a mountain home enlivened by so cheerful a friend, and my own imperfect stores of knowledge greatly augmented by the conversation of so eminent a philosopher.

"Whenever he finds occasion to enter into communication with others, it is done in a manner perfectly free and easy,—a cheerful familiarity blended with all-sufficient and graceful reserve.

"A small black leather bag, carried easily in the hand, would, as regards size or weight, have offered to him no impediment even to a long pedestrian excursion. 'I will stay and dine,' said his note, 'if Miss Sopwith will allow me to do so in a frock-coat.' He understands to perfection the art of being perfectly at home, and succeeds in placing every other person at ease as regards any attention due to himself. His views on this and similar matters accord with my own, and I trace with unerring certainty the admirable instance of perfect sincerity and a clear definition of view,—one of the highest and truest tokens of his supremacy as the 'prince of lecturers,' an appellation which he well deserves.

"Next I may advert to the extreme interest which he takes in matters of actual fact connected with the locality. The limits of these notes admit only of brief references ; whereas the field, and road, and everywhere, as well as 'table' talk of Faraday is suggestive to an extent which might form materials for many pages.

"The school drawings and exercises and the general principles of education as followed out at Allenheads met his warm approval. He was pleased with the office arrangements and with the practical results of good education which he there observed.

16

"In the evening we walked and talked—a long walk and a long talk—to Byerhope Reservoir, and in the garden. Seated at the end of Byerhope Reservoir, the conversation turned on subjects which I had at that very place once discussed with Robert Stephenson, and it is a pleasing memory ever to associate with that spot that it has been the scene of philosophical disquisitions, in which the minds of Faraday and Stephenson were freely opened on some of the most curious and wonderful problems which philosophy has ever disclosed. If I mention that at this place and on this occasion Faraday unfolded in a clear, perspicuous manner his views respecting centres of force, the undulations of light, the difficulties surrounding the received theory of atoms, and other similar matters, it will be readily understood how full of deep and engrossing interest such a conversation must have been. In clearness, in earnestness, in identity of view, how very closely did this conversation remind me of a like interview at this place and of a like discussion with Robert Stephenson ; and in companionship with these, and as connected not with one but with very many opportunities of conversation on the like subjects here and elsewhere in the Allenheads district, I cannot but place the name of my valued friend William George Armstrong, who, in addition to general science, has in this district placed abiding records of his engineering skill, and is now occupied in adding to the number of hydraulic machines which are already in operation. Nor do I ever forget that one of the highest compliments ever paid by one son of science to another was in the instance of Faraday, when I mentioned to him the delicacy felt by Armstrong as to his reception into the Royal Society.

"A long and most agreeable conversation in the garden was followed by some lively anecdotes and friendly talk over the fireside, which even in July has its attractions during the long-continued rains and dull weather which marked the present (so-called) summer. In this we were joined by part of my family circle, and much did we regret that

Ursula and Isabella were unable to be present owing to indisposition.

"When they returned, Mr. Faraday sat with me in my library and looked over some passages in my journals, the keeping of which he greatly commended."

"*July* 15*th*, 1856.—Pleasant walk with Mr. Faraday in Cleugh Plantation, where he admired the romantic combinations of woods, rocks, and rivulets.

"We drove to Allendale Smelt Mills, and on our way had a long conversation on the construction of the nine miles of flues which convey the smoke of the mills to the summit of the adjacent mountains.

"Mr. Faraday (which appellation he said he preferred to either Doctor or Professor) was much pleased by his visit to the smelt mills, and by a rapid survey of some of the processes He greatly admired the straightforward and candid manners and willing information of Mr. Steel, whose long-continued and very large experience of smelting gives much value to his practical opinions.

"At eleven we proceeded to Haydon Bridge and Hexham, where I parted with my much-valued friend.

"In the course of our conversation he remarked that he had seldom known method combined with imagination, and that he thought it a remarkably happy constitution of mind to have acquired so much method as he had seen evidenced, and at the same time to possess a playful fancy and lively imagination. But if he is correct in applying this observation to myself, it is one which I think is still more applicable to himself, his habits of reasoning, his careful and elaborate deductions from long and well-conducted experiments, being blended with a peculiarly light and happy expression in his general demeanour, whilst his general conversation is enriched by variety of anecdotes and amusing comments, which are alike diverting to young and old."

On July 25th there is an entry describing the first trial of the now famous Armstrong gun.

"I returned to Allenheads, and found the gun experiments in full activity under the immediate and most energetic direction of William George Armstrong. Five out of seven of the shells passed through the target at a thousand yards, and three successive balls passed through very nearly in a vertical line and not many inches apart. The arrangements by which the shell is exploded are entirely new contrivances of Mr. Armstrong's, and appear to me to be most ingenious and effective,—of the latter result we had abundant demonstration."

The description of the gun is followed by a short history of its distinguished inventor.

"Armstrong's boyhood was a continual study of electricity, chemistry, and mechanics. He was articled to be a solicitor. His devotion to practical science did not militate against his completing his clerkship and becoming a principal in one of the first houses in the north of England,—a partner in the firm of Donkin, Stable, & Armstrong,—nearly the utmost limit to be gained in a provincial town. In my own case the carpentry and other business concerns in which a few years of my youth were occupied were advanced to as great an extent as the case permitted, and I yet retain a principal position in what is now one of the largest establishments of the kind in the north of England.

"But the steps by which Armstrong has acquired an European reputation and an enduring name, and those by which I have attained a position of some significance in connection with mining, have been more arduous than most young persons are disposed to imagine. We both had to make our own way—to fight our own battle in a field where the conquerors are few and the vanquished are many. One feeling, I think, we have in common,—a strong faith in the power of real merit of whatever kind to make its way, and a hearty desire to lend a helping hand to any who evince an aptitude for the struggle, for such indeed it is."

CHAPTER XXIV.

IN the year 1856 we find Mr. Sopwith in what may be called the ripeness, not only of his years, but of his reputation. He was a Fellow of the Royal Society; a member of the Athenæum Club; a Fellow of the Geological Societies of England and France ; a member of the Geological Club ; a member of the Institution of Civil Engineers, and a Telford Gold Medallist of that Institution ; a member of the Royal Institution, proposed by Faraday ; a member of the Royal Geographical Society, of the Palæontological Society, of the British Association for the Advancement of Science, of the Society of Arts, of the Meteorological Society of England and Scotland, of the Statistical Society of London, and of the Archæological Institute and Archæological Association. By these bonds of fellowship he was connected with general science and literature ; geological, mining, engineering, and useful arts ; geography, meteorology, and natural history ; and statistics, antiquities, and the fine arts. In addition, he belonged to many local societies ; and in total was connected with no less than twenty-six learned institutions.

In the opening chapters of this work, I referred to the first interview I had with Mr. Sopwith at Hartwell House, in Buckinghamshire, the residence of the learned and eccentric Dr. John Lee. As this house is historical, and as the scientific visits which annually took place there for many years were in their way unique, it may be of interest to give from the diary a description of the house and of the one visit recorded.

"*September* 16*th*, 1856.—I left Leeds this morning, and went by rail *viâ* Tring to Aylesbury, where I found Dr. Lee's servant and conveyance waiting to take Captain Fitzroy and myself to Hartwell House, where we received a hearty welcome from Dr. Lee, and I had the great pleasure of meeting my excellent friend Mr. James Glaisher, who introduced me to the companion of the latter part of my journey, Captain Fitzroy, and to Mr. Perigal, Treasurer of the Meteorological Society.

"After dinner and music by Mrs. Lee and Mrs. Reade, another attraction was presented by the observatory, and by a clear atmosphere affording good views of the moon, of Jupiter, and of some other celestial objects.

"The Rev. Mr. Reade furnished a gratifying enjoyment by exhibiting several objects in his very excellent microscope, and especially some exceedingly small writing : inscriptions cut on glass with a diamond, and of a degree of minuteness almost surpassing credibility even when seen ; the Lord's Prayer, for example, occupying only the two-thousandth part of an area of one square inch, which is equivalent to 112,000 words or 436,000 letters in a square inch.

"The bedroom which I occupy possesses, in some degree, the associations of historical interest for which Hartwell is well known in connection with the exile of the royal family of France, and their sojourn in this place for seven years. Not the least interesting is a blank space in one of the walls in shape resembling the pheasants which form a prominent feature in the paper. The absent pheasant is said to have been cut out by one of the maids of honour as a memento of 'dear Hartwell.' The room next to mine was the Queen's state apartment, and a small apartment separated from it by a temporary partition has the melancholy interest of being the scene of her last moments.

"The earnest affection and deep lamentation of the King for her loss are certainly among the most touching of the memorials connected with Hartwell, and they occupy a yet higher place as lessons teaching in most expressive eloquence the supremacy of Nature and the hollowness of all earthly pomp."

"*September* 17*th*.—After meeting a very agreeable party at breakfast, we adjourned to the front of the house, and were for some time employed in witnessing the photographic operations of the Rev. Mr. Lowndes and the Rev. Mr. Reade, who arranged our party in a group and took a photographic picture of the same, with the fine architectural door of Hartwell House in the background.

"Dr. Lee had arranged a programme of occupation in Aylesbury, which was exactly carried out; it included a visit to the County Infirmary, the Church, and a miniature observatory in the premises of Mr. Dell.

"After luncheon we called at St. John's Lodge, a handsome house now occupied by Admiral Smyth and his family."

"*September* 18*th*.—A meeting of the Council of the Meteorological Society was held in the library this forenoon.

"After this meeting Dr. Lee very kindly offered to conduct any of the party who were desirous to see the house and its rich and varied scientific and literary stores, or to hear some details of the historical events connected with the residence of Louis XVIII. and his Court. We gladly availed ourselves of so good an opportunity; but the number, variety, and extreme interest of objects in almost every apartment is such that it was somewhat difficult to concentrate attention upon any specific point.

"To attempt any description of Hartwell would be to write a volume, and need not be attempted. The following memoranda are little more than a copy of rough notes made during our inspection, and they may serve as an index to connect my own reminiscences with the important and elaborate details given in ' Ædes Hartwelliana,' by Admiral Smyth.

"The mounting of the telescope in the observatory is very complete, and the clock by Vulliamy is one of two which he made with great care—the other is at Windsor Castle. The Equatorial Room possesses many points of interest. The telescope formerly belonged to Admiral Smyth at Bedford, and was used for the ' Catalogue of Stars and Celestial Cycle ' of that accomplished astronomer. The object-glass cost two hundred guineas.

"A large and handsome room is called the Library, but indeed the entire house merits the same appellation, as almost every room contains a selection of valuable books. This, however, is the principal library, and it contains a rich store of mathematical and other philosophical works of great value for reference. The walls and tables abound with diagrams and objects of interest, and I especially admired the busts of two most valued friends, distinguished for high intellectual attainments and moral worth,—Mrs. Somerville and Mrs. Smyth.

"Dr. Lee pointed out in the chapel a curious Egyptian sarcophagus in the form of a richly ornamented square case. Here also are a great variety of fossils found in the locality, the contiguity of the parish church having led to the disuse of the chapel for its original purpose.

"In a small library lived the Archbishop of Rheims during the sojourn of the French exiled Court, and here on Dr. Lee's table lay a great many prisms, lenses, and other specimens of glass made from Hartwell sand.

"In another library Louis XVIII. spent the chief portion of his time, a small room adjoining it with a passage and doorway leading to the garden. In this library he received the deputation which came to announce his restoration to the throne. He was attended by a single servant, and a sentinel or watchman kept a look-out at night.

" Dr. Lee conducted us to the top of the house, from the leads of which the views are extremely beautiful. Many traces remain of the alteration made during the residence of the French King. His retinue and Court together numbered about one hundred and forty persons; they amused themselves by forming gardens, and making pigeon-houses on the roof.

"On the upper floor are several libraries; one contains a rich collection of books, a good telescope, formerly belonging to Captain Smyth when at Bedford. A small and very plain barometer hangs on the wall, indicating the atmospheric changes now, as it did in the time of the French King, to whom it belonged. The books here are English history, Roman history, catalogues, works on agriculture, architecture, etc.

" In the second library on this floor the books are chiefly historical, many of them of great interest and value.

"The third library is chiefly filled with law books, of which Dr. Lee's ancestors, judges and others, had collected a great number, and he has made some additions. Dr. Lee kindly presented me with two volumes.

"The fourth with theological works, a curious Swedish Bible, and a great variety of sermons and tracts. The fifth contains works on geography, biography, and Chinese works.

" Dr. Lee mentioned a curious anecdote of a French lady, who visited Hartwell not long ago, and who had lived with the royal party. She had occupied this room, and was accompanied by a daughter about twenty years of age, to whom she pointed out a corner of this room as the place of her birth. ' Vous y fûtes naquit.'

" A sixth library on this floor contains, amongst many other works, a nearly perfect set of the great French Encyclopædia.

" A seventh room contains a complete series of the *Times* newspaper from its commencement in 1809 to the present time. The paper was first called *The Day*, a title which it retained from 1809 to 1817. It was then called the *New*

Times for two years, and afterwards *Morning Journal* until 1830, since which period it has retained its present name of *The Times.*

"An eighth room contains law and other books, some compiled by former members of the family. In all these rooms the books are neatly arranged and in excellent preservation ; many of them are of a very valuable description, and it would not be difficult to find in each of these separate libraries a choice store of reading on any of the respective subjects to which the general contents relate, there being a division of subjects into theological, legal, and other subjects ; nor is a hasty inspection sufficient to do more than give a very vague notion of the extent and value of this great collection of books, some rooms containing from one to two thousand volumes.

"The state-room of the Queen is still retained, and adjoining it is the small chamber in which she died. Several pictures remain, one of them a good portrait of Louis XVIII.

"The room which I occupy was the abiding-place of the ladies of honour in waiting upon the Queen.

" Dr. Lee related an anecdote of the Duke de Berri being reminded, when in a magnificent suite of apartments in a French palace, of his sojourn at Hartwell. 'Ah !' said he, ' I had only one room, but I was very happy in it.'

" A room originally built as a ball-room was formed into no less than thirteen separate apartments for the retinue of the French Court, and is now used as a museum. The collection is extensive, and well arranged into botanical, geological, and other divisions, a rich collection of local fossils, and a vast variety of miscellaneous curiosities. The Egyptian collection is exceedingly curious and select.

" In a museum library Dr. Lee showed us several ancient charters and admirably preserved MSS. in volumes. Amongst these are the original MS. of Dr. Pearson's great work on astronomy, and many MS. compositions of the indefatigable Admiral Smyth, certainly one of the most arduous veterans of scientific research and literature of modern times.

" A muniment-room is remarkable for its ancient oak carving; a picture-gallery; a picture-room, the contents of which are varied and extensive,—here is a closet with a medical library, which is considered a valuable collection.

" It would, however, be difficult to follow each particular room, and I have not yet noticed the principal apartments on the ground floor. My rough notes contain more than I have time to enter in these brief memoranda, and in continuation of Dr. Lee's explanations I may refer to Room 23—as we took it in order of our visit—as containing a very curious oil-painting of a hunt at Colworth, in which the grandfather and grandmother of Dr. Lee appear in the centre of a numerous equestrian group. A bookcase is here fitted with Oriental treasures, and we saw a fine copy of the Koran. In a closet is a collection of books relating to the army and navy. An adjoining room contains Egyptian books and Dr. Lee's 'firman' when travelling in the East. Another room contains many paintings and a medical library.

"Aylesbury Mechanics' Institution.

" Dr. Lee takes a very active interest in many of those institutions and societies which aim at general ameliorations or amendments. Those who have largely studied mankind, or who possess acute powers of observation, or who have been thrown into opportunities of knowing the inner machinery and guiding motives of some of those societies, directed as they often are by a few influential minds, must have painfully seen and felt that they are by no means free from imperfection in design and failure in result; while on the other side of the question there can be no doubt that the great majority of members and promoters are really actuated by good intentions and direct their views to solid and substantial benefits, which, however, are more easily aspired after than obtained. Mechanics' institutions are especially an illustration of this, as are also a yet higher class of literary and scientific institutions and public societies. This being the case, it is evident that such benevolent institutions, however slow in progress or attended with imperfection, have in the main a right tendency; and though some of them aim at results which appear difficult if not absolutely impossible of attainment, yet they promote some approaches thereto which are on the side of temperance and mutual improvement. There are two circumstances which appear obvious as regards the true use of these societies: one is, that to place solid information within their reach is the most likely means to displace the influence of mere pretension; and the other, that the patronage and encouragement of persons of wealth and local influence as well as of intelligence, when bestowed in the form of generous hospitality to the members of a mechanics' institution or any similar society (many of whom are of the middle or what is sometimes deemed an inferior station of life), are calculated to give a right tone and energy to their exertions.

" The party now at Hartwell comprises several who, like myself, have fought their way from a position of very moderate influence to some approach to usefulness in the world,—some who have carried with them a fair share of comfort as regards wealth and position, others who are yet striving by well-directed efforts to gain the true dignity of self-advancement.

" The members of a mechanics' institution in a small country town like Aylesbury are necessarily of a humble condition as compared with aristocratic society, and consist of schoolmasters, clerks, and shop-keepers, rather than of working mechanics.

" It may therefore be readily imagined that to the members of such a society an invitation to take tea and spend an evening at Hartwell House must afford an agreeable variety from the routine of their usual duties, and at the same time promote a kind feeling between different classes of society. There are some who object to this intermixture of classes in a private mansion; but it accords very closely with my own views and sympathies, and is, I believe, calculated to give a healthy and vigorous tone to social intercourse.

" The present occasion was considered by Dr. Lee as fitting

for such an invitation, and a series of addresses were arranged
to be given by some of the visitors now residing at the Hall.
This was very admirably carried out. Mr. Thomas Dobson
explained a beautiful series of diagrams of atmospheric changes
during three or four successive years, and their close connection and correspondence with coal-mine explosions.   Dr.
Richardson exhibited the heart of a young calf, which he
dissected as he illustrated and explained the machinery of the
circulation, and detailed at great length the successive steps
by which he was led to the discovery of ammonia in the blood.
Dr. Barker spoke on ozone.   Mr. Glaisher described a new
system of self-registering thermometer, and I said a few words
on improvement societies.

" Dr. Lee had made a careful programme, and the evening
was spent most agreeably until about eleven o'clock, when the
Aylesbury visitors returned home."

"*September* 20*th*.—On this day Dr. Lee had very kindly
made arrangements for a party comprising his visitors and
some of his neighbours to visit the place of the Hampdens
and of Cromwell, as also to see some of the finest scenery and
most extensive prospects in this part of the kingdom.   About
six carriages were put in requisition, and I had the pleasure
of being grouped with Dr. Lee, the Rev. Mr. Reade, and
Mr. Glaisher.

" We drove on to Hampden, admiring what Mrs. S. C. Hall
so well describes as ' tinted woods and uprisings of the
Chiltern Hills.' We first visited the church, containing some
monumental memorials of the Hampden family, but no separate
one dedicated to ' the Hampden ' whose fame gives a sacred
character to all around.   On the feelings of reverence and
respect created by a visit to this place I might say much, but
my own views and those of all who can rightly regard the
value of historical associations are admirably expressed by Mrs.
S. C. Hall in her account of 'The Burial-place of John Hampden,'
in her beautiful book of ' Pilgrimages to English Shrines.'

" We then visited the mansion, and were received with great

courtesy by Lady Vere Cameron. A photographic view was taken of the house by the Rev. Mr. Lowndes, and a group was formed as part of the picture,. in which Mrs. Lee, two of the daughters of Lady Cameron, Mr. Glaisher, and myself were included. Her ladyship provided refreshments in the dining-room, and we were much gratified by all we saw. We then proceeded a distance of two miles to the 'Chequers,' formerly the mansion of Cromwell.

"We returned to Hartwell at six, and I immediately left for London, where I arrived at 8.30 p.m."

It seems to me but a very brief period indeed since I had the pleasure of accompanying my friend in these excursions. At this time the great moon controversy was the topic of the day, the question being whether the moon turned on its own axis once each month, or whether she did not turn on an axis at all, but simply moved liked a rigid body with one face always towards us. Mr. Perigal, friend and ally of Jelinger Symons, took the rigid side of the question. The Rev. J. B. Reade, one of the brightest men of science the Church of England ever produced, and Mr. James Glaisher took the opposite and orthodox side. The controversies often got wild and furious; two or three, including Mr. Dobson, Captain Fitzroy, and myself, losing no opportunity of setting the combatants on whenever we could, to Dr. Lee's great delight. He appointed Sopwith umpire, and the sly humour which the umpire introduced into the summings up was most amusing; for although he went with Glaisher and Reade, he would sometimes, for the amusement of the thing, throw an argument to the other side, interposing calculations of his own of the most fanciful kind, such as how many moons would be required to keep up a perpetual eclipse of the sun; how a universal deluge could be produced in three days by a change in the movements of the moon; what would be the size of the inhabitants of the moon if there were any there, and what height they could jump; whether the moon was not Liliput, and so on,—topics which gave us amusing subjects for discussion from day to day. I was greatly surprised at the rapidity with which he learned new mechanical things. After my lecture on the heart of the calf, to which he has referred above, he asked me to give him a private lesson, and got up the whole subject with such precision that he could name every valve and part straight off; and when I showed him how the large valves rose when water was poured into the cavities his delight was great, for he knew of some piece of artificial mechanism to which the principle would apply. "You see we are both engineers," he added, "I an iron and lead engineer, you an animal engineer."

Photography was just then coming into use, and one of our party, the Rev. J. B. Reade, was amongst the first, if not the first, to lead the way to that great improvement. The Rev. Charles Lowndes, who held the chaplaincy at Hartwell, was great in the new art, and in the mornings we photographed everybody and everything. I have a capital photo still of Messrs. Glaisher and Sopwith sitting together examining a watch. Sometimes our fun was a little more lively. One day Mr. Glaisher and I had a wrestling match on the top of a hill, greatly to the amusement of Captain Fitzroy and Mr. Sopwith; they, so to say, being our seconds, Mr. Sopwith backing Glaisher and the Captain me. After a stiff tussle we both fell together, and rolled from the top of the hill to the bottom, much to the general amusement. Glaisher has been up in balloons since then, and I hope he never got a worse shaking. He is always a delightful memory.

At night in the drawing-room, as a variation to Mrs.

Lee's excellent music, Dr. Lee would call upon somebody to give a short lecture or tell a story. On one of these occasions Mr. Sopwith described the hypothesis of the development of living things from a primordial centre. That, said Reade, is rank Darwinism. It was the first time I had heard that word used. It had no reference to Charles Darwin, whose name at that period was not connected with the subject ; but it had reference to Erasmus Darwin, and to his original and fruitful observations. I name this incident as indicating that Darwinism, like everything else, is itself an evolution.

I have already described the morning discussion at Hartwell in the first chapter, to which these later memoranda, suggested by perusal of the Sopwith diary, are an appendix.

On returning home from this visit, Mr. Sopwith sent eighty pamphlets and books to Dr. Lee, either for himself or for the Mechanics' Institution at Aylesbury. The visit also set him on a new occupation. At Hartwell Dr. Lee had a meteorological observatory, the records of which were kept with great precision by his able secretary, Mr. Samuel Horton. Mr. Sopwith "took lessons," and at Allenheads soon commenced to practise similar observations, with special reference to rainfall. This leads to a note in his diary on the amount of rain on Tuesday, September 30th, after a series of continuous showers from the previous Saturday. The entry is rendered as follows :—

"*September* 30*th*.—The rain-gauge on this Tuesday morning shows that upwards of five inches of rain have fallen in three days,—Saturday, Sunday, and Monday, from 9 a.m. on Saturday to the same hour on Tuesday (this day). Conversing with Mr. T. J. Bewick on the large quantity of rain, I was led to enter on the following calculations, which present a curious view of the vast amount of water-power in the quantity which has fallen.

"The exact depth is 5·070 inches, which I call in round numbers five inches.

"There are 27,878,400 square feet in one square mile.

"Five-twelfths of this will be the number of cubic feet of water in one square mile, and this is found to be 11,616,000 cubic feet. One cubic foot of water weighs 62½ lb., but say 60 lb. Then 11,616,000 × 60 = 696,960,000 lb., which amounts to 312,482 tons, or in 100 square miles 31,248,200 tons of water.

"For an area of ten miles square in this locality: 100 square miles, the rain falls on lands which are elevated from 800 to 2,200 feet in height (this distance not including Cross Fell, which is 2,901 feet), and the average descent of water from these districts to the outlet by principal contiguous rivers, as the Tyne, the Wear, and the Tees, may be taken at 1,000 feet.

"Now if 33,000 lb. falling one foot in a minute be taken as the estimate of a horse-power, and assuming the above quantity to fall 1,000 feet in seventy-two hours, we have an aggregate fall of water equal to 4,888 horse-power per minute for one square mile, or in the area of 100 square miles 488,800 horse-power. Taking the mining districts, with Cross Fell and the adjacent hills, as including 400 square miles (the area assigned in my account of these districts), and calling the descent 1,000 feet instead of about 1,500 or 1,600 (which is equivalent to allowing only ⅔ of the rain), we have an escape or running away of a quantity of water equal to 1,955,200, or in round numbers 2,000,000, of horse-power exerted continuously over the whole seventy-two hours. This is equivalent to the united power of 10,000,000 men employed at the limit of their extreme strength for nine days at eight hours a day.

"Another mode of bringing this extraordinary quantity

of water under consideration is to suppose it piled up or contained in a square pipe of twelve inches clear dimensions inside. Such a column twelve inches square would be 220 miles high to contain the rainfall of five inches over one mile ; and in the mining districts of 400 square miles, the quantity of water would require a twelve-inch pipe of no less than 88,000 miles, which is more than one-third of the distance from the earth to the moon.

"As about ten times the above quantity of rain, or fifty inches, is a moderate estimate of the annual rainfall in these districts, it follows that a twelve-inch square pipe to contain the whole rainfall in one year over the 400 square miles would be 880,000 miles in length ; and in some years—1852, for example, when nearly one-half more rain fell (72 inches)—the length of the twelve-inch pipe would be upwards of 1,200,000 (one million two hundred thousand) miles.

" It is only by calculations of this kind that any exact notion can be formed of the magnificent scale of the operations of nature. Or, if we suppose the last named quantity of water to be placed in a canal 100 feet wide and 10 feet deep, the length of such canal would be 1,200 miles."

In the closing part of this year Mr. Armstrong renewed his gun experiments at Allenheads, when Mr. Robert Stephenson paid a visit there, and Mr. Sopwith, after having retired from the business with which he had been so long connected in Newcastle, started on a tour to Egypt, then a much more formidable undertaking than at this date. He had for his companions Mr. Robert Stephenson and Mr. Lee, R.A. On their way through Paris they met M. Paletot, the distinguished engineer ; M. Didcon, a director of the line of railway between Paris and Bordeaux, an accomplished scholar and Shakesperian ; Mr. Locke, M.P., Mr. Brassey, and many other eminent friends. From Paris they went to Lyons and Nismes, with which they were greatly delighted. From Nismes they travelled to Marseilles, and from Marseilles to Toulon, where they went on board the *Titania* yacht in the harbour there.

On Tuesday, December 2nd, they set sail for Alexandria, where they arrived after a delightful voyage on Saturday, December 13th. After staying in Alexandria three or four days they went by the first " Mussulman Railway " to Cairo.

To Mr. Sopwith this bit of railway journey was one of the events of his life; and his description of the men who were engaged on the railway, and the manner in which, as in ancient Egypt, they were forced to leave their crops and all other works at the call of their task-masters is very striking. The mode of work of these men, their " cat-like facility and surety," and their wonderful powers of endurance were, he thought, sur-prizing, for they could compete for a whole day with a horse going over thirty or forty miles at a moderate speed. The ferry-boat which Robert Stephenson planned for crossing the Nile where it is 1,200 feet in width is described with great care and admiration. This was the first opportunity Mr. Stephenson had enjoyed of seeing his work in operation,—a fact which added naturally to the freshness of the visit.

CHAPTER XXV.

1857-59.

N landing in England from his Egyptian tour on January 22nd, 1857, Mr. Sopwith proceeded direct to Allenheads. On February 26th he revisited London, and dined with Sir Roderick Murchison to meet Dr. Livingstone, who was then in the metropolis. On the following day, with his daughters Anna and Emily, he went to the Royal Institution to listen to one of the remarkable lectures of Faraday on the Conservation of Force. Prince Albert was in the chair, and the lecture was received by all with the profoundest attention.

During this visit to town (on March 2nd) some differences of opinion between Mr. Sopwith and Mr. Beaumont led Mr. Sopwith to tender his resignation of the agency of Allenheads. It was a painful decision for him, tempered, however, by the complimentary offer of the Council of the British Meteorological Society that he should be President of the Society, an offer he was obliged, reluctantly, to decline on account of the distance at which he resided from London.

The difficulties between Mr. Beaumont and himself were temporarily made up by his acceptance of the office of non-resident agent of the W. B. Mines. On August 1st, 1857, he left Allenheads, as he believed, for good, and removed to London. Here he took up his residence at 43, Cleveland Square, a house furnished, almost exclusively, under the immediate management of his "dear Ursula." In October he paid a visit to St. Leonards, in company with Mr. Decimus Burton, and in November of this year had conferred upon him, *Honoris causa*, the degree of M.A. by the University of Durham.

On December 8th, at the Institution of Civil Engineers, he read a paper on the Ferry at Kaffre Azzayat, on the river Nile. The paper was rather novel at the Society, as it infused a little landscape and picturesqueness; but it went off well, Sir John Rennie and the beloved Robert Stephenson expressing their approval. The isometrical drawings with which the paper was illustrated were much approved.

His retrospect of this year, 1857, ends as follows :—

"On December 29th I spent the forenoon at Millwall at the *Great Eastern* or Leviathan ship, and the afternoon at Faraday's lecture, where the Prince of Wales was present. On the 30th I had a conversation with Mr. E. J. Smith on matters of great concern as regards the Weardale mining districts, and on the 31st the evening was spent and the year ended at a most agreeable party at Mrs. S. C. Hall's, my return from which brought me home about midnight; and thus I commenced the early hours of the New Year in the much-loved company of my dear children, all of whom are now sojourning at No. 43 in Cleveland Square as residents, with the exception of my son Tom, who is on a three weeks' visit for the enjoyment of his Christmas holidays.

"It is with much interest that I thus draw up a brief epitome of some of the more prominent features which have marked the events of the past year.

"The retrospect is one which furnishes abundant food for deep reflection, and let me say, for deep and lasting gratitude. Of my own weakness and infirmity I am too conscious not to know and feel that in the ordering of events by the unseen and mysterious Providence which guides and governs the world I have been permitted during the past year to possess privileges and to enjoy benefits to which, as of my own merit, I could lay no claim, and which therefore I ascribe entirely with devout gratitude to the undeserved bounty of the Giver of all good. I care not how others may choose to express the sentiments they feel in connection with what may be deemed a religious view of life ; I purposely abstain from all save general expressions, and I honour and respect every variety of form in which sincere feeling is clothed. That clothing depends much on the conditions of early training, on long-continued habits and associations, and I therefore deem it important not to interfere or comment with reference to special views on sectarian differences.

"That 'the goodness of God endureth yet daily' is one of the chief articles of my belief, as it also is the strongest pillar of an unfaltering trust in God, and a confidence in the wisdom and goodness of the government of the world, however deep and mysterious the apparent contradictions may be. A year of perfect health, of reasonable prosperity, of great variety of scenery and occupation, and blessed with overflowing abundance of the rich treasures of valued friendship ; what broad outlines are these of as much felicity as can be reasonably desired ! My change of residence from Allenheads to London has been one of the marked conditions of the year, and this change has led me into a new range of duty and a wider sphere of enjoyment. The circumstances which gave rise to it led to some anxiety, but on the whole I am inclined to believe that friendship and confidence, as between Mr. Beaumont and myself, have been placed on a firmer basis than before.

"The magnitude, the number, and the great variety of my duties connected with his service occupy my whole time and attention, and I have declined all other business.

"I have received in very many quarters the most earnest and friendly sympathy and regard, and in concluding the notes of this year I desire to express, as I have often before done, a sense of deep and fervent gratitude, mixed with a consciousness of my own inability, yet with a humble and hearty trust in the unfailing goodness of God."

1858.

The year 1858 seems to have gone on very smoothly. On June 9th Mr. Sopwith gave a lecture to the students of King's College on geological plans, sections, and models, and on the following day he was gratified by a visit from George Coombe, the author of "The Constitution of Man." On the 19th he was at luncheon at Mr. Robert Stephenson's to meet Professor Wheatstone and Frank and Miss Buckland, both of whom were now lamenting the death of their distinguished father, the Dean of Westminster. On this occasion Frank Buckland gave him a Memoir he had written of the Dean for perusal. On July 24th he was at dinner at Sir James Duke's to meet Mr. Alderman Mechi, "well known in connection with his agricultural improvements in experimental farming at Tiptree." On August 25th he was busy at a meeting of mechanical engineers at Newcastle. On September 22nd to the 27th he was equally busy at Leeds at the British Association for the Advancement of Science, and on September 29th Mr. W. G. Armstrong, of Newcastle, took him in his brougham to St. Nicholas' Church, where he was married to Miss Anne Potter, of Heaton, by the Vicar of Newcastle; after which the bride and bridegroom started for Lincoln on their wedding tour.

In the diary of 1859 a valuable entry gives us an idea of the quick, keen and sound appreciation of natural facts by Mr. W. G. Armstrong.

"*January* 30*th*.—I spent the evening with Mr. W. G. Armstrong at Jesmond. I was truly glad to learn that the Government, in due appreciation of Mr. Armstrong's services, have given him an appointment to be 'Engineer of Rifled Ordnance' with a handsome salary, together with a large order for guns, and offers of personal honours which are well deserved, and which mark the favour of the Sovereign as well as the approval of her Government. In all this I sincerely rejoice. I have had many opportunities of witnessing his devotion to Science, and his marvellous aptitude in adapting the power of natural forces to any required mechanical purpose. I accompanied him on his first visit to and examination of the boiler at Seghill, where the curious phenomenon of electricity developed by steam was discovered by one of the workmen, and made by Armstrong the foundation of his rapid and brilliant researches, ending in the construction of the well-known electrical steam-engine.

"At Gateshead, in 1840, I witnessed some of the earliest experiments with a hydraulic engine, and both in London, at Allenheads, and Newcastle have again and again been delighted by his extraordinary powers, as may be seen in many former pages of this journal. Speaking this evening of 'tails,' *i.e.*, distinctive letters after a name, he jokingly said that he valued none more highly than M.D., which he thought he might assume as an abbreviation of the title bestowed on him by an Allendale miner of 'Maister o' th' Drallikers,' by which was implied his mastership of the men employed in putting up the hydraulic engines which are not among the least of his eminently practical and scientific works."

The honours soon followed, knighthood being conferred

on Mr. Armstrong about the 20th of the succeeding month; and on May 11th there is a brief record of a dinner to Sir William in memory of the event. The dinner was given at the Assembly Rooms, Newcastle. Sir George Grey occupied the chair, and Mr. Robert Stephenson, many other notabilities, and about two hundred local gentlemen took part in the ceremony.

On May 12th there is a curious entry of an interview which Mr. Sopwith and Robert Stephenson held as railway travellers from York to Doncaster with George Hudson, the famous railway king. Hudson at this time had lost both wealth and power, and had just been dispossessed of his seat for Sunderland. Towards him Mr. Sopwith was affected in a twofold sense. He could not withhold sympathy with the man in his misfortunes, and he could not doubt that those misfortunes were the natural results of his own lines of procedure.

A visit to the Isle of Wight, visits to the Birkbeck Schools, a lecture at King's College, and continual active business between London and Allenheads, made the days go very pleasantly in the early part of 1859. In this year an arrangement was made by which Mr. Thomas Sopwith, Mr. Sopwith's son, commenced to undertake duties at Allenheads under Mr. Bewick, who was now practically acting as agent. The arrangement was very satisfactory.

In the diary of August 21st, 1859, there is an abstract of his views on the subject of taxation as the basis of voting.

"*August 21st.*—In the evening I dined with Mr. and Lady Margaret Beaumont, the Duke de Richelieu, the Countess of Cork, and Sir John Shelley. In the drawing-room the conversation turned on the ballot, which I contend would be rejected if its essential principle of secrecy admitted of being made compulsory. This public duty I consider should be performed in a public manner by those most competent to understand its obligations. I also named my opinion that taxation is the proper basis in proportional value according to the number of pounds sterling paid for taxes, rates, or other similar contributions. Every man, and even every woman and child, might thus contribute and be enabled to assist, to the proportional value of their payments, any candidate for the representation. Due influence would thus be given to intelligence and solid interests as represented by the more opulent members of the community, who would be utterly swamped in any system of equal voting and universal suffrage. This theory finds small favour with Sir John Shelley, who has not yet joined the ranks of what are called ' retarded ' Liberals, men who, in practice, are not far apart from the ' advanced ' Conservatives. It is, however—I am persuaded, that it is—only on some such basis that a large extension of voting power can be combined with stability."

Another entry on September 6th refers to an important improvement in the construction of submarine cables.

"I dined with Mr. Sillick at Claremont Place to meet Mr. William Hooper of London, with whom I have had occasional interviews and some correspondence on a recent improvement he considers himself to have effected in the insulation by india-rubber of electric wire for submarine cables, and which, so far as I can judge, appears to possess undoubted claims to great consideration. It is worthy of notice, as an index to the large character of some of the modern works of ingenuity, that the average quantity of cable used per week by one firm (Messrs. Newall & Co.) is about one hundred miles, the cost of which at a minimum may be about £8,000, or more than £400,000 yearly."

A note on September 18th, 1859, relates to the death of the distinguished I. K. Brunel.

"*September* 18th.—On Wednesday last I heard mentioned the serious illness of Mr. I. K. Brunel, who died on the following

evening, Thursday, September 14th.   He was brought home
from the *Great Eastern* steamship at midday on the 5th in a
very alarming condition, having been seized with paralysis,
induced, it was believed, by over mental anxiety, from which
his health had materially suffered for some years past.   Brunel
occupied day and night alike in continual and earnest mental
exertion, and thus his death took place at the comparatively
early age of fifty-four.   He has for many years occupied a very
prominent and influential position as an engineer, placed by
some at the head of the profession, but not so recognised either
by the public, or by the profession ; but all who for the past
thirty years have known intimately the progress of civil engineering in this country, will remember Telford as the chief
head and representative of an old school which expired with
him and the two Stephensons, father and son ; and Brunel
as the leader of a new and vastly extended school of which
railways and locomotive engines have been the great features,
with their concomitants of tunnels, bridges, telegraphs, and
steam navigation.   At the present time hydraulic machinery
and gunnery have assumed a prominent place, and no name
in 1859 is more extensively recognised than that of Armstrong.
The associations of the present moment are seldom much thought
of, and still seldomer deemed worthy of being recorded, but
in after years it may be curious to remember that the illness of
Brunel was the subject of conversation at Armstrong's dinner
table, and his death took place at the very hour when my friends
and myself were separating after spending the evening at
Jesmond.   Constant occupation and anxiety seem at present to
be telling upon Armstrong's health, which I fear is far less
robust than was Brunel's a few years ago ; and on every side I
see examples of premature decay and death, induced by undue
pressure of mental exertion."

On October 12th is a still more sad entry made at
Newcastle.

"*October* 12th.—At ten minutes past twelve the world lost

Robert Stephenson. Of this sad, but not unexpected, event I did not receive intelligence until the arrival of my letters the following morning. I went to Bretton Hall, and was engaged some time with Mr. Beaumont on business matters. There was a large party to dinner, amongst whom were the Earl of Sefton, Lady Mary Fox, and others.

"*October* 13th.—This morning's post brought me a letter from my dear Lallah. It conveyed the sad news already mentioned, that Mr. Robert Stephenson was no more. When the intelligence reached Newcastle universal sorrow prevailed. The bell of St. Nicholas' Church tolled for a long time during the afternoon, and the colours of vessels of all nations in the Tyne were hoisted half-mast high. Mr. Beaumont, with generous sympathy, left me for a short time, and I deeply felt how great a loss I had sustained in the death of so revered a friend. Controlling those feelings, I went into the consideration of such urgent matters as admitted not of delay, and was thus enabled to leave Bretton at noon, and to arrive at home at six in the evening.

"*October* 14th.—I called at 34, Gloucester Square, where I saw Mr. George Vaughan, and learnt from him some interesting and affecting details of the illness and death of our mutual and greatly beloved friend. It is within a day or two of one month since Brunel died, and since Stephenson returned, seriously ill, from Norway. The latter had suffered much from illness and sea-sickness on his outward voyage to Christiania, where also he was much indisposed, but was nevertheless able to attend to the decision of some weighty matters of business left in his sole arbitration. Some apprehensions were entertained on his return as to whether he would survive the voyage, and on reaching Lowestoft he had to be lifted into his carriage. He suffered little pain, was visited only by his medical attendants and nurses, and was, for the most part, and especially during the two days preceding his death, calm, composed, perfectly conscious of, and fully resigned to, his approaching dissolution.

" He was much interested in passages of Scripture read to

him by Mrs. Bidder, who attended him with affectionate and unremitting care, and his own prayers were described to me as having been most impressive and appropriate, as well as consistent with those deep sentiments to which, in the vigour of health and strength, he had so often given expression. At the moment of his death he was resting in the arms of his housekeeper, in whose arms his wife had breathed her last. Such, at least, are some of the circumstances, as I understand them to be, described by Mr. Vaughan, who is now placed in charge of the house by Mr. George Robert Stephenson. I need scarcely say how deeply interesting is every incident connected with the last moments of so truly great a man.

" Every letter I receive is full of corresponding eulogium, and I this evening received one of which this may be truly said. It is a letter from one whose opinions are as sound as his feelings are deep and earnest—the biographer of George Stephenson. In this communication he so well portrays the more prominent features of the case that I transcribe it at length as follows :—

" It is dated this day, October 17th, 1859, from 6, Granville Park Terrace, Blackheath, S.E., and thus proceeds :—

" ' MY DEAR SIR,—

" ' I was much grieved to hear of Mr. Robert Stephenson's dangerous illness, and soon after of his death. I was informed at his office that his medical advisers required him to be kept perfectly quiet, otherwise I should have endeavoured to see him once more before he died. But perhaps it is better not, as I shall continue to see him before me, and to think of him with his fine, cheerful, frank, and open countenance as he used to appear among his friends, and not wasted by disease nor distorted by dropsy. Although he has died young, comparatively speaking, he had lived much ; and the works he has left behind him, massive and majestic beyond precedent, are grandly stamped with power, the Britannia and High Level Bridges especially so. There may not have been the same interesting originality about him as there was about his father, for he represented the highest educated and polished intellect of his day; but there was quite as much force of character and energy of purpose. And then, what a noble, gentlemanly nature he was; so modest, so kind, so considerate, so generous. I have heard of many beautiful traits of character in Robert Stephenson which make me rank him even higher as a man than as an engineer, though there he was the first, the acknowledged chief.

"'I shall be exceedingly glad to have an opportunity of renewing the intercourse with you which began so pleasantly at Mr. Stephenson's table; and I shall esteem you all the more that I know he entertained so high an opinion of your qualities as a man and your accomplishments as a pursuer of science.

"'Believe me, my dear sir,

"'Yours truly and sincerely,

"'S. SMILES.'

"'T. SOPWITH, ESQ.'"

A further entry describes the funeral of the great engineer.

"ARRANGEMENTS FOR MR. R. STEPHENSON'S FUNERAL.

"The arrangements of the funeral are of a most extensive and delicate character. The Duke of Cambridge has given permission for the procession to pass through Hyde Park on its way to the Abbey; more than two hundred and fifty applications from the nobility and others to send carriages have been declined, and the cards of admission exceed two thousand, in addition to the parties forming the funeral procession. The latter are confined to the immediate relations, some friends, and several noblemen and persons of official rank and station, and a deputation from Newcastle to represent the Corporation.

"October 21st.—Sir William Armstrong came to breakfast, and we had a very long and careful conversation on the Slitt Mine requirements. We walked soon after ten past the residence of

the late Robert Stephenson. As we were passing, the hearse
was moving from the door, a large crowd was assembled, and
about a dozen mourning coaches and forty carriages were in
attendance. I drove with Sir William to Great George Street,
when he went to join the Council of Civil Engineers, and I
reached the Abbey a few minutes before eleven. A large
number of persons were already assembled, and I took a place
beside Mr. Decimus Burton, close to the entrance to the Choir.
From this time until twelve the numbers were greatly augmented. Men of every profession, many of them of the most
distinguished rank in their respective walks, were to be seen.
Every art and science was thus represented ; and it would
be difficult to imagine a crowd composed of more intelligent
and well-known characters. On every face sincere grief and
marked respect, nay, reverence, seemed to be impressed ; and at
length, a few minutes after twelve o'clock, the solemn pealing
of the organ, the chanting of the choristers, and the deep-toned
funeral bell, indicated the arrival of the funeral procession.
What a moment of intense interest was it when first the
stream of music flowed through the vast aisles, and the majestic
tones of the organ were reverberated from the lofty roof.
Slowly onward came this most impressive and awe-inspiring
melody. It seemed the very essence of the beauty of holiness,
and well accorded with the import of the words to which so
powerful and impressive an expression was given. The
choristers, preceded by some of the officials of the Abbey,
walked slowly past, then came the mayor and sheriff and two
aldermen from Newcastle, who, in official costume, walked in
front of the coffin. Mourners, many and sincere, followed, and
the Burial Service was continued in the Choir. The chanting of
the thirty-ninth Psalm was most solemn, and so indeed was
all the musical service, the sublime anthems and the *Dead
March* exceedingly so. The words as well as the music were
most impressive. Of Robert Stephenson it was truly to be
said that he delivered the poor that cried, the needy, and
he that had no helper. Equally true and solemn were the

words of the concluding anthem, ' His body is buried in peace,
but his name liveth evermore.'

" At the same time that these sad ceremonials were taking
place in Westminster Abbey, similar respect to the memory of
Robert Stephenson was paid in many other places, and especially
at Newcastle and Shields, Sunderland and Whitby. In the former of these towns divine service was celebrated in St. Nicholas'
Church, and attended by about 1,600 men from the factory, all
in deep mourning. This deep manifestation of public honours
was made before any intelligence arrived of the munificent
benefactions given to the Infirmary and Literary and Philosophical Society, the one of £10,000, the other of £7,000, which,
with a recently given gift of £3,000, makes £10,000 also to the
last-named institution.

On December 23rd Mr. Sopwith attended at the
Society of Arts in London a meeting of the Committee
on the subject of a Normal Diapason.

The great need of uniformity on this subject having
been affirmed by the general meeting held in August
last, a sub-committee was then appointed, and this was
its first meeting. The duty assigned to it was the definition of such diapason. Several eminent musical men were
present, as Sterndale Bennett, Blagrove, Goss, Goldsmidt,
Davison, and Hullah who presided.

The present prevailing pitch was defined, and in
moving a second resolution Mr. Sopwith affirmed that
in selecting any uniform pitch regard should be especially
had to the capability of the voice, and this after some
discussion was carried. That any compulsory uniformity
could be effected was out of the question; much difference of opinion prevailed, and eminent instrumental
manufacturers and performers viewed the matter with
regard to the brilliancy of concert effects from the
high pitch at present in use, rather than in regard to

the strain on the voice which is thereby caused, and of which Madame Goldsmidt (the far-famed Jenny Lind) had given strong testimony at a previous meeting.

On December 28th there is an entry on a new London music hall.

" This evening I walked with my son Tom to Canterbury Hall. It is very rarely indeed that I visit any place of public amusement as such, and my object this evening was rather to study a problem of social economics than to seek any enjoyment. When in Paris, Marseilles, and other towns in France, I had been much interested by seeing the entertainments provided in what may be called the singing coffee-house (*café chantant*), and Canterbury Hall being of this character, I was anxious to see how it was managed. This place is truly one of the signs of the times, and merits more than a brief mention. There are many similar establishments in London, but this, the earliest, is also, so far as I know, the best.

" We enter the door of Canterbury Hall,—so called, I presume, from its close proximity to Lambeth Palace,—we pay sixpence for admission each, and at once enter a sort of spacious vestibule ornamented with some large oil-paintings, pier-glasses, and with a rich array of refreshments of various kinds on a stall or table of considerable length. Open archways in one of the walls enable us to see that the ground floor of the ' hall ' is crowded; the balcony above is well filled, and by paying an extra sixpence we gain admission to this narrow gallery, running round three sides of the room. Here we can see the proportions of a stately room painted a light stone colour, and of very chaste and ornamental design. The general effect is exceedingly good, and for purity of style and elegance of architectural character the Hall might be a portion of a palace. It is brilliantly lighted by glass chandeliers of uncommon magnificence and beauty. Refreshments are supplied of good quality, and at moderate prices, according to a printed tariff.

18

Thus artisans, soldiers, small tradesmen, and others in a similar walk of life can spend the whole evening for a moderate admission fee of sixpence, taking more or less of refreshments, or if so disposed, none at all. A constant succession of performances takes place on the stage, chiefly songs with accompaniments, recitations, dancing, etc. A book of words is sold for a penny; it contains fifty-five selections from operas. All is in good order and in good taste. The whole might pass for an aristocratical concert, but for the *pipes* on the ground floor and cigars above, which sorely test the admirable ventilating qualities of the room.

" Leaving the crowded hall, we pass into a splendid picture gallery, well lighted, and containing two hundred and forty pictures. Among them is the original Horse Fair of Rosa Bonheur."

Turning to another and very different topic, there is a short commentary on Faraday.

Everything relating to Faraday had a special charm for Mr. Sopwith, but nothing in relation to the philosopher pleased him so much as the truly childish simplicity and purity of that charming and philosophic life. "I do not know which I admired most in Faraday," he said to me, " his simplicity or his profundity. There will never be another Faraday in our time." We all know the truth of this prediction, and that the mantle of Faraday was buried with the man. But perhaps my friend was right in saying that his simplicity was as conspicuous as his profundity. He goes on to speak of something illustrative of this in a note at the close of the year 1859, bearing upon one of the juvenile lectures which the brilliant Professor was accustomed to deliver annually at the Royal Institution. On the last day of the year the first of one of these courses of six lectures was delivered. The subject of the lecture was "The Forces of Matter." Mr.

Sopwith arrived about fifteen minutes before three p.m., and found the room so crowded he had to sit down on one of the steps. As the clock struck the hour the lecturer appeared, welcomed by general and sincere applause. A few graceful sentences of explanation and apology for having been obliged by indisposition to postpone the lecture from the 27th were followed for an hour by a plain and purposely elementary series of illustrations bearing on those phenomena of gravitation which are wonderful when made subjects of contemplation, but which, like all the vast and magnificent arrangements common to constant observation, we are but too apt to pass unheeded by.

Summary of 1859.

In the summary of this year, 1859, Mr. Sopwith enters into a general epitome of the chief occupations and events which came across his path and occupied his time. It is a cheery little record. He rejoices in buoyancy of health, in the enjoyment of as much of domestic comfort as can reasonably be expected, in the affection and solicitude for his happiness which his " dear Anne " has evinced in every possible way, and in the love of all his children. He has been a great deal from home with work divided between London and the North, and has found his chief enjoyment in close attention to duties, with consciousness of many imperfections from inevitable want of power, and with some anxieties and distress— shades of doubt and difficulty—which, like clouds, seem to have passed away.

CHAPTER XXVI.

1860-61.

IN the year 1860 events ran on in the usual course, unbroken by anything special until February 22nd, when Mr. Sopwith commenced to take an active part in the organisation of the great Exhibition to be held in London in the year of 1862.

In company with a deputation, although he was unwell, he waited on the Prince Consort at Buckingham Palace, to explain the views of the Society of Arts in regard to the Exhibition. Sir Thomas Phillips acted as spokesman, and many points of organisation were agreeably discussed.

In the early part of June Mr. Sopwith resumed his residence at Allenheads, by a new arrangement made with Mr. Beaumont. He does not seem to have relished much the change from London life, for London to him was ever a centre of attraction. On May 21st he was again in London, and on the 22nd was in attendance at the funeral of Sir Charles Barry, who was buried in Westminster Abbey, close by Telford and Stephenson.

On the 27th he paid a visit to Mr. Babbage, at the well-known house in Manchester Street, and found that learned man occupied in some analytical amusements, one of them being the solution of an anagram. " I tore ten Persian MSS." into " Misrepresentations."

This was a favourite amusement with Babbage. He once gave an anagram to me after I had benumbed, by local anaesthesia, one of his teeth, that Mr. Matthews, the dentist, might extract it painlessly. I think it was the very same anagram.

On June 22nd I find a note relating to a dinner at which Mr. Sopwith met Mr. Disraeli. He adds a note relating to the oratory of the distinguished statesman.

" *June 22nd*, 1860.—I dined with the Society of Arts at St. James's Hall, Benjamin Disraeli, Esq., in the chair. He spoke at great length on the origin of the Society above a century ago, of the then state of the world, of subsequent decline and decay until fourteen or fifteen years ago, of the revival caused by attention to manufactures and commerce, of the Exhibition of 1862, and of examinations in country institutions. On all these and similar topics he spoke well and in great clearness of detail; but I was particularly struck by the repetition not only of subjects but words, so much so that it appeared to others as well as myself to have been a tale thrice told."

In the course of this year Mr. Sopwith occupied his leisure in encouraging the Allenheads Rifle Volunteers, of which corps he had been one of the founders. He also projected a series of Meteorological Coast Stations, an organisation which has proved of the greatest possible value. On September 22nd and 26th the following notes occur on this last-named subject :—

" *September 22nd*.—Occupied all day chiefly at the office, and

occasionally with Mr. Glaisher, in the consideration of various
meteorological details, and conversation.   Mr. Glaisher has been
unwell for the past two days.   I obtained from him an account
of all his operations, and prepared in a tabular form a statement
of the various stations, of the instruments placed at them, and
of the names of the several observers.   The following is an
epitome of the same :—

  1. North Shields, barometer, thermometer, and rain-gauge.
  2. Tynemouth, ditto, ditto.
  3. Cullercoats, ditto, ditto.
  4. Newbiggin, ditto, ditto.
  5. Hauxley, ditto, ditto.
  6. Amble, ditto, ditto.
  7. Alnmouth, ditto, ditto.
  8. Alnwick, thermometer and rain-gauge.
  9. Boulmer, ditto, ditto.
10. Craster, barometer, thermometer, and rain-gauge.
11. Newton, ditto, ditto.
12. Beardnell, ditto, ditto.
13. North Sunderland, ditto, ditto.
14. Holy Island, ditto, ditto.
15. Spittal, barometer.
16. Berwick-on-Tweed, barometer, thermometer, and rain-gauge.

"*September* 26*th.*—I wrote a draft report on the Northumberland coast stations, embodying the general results of
Mr. Glaisher's recent operations in that (meteorological)
service.

" The following are extracts from this report, which I reduced
to the form of a letter to Frederick Holland, Esq., for the information of the Duke of Northumberland.   In copying some
portions of this letter, I do so under distinct headings, which
are not inserted in the original, in order more readily to refer
to them, as well as to direct attention to the subject of each.

"I. Mr. Glaisher's Valuable Aid.

" This successful progress is almost entirely owing to the
services of Mr. Glaisher having been most promptly and

willingly rendered, not only in studying the best modes of construction for the instruments and the requisite forms for registration, but also by having at several interviews with me in London, and for upwards of a fortnight in Northumberland, devoted his time and his whole energies to the carrying out of this useful work.

"Mr. Glaisher's great skill and untiring zeal have, I am convinced, conferred very great benefits on science in general, as well as upon the local interests more immediately concerned.

" II. INSTRUMENTS.

"The barometers have been purposely planned by Mr. Glaisher, so as to be plain, strong, easily read, not easily injured, and as moderate in price as is consistent with the care and skill required; the makers, Negretti and Zambra, are well known for the accuracy and excellence of their work.

"The Duke of Northumberland has been very desirous that the instruments used should be strong, very plain, not easily damaged in moving, and without any but the most plain and practical indications, as also that they should in every instance have been examined by Mr. Glaisher.

"III. CO-OPERATION OF OTHERS.

"At Berwick we received every kindness from the Rev. G. W. Hamilton, the vicar of that town, as also from the Rev. Messrs. Irwin and Durham, and from Mr. Alex. Lowrey. To Captain Popplewill also our thanks are especially due for the very kind interest he has taken in the subject, and which has conduced most materially to its success. The Mayor of Tynemouth has, from the first mention of the subject, taken a most lively interest in it. The Tyneside Naturalists' Field Club, and the active secretary of that society, Mr. Mennell, have most cordially united in giving their friendly aid, and also subscriptions from some of their members.

"The present operations as commenced in Northumberland appear likely to result in an extensive adoption of them in

various parts of England, as examples of which I send copies
of a letter from Suffolk, and of my letter to the writer of it,
who dates on the 20th and 21st inst. A similar application
reached Mr. Glaisher from Torquay, for the express purpose
of aiding the fishermen there.

"IV. The Fishermen.

"But most of all is it gratifying to be able to state that
the fishermen generally along the coast have shown not only
a friendly reception of the instruments, but an intelligent
appreciation of their use, and I am glad to say that these
were evinced by expressions of gratitude and respect which I
believe to have been truly honest and sincere.

"V. Printed Forms.

"The requisite printed forms are in progress ; they are of so
plain and simple arrangement as to admit of being much more
easily attended to than the usual registry of observations prepared for the Meteorological Society, which are adapted for
more minute details than it would be either useful or reasonable to expect from gratuitous observers on the coast.

"VI. Indicators.

"Mr. Buddle, the joiner, is making other two forms of
indicators in conformity with the wish of Captain Washington.
The cost of these, and also of the indicator removed from High
House, will be met by the Admiralty.

"VII. Future Progress.

"Although I am unwilling to mention any suggestion that
may seem like an appeal to any further generosity on the part
of His Grace, I yet feel it consistent with the eventual success
of the plan to remark that another survey of the stations by
Mr. Glaisher in the course of a few weeks would be of great
service, and that some small annual expenses to meet breakage,
or in occasional visits to the stations, may be found indispens-

able in addition to the general supervision which the Meteorological Society willingly undertakes.

" VIII. Results.

" In conclusion, I may beg to add in the most respectful terms my best thanks for the kind attention which my communications have received from the Duke, who, by encouraging the present efforts, has, I am convinced, done great service to a science as yet in comparative infancy, but which in its more mature growth has in it the capability of unfolding many important physical facts, bearing on the local conditions of climate, on the cultivation of crops, on the planning of farm labour, as well as on the foretelling of storms and on the improvement of agriculture, not less than the safety of life and preservation of property."

On October 25th we discover Mr. Sopwith taking the lead in what has since become one of the greatest social movements of the century, namely, the establishment of the United Kingdom Alliance, and the inception of the Permissive Bill, for permissive legislation in the sale of intoxicating drinks.

" *October* 25th.—I presided at a meeting this evening, the object of which was to promote the objects of an association called the United Kingdom Alliance, for the total legislative suppression of the liquor traffic. Mr. Wilson, who attended as agent of the society, gave a very clear explanation of the evils resulting from the indiscriminate sale of intoxicating liquors.

" No doubt it seems on a first view a very unlikely plan to bring into operation ; but the true point of view is to suppose that it was carried into effect, and weigh the disadvantages with the benefits. The latter, I feel assured, would very greatly predominate. Indeed, the poverty and crime and utter wretchedness caused by drink are beyond all calculation, and justify any attempt to provide a remedy.

"Within my own recollection a very great amelioration has taken place in the drinking usages of society. Some further improvements may reasonably be hoped for as education and sound social reforms are promoted; but so long as it is the custom to offer intoxicating drinks as an indispensable hospitality, and so long as ale-houses are places of easy access and of popular resort, it is hopeless to expect any important diminution of the awful and alarming evils which now exist.

"As chairman I introduced the subject by a few general observations of this nature, but without identifying myself with specific details. If ever the question is really entertained where I am interested as a resident, I should decidedly vote in favour of it as a boon of inestimable value to the community at large, and most especially so to the great bulk of the labouring classes."

In the early part of 1861 Mr. Sopwith read an important paper at the Meteorological Society on barometer indicators. This was on January 16th; and on Sunday, the 20th, he visited Exeter Hall to hear Mr. C. H. Spurgeon, then rising towards the zenith of his reputation. Mr. Sopwith's comments run favourably for the the great preacher.

"*Sunday, January 20th.*—I went with Mrs. S., Mrs. Christiansen, and two of my daughters to Exeter Hall, and heard the Rev. Mr. Spurgeon preach. I was much interested by hearing for the first time so celebrated an orator.

"The first impression, after he commenced speaking, was that of admiration of the clearness of his voice and the distinctness of his utterance. He maintained a seriousness of manner, a high respectability of demeanour, an argumentative and emphatic eloquence which is very attractive, and to many minds must be very impressive. I had heard many accounts from former hearers, most of them tending to the opinion I am here expressing, and I was gratified to find that the extraordinary popularity of Mr. Spurgeon rests on a basis of great talent and great earnestness."

The diary of February 11th records a little adventure at Allenheads.

" *February* 11*th.*—The weather very stormy, and very heavy showers of snow fall at intervals.

"To-day about noon Mr. Ralph Murray (one of the agents in this office) and a mason lost their way on the moors. For about six hours they wandered on the western slopes of the mountains under the conviction that they were descending the eastern side to Allenheads. Fortunately they arrived at the vicinity of Carshield, and followed a road which took them to Coalcleugh, where they remained, it being then past midnight, heavy showers of snow falling on the ground, already about two feet deep, and many drifts of eight or ten feet in height on the fells. At eleven o'clock at night my son Tom, accompanied by twelve stout fellows, went in search of Murray; they followed the tracks over the various windings from the top of the mountains to Carshield. As no tidings could be learnt there, my son and six of the party (six having gone in another direction) went to Coalcleugh, and arrived there at five in the morning, and were glad to find the objects of their search.

" In the meantime Mr. Bewick, who had sat up all night in anxious suspense, gathered other twenty men, who, with him, set off in search of the others, and met them soon after daybreak on their return."

Touching the origin and development of electric telegraphy there is an interesting entry on March 21st, 1861.

" *March* 21*st.*—In the evening I dined with my excellent friend Mr. Decimus Burton and a few friends. The conversation embraced many of the most advanced matters of science, and I had a very pleasant talk with Wheatstone on his new telegraph. By the new telegraph I mean the operations of the 'London District Telegraph Company,' the wires of which are rapidly increasing over the house-tops and across the streets of this great city. A message of ten words is sent for a charge of fourpence (including delivery). Message and reply of ten words, each sixpence. Message of twenty words, sixpence.

"It would be a most curious catalogue, as I suggested to Mr. Wheatstone, if he would draw up a list of his various inventions. To him, in conjunction with Mr. Cooke, the world is indebted for that greatest of all inventions, the electric telegraph; and the respective interests of each of these parties were defined by a memorandum in 1841, drawn up by Brunel (the elder) and Professor Daniell, with both of whom, as well as with Cooke and Wheatstone, I had the pleasure of occasionally meeting, as also with many others of the leading 'men of the time,' with whom about that time the idea of a great National Exhibition originated, the chief concentration of that design being at the Society of Arts, where a committee (of which I was a member) was appointed in 1844."

In the same month there is notice of an original design for meteorological charts which deserves record.

"*March* 26*th*, 1861.—This evening at seven I went by appointment to the *Morning Chronicle* office, where I met Mr. Glaisher, Dr. Tripe, Mr. Beardmore, and Mr. Perigal, at a consultation on some meteorological details connected with the establishment of a new paper devoted to meteorology, as bearing upon great commercial as well as scientific interests. One important feature of this daily publication is to be a map, whereon, by pictorial remarks, the state of the weather and direction of the wind, etc., are to be shown. Much care is requisite in the selection of characteristic signs, both with a view to convenient and rapid manipulation, and also for the sake of the public, who would be perplexed by any attempt at too much nicety of detail. It is far more important to show the more prominent indications plainly than to exhibit a great variety of states of weather. The principal matters that concern the merchant, the mariner, the farmer, or even the public generally, are whether the weather is fine, dull, wet, or stormy. Nothing shows bright or fine weather better than marks in a certain sense pictorial, as showing a sun with rays, a disc of the sun without rays, shade or clouds by oblique lines, rain or descending clouds by vertical lines of greater or lesser strength, and snow by its somewhat crystalline form of hexagonal radii, rudely indicated by a cross, and arranged in lines. Each kind of weather may thus have, say, sixteen varieties of direction of wind, and the wind in each may be very slight or calm, brisk, violent, or a hurricane, and these might be represented by arrowhead-like forms, moved in any of sixteen directions. There may thus be six varieties of weather, viz., (1) bright, (2) fair, (3) dull, (4) showery, (5) rainy, (6) snowy; and six varieties of wind, (1) calm, (2) gentle breeze, (3) brisk, (4) a gale, (5) violent, (6) hurricane. These make thirty-six variations; and if each type were movable in sixteen directions, we then have, with thirty-six types, as many as five hundred and seventy-six variations, by placing them according to any of the sixteen directions of the wind. This rough outline is founded on the consideration of some of these details many years ago. I mentioned them briefly, and proposed to explain them more fully next Saturday."

À *propos* of London society, he says, on the date of April 25th,—

"*April 25th.*—The vicar of Newcastle and Mr. Woodall, junior, of Scarborough, dined with me at six,—the vicar, frank, hearty, and open, in general conversation, and Mr. Woodall remarkably intelligent, and possessed of much information of a very practical character. The company of one or two agreeable friends is, in my opinion, quite as enjoyable, and often more instructive, than a larger party, where conversation is cut up into shreds and patches, and cannot be long concentrated on any one subject. Both have their attractions; but in London the tendency is generally towards a large party—by which I do not so much mean a great number, as exceeding the quiet limits of two or three. The boundary-line between what I call large and small dinner companies is the number eight, which is accomplished in a family by an addition of two, three, or four to the usual circle; and this I think is the maximum of small parties in so quiet an establishment as my own. To evening parties my objection is very great when they are so numerous as to cause crowding and want of ventilation. Such inconvenient and unhealthy assemblies are unfortunately too fashionable to be wholly avoided; but I endeavour always to avoid them, to keep clear of what I consider 'vulgar errors' on so large a scale; and my family, knowing this aversion, assist in keeping me aloof from them. At my own house I always desire ample space for dancing, comfortable seats for all, and the endeavour to bring together those who are likely to enjoy each other's society. I make no allusion here to either dinner parties or evening assemblies of the higher ranks. I confine my remarks to my own walk of life, and I always rejoice when cheerful and kind feelings appear to prevail among such friends as favour me with their company."

Amongst the acquaintances whom Mr. Sopwith delighted to recognise for his sterling qualities and great learning, the late Sir James Kay-Shuttleworth holds a first place. On May 3rd of this year he met Sir James and Mr. John Simpson, together with his own son Arthur. Sir James is here called upon to explain some mining conditions, which he does with much skill. It afforded " a good example to the youths, as showing how clear a knowledge of technical subjects can be attained by an intelligent gentleman who had not been professionally educated on the subject. It also showed the conciseness, yet abundant illustration, which marked the verbal explanation of Sir James." The commendation is not a word too strong. Sir James Kay-Shuttleworth, originally Dr. Kay, was a man great in all things he undertook to master. His experimental essay on asphyxia, written while he was a young medical inquirer, showed an originality and a resource of research which makes one almost regret that even good-fortune took him out of the ranks of practical medicine, and led him from pursuits towards which, to the very close of his life, his highest intellectual powers leaned ; as I discovered with great delight, when I once had the pleasure of dining in his company at the hospitable table of the late Sir Thomas Watson.

The autumn of 1861 was diversified by a visit at Alnwick Castle to the Duke of Northumberland, followed by a tour in Italy, Switzerland, and France in company with Mrs. Sopwith, and including an inspection of the works in progress in the famous Mont Cenis tunnel.

They travelled two thousand five hundred miles in twenty-five days, at the rate of one hundred miles a day, and yet were able to see so much that the travelling was felt to be the least part of the whole journey.

A good deal of the diary at this stage is taken up with reports on the Nova Scotia Gold-mining Company, and on the second Great Exhibition (1862), then in progress. On the first of these topics public interest has faded ; on the last it still remains.

The leading spirit in the Exhibition movement was Mr. (afterwards Sir Henry) Cole, to whom Mr. Sopwith pays a graceful tribute.

" *December 7th*, 1861.—Walked to the Exhibition buildings, and reached the entrance just as Mr. Cole and a party of his friends were entering, and with them I walked through several portions of the edifice, and had some conversation with Mr. Cole on the present state and probable completion of the works. ' It will be done in time,' said Mr. Cole, and I have confidence in his prediction, for he is one of those who accomplish much in a quiet and steady way. Now a hint—now a few words—now a resolution or a newspaper paragraph. These are the first indications; weeks pass on; progress is being made,—persevering, untiring progress; and a footing is gained; the opinion of influential men is attracted; that influence is brought to bear. The germ of some great design appears in a humble form; it steadily increases; and in a few years the dimensions are vast, the utility (for in that lies the secret of the whole) is made manifest, and in after-time Sir Henry de la Beche and Mr. Cole will be assuredly recognised as founders of two great institutions, or rather two designs merging into one. The Museum of Practical Geology, and the South Kensington Museum and its extensions (mark the words, for they are of significance), will be lasting monuments of their skill and untiring zeal in administrating to the great cause of improvement in knowledge and taste."

The diary of the year concludes with several references to the exceedingly painful event of that time,—the death of the Prince Consort. The loss of this illustrious man was felt by everyone, but by none, I think, so much as by those who were engaged in scientific and artistic labours,—labours which he had made specifically his own. Mr. Sopwith, who had met the Prince personally, and had conversed with him on subjects of equal interest to both, was naturally much affected, and to the end of his life never ceased to speak of the Prince without expressing his earnest regret at his early death, "just at the time," he once observed to me, "when his great knowledge was maturing into excellent wisdom."

CHAPTER XXVII.

1862-65.

N article written by Mr. Sopwith for *St. James's Magazine*, at the request of Mrs. S. C. Hall, forms the first subject of notice in the year 1862. The article brought under review the depressing incidents of a lamentable calamity, under the title of "A Place of Darkness and in the Deep;" but it also dwelt on prevention of similar accidents, and on the conservation of coal in reference to economy and durability from a national point of view.

In March (the 10th) there is an account of an interesting visit to John Bright, M.P., in which that distinguished orator made an unexpected prediction. "If I had to begin life again," said Mr. Bright, "I would certainly choose the profession of an engineer. It is the engineers who are doing the great work of the time; they are the true statesmen, and are guiding the destinies of nations and of mankind by the influence of their works." With this view Mr. Sopwith generally concurred.

A little later—namely, March 25th—he records the particulars of an evening spent with Mr. Cobden, in the course of which nearly all the subjects he—Mr.

19

Sopwith—was most familiar with were touched upon, but the most interesting topic was the Suez Canal.

"The Canal of Lesseps.

"*March 25th.*—Mr. Cobden was desirous to know if I possessed any information as to this work. I described what I had seen of the places and surroundings of it on board the surveying-ship *Tartarus* when at Alexandria. Mr. Cobden said Lord Palmerston's opposition on political grounds had been the making of Lesseps. We had much conversation on Robert Stephenson's opinion of it.

"' He did not,' I said, ' consider it as absolutely impossible, but as utterly beyond the pale of prudent commercial enterprise.' Mr. Cobden said he agreed in that, and alluded to the difficult navigation of the Red Sea, the inevitable exorbitancy of tolls, etc.

"Mr. Cobden's recollections of Egypt, the ascent of the Pyramids, the character of the prospect from the Pyramids, and his vivid recollection of the Nile like a narrow ribbon in the midst of green plains, bordered on each side by the brown desert, he described with much force.

"The Roman Wall was for some time a subject of lively conversation. The name of Wallsend as associated with coal and the Romans was new to Mr. Cobden."

As a juror of the National Exhibition of 1862, Mr. Sopwith was present at the opening ceremony on May 1st. In the working of the Exhibition he took, all through, a prominent part, suggesting many important details for the consideration of the jurors.

1863.

A number of current details are touched upon in the opening of the year 1863, including a scheme, unfinished, for the formation of model workmen's homes ; an interview with Mr. Brassey, whose society is always enjoyable,

—so open, genial, courteous, frank, and, withal, cordial and hearty; a long conversation with Sir Charles Bright on telegraphic communications; the opening of the metropolitan railways to the public on January 10th; a visit to Mr. Decimus Burton at St. Leonards, and a visit to the Royal Institution to hear Cardinal Wiseman lecture on Science and Art. On February 10th, 1863, there is an entry, of much interest to all his family circle, as well as to many relations and friends, namely, the marriage of his daughter Isabella to Mr. James Hall, of Newcastle, and of his daughter Anna to Mr. W. Shelford, at Christ Church, Bayswater.

March 4th gives us a little picture of Bishop Colenso at an "At Home" given by Mrs. Heywood. He considered Colenso eminent as a mathematician, and from many sides heard, even from those who were opposed to his theological train of inquiry, the most favourable account of his amiability. He describes the Bishop as tall, very young-looking for a bishop, with an intelligent and firm expression of countenance, and apparently a mild and reserved disposition. In another entry the Bishop is further described.

"*April 1st.*—In the evening I attended a meeting of the Geological Society. After the meeting we had tea downstairs, as in former times, and I had some conversation with Bishop Colenso, Mr. R. Chambers and Mr. Ramsay also joining in the same, which had relation to the works in which the Bishop is now engaged. Whatever differences of opinion may exist thereon, I am satisfied that the Bishop is actuated by a stern love of truth, and he expressed very feelingly how much the conversion of the heathen nations is impeded by too rigid an adherence to strict literal interpretation."

In April of this year Mr. and Mrs. Sopwith, with some other members of the family visited the Continent, to see

Mr. Thomas Sopwith at Aix-la-Chapelle, where he was residing for his health. On his return he proceeded in June to Mr. Hooper's works, to see the manufacture of the Hooper electric cable. Towards the latter part of June he was again on the Continent, visiting the Rhine and passing into Switzerland. The journey was brief, and early in July he was back to business, public and private, including a more complete examination of Mr. Hooper's Cable Works at Mitcham, and an attendance, in company with Lord Brougham, at the Annual Meeting of the Working Men's Club and Institute Union, over which Lord Brougham presided, "and spoke very sensibly, giving great clearness to his views by simplicity of language and force of expression."

On July 18th we get a glance at another very interesting man of science, Mr. Cyrus Field.

"*July 18th*, 1863.—I went to Regent's Park, and called on Professor Wheatstone. Here I met Mr. Cyrus Field, and had the great pleasure of hearing Mr. Wheatstone explain some of his recent improvements in telegraphic communication, and especially a method of transmitting from six to seven hundred letters per minute. Mr. Wheatstone's obliging and clear description of all the various manipulations was a very great intellectual treat.

"During this interview I took an opportunity of mentioning the cable of my friend Mr. Hooper, and I read the results of Bright and Clarke's experimental tests. Mr. Cyrus Field expressed an earnest wish to see Mr. Hooper, and I wrote to make an arrangement for their meeting on Mr. H.'s return to town."

On August 26th, 1863, the British Association opened for the second time at Newcastle, Sir William Armstrong being president. This time a visit to Allenheads formed one of the excursions. It was a wet day, and the *Times* called the excursionists "the dripping savans," but the meeting passed off satisfactorily nevertheless.

1864.

In April and May 1864 Mr. Sopwith made a journey to the mines of Linares, and to various other places in France and Spain. The journey extended through May, and was full of incident, including a sketch of a bull-fight.

"*Seville, May 2nd*, 1864.—I was unwilling to lose an opportunity of seeing that most renowned of all Spanish amusements, a bull-fight—the more so as the bull-ring of Seville is the largest in Spain, and the bulls of this district are said to be peculiarly wild. Moreover, the performance was to be for a charity. The Duke and Duchess of Montpensier were to be present, and the most eminent bull-fighter in Spain had volunteered his services. So, having in the morning obtained a ticket for the shady side of the balcony, in the first row, I went at 4 p.m. on Tuesday, May 3rd, and was at once shown to my seat. Two gentlemen alongside spoke sufficient English, and were good-natured enough to explain to me the principal incidents of one of the most remarkable scenes I ever beheld.

"I shall not here enter the details of a bull-fight, for I should never read them but with horror and with deep sorrow. Suffice it to say that, although I left long before the close of the performance, I saw four bulls and five horses killed amidst the plaudits of the admiring crowd of spectators. I shall not presume on one single visit to be able to analyse what may be merits or demerits. There may be some advantages which I do not understand, and if there be none it seems difficult to understand why the so-called amusement is so nationally popular. I shall only record my own impressions: the sight of the vast and eager company; the introductory pageantry of asking for and receiving the key of the ring; the brilliant dresses and brave demeanour of the chief artists,—all disposed me to look on the performance so as to form a fair conclusion apart from all previous prejudice. I looked on with painful interest—then with horror—then with shame, and I left with very acute feelings of sorrow blended with astonishment, and with a firm determination never again to be a willing spectator of a Spanish bull-fight."

Much more pleasant is another entry of the same date bearing on Spanish workmen, and of a visit to some large works under the superintendence of Mr. Pickman.

" I was much interested by the several commendations which Mr. Pickman made to me relating to Spain and the Spaniards generally, and of this conversation I said to him that I would enter a few memoranda in my journal, and this I do now :

" 1. Mr. Pickman strongly confirms the opinions I have heard expressed by many, that the working classes of the Spaniards make excellent workmen, that they learn readily and willingly obey, that they are industrious, but have a rough-and-ready sort of independence which has to be met by patience, tact, and sometimes indulgence. In short, they are easy to lead, but hard to drive ; and Mr. P. speaks of them as workmen with much commendation.

" 2. In twenty years, during which the whole of this concern has been under Mr. Pickman's superintendence, he has never had occasion to discharge a single workman for intemperance.

" 3. Mr. Pickman speaks most favourably of the honest and honourable dealing shown by the great number of persons to whom credit is given—often with slight means of correct information as regards wealth or position or character. ' In sixty thousand pounds of credit,' said he, ' we have not three hundred pounds of bad debts.' These commendations of industry, temperance, and correct dealing in trade are valuable testimony as coming from one like Mr. Pickman, who speaks from a large experience as well as from a sound judgment."

By an entry in the diary dated July 14th, 1864, I find that Mr. Sopwith was observing some experiments by

Mr. Redy in blowing up rocks at Allenhead with gun cotton fired by electricity. The results appear to have been satisfactory, and were a matter of great surprise to the miners, who had hitherto blasted with gunpowder. The experiments were repeated on July 19th, and with still more success.

At this period what was called spirit-rapping was in fashion, and the battle royal was being fought on the subject between the men of science headed by Faraday on the one side and the spiritualists on the other. Mr. Sopwith was disinclined to accept the many claims that were made by the spiritualists, but on September 7th he was induced to see Mrs. Marshall, a "medium" living at 10, King Street, Bloomsbury Square. " A spirit there rapped out his own name and the maiden name of his mother, the Christian name of his father, and the place where he was born." Beyond stating what occurred, he has nothing to say, no hypotheses to offer, only that he could not believe there was any possibility of collusion. He recorded no more than what he distinctly saw and observed, and added that the seeing of this table movement and receiving this seemingly mysterious communication did not produce any feeling different from that with which one is accustomed to view any curious experimental result.

On October 6th he was at the Mining Institute, Mr. Nicholas Wood in the chair, when a paper which he submitted on the lead mines was brought under discussion. After this he returned to Allenheads to receive the members of the Gun-cotton Committee, who arrived there on the 17th. This Committee, of which General Sir Edward Sabine, F.R.S., was President, was well represented on the occasion of the visit. Mr. Sopwith also was a member of the Committee. In the latter part of this year he took

up a London residence in Victoria Street, Westminster,
which residence he held until the time of his death.

1865.

In April 1865 he revisited Spain, spending some time
at the lead mines of Linares, where Mr. Thomas Sopwith,
jun., was residing.   There is a note on May 1st of a ball
at Mr. Thomas Sopwith's, and several other entries recording pleasant visits to Madrid, Barcelona, and other
famous places in Spain.

Under the head of reminiscences, bearing date of this
year, 1865, Mr. Sopwith gives the following epitome of
twenty years' experience of mining life at Allenheads.

The epitome forms a kind of simply-expressed autobiography.

"REMINISCENCES.—TWENTY YEARS AT W. B. LEAD-MINES.

"*July 1st,* 1865.—I was occupied until twelve o'clock last
night with papers relating to the inclosure of Allendale
Common, and thus ended the twentieth year of my connection
as Chief Manager of the W. B. Lead-mines.   This morning at
nine I resume the study and carrying out of the usual routine
of my duties, and take an hour or two during the day to enter
a brief review of some of the more prominent circumstances of
the last twenty years.

"When, in 1845, I entered on the management I received a
friendly letter from the late Mr. John Taylor, in which he
spoke of the generally-received opinion that these mines were
nearly exhausted.

"An examination of details showed that expenditure in raising
ore was rapidly increasing, whilst no outlay was made on repairs
or improvements beyond such as were absolutely inevitable.
I was informed that my predecessor contemplated that actual
loss would arise during the first year of my agency, and these
were not only the discouragements of mining, they were
indicative of other and serious obstacles which were laid in my

path, but to which I will not now advert in any detail. Many
of the parties who then moved within the sphere of action in
which my new duties lay have gone to their rest. I have
endeavoured wholly to forget whatever was unpleasant, and
more willingly dwell with satisfaction that feelings of friendship
largely predominated even where differences of opinion prevailed,
and I can find employment enough in tracing my own errors,
without finding it necessary to remember what I may have
deemed the errors of others.

" So far from being exhausted, the value of the produce of the
W. B. Lead-mines in lead and silver has approximated during
the twenty years to more than £500 per diem, and a fair
amount of steadiness of produce has been maintained, ranging
from eight to ten thousand tons of lead per annum. This is
the first and most prominent feature in this short retrospect,
and I shall now recapitulate some of the leading circumstances
to which my attention has been given, with a brief remark or
two in passing them under so hurried a review.

" By far the most important features of my early labours were
various works of exploration and improvement, for which I
obtained from the late T. W. Beaumont a special grant of
upwards of £6,000 per annum.

"This liberality in beginning and continuing new works was
continued and largely exceeded by the present owner of the
mines, Wentworth Blackett Beaumont, Esq., and it would
occupy a volume to describe the various works in detail. The
very face of the country at and near Allenheads has been absolutely changed. Old and ruinous and imperfect works have
been replaced by new and substantial buildings, machinery,
roads, etc., of the most improved construction. The deep
drainage of the mines at Allenheads was closely investigated by
me, with the valuable aid of Mr., now Sir William, Armstrong,
and the hydraulic engines placed in the mines by him met
with unqualified approval and high commendation from Robert
Stephenson and other competent authorities.

" A still higher testimony to ¦their value has been the

uninterrupted efficiency of the work performed by them, and the exceedingly small cost by which they have been kept in repair, a merit which appertains to all the extensive works of machinery which have been put up by the eminent firm of which my greatly valued friend Armstrong was the sole originator, and is yet and I trust long will be the greatly honoured head and chief conductor. In the erection of the various engines and machinery, and in the construction of all the engineering works generally, the greatest and my warmest thanks are due to Mr. Thomas John Bewick, who came to me as a pupil, and has ever since either been directly in my service or acting under me in the service of W. B. Beaumont, Esq., as resident engineer of these important mines.

"New workshops on a very complete scale have been built. A new crushing mill and improvements of the dressing floors have resulted in a rich economy of labour, and an increase of produce so remarkable that the percentage of lead now obtained is the greatest in the kingdom, whereas when I came in 1845 it was the least. In this alone has been an element of value to the extent of several thousands of pounds yearly. Great improvements were made in the reservoirs, and the extension and renovation of Byerhope reservoir, estimated by several experienced engineers as a work of £2,000, cost less than one-third of that sum, and this I mention as an index to the comparative economy of many other works.

"In 1855 the Blackett Level was planned and commenced, having during the previous ten years been more or less a subject of consideration. The idea was not original, it was only an extension, and in that degree an improvement on designs contemplated long ago by my predecessor Mr. William Crawhall, who in like manner was preceded (ninety years ago) by Smeaton in his Nent Force Level. This great work has been continued in accordance with the views entertained and the rate of expenditure sanctioned by Mr. Beaumont, who has taken a most able and lively interest in this undertaking, of which it is yet difficult to form any accurate conjecture as to eventual success. The hydraulic engines on this work have been much, and as I think very deservedly, admired. In 1856, on my suggestion, and indeed, as Mr. Beaumont kindly put it, at my request, the opinion of Mr. W. Warrington Smyth * was taken on the general character and prospects of the Blackett Level, and the experience of ten years has not shown anything at variance with the views expressed in a clear and, as far as it goes, a very accurate report. In 1856 I had a correspondence with Captain Collinson on the subject of boring rocks by machinery, on which also Mr. Edward Beaumont when at Allenheads expressed a strong opinion of its applicability ; but from time to time the conviction has been forced upon me that in a large concern like the W. B. mines it is better to adopt completed and successful inventions than to institute those experimental researches which, being in themselves very costly, are also for the time being not unfrequently a positive hindrance rather than an advancement of practical mining operations.

"Some interesting trials of boring machines have been made in the last two years by the express desire of Mr. Beaumont, and the results are not at this time sufficiently established to enable me to say whether either of them will be especially applicable to lead mining works.

"In West Allendale and in Weardale many works of exploration and improvement both on the surface and in the mines have been carried out. All the details of these works were very accurately recorded in a series of reports, without which I could not have retained any clear and long-continued views relating to so great a number of operations conducted in various parts of a mining district embracing more than two hundred square miles of superficial area. It is in this method of written instructions, memoranda, and reports that I have been thought (although in a very friendly and considerate manner) to have exceeded rather than fallen short of what my duties might seem to require, and in deference to the opinion of one who has the undoubted right to offer any such suggestions

* Afterwards Sir W. Warrington Smyth.

I have of late years relaxed, and to some extent entirely abandoned, the attempt to preserve rigid and exact data of the principal details. In so doing I have been more convinced of the utter inability of myself, or of any one person, to preserve such written details, rather than of the inutility or impolicy of the system, which appears to be almost indispensable in multifarious concerns of great magnitude.

"The subject of education has had especial notice bestowed upon it, both by the late and present owner of these mines. The liberality of W. B. Beaumont in the building and supporting good schools is beyond all praise, and I firmly believe as well as hope that he and his family will reap a rich reward in the virtue and intelligence which have been so ably diffused amongst the people of this district. In referring to this subject I must mention with special praise the efforts of Mr. and Mrs. Fisher at Allenheads, from the commencement of the school (1848) to the end of 1864, and much credit is due to many others who have had charge of the schools so liberally encouraged by Mr. Beaumont. The new and handsome schools built at Allenheads, Carshields, Brideshill, and Newhouse will remain a lasting monument of the zeal as well as good taste with which Mr. W. B. Beaumont has promoted education in these mining districts.

"When I came to Allenheads one small room sufficed for an office. New and spacious and exceedingly convenient offices have been built, and further additions, made to them a few years ago, render them, as I think, absolutely perfect. In them I have spent a large portion of my time, and the facility with which I can at once refer to the several sub-agents and clerks, and to their respective books, plans, etc., is very great.

"The well-being of the large body of miners and other workpeople, men and boys (for no women are employed on the mines or works of any kind), has had my constant and earnest care. It is true some differences with the miners at Allenheads led to a separation or 'strike' of four months' duration (in 1849), but I gained the point at issue, viz., the observance of the terms of the bargains in respect of time, and a temporary ill-feeling, and some acts of violence and of malignant censures in newspapers, handbills, and songs, were soon replaced by a friendly confidence which has ever since continued, and I trust is not now likely to be disturbed. Important ameliorations in the matter of wages, etc., were made, the comfort of the men in many respects attended to, and above all a fair effort has always been made to deal with them justly and equitably. Neither in West Allendale nor Weardale has any interruption of good feeling taken place, and as regards all of them I have ever met them as friends, and have on many occasions received from them the kindest testimony of approval. The establishment of Improvement Societies in Weardale was for a time a great benefit, and I can in many cases trace very distinctly the highly favourable results.

"The roads in the district have been in many respects improved during the last twenty years. In 1850 I had a plan and section of a railway made up East Allendale and Swinhope, and prevailed on the directors of the Newcastle and Carlisle Railway to visit the district. It was too late—the Alston line had been decided on, and the matter remained until 1864, when, on the subject being named by Mr. Beaumont at a public dinner, the public feeling was roused, considerable support was promised, and soon after liberally subscribed. Surveys have been made by Mr. Bewick, and the royal assent has been given to an Act for making the railway.

"Much attention was given in the earlier years of my agency to applications for 'tack bargains,' or workings out of the ordinary routine, conducted by parties holding a grant or lease for a term of years. The most important of these were the working of lead ore in conjunction with iron stone, by Messrs. Attwood & Company, and the driving an exploration level at Fallowfield by Mr. Jacob Walton, and now, since his decease, by his son and partner. The system, however, is not found to be a convenient one for general adoption; the damage to private lands, the time and cost of preliminary meetings and of subsequent inspections and surveys, in most cases far outweigh the probable advantages, and in cases of entire failure these difficulties are often increased by unreasonable delays or objections to a fair settlement.

"I have from time to time collected many printed and written books and papers relating to mines. These are found to be useful for reference, and the method might perhaps be extended. I have also arranged a very capacious cabinet for the collection and preservation of mineral specimens, to be used as a place of study for the agents, and as a means of preserving data relating to the discovery of mineral veins.

"The supply of materials for the mines has been gradually brought into a form of great regularity. Printed order-books have been introduced, and all orders now go from this (Allenheads) office, and are examined and signed by myself as well as by the resident engineer. The drawing of work from the mines, and the carriage of ores, lead, and of all timber and other materials, has been also placed on a proper basis.

"There is perhaps no subject affording more gratification than the great rarity of serious accidents in the mines during the last twenty years. They average less than half a life per annum, and that in a body of more than two thousand workmen.

" In a remote district like Allenheads the selection of proper clergymen to attend to parochial duties devolves on the owner of the mines, who is patron of the parish, and in some of these matters I have been consulted.

"The engineering duties have been attended to by Mr. Bewick, as already named, and for some years past (seven) Mr. J. C. Cain has acted as general surveyor of the mines. Among the numerous body of inspectors I must especially record my regret for the recent loss of Mr. William Curry, whose earnest attention to his duties and friendly regard for all my advice and instructions I shall always remember with respect. He is worthily succeeded by his brother, Mr. John Curry, assisted by Mr. John Ashman.

" The taxes, highway and poor rates, are of some considerable amount, and a supervision of the several details is at all times necessary. In cases where any difference of view has arisen, I have had the good success to have my own propositions approved and confirmed by the Commissioners of Stamps and Taxes in London, and by the chief surveyors at Darlington and Hexham, from one of whom I received a most complimentary letter on the promptness and exactness of the W. B. mines' arrangements in this department.

"The 'subsistence,' or money paid monthly on account to the miners, was advanced from 7s. 6d. to 10s. per week, and all the accounts and details of payment have been greatly improved. The 'pays' or settlement of the balances are now made half-yearly instead of yearly, and all tradesmen are regularly paid once a quarter instead of once a year. The mode of letting bargains has also been gradually amended, and the arrangements with the men are as far as possible based on a desire to deal fairly with them, and to give them fair wage for due work.

"The establishment of libraries has been a great benefit, and there are now four of them, viz., at Allenheads, Coalcleugh, Weardale, and Allen Mill. I take to myself any merit that may belong to what I have called children's libraries, accompanying the ordinary collection of books, the object being to afford young children a good selection and frequent change of amusing books.

"Benefit societies have had a large share of my attention, and by the very able assistance and kind co-operation of Mr. Bewick both these and a benefit building society have proved of great advantage. The liberality of Mr. Beaumont has been most effectually bestowed in a proportional encouragement of the Allendale Benefit Societies, by giving them donations yearly of 5 per cent. on the amount of money subscribed in each year, and 2 per cent. on the amounts invested, thus giving the members the advantage of full 5 per cent. interest annually, as they receive 3 per cent. from savings banks or Commissioners for Reduction of the National Debt.

"At Allenheads there have been during the last ten years, 1856-1865, both inclusive, an average of 395·4 members, and the increase has been from 314 in the first of the ten years to 491 in the last. The average number receiving sick pay has been 48·3, and the average time of sickness of each sick member has been 12·2 days. The cash paid in the ten years to sick members has been £2,486 5s., and the average to each sick member has been £5 2s. 11d. Payments at death have amounted to £220, making the entire payments £2,706 12s. 6d., or an annual sum of £270 12s. 6d. The total amount expended in fifteen years since the commencement has been £3,466 7s. 0½d.

"There is a difference in the amounts paid by the W. B. workmen and by persons not employed in the mines and works. I find this difference, taking five cases of different ages, and ordinary rates, to amount to about 11s. 4¼d. each member (yearly), or £5 13s. 9d. in ten years.

"The value of Mr. Beaumont's contributions has averaged in the same period nearly £20 a year in respect of the annual contributions, and rather more than £40 a year in respect of moneys invested, the total average being above £62 a year, or in the ten years £622 7s. 8d. The value of this contribution to each member has been about 3s. yearly, or £1 10s. 10¾d. in ten years.

"The inclosure of Allendale Common has been mooted at various times, and some agitation has been promoted by parties desirous to effect a division.

"In the cash transactions, which have been large, and amounting in the aggregate to upwards of three millions sterling, I have, during the whole period of twenty years, had the great satisfaction of corresponding with the highly-eminent house of Findlay, Hodgson, & Co., of London, and of enjoying the friendship as well as confidence of the late John Hodgson, long the senior of the firm, and a warm friend and zealous promoter of the interests of the Beaumont family; as also of his sons Kirkman Daniel Hodgson, M.P. (recently

Governor of the Bank of England) and J. E. Hodgson, Esqrs.
The extreme punctuality and exactness of all those transactions has been a source of constant satisfaction, for it need
scarcely be observed how much financial exactness lies at the
very root of so extensive a mining and smelting concern.

" The landed property belonging to Mr. Beaumont, in the
mining districts of East and West Allendale, has been vastly
improved, many cottages have been built, lands drained, and
plantations reared. The area of the land estate in Allendale
has also been considerably augmented by purchases made from
the profits of the mines.

"In the general financial business of these mines I have had
frequent occasion to spend much time at the W. B. Lead Office
at Newcastle, where, for many years, I had the valuable and
skilful aid of my much lamented friend, John George Anderson,
and, in later years, I have found Mr. Fothergill most kind and
attentive, as well as most assiduous in the discharge of his
duties.

" In legal matters I have had the advantage of consulting
several solicitors who were my personal friends as well as
professional advisers of the Beaumont family; and, I may
mention the names of Donkin, Stable, Armstrong, Bell, Dees,
and I. and R. Gibson. All my recollections of them are
associated with much respect for their courtesy and candour as
well as for their legal ability.

" The ordnance survey of this district has been made within
the period I am now adverting to, and a very great number
of surface and mining plans have been constructed in this
office under the immediate care of Messrs. Bewick, Coates,
Ridley, and others, acting under my general directions.

" I venture to say of these plans generally that they are
models of excellence, and they accurately delineate what has
been most carefully surveyed. These plans have been of great
use in many respects, both in mining and in many surface
improvements.

" The retrospect of the last twenty years is not wholly

destitute of incidents more allied to military than to mining
matters.   Amongst these are to be classed the numerous
experiments in gun practice by Mr. (now Sir William) Armstrong; the experiments on gun-cotton by the Government
Commission (of which I am a member), and the establishment
by Mr. Beaumont of a regiment of Rifle Volunteers, commanded,
in the first instance, by my son Thomas Sopwith, junior, and
since he left Allendale by Mr. Bewick.

"There are many other incidents I might mention, such as
the effectual repairs of Allenheads Chapel (to which I willingly
contributed one-third of the cost), the regular keeping of
meteorological observations, the Exhibitions of lead and silver
in London in 1851 and 1862, and in Paris in 1855, at all of
which medals were awarded in recognition of the interest of
the objects exhibited; and, though in 1862 I could not (as a
juror) receive the awarded medal, yet it was specially named,
and I received a medal as a juror in Class I. of that great
Exhibition.

"In concluding this little epitome I may observe that
during ten years I resided in the house built by the late
T. W. Beaumont in conformity with arrangements made
before I undertook to give up my profession and undertake
the agency.   The scale of dimensions and expenditure were at
first meant to be included in an amount of £4,000, which
entirely met my views; but, by the special instructions of Mr.
T. W. Beaumont, the matter was not placed within my control,
and the cost, I believe, exceeded double the above-named sum.
During two years previous to its completion I occupied the
house in the village, so that my period of residence has been
twelve years, and of partial residence eight years.   Of the
latter period my family abode has been for seven years in
Cleveland Square, and one year in Victoria Street, London.

"There is nothing in all my remembrances of this twenty
years' period that I record with greater pleasure and gratitude
than the great amount of domestic happiness I have enjoyed
at Allenheads, and in my London home, as also amongst

many most valued friends at Newcastle and elsewhere. True it is that dark shadows fell upon my path in the middle period of that time. Time, which softens the pangs of affliction, has only given strength to all my memories of devoted affection and of worth, which were duly and very highly estimated by all who knew the truly good and loving mother of all my surviving children.

"The death of my eldest son in India, not long after I came to Allenheads, was a very sudden, but a very heavy, blow, alleviated by some considerations arising from the fact that in his mind, a highly accomplished one, there were tendencies which had caused his friends and himself much sorrow, and no one could say whether in a longer life the good or evil tendencies would most have prevailed. Of all my other children I have only to speak in unmeasured terms of affection and approval; and in like terms I have to commend her who has become the partner of my life, the sharer in my joys and sorrows, the active, intelligent, and agreeable companion of my travels, and the affectionate friend and adviser of my family. In a wide circle of friends it would be most difficult to make any selections, but I may mention the names of Robert Stephenson, Robert Chambers, Michael Faraday, and James Pillans, as honoured visitors during my abode at Allenheads. The warm and steady friendship of William Ord, of Whitfield, was for many years a great source of enjoyment, and his beautiful house at Whitfield was one in which I spent many days with much, and always increasing, regard for its worthy inmates. Amongst those in whose society I have found a congenial feeling and candid reciprocation of views I may mention James Sillick, T. M. Mackay, and Robert Simpson; and to these I might add a large number of my friends whose opinions and character I most highly esteem.

"Last and not least, but, on the contrary, held by me in constant remembrance and regard, are the many, I may say the almost daily, proofs of confidence and friendly feeling exhibited towards me by the late and present owners of these

mines, the late Thomas Wentworth Beaumont, and his son
Wentworth Blackett Beaumont.   Some few differences of
opinion arose eight years ago; and in these, perhaps, my own
impatience was at fault, even though I deemed myself safe in
the judgment of so able and impartial a person as Robert
Stephenson; yet these little passing clouds have been of small
import as compared with the steady and solid friendship shown
to my son as well as myself, and in return for which a steady
devotion of my best efforts is due.   I had almost forgot to
mention, as one of those proofs of confidence, the important
arrangements whereby my son was enabled to make a mining
tour through Europe, and to be placed in charge of valuable lead
mines in Spain; but this is because my present observations have
reference chiefly to Allenheads and to circumstances connected
with it.   In these few pages I have inserted such memoranda
as recall to my mind many leading incidents, many important
improvements, and many sources of enjoyment, during the
period of twenty years which have been chiefly spent at
Allenheads, at which place, on this the 1st of July, I have
entered these memoranda.

" (*Signed*) THOMAS SOPWITH."

Towards the close of the year 1865, November 22nd, Mr.
Sopwith presided at a meeting held to establish colliery
insurances.

The diary of the year 1865 ends with entries referring
to a very pleasant task, that of arranging the library in
the new house, 103, Victoria Street, Westminster.

CHAPTER XXVIII.

SPECIAL entry in the diary on January 3rd, 1866, is headed, " My Birthday, and Friends at Dinner." It supplies a little commentary on the sensation of entering the sixty-third year, the close of the third section of three maturities. It then passes to describe the dinner, at which were present Mr. Robert Chambers, Dr. and Mrs. Priestley,—the last-named, the beautiful and accomplished daughter of Mr. Chambers,—Mr. and Mrs. Joseph Cubitt, Mr. W. Warrington and Mrs. Smyth, Mr. T. M. Smith and Mrs. Smith, Mr. Julian Hill and Mrs. Hill, and the Sopwith family circle. Speaking of some of these, he says :—

" *January 3rd.*—Mr. T. M. Smith was associated with me in professional matters about twenty years ago, and I had known his excellent and kind-hearted mother some time previously.

" Mr. Julian Hill is one of the well-known family which has gained world-wide renown by the Penny Postage Reform effected by Mr. (now Sir Rowland) Hill, whom it has been my good fortune to know very intimately, as also Mr. Arthur Hill. With Mr. Julian Hill I have been long and very intimately acquainted, and have often experienced the hearty hospitality of his amiable lady and himself.

"Such, therefore, was my birthday party—realizing much of that true wealth of friendship and regard which I have treasured through life with an anxiety which has never been bestowed upon mere worldly wealth, although not insensible to the duty as well as the advantage of a reasonable attention thereto.

"The term of sixty-three years is an interesting one. It completes three periods of twenty-one years, and each of these periods has been singularly marked by material differences as regards my home, my occupations, and my connections. The first period, from 1803 to 1824, was entirely spent at home. It was in 1824, when twenty-one years of age, that I left the home of my birth, my infancy, my childhood, my boyhood, and my ripened youth. In that year also I became engaged, but could not then with prudence contemplate marriage in less than four years. Then, in 1828, I married, and in 1829 lost, in a few short months, both my father and a beloved wife. In 1831 I again married her who became the mother of all my now surviving children. For other fourteen years I was most actively engaged in my profession at Newcastle, London, Gloucestershire, South Wales, and in other parts of England and Scotland. I acted as Commissioner for the Crown for Dean Forest from 1838 to 1841, and undertook some extensive professional services in Belgium, where I had as colleagues the well-known George Stephenson and William Cubitt.

"I had offices in London and in Newcastle, and my time was a good deal directed between these places. I enjoyed over the greater part of this period the intimate friendship of John Buddle, of Dr. Buckland, and of many eminent men in various departments of Art and Practical Science.

"In the third period, from 1845 to 1866, I have had the chief agency of the W. B. Lead-mines belonging to the Beaumont family, and during twelve years resided at Allenheads. The last nine years have been nearly equally divided between Allenheads and London, living for seven years in Cleveland Square and two in Victoria Street, Westminster, where I am celebrating the day on which all these three periods culminate in what is called The Great Climacteric of Life.

Under the date of January 4th, 1866, the diary contains a long entry on a discussion at a dinner at Mr. Peter Graham's ; Mr. Owen Jones and Mr. Routledge being present as well as Mr. Sopwith. In the morning of the same day Mr. Sopwith had had a very agreeable *tête-à-tête* with Mr. Delane, editor of the *Times*, to whom he jocularly communicated that he also had become a newspaper proprietor, namely, of the *Hexham Courier;* and at the dinner in the evening various subjects of current social and political interest came up. The subject of Reform was now on the *tapis*, and the great speech of Mr. Bright at Rochdale came in for review, with a glance at the ballot. Mr. Sopwith urged for universal voting " on the proportional basis, say in pounds sterling of actual taxation." To this Mr. Graham objected that would never do, because " wealth does not represent intelligence." " Then does poverty ? " asked Mr. Sopwith; " is it not almost entirely by industry and intelligence combined that wealth is accumulated ? "

The anatomy of a strike was another of the subjects discussed, in which Mr. Sopwith detailed his own practical experience of a strike, assigning as an almost invariable cause the persuasive arguments of one or two individuals who influence the mass. Thence the debaters passed to modes of providing good and healthy homes for all working men. To secure cleanliness of person and improved dwellings were the two great reforms required. For this organization alone was wanting. The work would be one of pure self-support as regards money; and the appropriation of all profit above 5 per cent. to the increased comfort and accommodation of the inmates would, Mr. S. was persuaded, soon make dwellings won by wages investments as solid as the public funds.

On March 6th of this year, at the instance of Mr. Walter, Mr. Sopwith gave evidence before the Committee on Education, over which Sir John Pakington presided. The inquiries made of him were chiefly directed to the difference between certified and uncertified teachers, as to more extended means of education, and as to the teaching of religion in schools. On this latter point he suggested the inculcation of plain and practical matters of duty, without entering into the details of doctrinal points. He further suggested that educational commissioners representing the Government ought to be a moving body, and not to be stationary in London. They should be persons who would give the greater part of their time and attention to education in different parts of the kingdom, and acting under them there should be local commissioners. Local rates ought also to be established, the funds from which should be supplemented by grants from the Central Department. Referring to the Allenheads School, he said it was so good his own son went to it with advantage.

On April 27th there is a touching reference to the decline of the illustrious Faraday, who, after his lecture, was obliged to leave leaning on Professor Tyndall's arm : "If anything could strongly impress the transitory glories of an earthly state it is surely such a scene and such an association."

In the middle of June of this year Mr. Sopwith began to experience what he called " some symptoms of central failure," for which he consulted the late Dr. Bence Jones, who wrote to him on June 20th, telling him that his heart would not bear the strain he was putting upon it. He thereupon, with his usual common sense, determined to measure his work as well as his time, and take things more easily. In July he paid a visit to the Isle of Wight; in August he went to Harrogate; and afterwards to the British Association at Leamington. Between October 4th and 19th he made a tour with Mrs. Sopwith on the Continent of Europe. In his notes he dwells with much satisfaction on two or three particular events: the marriage of his son Thomas, on March 1st, to Lydia Gertrude Messiter; his completion of twenty-one years' supervision of the works at Allenheads, and, most agreeable recognition, a letter from Mr. W. B. Beaumont, congratulating him on attaining his majority at Allenheads, and asking his acceptance of a picture of Warkworth Castle, by Richardson, a picture he had once much admired. On July 5th he notes that he made his Will, the provisions few, simple, easily understood, and easy to be carried out.

1867.

The diary for 1867 contains some matters of interest, although less crowded with details than that of any preceding year. A touching reference to the death of the Dean of Hereford, and a delightful recognition of the early literary efforts of Frank Buckland, son of the distinguished Dean of Westminster, stand well out. Several pages are devoted to the description of an arbitration on electric affairs, between Messrs. Hooper and Elliott, in which Mr. T. Brassey and Mr. Sopwith were the official arbitrators. In May the scene changes, and a description is given of a visit to Paris and the volcanic district of Auvergne. On August 25th there is an entry dated Saltburn, in which reference is made to a letter " from my son Tom," respecting the skill of foreign workmen at Moresact. "Everything about the mines there is really a long way ahead of England, and it is a great pity it should be so; but the next generation will find it out if we do not." On this Mr. Sopwith makes the following comment :—

" All this is in accordance with the opinions which, in the last few years, have been forced upon me (rather than adopted) from observation of Continental as compared with English progress. At the root of all is education,—not only education of the head, but of the hands. I am much afraid that in this most important particular England is not only not keeping pace with the Continent, but is receding, whilst other lands are advancing.

" When, about twenty years ago, I had occasion to consider the red-tape system of the National School, as carried out at Allenheads, I met the generous support of the late Thomas Wentworth Beaumont, Esq., in replacing it by a school based on a generous desire to extend and promote useful education (which support was much increased and extended by his son, W. B. Beaumont, Esq.). I thought the system of administration of schools by Government in many respects defective, and subsequent and larger experience of it has strongly confirmed this view. The present Government system appears to me to be needlessly complicated, to entail a vast amount of useless correspondence on trivial points; and in all this correspondence there is a transparent fallacy which deprives it of the great and essential feature of truth. Each letter professes to be written as by authority of the Lords in Council forming the Committee on Education; and that it should assume this character of Government authority is proper. But in matters of trifling detail relating to a floor, a fireplace, or other petty alterations or repairs, or to the defective reading or writing of a few scholars in a small country school, it seems to be uselessly magnificent to say that ' My Lords ' disapprove, or ' My Lords '

expect so and so. The opinion which professes to be that of
their Lordships is often based, as I have had some opportunities
of observing, on a very cursory examination, and without much
inquiry. At certain schools, where fire-brick floors have been in
use for periods of from ten to eighteen years with comfort and
satisfaction, 'My Lords' consider them cold in winter, and ask
that they be replaced by wooden floors. In like manner the
examination of teachers for country schools appears to be most
unsatisfactory in operation. Of three excellent teachers two
were rejected, and as I have had for many years a good
opportunity of knowing their proficiency in study, their
diligence in teaching, their great respectability of character,
this rejection, based on paper returns apart from personal
observation, has appeared to me a gross injustice and a serious
impediment in the way of Mr. Beaumont's generous efforts to
promote good schools. In all this I believe England is really
far behind some other nations. I cannot but think that, however useful centralization may be, and I believe is, in such a
matter, yet it ought to be accompanied and supplemented by
much more of local observation and local influence than are
generally brought to bear on the subject. Local rates, local
supervision, and compulsory education, may, I believe, be
accomplished if a due regard is had to the requirements of the
case. Gardens, fields, workshops, may become accompaniments
of properly conducted public schools. In these at certain hours
instruction in gardening, in farming, in mechanical pursuits,
might be blended with instruction at other hours in reading,
writing, and other studies. For such work food might be
given, food cooked by pupils, and the relief of poverty might
thus go along with the removal of that fearful amount of
ignorance which, by continued accumulation, must end in
national disaster. Under existing systems, both of schools
and colleges, of workshops, farms, mines, and manufactories,
it is only in exceptional cases (and these brought about by
legislative measures) that training in industrial occupation and
mental instruction go together.

"There seems no reason why heads and hands should not be alike trained from an early age—the fatigue of bodily exertion relieved by mental study; the confinement and bodily inaction of study relieved by active and useful exercise.

"This is the direction which education must take if it is to enlist the sympathies and secure the cordial support and co-operation of the great mass of the people."

In August (28th) there is a comment on the able memoir and leading article in the *Telegraph*, on the "late Professor Faraday." Of this illustrious philosopher Mr. Sopwith never could say too much, although all that he said was in such good taste and feeling that Faraday himself might have heard it without a blush. Faraday, on his part, was equally pleased with his generous friend, whom he would, after lecture, invite to the simple family supper, in which bread and cheese formed the staple of the refreshment. In September (the 30th) Mr. and Mrs. Sopwith visit Sir William and Lady Armstrong at Cragside. They drive to Rothbury and Thropton, where some new schools have been opened, and where, in accordance with arrangements previously made, Mr. Sopwith gives a lecture on Education, and Sir William exhibits some beautiful electrical experiments. The visit gave great delight, notwithstanding the "awful punctuality" which prevailed in everything.

On November 26th, 1867, Mr. Arthur Sopwith took his departure for India.

1868.

The opening passages of the diary of 1868 give rise to some reflections which show in an expressive way the gentle tone and quality of their author.

"*January 12th*, 1868.—In writing these few remarks, on a quiet Sunday evening, I cannot but reflect on the soothing and agreeable influence which is exerted by the objects around me. They seem to provoke, as it were, a sentiment of gratitude and contentment; to separate the mind of anxious cares; and, looking back on the past, I find some sources of comfort which I fain store for the future. That, however, is hid in darkness. Time only will slowly draw the veil and disclose events whether for good or seeming evil; whether of continued health and comfort, or of infirmity and anxiety. All that is hidden, and wisely hidden, and it only remains to humbly hope that my enjoyment of the future may correspond with my content and thankfulness for the past.

"I pursued, for some time, this train of thought. It was in harmony with all around me. In arranging the contents of the drawers of my writing-table I came upon the first railway section I had made (part of Newcastle and Carlisle Railway surveyed by me in 1825), and many plans, lectures, and reminiscences of the most active period of my life. They recall much to my memory, and suggest longings for the same ardent and active life I then led. But this cannot be, and I feel that continued health can only be preserved by giving up some of the long hours, close writing, and active energy of younger years."

Under a later date some similar reminiscences convey a similar portrayal of the man.

"*February* 22*nd*, 1868.—I resumed my usual occupations in my office at 103, Victoria Street. The various matters which require attention at the W. B. Mines fully occupy the time usually devoted to business; and not only so, they intrude on other hours, early and late, and when I review the number and extent of such business affairs I feel how important it is that such attention should be given. This prominence, which it is alike my duty and my interest to give to business affairs, has not entirely excluded the love of science and art, but it has prevented my giving either to them or to literature that devoted care which can alone secure eminence, and my coming

to Allenheads nearly twenty-three years ago rendered it
absolutely necessary that I should forego the chances of distinction which the pursuit of science, art, or literature may
lead to.   My position in society has, from my birth and early
progress, been essentially that of business.   My acceptance of
the W. B. Mines agency caused my retirement from the Council
of the Institution of Civil Engineers ; and attention to its duties
was also the cause of my leaving the Councils of the Geological
Society and the Society of Arts.   To none of these could I
possibly give the attention due to them.   I willingly give up
all ideas of the honours due to those who can give more time,
and who also bring to such duties a higher amount of intellectual energy and accomplishment than I can lay claim to.
If, therefore, I see many who, some thirty or forty years ago,
were my juniors raised to an elevated rank in their respective
professions, I can heartily join in approving and admiring the
industry and talent whereby they have achieved success.   Work,
hard work, has been the only road by which they have won
their way ; and work, hard and unremitting work, has been
my only means of discharging duties connected with extensive
mines and numerous people under my direction.   Indeed, when
I consider how much the task of actual labour was, in my
early years, an absolute necessity, I rather see some reason for
surprise that I also found leisure for what may be deemed
intellectual pursuits apart from business occupations.

"My love of drawing was a means whereby I could be
useful to two of the most eminently gifted men in the north
of England—Hodgson and Surtees, the historians of Northumberland and Durham.   And this not only procured me their
acquaintance, but their friendly offices ; and it was not a little
gratifying to me to be occupied in illustrating works which
were adorned by the highly artistic productions of Edward
Swinburne and of Edward Blore.   I had also the friendship of many artists, and when thirty years of age I was
urged to become President of a society of all the principal
artists of my native town.   Music was also a great enjoyment ;

and, although I never learnt it as an art, yet I indulged in amateur performances, which had their culminating point in the performance of an entire service in the Church of St. Nicholas, in Newcastle.   In architecture, which I had studied only as an amateur, my first attempt in composition gained a prize and much commendation.   In engineering, civil and mining, I won my way with great satisfaction through many undertakings, which brought me into competition or contact with many leading men of the time.   My surveys in Alston Moor made me well acquainted with lead mining, and introduced me to John Taylor, certainly at that time the head of mineral mining.   A road which I projected from Newcastle to the Scottish Border, on the way to Edinburgh, was preferred to one which McAdam had proposed; and in railways I had many years of successful practice, and an acquaintance with nearly all the eminent men who carried out the vast systems of railways in the last forty years.

" My connection with public societies has been a source of great enjoyment, and in several cases has originated in a manner which I remember with pleasure.   It was my good fortune to be proposed at the Institution of Civil Engineers by Telford, the founder and first President, who volunteered to do so.   My introduction to the Royal Society was first suggested by the then President, Lord Northampton.   I have been a Member of the Council of the Geological Society, in the Society of Arts, etc., and President of the Meteorological Society, as also of many local societies in the north of England.

" My business occupations have been throughout life of a nature congenial to my tastes, and it is now approaching to a quarter of a century that I have had extensive charge of mining concerns in the very districts where I first commenced my professional duties—a boundary line only separating Allendale and Weardale from Alston—where I went forty years ago.

" My occupations have been varied by travels in various countries, in Norway, Denmark, Holland, Belgium, Prussia,

France, Spain, and Egypt; and, above all, in addition to the comforts of home I have enjoyed the friendship of many eminent and greatly esteemed men.

"All these (and I might add many more agreeable re-membrances) form an aggregate which I suppose to be much above, rather than at all below, the average enjoyment of life amongst the members of what may be called the middle classes, and, at all events, I look back to the retrospect of them with fervent gratitude to the Giver of all good.

"I look back on many sad shortcomings, on wasted opportunities, on infirmities of purpose, and on neglect of duties. Every-one who honestly looks into the past must, I fear, see much to regret, and much that would bear amendment. Of each other we cannot judge, for all the data on which a true decision can be formed are hidden from us; but of ourselves we are bound to analyse our secret motives as well as outward actions.

"In the multitude of blessings I have enjoyed I am desirous to acknowledge the great and unfailing goodness of God, and humbly desire that, amidst all the cares and anxieties which may occur in this ever-changing scene, I may repose an un-failing trust in the continuance of that goodness."

In the spring of the year, May 5th, Mr. Sopwith took Lantern House in the Isle of Thanet for four months, where, with some members of his family, he passed an agreeable vacation. During this time his son Arthur, who had returned from India, set out for Brazil.

The visit to Thanet was continued until the early part of September, when Mr. Sopwith started for another tour through Central Europe, in company with Mrs. Sopwith. Of this tour he has published a concise little volume, beautifully illustrated throughout: a summary of it, therefore, is alone required.

In the course of this journey visits were paid to Brussels, Prague, Aschaffenburg, Nuremberg, Franconian Switzerland, Baurberg, Leipsic, Dresden, Saxon Switzerland, Freiburg, Berlin, and Potsdam. The return was made on September 30th, when work was resumed in the usual form. On October 12th there is a note relating to a subject on which Mr. Sopwith often spoke, and almost with enthusiasm, the goldfields of Nova Scotia. He was of opinion that a great field for enterprise was open in this direction, and in the entry to which reference is made he says :—

"*October* 12*th.*—I completed some notes on the Nova Scotia gold regions, to which the attention of Messrs. Shelford & Robinson has been drawn, with a view to Mr. Robinson going out early in November to inspect a property at Lawrence Town, known as 'Werners,' and comprising upwards of two hundred acres which have been partly explored, but which would require larger capital to develop the deeper portions of the veins or lodes. Gold mining has made a steady progress in Nova Scotia, and the evidence adduced with reference to this property appears to be worthy of attentive investigation. In Memorandum 117 I have noted such points as seem to require attention."

On November 25th he adds an interesting reflection on party politics.

"*November* 25*th.*—I learnt from the newspapers that Mr. George Elliot headed the poll yesterday, Sir H. Williamson being second, and Mr. J. L. Bell not elected.

"It is really absurd to hear the exaggerated terms in which extreme party men speak of each other, as if difference of political view necessarily indicated more or less of moral depravity. In my own path I avoid as much as possible all connection with extreme party views. Well has 'party' been defined, 'the madness of many for the gain of the few.' It really amounts almost to a species of temporary insanity in many persons of humble position, whose zeal would be equally great on one side or the other according as accidental circumstances have thrown them more in the way of one candidate than another. Nor is it at all an uncommon incident for me to meet with patriotic and liberal candidates denouncing the absolute robbery and jobbery enforced on them in a 'liberal' candidature. Some of the most consistent and advanced members of the Whig parties gradually became far more conservative, restrictive, and reserved, than the most extreme Conservative of the present time ; and among the much-abused Tories I have known men of the most exalted and refined liberality and usefulness. Indeed, I scarcely see any line of demarcation between a Conservative Liberal and a Liberal Conservative, and that both parties should have their political creed tempered and moderated there is no doubt."

1869.

A note on February 14th, 1869, describes a visit to a home which everyone remembers for life who had the pleasure of entering its doors, namely, Maryland Point, Stratford, the residence of the late accomplished and earnest Sir Antonio Brady. "In few houses," says Mr. Sopwith, "is there a greater number and variety of curious and instructive objects than at Maryland Point. A good collection of plants, a remarkable set of gigantic fossil bones, a fine collection of minerals, with paintings, drawings, books, and microscopes."

On March 8th a tour commenced to Paris, Cannes, Mentone, Geneva, Genoa, the marble quarries of Carrara, Pisa, Leghorn, Lucca, Florence and Bologna, Modena, Parma, Nice, Montpelier, Barcelona, Tarragona, Valencia, Linares, Madrid, and Biarritz. The journey altogether was one of extreme pleasure, and afforded ample instruction of a scientific as well as of a social character. He returned to England on April 27th.

An entry on June 30th, made at Durham, is interesting in regard to a presentation to Professor Chevallier.

"*June 30th.*—At ten I attended service in the Cathedral. I called on the Rev. Professor Chevallier, who resides in one of the stately and comfortable residences immediately under the shadow of the western part of the Cathedral, and commanding a most charming view of the river and of the woody banks. Here I found several friends of the Professor, who had come— as I also had done—to congratulate him on the well-won honour about to be conferred on him by the public presentation of his portrait, and among them was my much esteemed friend the Venerable Archdeacon of Lindisfarne, and his young and very beautiful bride. We accompanied the Professor from his house to the Castle, and in the ancient dining-room, amidst a very large concourse of clergymen, ladies, and gentlemen, the portrait was formally presented."

On July 15th he was gratified by a kindly letter from Mrs. Somerville, in which that scientific lady expressed her opinion in favour of gun-cotton for blasting purposes over its rival nitro-glycerine. She considered gun-cotton the safer explosive.

In August there was a Congress of the Mechanical Engineers at Newcastle, before which body Sir William Armstrong delivered a characteristic address. The members of the Congress visited Allenheads and received a cordial reception.

In November (28th) one or two anecdotes relating to Mrs. Somerville and Dr. Buckland are neatly told.

"When Mrs. Somerville was introduced to Laplace he complimented her as the authoress of the 'Connexion of the Physical Sciences,' and as the second most learned lady in the world. 'I give' (so I understood him to have said) 'the first place to Mrs. Grieg.' It was under this—the name of her first marriage—that Mrs. Somerville had performed her great work, the translation of the very abstruse and elaborate 'Mechanism of the Heavens,' by Laplace.

"Of Dr. Buckland one or two anecdotes are listened to with attention and amusement, such as his comment on Mrs. Probyn's picture of the Queen, 'Deplorably like.' Another is as follows : ' Soon after the Great Western Railway opened some attention was called to the inclination of the Box Tunnel being nearly in the same direction as the bedding of the strata, by which very thin wedge-shaped edges would, by exfoliation and the action of the air, become liable to be separated and fall down, which separation might probably take place during the vibration which accompanies the passing of a train through a tunnel. On this subject Dr. Buckland made some observations at a meeting of the Institution of Civil Engineers, and this was followed by comments in the *Times* and other papers, by which the matter obtained some degree of public attention. About this time an elderly gentleman was travelling in a first-class carriage between Bristol and the Box Tunnel, which latter place the train was approaching. Several persons were in the carriage, and the conversation turned on the alleged danger of the roof of the tunnel. A smart young gentleman, who sat opposite to the gentleman already mentioned, said there was no danger, and freely ridiculed the nonsense which Dr. Buckland had uttered and written upon it. "So ignorant is the Doctor on the matter that he does not even know the shape of the tunnel, for he wrongly describes it." "You appear to be well acquainted with the subject," said the elderly gentleman to his youthful informant. " Yes," was the reply, " I am, and ought to be, for I am one of the engineers employed on the line." " Is this, then," said the elderly gentleman, " the shape of the tunnel ? " at the same time exhibiting a drawing of it on one of the pages of a memorandum-book. " Oh dear no ! " said the youth, " nothing like it—that's the shape Dr. Buckland has described, and he is all wrong, he knows nothing about it." "Well," said the elderly gentleman to the passengers who were listening, " I suppose we must pay great deference to this young gentleman, as he is an engineer on the line, and perfectly well acquainted with the tunnel. At the same time, let me say I am Dr. Buckland, that this sketch was made expressly for me this morning at my request, and that the engineer who kindly drew it for me in my memorandum-book was Mr. Brunel." ' "

At the close of this year and on the first day of the next year, Mr. Sopwith makes a curious series of memoranda of forty-seven New Year Days, namely, from January 1st, 1824, to January 1st, 1870, each day commencing a New Year, and reminding him of nine different homes, viz., (1) Pilgrim Street, Newcastle, 1824-32 ; (2) Loaming House, Alston, 1825-29 ; at different places at home and abroad from 1830-34 ; (3) Carliol Street, Newcastle, 1835-37 ; (4) St. Mary's Terrace, Newcastle, 1838-47 ; (5) Allenheads, 1848-49 ; (6) 17, Northumberland Street, Newcastle, 1850-52 ; (7) 1, Ridley Place, Newcastle, 1854-56 ; (8) 43, Cleveland Square, London, 1858-64 ; (9) 103, Victoria Street, London, 1865-70.

CHAPTER XXIX.

*A TOUR IN ITALY. MEMORIAL TO EDWARD POTTER.
DEATH OF MRS. SOMERVILLE. E. W. COOKE, R.A.
THOMAS TATE, C.E. THE HOOPER ELECTRIC CABLE.*

1870-73.

 N the spring of 1870, Mr. and Mrs. Sopwith visited Italy, spending some time in Naples, Rome, Florence, Bologna, Milan, Verona, and Perugia, and visiting the ruins of Herculaneum and Pompeii.

Under date of March 14th we have a final picture of Mrs. Somerville.

" *March 14th.*—We went to Sorrento and visited the house in which Tasso was born—viewed the ancient walls, etc.

" We spent the evening with Mrs. Somerville, with whom I had a long and agreeable conversation. At length came the hour of parting, perhaps for ever in this world, but we live in hope; and if spared in health and comfort it may be that another spring may find us again at Naples. We have seen much, but much remains to be seen, and all we have seen would well bear revisiting. We bade adieu with all the affection of old and sincere friends, and that this sentiment is mutual and reciprocal is to me a source of the highest gratification.

" Mrs. Somerville is now in her ninetieth year, and not only retains her memory and a fair share of good health and mental vigour, but is able to devote attention to the re-editing of some of her former works, and takes a lively interest in all that is passing. Full of kindness and amiability, of intelligence, of cheerfulness, of hospitality, and as much of goodness, simplicity, and truth as I have ever known combined in one character, she enters freely into conversation upon any topic that happens to be named. Many of her anecdotes are of personal reminiscences, such as her intimate acquaintance with Sir Walter Scott and others known only by their memories to many of the present generation.

"Our chief object in visiting Naples was to visit Mrs. Somerville, and most amply has this been carried out, for during a stay of less than a fortnight we twice called and saw her on afternoons, we spent three evenings from eight until near eleven, and dined with her and her family circle twice; dinner at six being followed by a few hours of most agreeable conversation. Very imperfect is the homage which any words of mine can express, compared with the inward homage of the deep respect and esteem which I entertain for her in my heart of hearts."

On Lady Day, being in Rome, he gets a view of the Pope.

"*Friday, March 25th.*—This being Lady Day is a great festival in Rome; every shop is closed, and evidences of universal holiday meet one in every street. It is an annual custom on this day for the Pope to go in state to the 'Church of the Minerva,' as it is commonly called, and thither we went immediately after breakfast. After waiting an hour in the midst of a dense crowd in the centre aisle of the nave, we saw the procession, and had an excellent view of the Sovereign-Pontiff, as he slowly passed immediately in front of where we stood. He wore the golden triple crown and robes of white and gold. The throne or chair of state was carried by men, and thus elevated, the whole of the Pope's person could be seen. He is a portly, benignant-looking, and well-conditioned looking personage, and appears remarkably stout and well for his advanced age. It added much to the interest of the occasion that the King of Naples, the Corps Diplomatique (in state costume), and many archbishops and bishops, were present."

The return from Rome to England was made in the middle of April, and entries of every-day life continue, of little moment until August 23rd, when the marriage of Miss Emily Sopwith to Mr. William Hollis Luce is reported. The ceremony took place in St. Margaret's, Westminster.

On October 30th a picture of Mr. Holman Hunt's, called "Isabella, or the Pot of Basil," for which his son-in-law, Mr. James Hall, had given two thousand pounds, is commented on. He says of it :—

"It is admirably painted, yet it would be the merest affectation in me to attempt to pronounce any opinion of its merits. In the first place the subject generally does not enlist my favourable sympathies; there is nothing great or noble or even virtuous in a woman giving way to excessive and useless grief. As a representation of the female figure, and of the female face especially, I do not seem to discern either beauty or intelligence. Hunt is a great painter, popular and fashionable, and that the picture is really very valuable I have no doubt. Unable at present to see in it such attractions as would have induced me to give even one-tenth of the price, I reserve all expression of opinion of its merits until I shall have seen it a number of times. Repeated inspection is the true test by which inexperienced observers can judge. The connoisseur can at once decide, but to less critical eyes a really good picture seems on each repeated visit to present some new point of merit, some hitherto unnoticed charm, and to this test I trust I may be able to submit this curious and costly work of art."

An entry a few weeks after this date records the death of his old friend, Mr. Thomas Brassey.

"*Saturday, December 10th*, 1870.—I read with much concern in the *Times* a notice of the death of my greatly honoured and respected friend, Mr. Thomas Brassey, at the comparatively early age of sixty-five years. Of him most truly may it be said, 'A good man has gone to his rest.'

"It cannot but be a matter of deep regret that one so eminently useful, so remarkably successful, so truly benevolent, and so charmingly agreeable in his manners and conversation, should be so soon and so suddenly removed from the sphere of his extensive and prosperous labours. I shall ever remember with satisfaction many opportunities I have had of enjoying the society of Mr. Brassey since my first meeting with him at the house of Mons. Paulin Talebot in 1856. I have often enjoyed his cordial hospitality, have had the pleasure of receiving him as a guest at my house, and have also been associated with him in some professional matters. Every interview and every transaction inspired one with increased esteem and regard for his frank, hearty, straightforward, and sensible conduct. His memory will be honoured by all who knew him."

1871.

In the early part of 1871 a return of indisposition led Mr. Sopwith to feel the necessity of retiring from active life, and resigning the important agency he had held so long. He had now been engaged fifty years in professional work, and felt that it was time to cease. The death of his friend, Robert Chambers, on March 17th, at the age of sixty-nine years, affected him very much, and led him to think that if the writer of the "Book of Days," and of other important works, succumbed, with his rich powers, at so comparatively early an age, it would be wise for himself to be more careful of such strength as remained to him. To the note referring to Robert Chambers he appended a few words relating to the brothers William and Robert Chambers, to the effect that in his long acquaintance with them he had arrived at a firm opinion that they will, in the estimation of posterity, occupy a larger space in the history of their times than they have attained amongst their contemporaries. So far they have been prominently before the public in their business capacity in the publishing department, which condition had kept out of view, in no small degree, the remarkable—one might almost say astounding—breadth and vigour of mind displayed by both the brothers in their various original works.

The retirement is recorded by Mr. Sopwith as follows:—

"*June* 30*th*, 1871.—At length the day has arrived when, according to the arrangements mutually agreed upon as between W. B. Beaumont, Esq., and myself, my term of agency expires—this day, Friday, June 30th, completing twenty-six years of service as chief agent of the W. B. Lead-mines in Northumberland and Durham.

"I examined bargain sheets, and signed receipts for subsistence, £5,156 18s. 2d., and at half-past nine this evening I make the entry at the close of my chief agency of the W. B. Mines."

On July 19th, 1871, a presentation was made to him, originated by the body of miners and other workmen of the W. B. Mines. It included an address and a magnificent silver tankard, two elegant stands for flowers or fruits, three Grecian figures, and an elaborate writing-desk. The day of presentation was spent as a general holiday. The account of this hearty recognition ends with a description of the way in which he parted from a place he had occupied so long.

"At 3 p.m. I left Allenheads in my own phaeton, and had the company of Mr. Thompson and Mr. Cain as far as St. John's Chapel. The band of the 7th Northumberland Volunteers played a tune or two ending with the 'White Cockade' in front of the carriage a short distance along the road, and thus I made my farewell parting from a district which for more than a quarter of a century has been very much a home in the way of residence, and which has had almost the sole occupancy of my thoughts, so far as professional matters are concerned, in relation to its important mining interests. I leave it with many deep emotions—esteem for my many friends prevailing over all other feelings."

As was common with Mr. Sopwith after any important event of his life, he paid a visit to the Continent. This time, accompanied by Mrs. Sopwith, he made his way to Bavaria, in order to witness the *Passion Play* as it was then performed, and which he thus describes :—

"*August 26th*, 1871.—I commenced this Journal (No. 131) in the upper room of a small but comfortable and picturesque cottage in the village of Ober-Ammergau, in Bavaria, to which place my dear Annie and I have come this day, as have vast numbers of people, with the intention of witnessing the now celebrated performance called the *Passion Play*, which is appointed to be performed in this village to-morrow.

"*August 27th*.—At half-past seven we went to witness the performance of the now far-famed *Passion Play* at Ober-Ammergau, which commenced exactly at eight in the morning and continued until near five in the afternoon. The exact duration of the play was eight hours and a half. That an audience of not less than six thousand persons should sit in profound silence and attention during so long a period is perhaps as striking a proof as any that can be adduced of the interest it excited; and I am satisfied that this attention was, if not universally, yet in a very large degree, due to feelings of

sympathy and reverence for the subject of the representation.
If there were in this or any former occasions of the performance
any exceptions to this remark I have not heard nor read of
them ; whilst on the other hand I have met with many written
and verbal opinions strongly concurring in the respect and
reverence as well as admiration which the performance is
calculated to excite.   I do not here attempt to base this on
the peculiar history of the *Passion Play*, further than to
observe that it originated in fervent piety, and is continued
under the powerful influence of a strong religious feeling.
Viewed in this light it appears to me to present one of the
most extraordinary examples of dramatic representation that
the world has ever seen, and certainly no public performance
that I have either seen or heard of in modern times has excited
so much attention.   The Derby Day in London, the races at
celebrated places in English provinces, and public pageants and
ceremonies, no doubt attract thousands and tens of thousands
of admiring spectators ; and in large cities many occasions arise
where a much greater number of people are assembled : but it
is not so much in the number of spectators as in the character
of the performance and of the performers, as well as in the
nature of the locality, that we find reason to be astonished ; and
the more these elements are duly considered the more profound
must be the impression of surprise and admiration.

    " The performance aims at a representation of some of the
most profoundly awful and important events recorded in the
annals, whether sacred or profane, of the civilized world.   The
death of Christ on the Cross, and the attendant circumstances
immediately preceding it and following it, have exercised an
influence on the destiny of nations, and of individuals of every
class, far beyond that of any other event ; for, whatever may be
the differences in dogmatic beliefs or in the adapted creeds, or
mental inferences as to details of doctrine and the observance
of ceremonial worship—the one great fact stands out prominently before all others, that in the sufferings and death of
Christ all that is precious in the enlightenment and improve-

ment of mankind has its origin. Such is the character of the performance, such the events which form the subject of the *Passion Play* as performed at Ober-Ammergau.

"Such being the lofty aim of the performance—an aim, it might be supposed, far beyond the powers of the most able dramatic performers—let us now consider who and what are the persons by whom the attempt is made. Truly by none other than the very class of persons who, as humble peasantry or the followers of some industrial occupation in the humble walks of ordinary village life, are so clearly delineated in the Scriptures as the founders of Christianity. The inhabitants of a small village in the midst of mountainous recesses aspire to represent the personal aspect and demeanour, as well as the historical conduct, of Christ and His Apostles; and so far there is a seeming fitness that characters and events relating to humble life should be represented by persons of corresponding meekness and lowliness. But in the *Passion Play* the peasant villagers of Ammergau represent some of the great ones of the earth—men of pomp and power in the exercise of high authority, and in this they succeed in a degree which can only be duly appreciated by witnessing the performance."

1872.

On March 10th of this year a very interesting letter reached Mr. Sopwith from Mrs. Somerville, still at Naples. It is a characteristic document. Mrs. Somerville accuses herself of being a lazy correspondent, but she never forgets her early and valued friends. She is sure that Mr. Sopwith is as active as ever, and that his Journal has been continued with all the originality and profound thought which characterised the parts of it she had the pleasure of reading. She expresses herself warmly on the universal and enthusiastic loyalty manifested on the recovery of the Prince of Wales, which shows that we are in no danger of revolution. She is very deaf and weak, but still reads without spectacles, and keeps herself up to what is going on in the scientific world, especially the mathematical; and, as she drives out every good day, her time passes very pleasantly. Mr. Sopwith's reply to this letter, equally characteristic, appears in copy in the diary.

"*March* 23rd, 1872.—In writing to Mrs. Somerville yesterday I replied in some detail to her kind inquiries as to the health of my family and myself, and I here insert one or two passages of my letter.

"'Although I am only a youth of sixty-nine, I begin to think that hills are steeper than they were forty years ago; that books are in smaller print; that people don't talk so clear and loud as they used to do, and that miles of walking are a *little* but *not much* increased in length, for I manage seven or eight miles without fatigue, and last autumn walked down the Rigi from the very summit to the base at Weggio.

"'I continue my Journals, and vol. cxxxv. is lying before me. I find much amusement and perhaps even some instruction both in writing them and in reading clear records of occurrences since I was eighteen. I thus again seem to travel to Alston in 1824; to meet there with Trevelyan, Pillans, and others; to climb mountains, and plunge into mines. In 1829 I was superseding McAdam, and my line of road (Newcastle to Edinburgh by Carter Fell) is adopted in preference to his; and thus from year to year I can follow every movement, and rejoice in the rich luxury of many valued friendships, yours among them, but I cannot condense them in the compass of a letter.

"'I delivered your message to General Sir Edward Sabine and his good lady; the former hearty, well, and vigorous; the latter very cheerful, but has recently suffered from cold and cough. Both of them delighted to hear of you. . . . I sometimes amuse myself in considering the problem we had some talk upon, *i.e.* of perspective intelligence capable of following with instantaneous rapidity the remote regions of space, and perceiving, as by parallel rays, isometric images of objects irrespective of distance and *viewed in any selected ratio* as to past and present. Passing in one moment from earth to a star (a position), to traverse the distance of which light requires a thousand years, such an intelligence may now view the defeat of the Danes at Ashdown (871); Stonehenge would wear the modest antiquity of three hundred years; after twelve years Alfred would be seen in 884 improving London; and, after thirty years Charlemagne crowned Emperor of the West. Taking a stretch backward of seven or eight hundred years of light's travelling, Pompeii and Herculaneum would be seen in all their magnificence. A flight equalling three thousand years of light, and we see Cheops building his pyramid. But six thousand nine hundred years of light would be required to see a newly-discovered Egyptian monument which Sir William Armstrong saw, bold and clear in colour and inscriptions, and a clear chronology of six thousand eight hundred years. Then, at any time a retracing of the path back to the earth, with continuous observation of rays of light met on the way, would represent six thousand years in six hours, in six days, in six or sixty years, according as our intelligent and perceiving atom willed its flight. I named this to our good friend Owen, who rejoices in the hope of seeing all his stud of big beasts in full vigour.'"

Under date of April 16th he records :—

"The marriage of my dear son Arthur to Catherine Susan Shelford at the Church of St. Matthew, Upper Clapton, on Tuesday, April 16th, 1872."

In a later entry there is a most pleasurable account of a visit to the late Mr. E. W. Cooke, R.A., a report which all of us who knew that illustrious artist will willingly endorse as photographic of the man.

"*May 10th*, 1872.—Whitsuntide was spent at Glen-Andred, the residence of the well-known artist and Royal Academician,

Mr. E. W. Cooke, and of his mother and sisters. The pleasure with which I had looked forward to this visit was more than realized, nor will it be forgotten as long as any powers of memory remain in a mind which is so disposed to treasure up all recollections of worthy and greatly esteemed friends, and of beautiful and romantic scenery. The general conduct and disposition of our host are such as to have gained him the esteem of all who know him, but it is in the happy sphere of home life that his worth and amiability are most fully developed. For his artistic talents I have the highest admiration, and much as these are known and appreciated by the public and throughout Europe, yet it is only in his home that anyone can become fully acquainted with the merit, the variety, and astounding number of his productions. It is not alone as an artist that Mr. Cooke's attainments are remarkable. He is possessed of much scientific knowledge, together with a large share of general information ; and of natural history his acquaintance is very extensive, more especially as regards trees and plants and flowers. He is a most devout and cheerful worshipper in the temple of Nature. In his character of host he greatly excels. Every possible comfort is provided by the unwearying assiduity of his worthy mother, his sisters and himself. Every wish seems to have been anticipated, and hence our stay of three days was one continuous round of enjoyment.

" At noon on Monday our party—consisting of Professor Owen, Mr. Cole, Q.C., and his lady, my dear Annie and myself —was increased by the arrival of Sir Antonio Brady, whom I had the pleasure of introducing to Mr. Cooke a few months ago. In the evening, Lord De la Warr was one of the party at dinner.

" It would be difficult, I think, to imagine in three days a more pleasant combination of circumstances than those by which we were surrounded. All the charms of friendly hospitality, of accomplished skill in art and science, romantic scenery, and all the delights of a happy English home.

" We returned to London on Wednesday, May 22nd, 1872."

The death of Mr. Tate, with whom he had been on terms of close intimacy for many years, on July 3rd, leads to a special series of notes in the diary.

"*July 8th*, 1872.—I received a card informing me of the death of my dear and good old friend, and formerly a much loved and instructive companion, namely, Thomas Tate, C.E., of Warrington. He died on July 3rd, 1873, aged eighty-one years. It is now half a century since I was on terms of intimate acquaintance with Mr. Tate. He entertained very liberal views, so broad indeed as to offend my early impressions, the more so as I thought his mode of speaking somewhat satirical; but this failing is one into which I have often fallen, and I think it quite possible, and even probable, that my own errors in this respect have been far greater than his.

" On looking into my Journals written nearly fifty years ago I find some entries relating to this excellent, clever, and large-hearted man.

" On January 7th, 1824, in mentioning Mr. Tate as one of the speakers at a debating society in Newcastle, I find the remark of his being 'very ingenious, uncommonly mild and even accomplished in his manners, agreeable in person, and intelligent and logical in argument.' Again, in April of the same year, I speak of him as being 'the ablest speaker and in every respect the brightest ornament of the society;' and again, about the same period, I wrote as follows: 'To a very candid and amiable disposition are added very extensive attainments, possessing considerable mechanical and scientific knowledge, which he communicates with great plainness and sweetness of manner, an agreeable smile relieving the dryness of philosophical disquisitions.'

" When employed all day he sometimes, at his rooms in the Low Bridge, Newcastle, had classes, to whom he gave lessons in geometrical and architectural drawing.   His proficiency in such drawing, and especially as applicable to oblique bridges, opened a way for him in the more important and profitable department of civil engineering, in which, during his long and active and most useful and prosperous life, he has not only been extensively employed, but also gained the warm friendship and entire confidence of several of those chiefs, George Stephenson among them, who were then commencing the great railway works which now abound in all England, as in every other civilized nation.

"In the last few years I sought an opportunity of renewing our former friendship.   I paid two or three visits to his hospitable abode, and had the pleasure of seeing him at my house in London.

"He retained in old age all that pleasing expression which I have mentioned as being so conspicuous when he was about thirty years of age.   I have seldom if ever seen a happier old age, and now at a year over fourscore he sleeps the sleep of death.   Of so inevitable an event at so ripe an age the general sentiment of his friends must be that of rejoicing over his well-spent life rather than of lamenting its close."

On July 26th, *à propos* to a proposed memorial to Mr. Edward Potter, Mr. Sopwith wrote to Mr. W. A. Potter (Cramlington), giving his views concerning the proposed memorials of the late Edward Potter.   He thought that a clock and peal of bells would be extremely suitable for such a memorial.   They are for all time, and day by day and night by night their sound is going forth with impressive eloquence, deeply suggestive to thoughtful minds.

The small hours of morning indicate the time when, with watchful vigilance, the mines are examined to ensure the safety of workmen (not always grateful for heroic care); and this duty in early life devolved on Edward Potter.

Early hours of rising and the breakfast-hour precede the midday chimes, reminding one of many a livelong day of arduous duty. At noontide and at midnight, hours of brightness, hours of gloom, will the bells remind one of chance and change in the life of a brave and good man. When wedding bells peal forth a joyous feeling they will tell of one who, in his family circle, often was present at such festivities; and when sadder tones tell of more mournful missions, they will, to many, recall the remembrance of Edward Potter having been buried in the presence of many thousands. Some of these in life had opposed him during the period of unreasoning and tyrannous strikes, but in his death all truly mourned the loss of a true friend. Larger crowds may have gathered to view the pomp of royal obsequies, or the funerals of a Nelson or a Wellington; but few persons in the class of peaceful citizens have been buried in the midst of so large and so truly sorrowful a multitude. And thus the clock and its homely chimes, and the bells in more prolonged melody, may from day to day, from year to year, and even from century to century, be an ever-speaking monument, and a worthy memorial, more especially on Sundays, when "the sweet chimes proclaim the hallowed day."

Mr. Sopwith also suggested that each bell should have upon it Mr. Potter's name and some appropriate inscription. These will be as permanent as the bells themselves, yet in a lofty tower not often read. He proposed, also, that on the face of the clock there should be placed the initials E. P., with the years of his birth and death, and on the inner walls of the church a marble slab, whereon should be inscribed, "On the bells of the tower of the church are the following inscriptions," etc., etc.

In September and October Mr. and Mrs. Sopwith

revisited the Continent, taking in their route Cologne, Heidelberg, Vienna, Prague, Carlsbad, Ratisbon, Wurzburg, and Brussels. He returned on October 13th to the usual routine of home life in retirement.

He rose soon after eight o'clock, and breakfast at nine, preceded by a short service of prayers, at which the servants and family attended, spent an hour in reading the newspapers, and remained until one o'clock in the office—as he, from long use, called his library—engaged in writing and correspondence. The afternoon was variously occupied, sometimes at the desk, at other times in exercise and recreation, or in visits to Kensington Museum or the Athenæum Club. Dinner took place at seven, and the evening, for the most part, was devoted to rest, conversation, and sometimes a game of whist or dominoes. He found abundance of occupation in correspondence, in reading, and in referring to journals and other data of former days. His duties as Director and Secretary of the Spanish Mines Company, and various other matters, furnished him with as much business occupation as he could undertake with due regard to the injunctions of his medical advisers against anxiety and over-exertion.

On November 13th (1872) he received from General Sabine intelligence of the death of Mrs. Somerville, on which event he has the following entry :—

"*November* 30*th*, 1872.—No words can fully express the deep feeling of regard which I entertain and will ever cherish for the great talents and still greater virtues of this most amiable and honoured and much lamented lady. During somewhat more than half of my past life I have had the privilege of her most valued friendship, and at times, only too few and far between, have corresponded with her on various subjects.

"In one of my latest conversations with her she expressed her admiration of a sentiment which I quoted from an Italian tombstone, to the effect that death to the wise is the evening of a pleasant day. In a long conversation which followed, the subject of a future state was considered, with reference to the probable extension of already known physical conditions, and some of these which I mentioned having the advantage of novelty, were accepted by my amiable friend as opening views which she considered well worthy of contemplation. I do not attempt, however, now to enter upon disquisitions which can be only understood after some study of and candid acquiescence in certain conditions of physical laws already known to us, and of changes of condition and extensions of powers quite capable of being brought within the limits of possibility."

1873.

On February 5th, 1873, he records receipt of two letters, one from Miss Frances Cobbe, the other from Miss Somerville, relative to the death of Mrs. Somerville.

"*February 5th.*—I have received from Miss Cobbe the loan for perusal of a letter received by her from the late Mrs. Somerville, from which the following extracts are made. It bears date October 11th, 1872.

"'God bless you, my dearest friend, for your irresistible proof of our immortality—not that I have doubted it, but as I shall soon enter my ninety-third year, your proof is an inexpressible comfort, for my belief has been intuitive. I cannot tell why I have believed.' 'The sacred thirst of the whole human race for justice would be wanting if there be no world beyond,' is the noblest proof of our immortality that ever was written. 'The "Life after Death" is by far the most important, and perhaps the best of your works. At all events it is very great. Besides, it comes at a time when Atheism is so prevalent in the scientific world. It is deplorable and inconceivable how men can believe that the glory of the heavens, and the beauty of the earth, with all its inhabitants, is not the work of a Deity.'

" This was written at Sorrento (forty days before her death), ' where,' she observes, ' we have been three months, and shall remain till November,' and then continues as follows : ' I wish Mary and you had been with us, for we have a terrace with a roof, but otherwise open to the air, from which we have an extensive view of the sea, the whole coast of Naples, Vesuvius, and a range of mountains that end in cliffs on the shore. On this terrace we have spent our summer both during the day and in the evening, reading and conversing till bed time, for the air has been so mild and calm that the lamp burned was not flickering.' . . .

" ' With regard to myself, I am really in good health for my age, but painfully weak. I cannot rise from my chair without help, and rarely venture to walk alone; but I sometimes drive out in the evening, being lifted into the carriage. I am quite deaf, but I see well, and my memory is only good in mathematics, so I amuse myself solving problems by the method of Quaterninons in the morning, and Martha beats me unmercifully at bezique in the evening.'

" What a pleasing picture of blessed old age—the lamp of life burning indeed with clear and steady light, and without flickering, too soon, alas ! to be quenched in night. Truly of these terrace scenes, thus simply yet gracefully described, the human race may be proud, for in them we contemplate the closing hours of a good and useful life. True indeed is the maxim on an Italian tomb, which I quoted to Mrs. Somerville in 1870, ' Death to the wise is the evening of a pleasant day.'

" I received also a letter, dated February 2nd, 1873, from Miss Somerville, ' expressing gratitude to Mrs. Sopwith and myself for our sympathy in their irreparable loss—a loss which they feel daily and hourly, so that life seems very flat and sad without that gentle, intellectual spirit, so full of love and sympathy. ' You are a very old friend. I say are, and not were, because I believe (and in time the belief will, I trust, prove a consolation) that communion with those we love is only suspended for a time, and that love and friendship will be continued in the other world. I repeat, then, you are a very old friend, and the love and honour you have for her is very pleasing to us.' 'Miss Cobbe is a person of immense genius and talent, and of the warmest heart. My mother loved her dearly.' 'To the last her mind was clear and bright. She died very nearly suddenly, yet not so much so as to prevent her from taking leave of us two, and of her old servants, who were so devoted to her, and, thank God, without suffering or illness. In fact, not two hours before she was in her usual place—you know it well—in the corner.'

A note on reminiscences is curious, under date of May 13th.

" *May 13th.*—In replying to a letter received from the Rev. James Wayland Joyce, thanking me for having sent him an introduction to Sir James Anderson, I said it was 'exactly in accordance with the sentiments of sincere respect and esteem which had made it quite a pleasure to attempt being of any service to him,' and I added, 'I remember seeing in 1814 the first steamboat that appeared on the rivers Tyne and Thames, and it is seven years *more* than half a century since I travelled in and wrote a description of the first steamboat built on the River Tyne. When a second boat was suggested, the wise ones of the earth shook their heads, 'One may do, but Two—will never answer.' There are now about two hundred! So much for surmise. It is on printed record (but whether based on fact or otherwise I know not) that a former President of the Royal Society absolutely pooh-poohed the very notion of a steamship being possible. It is pretty well understood that Davy doubted the lighting of streets by gas, and we know that Lardner derided a crossing of the Atlantic by steamers. In view of these and many other instances of erroneous judgment by eminent authorities, I set a modest value on my own notions *as a guide for others;* albeit I suppose it is out of the nature of things not to put my own trust in what I call an *instinctive conviction*, rather than an elaborate induction."

Under date of June Mr. Sopwith has some comments on the Hooper electric cable, a summary of which may be of value.

THE HOOPER TELEGRAPHIC CABLE.

In former pages of his journals are entries (commencing April 19th, 1859), in relation to Mr. Hooper's cable, the merits of which appeared so prominent, on a first inspection, he did not hesitate at once to bring the cable under the notice of the distinguished engineer, Robert Stephenson, who made several suggestions and inquiries, and who formed such a favourable estimate of its value, that if his life had been spared a few years longer it is probable Mr. Hooper would have found in him a very valuable friend, and a powerful promoter and protector of his interests. Many obstacles presented themselves, and for years Mr. Hooper had to contend with great difficulties. At one time Mr. Sopwith took up the matter as a professional service, and brought it under the notice of Mr. Cyrus Field, Sir C. Bright, and Mr. Latimer Clarke, and under the able guidance of the last-named the cable was in a fair way to success. In the cost of pursuing experiments Mr. Sopwith undertook to find £700 out of £2,000, but no sooner were the merits of the cable made apparent than friends and capital were forthcoming.

"*June 9th.*—But, alas! calm seas were not yet reached by Mr. Hooper, who for months, and even years, had to contend against head winds and stormy weather, and I was led once more into some intimate connection with the cable along with the late Mr. Brassey. Of all these troublous times there is only one recollection that I wish to preserve, namely, that if, under very perplexing and most complicated conditions, Mr. Hooper found it difficult to meet every expectation, and even caused me some annoyance, yet one long-continued and unbending attention was bestowed with great practical skill, with untiring industry, and an honest and earnest zeal on the improvement of the cable. These efforts, which reflect the highest honour on Mr. Hooper, have eventually been crowned with success. Of this success the present time seems a culminating point. A powerful company has been formed; a ship has been designed and built purposely to lay one of Hooper's cables in South America; and in this ship much of the cable is already placed. I do not attempt to enter upon details of construction, but some of them are marvellous, none more so than the completion of an enormous and admirably adapted ship in the short period of seven months. The credit of this is due to Messrs. Mitchell and Swan, of Newcastle, one of whose firm was present at a lunch given on board the *Hooper* (for so the ship is named) this day, June 9th, 1873. Invited by a card from the directors, and by a special note from Mr. Hooper, I accompanied that gentleman and some of his friends to Millwall by steamboat. A numerous company filled the spacious cabin, and a very handsome cold collation enabled every one to enjoy themselves. When the healths of Sir William Thomson and Dr. Gladstone had been proposed and responded to, Mr. Hooper mentioned my name to the company, along with that of Mr. Latimer Clarke; a conjunction of which I am proud. He referred to my efforts during the infancy and subsequent struggles of the cable, and in a few words I expressed the high opinion which I really entertain of the wonderful and successful perseverance of Mr. Hooper. In this most hospitable and festive gathering I contemplated the realisation of Mr. Hooper's views. I consider him to be most worthy of his well-won laurels. He has achieved the usual reward of patience and perseverance; a painful past is followed by a bright present, and it may be fairly permitted us to hope that so good a commencement will be followed by a long and prosperous career, and favoured with blessings from on high from the Giver of all good.

"If my luncheon on board the ship *Hooper* was a great enjoyment to me this day, still more so was it enjoyable to sit with my old and most honoured and most estimable friend Decimus Burton. In my youthful days I was an earnest admirer of his works, as exhibited in engraved views of places which I had not seen; but I formed in my mind a sort of instinctive admiration of his pure style and severe taste. An early acquaintance with Greek architecture had taught me even then to know something of the elements of classical composition.

"In this I thought Decimus Burton supreme, and what I then fancied has been solidly confirmed by all subsequent observations and experience.

"After three hours spent under the genial auspices of Mr. Burton's hospitality, I went to join my dear Annie and Ursula at a reception given by Mrs. T. Brassey at 24, Park Place; and here I ended a day fraught with much interest and enjoyment.

"The science of electric telegraphy, the art of modern architecture, based on the purest examples of antiquity, and worth and wealth are well represented by Hooper, Burton, and Brassey."

Amongst other friends of Mr. Sopwith should be named Mr. Prestwich, the geologist. Their friendship extended over a long period, and the feeling for Mr. Prestwich by Mr. Sopwith was always of the warmest kind. On a visit which he paid to this friend he makes the following entry :—

"*July 5th.*—This afternoon Annie and I went on a visit to Mr. and Mrs. Prestwich, at their pleasant residence near Shoreham in Kent, named Darenthulme. It would indeed be a difficult task to record in any adequate terms the pleasure I derived from this visit, or the number and variety of the objects which claimed attention. The mansion is in short the home of a geologist, who by his long-continued and most able labours has gathered a rich store of scientific treasures, and attained the highest position of geological science, he having immediately preceded the Duke of Argyll as President of the Geological Society of London. His wide fame has been truly won, and much as I honour and admire his skill, I admire and esteem still more highly the worth of his general character—the gentleness of his disposition, and I may add his abundant and generous hospitality.

" We were delighted alike with the place and with the agreeable and intelligent friends we met there."

On July 10th Mr. and Mrs. Sopwith, accompanied by Misses Ursula and Alice, started on a long tour through Norway, Sweden, and Denmark. The diary is full of picturesque details, which at that time were really original, although they have now been superseded by other and more elaborately published descriptions. Some of the observations on the country people, however, have still a touch of novelty. The chief feature in Norway, for instance, lies, in his opinion, in the virtue of its inhabitants. In them the simplicity of childhood is a dignity approaching the kingdom of heaven ; and he desires to pay his respects for the civility and upright-ness he has always found exemplified in every transac-tion he has had with the Norwegian people.

In arts and manufactures, in important matters of learning, in commercial and manufacturing pursuits, in political and scientific studies, Norway had not, he thought, attained to the celebrity nor dignity of some other European countries ; but she is on the march forward, and her exhibitions of works of native industry indicate how surely she is advancing to a solid and honourable maturity.

The journey lasted over a month, the return to England being made on August 30th.

On September 4th there is an interesting note, from which it appears that Miss Cobbe and other friends proposed to bring the remains of the late Mrs. Somerville to a final resting-place in Westminster Abbey. " Dean Stanley was not only willing but wishful that this honour should be given to one so worthy of it, and Sir William Fairfax, a family connection, offered to defray all the costs." The suggestion, however, that an application should be made from eminent scientific men was not taken up. " The Astronomer Royal declined, and the cold shade was thrown over this honourable intention towards the highly gifted and most estimable lady, to whose worth La Place, Herschel, and Sabine had testified."

The next entry, containing a criticism of a much-praised and much-blamed work of English art, calls for introduction as coming from one who knew practically many of the details beyond the knowledge belonging even to professed critics. It is the view of an actual workman on the work presented to his sight by the artist.

" *Saturday, December 20th.*—I went to see the new picture by Holman Hunt, called (but why so I do not understand) ' The Shadow of the Cross.' This led me to expect something solemn and gloomy—some deeply touching and impressive lesson relating to that dark shadow of death through which all must pass. With only the painting before me I should have seen in it a somewhat garish but minutely painted picture of a carpenter's work-room, with a swarthy Syrian athletic youth who seems to have just ceased from sawing a deal board to utter some expression of anguish, to which a female figure (whose back only is seen) is seemingly paying no attention. These figures are meant to represent Christ and

His Mother. Many points of detail appear to me to be doubtful as regards accuracy. The shadow from an eastern sun would, I think, be darker. The crown and costly draperies seem out of place. The picture is without repose, and it is to me more like a map or even model of comparatively trivial objects rather than an impressive combination of well-adjusted light and shade. The shadow of a crimson wreath or 'Aghal' seems out of perspective, and looks as if caused by slanting rather than horizontal rays. The meagre costume of the principal figure appears much more elegant and costly than beseems any workman I have ever seen in the East, where the raiment, of coarse material, is often thrown round the figure with a graceful disposition of folds, which great masters have gladly and ably imitated.

" I looked in vain for the saw-dust which would be strewn on the floor under the recently-made incision, but of this it is futile to complain in presence of so extraordinary abundance of shavings. Before, behind, and at each side the floor is covered with shavings, from which it is to be presumed that much planing has been in progress in some part of the shop not represented in the picture. As to minute fidelity in the details, it is wonderful.

" I have briefly but honestly expressed what occurred to me on a first view of this work,—not a transient view, for I sat more than an hour in most attentive examination of it, both as regards the general aspect, the expression, and the amazing delicacy and model-like accuracy of the details of drapery, jewellery, and carpenter's tools. But no one, I think, can trust their judgment to come to any absolute decision on a great work at first view, the more so when the immense value assigned to the picture seems almost to provoke a desire to find whether imperfection can be detected in a work which ought in its way to be as nearly perfect as human art can achieve. Certainly my first view of it was disappointing."

CHAPTER XXX.

1874-79.

N the beginning of 1874 Mr. Sopwith was in
Paris, with Sir Antonio Brady. The season,
January 1st, led him to some reflections on
the course of events for the past fifty years,
on which he observes :—

"The period from 1824 to 1874 has been one of greater
progress than the world has seen in any preceding half century.
Even a bare enumeration of the leading incidents of such
progress would require many ample volumes ; how brief, how
imperfect then must be any attempt of mine to marshal them
forth in the brief pages—as I may say, mere shadowy outlines—
of a journal like this.

"Sixty-five years ago I witnessed the celebration of the
jubilee of George III., and of some of the incidents of that
day I have as clear a memory as though they had happened
only yesterday.

" Five years passed on ; and gas, first invented or brought
into use in 1803, was adapted as a means of lighting the
streets, and expelling for ever the 'darkness visible of the oil-
fed lamps.' And, at this period I witnessed the advent of

steam navigation. I saw the first steamboat that was seen on the Tyne. In 1816 I was instrumental in providing suitable arrangements for the exhibition of a locomotive engine in Newcastle; and five years before that my friend, Sir Charles Menteith, had heralded in print the engineering forethought of Mr. Buchanan of Edinburgh, that steam locomotion would become the means of conveying passengers more rapidly than by coach and horses. Not until 1824 was this expectation realized, and from that year is to be dated the commencement of the railway system. This I apprehend will be found to be the most effective promoter of human progress that has been known up to the period at which I write.

"Of the advances made in engineering, in astronomy, in geology, in chemistry, in arts, in literature, and in every department of human knowledge it is impossible to write without a feeling of wonder and admiration.

"Of this great march, as I may call it, of the human intellect I have in some few respects been a humble participator, but my note-books may hereafter possess some interest, inasmuch as they contain many allusions to men whom I have known intimately, and whose names must ever be enrolled among the great benefactors of mankind.

"Of engineers I have personally known Telford, Chapman, Walker, Cubitt, Brunel, and many others, but more especially the two Stephensons, father and son.

"I knew Dalton, the father (worthily so called) of chemistry; William Smith, in like manner the father of geology; and so I might continue to record a long list of honoured names.

"At the close then of half a century (dating from the beginning of railways in 1824) I feel it to be a privilege and blessing of the highest order to be able to record, as I now do, my humble but earnest and most sincere gratitude for having been permitted to be an eyewitness of the wonderful progress of the last fifty years."

The election of Mr. Burt to Parliament as a working-man candidate leads to one or two characteristic notes on working men in the House of Commons.

"*Sunday, February 22nd*, 1874.—The introduction of working men into Parliament is a circumstance that cannot fail to attract much attention. Take, for example, Mr. Burt, who is a direct representative of the pitmen in the vicinity of Morpeth, in Northumberland, succeeding Sir George Grey, who retired from the representation of that borough. I have no doubt but that the House of Commons, with instinctive right feeling, will show much indulgence to a speaker who directly represents ' the masses,' as it is usual to call them ; but I think it probable that indulgence will not be required, and that Mr. Burt will make himself heard and understood. If this should prove to be the case, it would probably lead, if not to a new party, at least to an extension of liberal views, with which the hitherto liberal parties have not been made acquainted. There is another and important influence which working-class members may exert, and that is an influence on the working classes generally, tending to convince them that improvement and advancement can only arise from sound education and prudent conduct. A sense of justice and love of fair dealing are lessons which pitmen have been taught by one of the people, who not long ago expressed such correct views that the employers themselves gave currency to them. The railway and telegraph afford means of communication very much more effective for progress than any which has hitherto existed, and I feel persuaded that in a few years the results will be much in favour of the so-called masses, if they as a body can be brought to imitate the example of many individuals of their class who have ascended the social scale."

On July 11th, 1874, there is an entry of a visit paid on the occasion of the golden wedding of Mr. and Mrs. S. Carter Hall; followed by a description of another visit to the Continent, and of excursions through Switzerland,

with a long account of all the places visited, together with
an excellent map of the journey. Of this journey to
Switzerland Mr. Sopwith published a very useful little
work, illustrated with a design, showing the approximate
heights of English and Swiss mountains.

In October of this year Mr. Sopwith revisited Leeds,
and his diary at this point contains an entry describing
a local institution called the Conversation Club. At this
club, which has existed many years, some special subject
is brought up for conversation rather than debate. I
remember attending one of these meetings with my old
friend, Mr. John Morley,—then little dreaming of being
a Minister of State,—when, under the presidency of
the late Mr. Kitson, capital punishment was the subject
for conversation. At Mr. Sopwith's visit on October
25th, 1874, the club met at Mr.—afterwards Sir Edward
—Baines's at St. Anne's Hill. The subject of conversation was " *The most useful form of memorial of eminent
men.*" Several propositions were made, Mr. Sopwith's,
which met with most approval, being a Memorial Hall,
containing a statue or bust of the person to be honoured,
adorned with frescoes, paintings, or engravings representing his achievements, with a library and reading-
room, and, when convenient, a lecture hall.

Under date of September 19th are some remarks sent
by Mr. Sopwith to G. Harris, Esq., furnished in reply
to an enquiry he made respecting the combined effects of
genius and energy :—

"*September* 19*th.*—Intellectual characters may be unfairly
estimated if the results which they accomplish are attributed
to energy and perseverance, and not to genius or skill.

"This leads to a consideration of these several qualities, both
as regards their own nature and the relations in which they
stand to each other.

23

"Genius is a gift interwoven with the natural mental character. Skill is as much of the nature of genius as can be acquired, and both genius and skill may be considered as included in the word talent.

"Energy is an impulse to work with power in efforts not necessarily continuous or lasting. Perseverance is akin to energy, but differing in this respect, that it is in its nature steady and enduring, and the objects to which it is applied are not necessarily of so great and powerful a character as those which are overcome by energy.

"Neither energy of mind, in its powerful efforts, nor perseverance, in its own more patient labours, are in themselves a proof of great talents being combined with them, nor do they necessarily result from the possession of great gifts of mental endowment. On the contrary, they are found in minds destitute of high endowments, and are sometimes wanting in minds of great and varied talents.

"Of this I will endeavour to give some illustration.

"In many cases of ordinary trading operations much energy and perseverance are absolutely indispensable for acquiring a requisite proficiency in pursuits in which no high endowments of genius are required.

"This is especially so in the case of acrobats, who are trained year after year in daily exercises of persevering energy—they excel in what Channing calls 'the greatness of action.' Yet, however successful in the energy and perseverance of muscular activity, they do not necessarily possess any rare endowments of mind; of the absence of which their constant occupation seems in itself sufficient proofs.

"On the other hand, instances are not wanting where genius and skill, or, in other words, great and varied talents, have existed without the accompaniment of energy or perseverance.

"In such characters occasional efforts prove how great is the talent, and the distance of such efforts from each other proves the want of energy and perseverance.

" Byron, who was a deep student both of his own highly gifted mind and of the character of others, ascribes to genius and energy a common origin when he writes of—

" ' Every fault that daring genius owes
Half to the ardour which its birth bestows.'

" Assuredly in many, probably in by far the greater number of cases, genius does ' give birth ' to ardour, which, as here used, is only another name for energy or greater mental activity.

" Most commonly they are thus united, and separately they are of little use in promoting any really high or important result. Talent without energy is little known, and energy without talent is only suited for ordinary or it may be even for trifling occupations.

" In any estimate of intellectual character of a high order, it is proper to value energy and perseverance as usual and most important accompaniments of genius, though not invariably combined therewith. They are the sword and the shield with which genius goes forth to battle, and without which but little conquest can be looked for. If the champion, however valiant, is without these arms he is almost powerless.

" Genius is not proved to exist by the exertion of vigour, but when energy is present then it is guided and concentrated by that pure light of genius which in its essence is of a higher and more spiritual character than any qualities which are common alike to genius and to efforts of a much more noble character."

1875.

The diary through 1875 is that of a man of leisure, living in London, and filling up his time by watching all current events, and taking part in some. There is a brief description of the death and funeral of Sir Charles Lyell ; a short defence of Dean Stanley from the attacks of the *Saturday Review ;* an account of a dinner-party

where George Cruikshank was present, " in which that
remarkable artist expressed himself without reserve in
favour of Temperance ; " an account of a visit, for the
first time, to Ascot ; a list of pleasant occupations, with
the outline of a day of refined pleasures. In August
of this year he made another visit to Holland, and on
September 27th he attended at the fiftieth anniversary of
the opening of the Stockton and Darlington Railway, the
jubilee of railway locomotion. At the Social Science
Meeting at Brighton he was one of the adjudicators of
the Sanitary Exhibition, and in his notes on the progress
of sanitation he describes Mr. Edwin Chadwick, " whose
name," he says, " will be remembered as one of the most
active, useful, and benevolent men of the time."

1876.

The year 1876 was marked by a very instructive tour,
in company with Mrs. Sopwith, through Normandy and
Brittany. Of this tour Mr. Sopwith has published a
short essay, giving a most careful description not only of
the various places visited, but of the manners and customs
of the people. History and superstition are, he thinks,
blended here more than in most places, where the marvellous legends which abound are implicitly believed
by many. The history of the church of Folgoet is cited
as a wonderful example of this fact. Later in the year
he made a tour in Scotland, and paid a visit to Mr.
William Chambers at Glenormiston. A short picture of
this visit is given under date of September 23rd.

"*September 23rd*, 1876.—We left Edinburgh this morning,
and had a pleasant railway journey to Innerleithen, where
Mr. William Chambers was waiting ready to receive us, and
we accompanied him in his carriage to his beautiful mansion
of Glenormiston.

"It is twenty years or more since I was here, and many and great are the improvements which have been made since then. We had a leisurely saunter through the grounds, which are laid out with great taste, and saw many of the operations of the active and enlightened proprietor, resulting in very satisfactory and beautiful works.

"It was with great interest that we heard our good friend (who is nearly three years my senior) describe these improvements. They reflect the highest credit on his taste, his engineering and architectural skill, and benevolence. They are works of a truly great and good man, whose name, along with that of his brother Robert, will rank among the most solid and persevering benefactors of mankind in a period of more than half a century.

"At three we had dinner, and both before, and at, and after that meal we had a great deal of conversation on a variety of subjects, interspersed with anecdotes, and with my imperfect rendering of the local song of 'Canny Newcastle,' the dialect of which is intelligible in Scotland, though not so in England generally, except in the north.

"The visit to Glenormiston has afforded us very great pleasure."

Visits of this nature gave Mr. Sopwith the liveliest gratification, and led him in another note to reflections bearing upon his experience of the happiness which is to be found in different classes of society.

"*October* 11*th.*—In my voyage through life it has often been my habit not only to reflect seriously on passing occurrences, but also to record such reflections with the hope that they may be interesting and perhaps instructive at future periods. At the present time the transition I have made from one house to another is suggestive of many considerations.

"I have never been able to discover that happiness (which has been justly called our being's end and aim) is in any material degree dependent on external conditions as regards wealth or poverty, splendour or a humble state. Of the extremes of these, in the exaltation of regal pomp or in the sad abodes of the miserably poor, I do not here desire to speak, inasmuch as my experience of either of these opposite conditions has been very limited; but in that wide range of English and continental society which has come within a nearer range of observation and experience, I have witnessed the diffusion of happiness in many forms and under a great variety of circumstances.

"It has been my good fortune through life to be thrown by professional and other circumstances into opportunities of visiting the homes of both wealthy and poor persons, and of enjoying the society of many highly accomplished persons of eminence in science, art, and literature, some in prosperous estate and others in moderate circumstances. Under all these varieties of human existence, I have found that the qualities which constitute friendship and mutual esteem are essential to true enjoyment. These qualities give to life its most exquisite and enduring enjoyments, its 'glowing charm,' as the learned historian of Northumberland has well expressed it. Fifty years have passed since I gave a strong expression of these views, and every year of that half-century has convinced me of their truth and value."

1877.

On February 23rd, 1877, he was much gratified by a visit from the Dean of Westminster (Dean Stanley), who called with Dr. Stoughton to look at some letters by the Rev. John Wesley. The interview seems to have been extremely pleasant on both sides, for the Dean was one of those Broad Churchmen towards whom Mr. Sopwith felt the warmest regard. The following day he started for Spain, through which country he made quite an extensive series of excursions, during a period lasting nearly three months.

On June 6th he makes a note of his having accompanied

me, in my capacity of President of the Council of the Royal Historical Society, to an audience granted by the Emperor of Brazil.

" We were shown into a drawing-room at Claridge's Hotel, where several ladies were in attendance on the Empress, and several gentlemen were assembled for interviews on various objects. The Emperor entered the room at the corner where we had been placed, and Dr. Richardson, in an appropriate address, presented the Diploma of the Society and five volumes of *Transactions* to the Emperor, who appeared to be gratified by the compliment, and after a short conversation he shook hands with the several members of the deputation, eight in number.

" Both he and the Empress signed their names in a book, and the latter exchanged parting compliments with the members of the deputation.

" Nothing can exceed the industry of the Imperial pair, in seeing every person and every place and every process of manufacture of a distinguished or remarkable character."

1878.

A series of leisurely and yet useful days leads us up to June 11th, 1878, when the diary records the marriage of Mr. Sopwith's beloved daughter, Ursula, to Mr. David Chadwick, M.P. The marriage was celebrated at the church of St. Andrew's, at Ashley Place, the ceremony being performed by Dean Stanley. The note appended to this event expresses the happiest hopes in truly felicitous terms, to which he adds,—

" These notes must ever possess a deep interest as long as I am spared in sufficient health and memory to read them, and to realize some of the pleasing associations which, in a great degree, reconcile me to the separation of my daughter from my home."

The rest of the journal during this year (1878) is

somewhat irregularly kept, and is interspersed with notes dwelling largely on the depressed condition of trade and the unfortunate state of the times. It was my duty during this year to visit Mr. Sopwith professionally, and I was obliged to observe that, although he made every effort to maintain his cheerfulness and serenity, an effort was required. He took an interest still in public affairs, but only for brief periods, and he began to tell me that the labour of carrying on the diary told upon him so much that he thought he should not continue it beyond the current year. I was obliged also to notice that the failure of his heart, which had at intervals been a cause of anxiety, was now almost a permanent failure. Towards the close of 1878 I recommended him to go to Bournemouth for a change, from which place he wrote to me, two or three times, quite cheerfully. He spent Christmas at Bournemouth, in a manner, he reported to me, not wanting in social enjoyment, in company of valued friends, to whom his song of "Canny Newcastle" was cheerfully rendered. On New Year's Day, 1879, a little before midnight, a sleepless state was followed by a paroxysm of difficult breathing. The next day he returned to London, and on January 3rd, his birthday, he completed his diary, and marked it, "The End."

CHAPTER XXXI.

MEMORANDA AND LITERARY NOTES. THE GLACIAL THEORY. ASCENT OF CHAMOUNIX. GIBBON AND LAUSANNE. CALVIN AND HUMPHRY DAVY. ROMAN BATHS AT TREVES. MINING AT FREIBERG. A GEOLOGICAL PIONEER. CHURCH OF THE FOOL OF THE FOREST. DANISH WATCHMAN'S CURFEW.

IN addition to his diary Mr. Sopwith was fond of jotting down memoranda and literary notes, some of which he printed for private circulation. They are as varied as the information which he had stored up in his capacious mind, and they afford admirable touches, here and there, of the judicial wisdom with which he could comment on different subjects, as well as of the acuteness with which he was able to record passing observations. The picture of him would not be complete without a chapter containing a few selections from these incidental notes.

THE GLACIAL THEORY.

In a chapter on Chamounix, published in a small treatise entitled "A Month in Switzerland," he gives us the following passages on the Glacial Theory :—

" For some time the glacial theory made slow progress, but Dr. Buckland took up the subject with great energy, and proceeded to investigate the evidences which Agassiz had contended would be found in various parts of Great

Britain and on the Continent, in situations where no one had even suspected the existence of any such features. I accompanied Dr. Buckland to various places in Northumberland, Durham, and North Wales, and the search for rounded and furrowed rocks—the work of glaciers—was very successful.

" In later years glacial action has been recognised by geologists as an important agent in many phenomena relating to the transport of large boulder stones, the formation of moraines, and the rounding and polishing and furrowing of rocks. The physical conditions under which these enormous masses of ice descend the Alpine valleys have been learnedly investigated by Saussure, Forbes, Tyndall, and others, and various communications to the Geological Society and numerous works on the subject have now made it one of popular interest. Here, at Chamounix, the tourist is within easy reach of glaciers which yet remain, and finds it difficult to realize that such masses of ice formerly existed in Great Britain. A comparison of the effects produced by the movement of ice with the features clearly shown by rocks in many places in Great Britain leaves no room for doubt as to the identity of the cause and effect in both cases, and glaciers which a century ago were thought to belong exclusively to high mountain ranges are now found to possess a much wider and more home-like interest.

" ' At what period, then, of the earth's history were English valleys filled with ice ? ' This inquiry, which is naturally suggested, may perhaps be best answered in words used by De la Beche with reference to some geological features. ' If,' said he, ' I am to be hard pressed on the subject of time, I should say that I consider these remains to be of very great antiquity as regards historical periods, and very little antiquity as

regards geological periods.'   For lessons of geological
time no pages are more instructive than those presented
by the vast masses of mountains in the district of which
Chamounix is the most accessible centre, and whoever
from England reads them with attention will learn
lessons which, on returning to his home, he may improve
by the study of English glacial phenomena."

THE ASCENT OF CHAMOUNIX.

"It is curious to reflect that, of all the centuries of
known history, in one only has this mountain been an
object of attraction to tourists.   In the middle of last
century the vale of Chamounix, although it had been
inhabited some five or six centuries, was dreaded as a
dangerous place, and its grand scenery known as 'The
evil mountains.'   One hundred and ten years ago (1764)
Saussure, that truly eminent philosopher and ardent
explorer, first commenced his well-known researches on
the glaciers.   The ascent of Mont Blanc was accomplished
for the first time on record in 1786, since which time up
to the end of the year [1874] the total number of ascents
has been 726 (exclusive of guides and porters).   Of these
only five were made in the last century.   During the
first forty-five years of the present century few ascents
were made, and these chiefly by Englishmen.   In ten
years between 1847 and 1857 all the excursionists were
English, and in later years the register at Chamounix
records the following number of ascents :—

1861	.	. 42 ascents.	1868	.	. 33 ascents.
1862	.	. 24 ,,	1869	.	. 54 ,,
1863	.	. 55 ,,	1870	.	. 14 ,,
1864	.	. 63 ,,	1871	.	. 22 ,,
1865	.	. 66 ,,	1872	.	. 57 ,,
1866	.	. 25 ,,	1873	.	. 59 ,,
1867	.	. 42 ,,			

"The following is a statement of the nationality of those who made the ascents :—

British	.	.	.	449
French	.	.	.	105
American	.	.	75
German	.	.	34
Swiss	.	.	.	30
Italian	.	.	.	8
Russian	.	.	.	6
Dutch	.	.	.	4

Austrians	.	.	4
Spaniards	.	.	3
Poles	.	.	.	3
Livonian	.	.	1
Belgian	.	.	.	1
Swede	.	.	.	1
Norwegian	.	.	1

It appears, therefore, that in the first sixty years of this century the number of ascensions was 165, or an average of rather less than three persons per annum. These records are satisfactory, as indicating the spirit of enterprise and hardihood of our fellow-countrymen."

Gibbon and Lausanne.

Amongst the favourite authors of Mr. Sopwith, Gibbon held a first place, in which sense of literature he and I had the same taste. We often compared notes, as he called it, on this author ; and I remember once how I envied him that I could only gather from his vivid description an idea of the home at Lausanne. I wish I could remember that description as he gave it. I cannot, but here is a fragment from the little work already quoted :—

"We did not attempt to realize the exact spot where he is said to have finished his great work, for the locality is so much altered that clear definition of such details is no longer possible. Enough it is to know that here and hereabouts was the place where day by day and hour by hour the great historian penned his work, in full view of the beautiful lake and mighty mountains which, from any part of this immediate locality, still present the same aspect as that on which his eye must so often have rested. These great and sublime and beautiful features we saw to great advantage on a lovely morning and in an atmosphere—how still and lovely."

Resting-Place of John Calvin and Humphry Davy.

In the cemetery of Geneva Mr. Sopwith made two notes:—

"The resting-place of Calvin is near the south corner of the cemetery, and (in conformity, it is said, with his own desire) no stately monument is reared to his memory. The place where he was interred is marked only by a stone rather less then a cubic foot in its dimensions, and bearing on it only the initials J. C.

"Here also is a monument erected to the memory of Sir Humphry Davy, who was buried here."

Roman Baths and Masonry at Treves.

In another treatise, entitled "Three Weeks in Central Europe," we get a graphic and original account of Roman baths and Roman masonry at Treves :—

"The 'Roman Baths' are situated at the south corner of the city, which in shape is nearly square, one of the diagonals nearly corresponding with a meridian line. These ruins are of great extent, both above and underground, and the adjacent surface is well wooded. It is impossible to repress feelings of astonishment as successive portions of this extraordinary mass of buildings are gradually disclosed to view. The walls have been built of amazing strength, and many of the arches consist of five or six ranges of stone. Some of the walls are very high, as well as enormously massive, and with the surrounding trees and ivy the general effect is very picturesque. We threaded our way through numerous vaults and subterranean galleries, which forcibly reminded me of similar excavations at Richborough, in Kent, and, like them, the full extent of these passages has not yet been ascertained. It is only during the last fifty years that the earth and rubbish which concealed the Roman Baths of Treves have been removed; even the upper walls of the castle or palace were much hidden by the earth-works of the fortifications surrounding the city. Curious as these ruins are they are far inferior to the Baths of Diana, at Nismes, where graceful arches and ornamental columns attest a more advanced stage of luxury.

"It was curious to observe that in four works of the Romans in this city no less than four different modes of building have been adopted. In the Basilica *brick and cement* only are used. The Palace and Baths are built of *stones* of *medium size, with layers of brick-work.* In the Amphitheatre are *small stones with cement,* and in the Black Gate *large stones without cement.* This strange variety seems to indicate fertility of resource as well as mechanical skill, for examples of every one of these essentially different modes of construction have endured to the present time in a nearly perfect state, over a period not far short of two thousand years, and bidding fair, if carefully attended to, to remain intact for many centuries to come. I made sketches of the *brickwork* of the Basilica, the *stone and layers of brick* at the Baths, the *stone and cement* of the Amphitheatre, and the *massive masonry without cement* of the Black Gate."

IN the same little volume, "Three Weeks in Central Europe," there is an account of a visit to the district of Freiberg, situated about twenty-five miles in a south-westerly direction from Dresden.

The city of Freiberg is well known as the capital or chief place of a territory which for its mining capabilities and operations is famous throughout Europe. In such a spot Mr. Sopwith would naturally be at home. He gives us the following pictures : —

"Mining in this territory is of venerable antiquity, extending backward for many centuries, yet having had its fuller developments in the last two or three hundred years, and more especially in the present century. I looked with interest at a plan said to be one of the earliest known ; it is dated 1608, and its execution, rude and inartistic as it is, sufficiently indicates the great depth and extent of the workings then existing. What they are now can only be fully comprehended by means of detailed plans and sections, several of which were shown to me. They indicate works of vast extent and intricacy, such as can scarcely be appreciated by any general description.

"The surface operations are conducted under cover, that is in roofed buildings, to a greater extent than in corresponding works in England. This is due to two causes, namely, the greater intrinsic value of silver ores and the severity of the climate in winter. The value of the ores and the close intermixture of several valuable mineral substances render corresponding care necessary in the dressing processes, some of which are of great ingenuity. The English, justly priding themselves on many important works of engineering skill in recent times, are apt to forget how much the metallurgical and mining processes now followed in England were originally derived from Germany and other mining districts of Central Europe. It was, therefore, with extreme interest that I viewed a place so celebrated as Freiberg has long been, not only for the number and value of its mines, but for the scientific instruction combined with the practical operations. Over all these the names of some of the most distinguished men of science shed a lustre, the brightness of which will be more and more appreciated as advances continue to be made in mining industry, and in the numerous sciences allied with it. Of these it may be sufficient to mention James Watt, Werner, and Humboldt.

"The Mining College of Freiberg has been in full activity rather more than a century, having been founded in 1766. At that time little more than three thousand men were employed at the mines, and the annual value of the produce is stated to have been £33,000. Recently (1865) the number of miners was about eight thousand, and the value of the produce not far short of a quarter of a million sterling."

A Geological Pioneer—A. G. Werner.

In the cathedral at Freiberg, said to be the oldest in Europe, our friend found the "Golden Door" one of the most prominent attractions to visitors, but he chiefly mentions it because immediately in front of it and only a few paces from it is the grave of one whose name is for ever associated, not only with Freiberg and its mining district, but with the history of science, more especially of the sciences of mineralogy and geology :—

"Under a plain, flat gravestone, scarcely to be distinguished from the pathway leading to the church, lie the remains of WERNER, indicated by the following inscription :—

ABRHM GTTLB
WERNER.

Near to it is a neat mural monument erected by his sister, and inscribed as follows :—

HIER RUHIT ABRAHAM GOTTLOB WERNER ; DIESES DENKMAL
ERRICHT IHM SCHWESTERRLICHE LIEBE.   EIN
BLEIBENDERES ER SICH SELBST.

An affectionate memorial of one who truly erected a more lasting monument for himself in the usefulness and celebrity of his scientific labours.

"Accurate geological induction does not date back to a period much anterior to the present century, and public attention was chiefly called to it by the views of Werner and Hutton in theories which became popularly known as Wernerian and Huttonian. The difference between these consisted in the prominence given by the former to water, and by the latter to fire, as prime causes in the distribution of the strata which compose the crust of the earth. The one looked to the deposition of vast masses of strata by watery agencies ; the other attached more importance to what were called plutonic or fiery influences ; and, while the world was giving attention to this contest, the really useful labours of the founder of English geology were in a great measure neglected. This was William Smith, who, so early as 1801, constructed an admirable geological map of England, and by his long-continued services laid the foundation of geological science in this country on a basis the soundness of which, having been abundantly established, has well entitled him to the generally accorded name of the

24

Father of English Geology. The cotemporaneous labours of Werner and Smith may be regarded as having chiefly paved the way to the important advances since made in this department of science. Having been intimately acquainted with the founder of English geology, whose friendship I greatly valued, it was with much interest that I paid the silent homage of respectful remembrance as I viewed the tombstone of his great cotemporary."

The Church of the Fool of the Forest.

When travelling in Brittany, Mr. Sopwith stayed at Landernau, where he visited Folgoet, the site of a church around which hangs one of the mysteries which even to his staid and thoughtful mind had the charm of legend. He thus describes the place in his notes on Brittany:—

"At Landernau we took up our abode at the Hôtel de l'Univers, and after an excellent breakfast we went to visit the curious old church at Folgoet, distant about ten miles. The roads in all this part of France, so far as we have seen them, are excellent. The first view of the church is very striking, and the spire is so much in the same style as those at Quimper, that it seems to be the model from which the latter have been taken.

"The interior is remarkably striking from the bold and picturesque style of architecture, and especially so as regards a rood-loft and large east window. Both of these are of a highly ornamental character. It is in vain to attempt by any description to convey an accurate idea of the peculiarities which meet the view in the doorways, columns, windows, altars, and other parts of the church of the 'Fool of the Forest,' for such is the meaning of its name. In the minuteness and beautiful workmanship of the carving in stone I doubt whether a parallel is to be found in Europe. In Murray's hand-book there is a good enumeration of the objects best deserving attention, and to an architect gifted with skill in delineation, and with leisure to exercise it, this edifice is a mine of wealth. The tendrils of leaves, a dewdrop and insects, are among the sculptured objects which abound in the decorations of this church.

"History and superstition are much blended in many places, but in few, if any, more closely than in Brittany, where the marvellous legends which abound are implicitly believed by many. Seldom has this union been exhibited in a more definite form than in the legendary history of the church of Folgoet. A boy of weak intellect, it is recorded, used to beg in this neighbourhood, and his supplications to passers-by were always accompanied by expressions of devotion to the Virgin Mary. He lived to the age of forty years, and before his death (says the legend) the Virgin appeared to him and pointed out the place where a well, endowed with miraculous powers of healing, would be found. After his burial close to this well, a lily tree grew from his grave, and on the leaves of the lilies the name of Mary was impressed. These wonders came to the notice of John de Montford, who was then at war with Charles of Blois, contending for the Dukedom of Brittany. He, it is said, sent commissioners to examine into these reputed miracles, and they, after investigation, reported that the roots of the lily tree sprung from the mouth of the buried Fool of the Forest. In consequence of this the church was partly built by John de Montford, and finished by his successor. The high altar is said to be directly over the grave where the imbecile was buried, and closely adjoining the outside of the east end of the church is the well, which, we were told, is still resorted to on account of its supposed miraculous powers of healing. Such is the curious concurrence of events which caused this remarkable building to be erected. Great indeed must have been its beauty when perfect. It is wonderful even in decay."

Sir Walter Scott.

It will be remembered that in a previous chapter (page 33) Mr. Sopwith described an accidental meeting of Sir Walter Scott in one of his tours in Scotland, between Longtown and Langholm. That the great novelist had an ardent admirer in our friend must be admitted, and some allowance made, therefore, for a touch of enthusiasm. Nevertheless, as the note about to be given was written at a time when the living man was well known as a man as well as a writer, it is certainly deserving of record how he was then viewed by a young but good observer. While relating the beauty of his journey, Mr. Sopwith digresses, for a moment, to refer to the prince of fiction :—

"The favourable state of the atmosphere contributed much to the beauty of this delightful ride ;—as we advanced, the sun shone brightly on the green and brown slopes of the hills, and, as they receded from our view, their massive and picturesque outline was formed by a misty, aerial tint, approaching to a deep blue, which produced a most sublime effect. But what added most interest to the scene was the circumstance of meeting in this romantic solitude the most eminent man of his country, Sir Walter Scott, whose writings have so much increased the interest and added to the associations of the localities noticed in them, and whom even to have seen is well worthy of remembrance, especially as on this occasion it had the coincidence of its being my first day in Scotland, and in a situation where the poet was surrounded by so much of the poetry and sublimity of Nature.

"It is pretty generally known that this admirable and fascinating writer is not remarkable for any external indications of genius. A dull and rather heavy expression of countenance is, indeed, wonderfully brightened up by the vivacity of his social spirit in conversation; but his is not in its general aspect the "poet's eye," which Shakespeare has so loftily conceived, and so beautifully described. His manners are universally described as being extremely engaging, and his disposition open, candid, and generous. His courteous behaviour and great hospitality are well known; but, it is said, that these amiable characteristics have latterly had some restriction forced upon them by their tendency to induce his admirers to seek the charm of his society; and, when the rank and unlimited number of these are considered, extending from the throne to the cottage, and from individual to national admiration, such a regard to privacy seems quite indispensable. Whatever exceptions may be found in some minutiæ of his character and writings, Sir Walter Scott undoubtedly holds a most exalted station as a poet, historian, antiquary, and novelist. His disposition and conduct, too, have been such as to gain him a very high, and almost unprecedented, degree of private esteem and public admiration. By incorporating accurate and beautiful delineations of national scenery and manners into the productions of his fertile and luxuriant mind, he has conveyed a great mass of useful information amongst a numerous and respectable portion of society, to whom the more laboured and less enchanting details of the historian and topographical writer would have remained almost entirely unknown.

And where can more vivid or exact delineations be found of many eminent characters and interesting places and events, than those which abound in the beautiful romances of the author of 'Waverley'? By the great interest, also, which these works have created, as regards the national character and scenery of Scotland, they have contributed much to the union of national feeling, and have conferred most important benefits on Scotland by the numerous and opulent tourists who throng in crowds to visit the scenery consecrated by his muse."

The Danish Watchman's Curfew.

As told in the diary, Mr. Sopwith, in company with Mr. Robert Stephenson, visited Denmark and Norway in the autumn of 1854. In Copenhagen he seems to have been entertained with everything, from the early morning until the hour for the song of the watchman at ten p.m.; a song he translates in the following strain :—

> " I am the watchman ; the clock has struck ten :
> If the hour you would ask for, listen again—
> The clock has struck ten.
> Master, children, and servants know
> Now it is time to bed to go ;
> Do not forget to God to pray,
> Be careful of fire, put candles away—
> The clock has struck ten."

CHAPTER XXXII.

1879.

Y recollections of Mr. Sopwith extend over nearly twenty-three years, namely, from 1856 when we first met at Hartwell, to the last day but one of his life, January 15th, 1879.

The opinion I formed of him on our first acquaintance, recorded in the opening chapter of this book, never varied. Our acquaintance ripened into friendship quickly, a friendship which remained unbroken and unruffled. A more reliable man I never met, or one of calmer, more forbearing, or gentler nature, combined with firmness of character, decision, and expression almost abrupt in its decisiveness. His voice was gentle, and, when his sympathies were aroused, slightly tremulous. In stature he stood about five feet six, and he was of strong, full build. His temperament was a mixture of sanguine and bilious. His features, well pourtrayed in the portrait at the commencement of this work, were full, firm, and expressive. His head was a little above the usual size; the forehead well developed; and the whole head finely balanced. The phrenologists might well claim him as one whose cranial development corresponded splendidly to the richly endowed and, at the same time, admirably balanced mind. Professor Laycock's theory of a large ear lobe as a sign of an active brain was also well illustrated. In action he was deliberate, but at the same time quickly observant ; his small, piercing bluish-grey eyes seeming to seize every object brought before them with remarkable rapidity. When I first knew him his acuteness of hearing was equal to that of sight, and this especially for musical sounds, the merest discord being instantly detected by him. I told him once that at the theatre nothing pleased me more than the tuning of the instruments of the orchestra,—it was so like chaos passing into order ; " Yes," he added, " that is true, and order is harmony." He himself was the soul of order ; every-thing had its place with him, and the cabinet called the Monocleid, in his study, was his pride. It contained every paper he was working at, so arranged that he could put his hand upon the book or document he wanted as if it came at a call. I used to compare his papers to the Roman centurion soldiers who always came when they were called, but sometimes came when they were not called. " Nay," he said, " my papers even beat the soldiers : they never come when they are not wanted, but always come when they are."

Sopwith loved work ; with him work was play and play was work, so that he was never for a moment idle ; but his method was so quiet and unostentatious that it troubled no one about him. When he travelled he carried with him his wonderful desk, fitted up like a small monocleid, arranged to carry all books and papers he wanted, and " ready for work the moment a table, chair, and proper place could be found for it." This constant occupation of mind conveyed to him, as it does to others of the same type, that happiness which the world can neither give nor take away; so that his years, though they went swiftly as the shuttle of a weaver's beam, were borne on the wings of happiness and perfect peace. His religion was that of the heart, without outward profession of any kind. He belonged, I believe, nominally to the old Church of England; and all his predilections—historical, antiquarian, and social—were in sympathy with a Church he considered quite broad enough to hold in her pale men of all classes, even men of the most exalted science. He kept the commandments, and although he was not the most rigid of Sabbatarians, he liked the day of rest as a good social and healthful institution.

Of his friends and contemporaries Mr. Sopwith entertained at all times the most charitable views. With him life without charity was indeed sounding brass and tinkling cymbal, but he avoided bad men with instinctive aversion. To friends with whom he was most intimate, and whose abilities he admired, he was much attached, and of such friends he never could say too much. Indeed, if he had a failing in this direction it was that he sometimes let friendship over-estimate ability. He was all through, in fact, of a generous nature, and was ready at any time to give his best assistance to every good cause and case that was brought before him. These qualities endeared him to his large circle of friends, friends of the most varied casts of mind, thought, and learning. Dr. Lee said very correctly of him, " that he made friends of every one he met, and he could not conceive of Mr. Sopwith having an enemy." This was an opinion very generally entertained.

He was fond of society, was essentially a social man, both at home and from home. At home he was a most genial host, full of anecdote and humour, and ready at the proper seasons to indulge in all innocent merriment and fun. He had several stock stories, one or two in rhyme, and when he sat down to the pianoforte, though I believe he could not play from notes, he discoursed, from memory, excellent music. In society from home he was always respected and always popular. In the learned Societies he was an attentive and appreciative listener, and as the range of his knowledge was wide, his eye good for telescope and microscope, and his hand good for mechanics, his opinion was much esteemed; but he was rather a poor debater. He had not in speech the gift of perspicuity ; he could not think on his legs with facility was given, therefore, to wander away from his subject, and then, detecting what he had done, would sit down abruptly. When, however, he had prepared a paper, all was as clear and sharp as crystal, and sometimes in repartee there was a sparkle of humour in what he said which made its mark. But always in the learned Society he was inquisitive to the last degree in regard to every new idea and invention that came under his notice. He held a theory similar to that held by the famous Dr. Anderson, the founder of Anderson's College, in Glasgow—that whatever appeals strongly to the eye is irresistible, that it must attract observation and force its way into the mind. He said he had scarcely ever met a man, however poor and simple, or great and intelligent, who would not stop to look at the working of a piece of mechanism that presented some novelty. This observation came out of a conversation on ballooning, in which Glaisher and Coxwell's perilous and brilliant researches were the subject of discourse. " A balloon is a piece of mechanism, a rude mode of flight, still a novelty because incomplete for practical purposes; therefore everybody runs to see a balloon, and some in their excitement would tear the thing up if they could get at it, as if they

wanted to see what was inside it." "Is it the motion or
the mechanism that is the wonder?" I enquired of him.
"Would a man, for instance, who had never seen a watch
show the least interest in it if it did not go?" "Ah!
that," he replied, "is a nice bit of metaphysics, or mental
physics rather, which you doctors must find out. All I
know is that whatever *goes* interests, and that I myself
am not easily tired at looking at whatever is going, in
which I am like the rest of the world."

Up to the sixty-fifth year of his age Mr. Sopwith enjoyed a healthy life—a life broken by very few interrup-
tions of sickness; a blessing due to several favouring
causes. In the first place, he was always most temperate
in his mode of life. He was not abstemious in diet, but
regular and moderate. He took but little wine or other
alcoholic drink, and that, as he said, *secundum artem.*
Secondly, he was an early riser and a good sleeper.
Lastly, born of a happy disposition and simple in his
desires, he brought upon himself few unnecessary cares,
and met such anxieties as necessarily came to him with
such serenity that disease from friction of mind on body
was ever wisely tempered. He told me on one occasion
that he did not remember being a day in a position in
which he could not cover every debt he owed at an
hour's notice, a position the most favourable of all both
for health and for happiness.

About 1867 his robust health began somewhat to fail.
He felt, as he described it, some central failure. His
mind was usually as active as ever, but not "always."
He consulted the late Dr. Bence Jones, who detected
the "central failure" as being truly central, that is to
say, in the heart, and who prescribed very judiciously
on that finding. Some time afterwards, on the death of
Dr. Bence Jones, Mr. Sopwith placed himself under my

professional care. By this time the heart affection had become very distinct and decided. He had what we physicians call " mitral disease," under which the balance between the pulmonary and general circulations was easily disturbed by slight external causes, and especially by atmospheric changes. Under careful management, change of scene, and regulated diet, the dangerous symptoms that were foreseen were deferred for many years ; and under the unremitting vigilance of Mrs. Sopwith his life remained comparatively healthy and comfortable until the beginning of the year 1879. Then his mental energies commenced rather rapidly to decline, and after a slight cold, bronchial troubles supervened, under which combinations of depression he gradually sank, resigned and gentle to the last.

Mr. Sopwith's death—I should rather say his euthanasia —took place on January 16th, 1879, at 103, Victoria Street, Westminster. He was buried at Norwood Cemetery, where a granite slab, inscribed,—

THOMAS SOPWITH, M.A., F.R.S., C.E.,

Born at Newcastle, January 3rd, 1803 ;

Died in Westminster, January 16th, 1879,

declares his final resting-place.

The End.

INDEX.

INDEX.

25

Printed by Hazell, Watson, & Viney, Ld., London and Aylesbury.